# THE CONFESSION

# THE
# CONFESSION

## Charles Todd

*wm* WILLIAM MORROW
*An Imprint of* HarperCollins*Publishers*

P.S.™ is a trademark of HarperCollins Publishers.

HarperCollins books may be purchased for educational, business, or sales promotional use. For information please write: Special Markets Department, HarperCollins Publishers, 10 East 53rd Street, New York, NY 10022.

A hardcover edition of this book was published in 2012 by William Morrow, an imprint of HarperCollins Publishers.

FIRST WILLIAM MORROW PAPERBACK EDITION PUBLISHED 2012.

Library of Congress Cataloging-in-Publication Data has been applied for.

ISBN 978-0-06-201567-9

12 13 14 15 16  OV/RRD  10 9 8 7 6 5 4 3 2 1

*For Sally and for David,*
*with much love.*
*Rutledge is one county closer to Mill Barn . . . and next year will bring him even*
*nearer. As promised.*

*And for Carolyn Marino, and everyone at HarperCollins/Morrow, for being*
*the wonderful people you are.*
*With much gratitude.*

# I

*The Essex Marshes, Summer 1915*

The body rolled in the current gently, as if still alive. It was face-down, only the back and hips visible. It had been floating that way for some time. The men in the ancient skiff had watched it for a quarter of an hour, as if half expecting it to rise up and walk away before their eyes.

"He's dead, right enough," one said. "One of ours, do you think?"

"This far up the Hawking? It's a German spy," the second man said, nodding, as if that explained everything. "Bound to be. I say, leave him to the fish."

"We won't know who he is until we pull him out, will we?" the third said and leaned out to touch the corpse with the boat hook.

"Here!" the first man cried out, as if this were sacrilege.

The body bobbed a little under the weight of the hook.

"*He* doesn't care," the third man said. "Why should you?"

"Still and all—"

Turning the hook a little, he put the end under the dead man's collar and pulled. Under the impetus of the hook, the corpse came out of the reeds obediently, as if called, and floated toward the skiff until the shoulder of his dark, water-sodden uniform bumped lightly into the hull.

"A bloody officer."

"He's been shot," the third man said as the body shifted. "Look at that."

"Turn him over," the second man ordered, after peering at the back of the man's head.

With some difficulty, that was done, and all three stared into the dead face, flaccid from hours in the water.

"None of our fishermen," the second man went on. "Don't know him atall. You?"

The first man shook his head. "I dunno. There's something familiar about him. I just can't put a name to him."

"Let's have a look," the third man said, and reached out to clutch the front of the sodden uniform, pulling him close enough to thrust his fingers into the man's breast pocket. He came away with a wallet stuffed with pound notes. He whistled in surprise.

The second man was already stretching out a hand for the trouser pocket nearest him, swearing as the skiff dipped alarmingly, and he had to kneel in the bottom of the boat. As the skiff steadied, he managed to dig into the wet cloth and extract more pound notes. "I'll be damned!"

Opening the wallet, the third man searched for identification. "Ah." He pulled out a card from behind the wet notes. Squinting a little, he read, " 'Justin Fowler. London.' What's he doing here, dead, then?"

"I told you. A German spy."

"You've got spies on the brain," the third man snapped. "Get over it."

There had been a spy scare not long before. Several waiters in London restaurants bore German names, and it was reported to the authorities that these men had been listening to private conversations while guests dined, looking for information to be sent back to Berlin. Nothing had come of it, as far as anyone in this part of Essex could discover. Mr. Newly had not been back to the city to visit his daughter, and thus the source of this bit of news had dried up before the spies had been arrested, shot, or deported, allowing for considerable speculation in The Rowing Boat at night. Much had been said about what should be done with such men if they were caught out here, far from London.

"Who do you suppose killed him?" the first man ventured. "Someone who followed him from London? It's not likely to have been anyone from the airfield. I've never seen them this far upriver."

"Most likely whoever shot him shoved him into the water. Out of sight, out of mind." The third man counted the wet notes a second time. "There's almost a hundred pounds here!"

"Flotsam and jetsam," the second man said. "We found it, we keep it. Like a shipwreck." He gazed round at the desolate sweep of water and marsh and gray sky as if half expecting to see a ship's hull half sunk in the deeper reaches beyond.

It was an unfortunate reference. They knew, all of them, what a shipwreck could lead to.

"What do we do with Mr. Fowler?" the first man asked dubiously. "If we bring him in, we'll have to summon the police. Someone is bound to want to know what's become of his money."

"Tow him out to sea. Let him wash ashore somewhere else," the third man said, scrabbling in the bottom of the skiff for a length of rope. This he proceeded to loop around the dead man's neck, and then he ordered, "Pick up yon oars. I can't row and pull at the same time, now can I?"

The first man sat where he was. "We're towing him nowhere until there's some understanding here. The money is evenly divided."

"I saw him first," the second man ventured. "Finder's fee."

"The hell with that," the third man retorted. "Share and share alike, I say. And then there's no room for one of us to feel denied and start trouble. We're all in this together. If one must hang, we'll all hang."

"If I walk home today with this much money in my pocket, my wife will ask questions. What do I say, then?" the first man demanded. "She'll start the trouble, mark my words."

"Then don't march home with the money stuffed in your pocket, you fool. Put it by, and use it a little at a time. You don't go waving it about first thing. Think of your old age, or your daughter's wedding, when a bit of the ready will come in handy. This poor devil doesn't need pounds wherever he's gone to, and it's a sheer waste to let the sea have it. We've done nothing wrong, have we? We didn't kill him, we didn't leave him here to be found by a schoolboy looking to fish for his dinner, we just took what he'd got no use for. Simple as that."

Half persuaded, the first man said, "Still, I've never kept a secret from my wife. That'll take some doing." He picked up his oar from the bottom of the skiff and put it in the water.

The third man laughed. "You've never needed to lie before. Now there's a reason."

They began to pull against the incoming tide, heading for the mouth of the inlet, towing the body behind them. The first man scanned the shoreline as they passed.

"I don't see anyone about, looking this way. Do you think they can see what's at the end of the rope?"

"It just appears that we've forgot to bring the rope inboard."

"What if he comes back again?" the first man asked, glancing over his shoulder. He was finding it a struggle to row against the current with that sluggish weight pulling at the rope attached to it.

"He won't," the third man promised. "He hasn't been in the water all that long. You can tell, the fishes haven't truly got at him yet. But they will. And no one will be the wiser."

But there he was wrong.

# 2

Sergeant Hampton had brought the man to Rutledge's office, saying only, "Inspector Rutledge will help you, sir," before vanishing back down the passage.

The visitor was a walking skeleton, pale except for his dark hair and his pain-ridden dark eyes. Sitting down gingerly in the chair that Rutledge offered, he seemed to feel the hardness of the seat in his bones, for he moved a little, as if hoping to find a more comfortable spot.

"My name is Wyatt Russell," he began in a voice thinned by illness. "I'm dying of cancer, and I want to clear my conscience before I go. I killed a man in 1915 and got away with it. I want to confess to that murder now. There won't be time to try me and hang me, but at least you'll be able to close the file and I'll be able to sleep again."

Rutledge considered him. People confessed for a good many reasons, not the least of which was to salve their conscience before facing a more lasting justice than that of the Crown. Sometimes they confessed to protect someone else.

"I was in France in 1915," he said after a moment. "If this is where the murder occurred, you should speak to the Army, not to Scotland Yard."

"It isn't an Army matter," Russell replied shortly.

"Perhaps we should start at the beginning, if I'm to make use of your confession. Where do you live, Mr. Russell?"

"I have a house in the Essex marshes. I've lived there all my life, until the war. I have money of my own and have never needed to seek employment."

"Was the Yard called in to investigate this murder, or was it handled by the Essex police?"

The man smiled. "I really can't say. I didn't hang about to see."

"In that case, can you be certain you killed this man? He could have been wounded and recovered."

"Yes. I'm absolutely certain. You see, he's my cousin. I'd have known if he'd cropped up again later. His name is—was—Justin Fowler. Not to speak ill of the dead, but we had our differences, he and I, and in the end they were serious enough that I had to make a decision. That doesn't excuse killing him, I realize that. I'm simply trying to set the record straight."

"Was a woman involved?"

Russell was disconcerted. "A woman? Ah. A love triangle. Sorry to disappoint you, but it wasn't that simple. And I'm not prepared to go into any more detail. Suffice it to say, I killed him and got rid of the body. It was during the war. People were enlisting, going to work in the factories. A time of upheaval, change. No one noticed when he went missing."

"The more we learn about a murder, the sooner we can determine who is guilty and who isn't. Establishing motive is an important part of an inquiry."

"But I've just told you—I've confessed to killing him. I can show you how and where, and what became of the body. I can't believe you need any more than that." His face had flushed, adding ugly blotches of red to his gray complexion.

"You've come to the police," Rutledge said, wondering what was behind the man's sudden anger, "of your own free will. Now it's necessary for the Yard to look into your confession and draw its own conclusions. A motive will tell us to what extent you are guilty of this crime. What role the victim played in antagonizing you—"

"Damn it, man, dead is dead." He glanced around, as if expecting to find answers in the plain walls and dusty window glass. Or was he searching for a way to retreat from what he'd confessed to? Rutledge thought it likely, and Russell's next words proved him right. "I shouldn't have come. It was selfish of me. I just didn't want to die with this knowledge on my soul." His gaze returned to Rutledge. "If you can't help me, I'll leave and we can forget I ever walked through your door."

"You've admitted to murder—" he began.

"Have I?" The man's mouth quirked. "My doctor will tell you it's just the morphine speaking. I have hallucinations, you know. It's difficult sometimes to tell true from false." He rose to go. "I'm sorry to have taken up your time, Mr. Rutledge. Dying is not something to relish. It is something to endure. No matter what the poets may tell you."

He reached for the back of the chair to steady himself, then said, "I doubt we'll meet again."

He went out the door without looking back, a man in great pain, walking upright by an effort of will, Rutledge thought. Pride was sometimes the last vanity to go.

After a moment, Rutledge stood up and went after him. "Is there

somewhere you must go? Or will you have lunch with me?" he asked
as he caught Russell up.

"Lunch? I can hardly swallow a mouthful of tea without nausea."

"It doesn't matter. I'd like your company."

Russell considered him. "Why should you wish to sit across a table
from this gaunt wasteland of a man? If you think you'll convince me
to change my mind about coming here, you're wrong. I have a strong
will. It has kept me going longer than my doctors thought possible."
He smiled at that, transforming his face to a shadow of what it might
have been before his illness.

"I was in the war," Rutledge said simply. "I have seen death
before."

After a moment Russell nodded. "I'm at The Marlborough. They
do a decent roast lamb with mint sauce. I can enjoy the sauce still."

The Marlborough would not have been Rutledge's choice. He had
gone there last with Meredith Channing. It wasn't a memory he cared
to revisit. But he had a feeling that if he suggested another restaurant,
he could well lose Wyatt Russell.

The hotel was not very far away, but Rutledge drove them there,
and Russell sat beside him in silence. He got out of the motorcar with
some difficulty, but Rutledge wisely stayed where he was, offering no
assistance.

Inside, Reception was busy, but the dining room was still mostly
empty, since it was early for a meal.

They were conducted to a table in a corner, and Russell sat down
on the damask upholstered chair with a sigh of relief.

"I should take a cushion with me these days. Sitting on wood has
become a trial for me. Will you have something to drink? It's my treat,
because I shall be able then to set the rules."

"As you wish. I'll have a whisky." Hoping to loosen Russell's
tongue . . .

Russell nodded, gave the order for two, and looked around. "I don't know half these people. Before the war, I could have put a name to most of them."

"In London often, then, were you?"

"I was young, unmarried, just down from Cambridge. Full of myself. Full of the future. In love. Essex was dull, boring. London was busy, exciting. If I even thought about it, life seemed to stretch ahead in an endless golden haze, and I expected to be happy forever. Or at least, looking back on 1914, that's how I recall it now. It may not have been such a blissfully happy time, but it does no harm to think so. Were you in London then?"

"I was. I seem to remember it in the same way. Were you in the war?"

"Oh, yes, rushing to sign up before it was over, chafing at the bit, afraid the Kaiser would fold before I'd learned how to fight him properly. Writing letters home from training filled with patriotism and an eagerness to kill a people I'd never met. Well, I did know a few Germans at Cambridge. Nice enough chaps, I didn't picture them when I was hot to shoot the Hun. They weren't the sort to bayonet Belgian babies and rape Belgian women. My cousin was fond of one of them, in fact, but the man was called home shortly before hostilities were declared, and we don't know if he survived the fighting or not."

"If you were in the war, how is it that you were in Essex to commit murder?"

"Yes, that's a bit confusing, isn't it? I was sent to London with dispatches. The house had been closed up, but I went down to have a look at it. Fowler was there, we quarreled. Opportunity presented itself, and temptation did the rest. There was a temporary airfield nearby. Zeppelin watch and night flights. The only risk was that if the body was discovered, one of the new chaps would be blamed for what happened. But apparently I was lucky. No one stumbled over him."

"Were you married when you went to war?"

"Ah, too many questions."

Rutledge's whisky came. Still probing, he said, "I decided not to marry the girl I thought I was in love with. And a good thing—I think she loved the uniform more than she loved the man. The marriage wouldn't have lasted." And he was reminded again of Meredith Channing, whose marriage had lasted, on the cold ashes of duty.

Russell studied Rutledge for a moment over the rim of his glass. "Did it turn out well, your war?"

"Not at all well."

"Yes, it seldom does, I expect. I found that killing people wasn't to my liking after all. But I did my duty to my men and to my country. I was damned glad when it was over, all the same."

"Did being a soldier make it any easier, killing your cousin?"

There was a moment's hesitation. "The policeman again. Do you never leave him at home? It must be a bloody nuisance at dinner parties, wondering what subtle undercurrent of meaning there might be when someone asks you to pass the salt."

Rutledge laughed.

"What made you decide to join the police? Why not become a lawyer, instead, if you were hell-bent on punishing evildoers?"

"My father was a solicitor. I considered his profession, and then decided against it."

The waiter brought their lamb, and Russell inspected it. "I'm hungry enough to chew the table. But swallowing is another matter." He sopped up a little of the sauce with a corner of bread and tasted it. "Ah yes. I remember why I always liked this so much."

They spoke of other things during the meal, and Rutledge waited until they had finished their pudding before asking, "Why did you decide to come to the Yard in person, rather than to write a letter that would be opened after your death?" He had once known a murderer who did just that.

"The policeman is back, is he? We could have been great friends, save for him. All right, I suppose you deserve the answer to one question. It seemed rather cowardly to tell someone after the fact. I suppose I had a religious upbringing of sorts and realized that to confess was not enough. To admit wrongdoing and to show contrition while I was alive had more meaning somehow."

"And do you feel better, for having unburdened your soul?"

Russell frowned. "Do you know, I thought I would. I've kept my secret for a very long time, or so it seemed to me. Screwing up the courage to come to the Yard while I could still manage the effort was a test of my intent. My strength of character, as it were. But it wasn't quite—as I'd expected."

"Would you have been happier if I'd clapped you in irons and taken you to trial? Would hanging make a difference?"

"I had rather not hang, although it would shorten a lingering death. And perhaps I felt, after a fashion, that my crime was not as horrific as it had seemed at the time. That's the war speaking, of course. When one has killed thousands—well, hundreds, although it sometimes seemed like thousands—what's one more life taken? But do you know, it does make a difference. I think it matters because I had a choice, you see. I could have *not* killed him. And yet I did. And so I have come to you to confess and set the record straight. Only," he added, frowning at the remnants of his pudding, "it hasn't been set straight, has it? Are you quite certain that you must know more about *why* I killed him?"

"It will have to come out. If there is an inquiry. You'll be questioned. And if you fail to answer those questions satisfactorily, then we will go in search of the answers ourselves. It will not be pleasant."

"I hadn't expected it to be pleasant," Russell told him. "I had just not anticipated that it would be so very personal. Or public. Least of all, that anyone else would have to be involved. With any luck, I shall be dead before it reaches that stage. Tell the policeman to mind his own business until then. I've no doubt you'll not let this matter drop, but once I'm not there to answer your questions, you won't be able to do any harm." He signaled the waiter, and then said to Rutledge, "I'm very tired. It's one of the curses of my condition. I shan't be able to see you out."

"Is there anything that I can do? Help you to your room?"

"Thank you, no. I can still manage that."

Rutledge rose and held out his hand. "If you change your mind at any point, you know where to find me."

"Yes, I do. Thank you, Inspector."

Rutledge turned to walk away, and Russell said, "Actually—there is one thing you might do for me."

Facing Russell again, Rutledge asked, "What is it?"

"Pray for my soul. It might help. A little."

Motoring back to the Yard, Rutledge considered Wyatt Russell. If he'd been telling the truth, that he'd come to confess a murder that was weighing on his soul, why had he been so reluctant to tell the whole truth, and not just a part of it?

Was someone else involved?

And that was very likely the answer. But then why not simply continue to live with the secret, and die without confessing it? When Russell learned he couldn't have it both ways, he had retreated from that confession.

Was that someone else a partner in the crime? Or the reason for it?

As he got out of his motorcar at the Yard, he was examining a map of Essex in his head. North of the Thames, north of Kent on the other side of that river, it was threaded with marshes, the coastline a fringe of inlets and a maze of tidal rivers that isolated the inhabitants in a world little changed with the passage of time. Until the war, the people of that part of Essex had known little about the rest of their county, much less their country, content with their own ways, in no need of modern conveniences or interference in a life that contented them.

As Essex moved inland, it was a different story entirely, with towns, villages, and a plethora of roads. Basildon, Chelmsford, Colchester might as well be the antipodes as far as the marsh dwellers were concerned, as distant to their way of thinking as London itself. And Rutledge, nodding to the sergeant on duty and mounting the stairs to his office, was certain that a murder in villages even in that part of the countryside wouldn't go unnoticed. Unless, of course, Russell had been very clever indeed at disposing of an unwanted body.

Something had been said about an airfield.

Rutledge walked on past his office and went to find Constable Greene, who had served with a squadron based near Caen.

Greene, a spare, affable man with unruly fair hair that to his chagrin curled when the weather was damp, was thirty-three, coming late to police work. After the Armistice, he had decided to join the Metropolitan Police, and it wasn't long before he had come to the attention of the Yard. Before the war he had owned a bicycle shop in Reading that had just begun to cater to motorcars when hostilities broke out. He had been mad to fly, but heights had made him ill, and so he had maintained and repaired the machines he loved. In the constant struggle to find parts to keep his pilots flying, he knew most of the other airfields in France. He might well know one in Essex.

Looking up as Rutledge came toward his desk, he smiled. "Afternoon, sir. What can I do for you?"

"I'd like to borrow your memory. From the war." He described what little Russell had told him about the airfield and asked, "Can you possibly place it?"

Greene frowned. After a moment he said, "There were several out there. At a guess, I'd say you're looking at Furnham. On the River Hawking. They had a good deal of trouble there. Not the least from locals wanting them out."

"What sort of trouble?"

"Wind, for one thing, and low-lying mists on the water. And then there was the burning of hay ricks, sending smoke across the field.

Petty theft. Quarrels among the men posted there and their neighbors. Mind you, many of the local girls didn't object to the newcomers. That may've had something to do with it. From what I was told, Furnham is fairly isolated. Change wouldn't be welcomed."

"What became of the airfield when the war ended?"

"I expect it was turned back to the farmer who owned it."

Rutledge nodded. "Makes sense. All right, thank you, Greene."

"Anything come up about Furnham? I can't say I'd mind going there to see it for myself."

"Some mention was made of the airfield over lunch. I was curious," Rutledge said easily and went to his office.

He debated whether to initiate an official inquiry into the murder that Russell had confessed to, and then decided against it. He wasn't completely certain about the man's motive in coming to the Yard.

But his own curiosity had been aroused, and it would do no harm, he told himself, to look into it unofficially. If more information turned up, he could bring in the Yard.

Two hours later, the reports on his desk finished, he went to Somerset House to look up Justin Fowler and Wyatt Russell.

# 3

Set on the banks of the Thames below The Strand, Somerset House had become the repository of records for births and deaths and marriages in England and Wales. Named for a Tudor palace long since demolished, it had been designed with the intent to collect in one place offices of government formerly scattered across London, from Inland Revenue to the Admiralty. Nelson was said to have had rooms there, although it was unlikely.

Rutledge spent three-quarters of an hour looking for Justin Fowler. The name had been passed down through three generations in one family, and there were six more unrelated Fowlers who could also have been the murder victim.

Finally settling on Justin Arthur Ambrose Fowler, who was only two years older than Russell appeared to be, he discovered that there was no date of death registered. And no marriage.

Wyatt Russell was easier to find, again with no date of death. But he had been married to a Louisa Mary Harmon, who had died barely a year later in childbirth.

There appeared to be a connection between Fowler and Russell—their grandmothers shared the same maiden name—Sudbury. And from what Rutledge could determine, going back through records, the women were cousins. Fowler's parents died in the same year and within two days of each other, when Fowler was eleven.

Russell had been born at River's Edge in Essex, Fowler in Colchester.

He spent another half hour looking at various branches of the family but found nothing else that seemed to connect the two men in any way.

Thanking the clerk for his assistance, Rutledge went back to the Yard to find a map of Essex.

River's Edge was not shown, which very likely meant it was the name of a house, just as Russell had indicated, and not a village. But he did find Furnham at the mouth of the River Hawking, set on a hook of land that curled out into the water. Like the Thames, the Blackwater, and the Crouch, Zeppelin navigators used the Hawking to find their way to London for raids. But unlike the Thames, the Blackwater, and the Crouch, the Hawking had never become popular with yachtsmen or possessed a Coastguard station at its mouth. Until the airfield had been built, it had probably remained little changed for hundreds of years.

So far, it appeared, the story Russell had told seemed to hold up.

Where was Justin Fowler? Alive and well in Colchester, or even Cornwall, for that matter? Or was he dead, his body as yet undiscovered?

Rutledge considered the upcoming weekend. He'd promised his sister Frances to take her to a concert on Friday evening—she was an accomplished pianist in her own right, like their mother, and the program included Liszt, one of her favorite composers.

But once that duty was done, the rest of the weekend was his.

It turned out not to be as simple as he'd expected.

Frances enjoyed the concert immensely, as well as the light supper he'd arranged when it was over. Finishing her wine, she said, "Ian, do you think we could drive into Kent tomorrow to call on Melinda?"

Melinda Crawford was the elderly woman who had been a friend of Rutledge's parents. Rutledge had known her since he was a small boy fascinated by the treasures in her house. For she had lived in India until her husband's death and traveled widely thereafter, collecting whatever struck her fancy, from jewels to swords to ivory figures of Chinese Immortals.

He had avoided Melinda since the war, although he had been thrust into her company from time to time by unexpected events. She knew him too well. And he feared that she would read in his face more than he cared for her to know about his war. As a child she had survived the Great Indian Mutiny, and having seen death at first hand, she was not as easily put off by his assurances that he was whole. If anyone could have understood about Hamish MacLeod, it was undoubtedly Melinda Crawford. And yet Rutledge couldn't bring himself to confide in her. He still carried the shame of Hamish's death, and that was something he could not confess to anyone, much less the widow of an officer twice decorated for gallantry.

"I was thinking of driving into Essex instead," he said lightly.

His sister put down her glass and turned to face him. "Essex?" she said, and he could almost read the list of names passing through her mind as she considered their acquaintances. Failing to come up with a possible connection, she added, "Where in Essex?" And in her eyes he could see speculation that her unmarried brother had met someone of interest.

He laughed. "The marshes. Out along the River Hawking."

"Then it's related to Yard business."

"No. Put it down to curiosity."

Intrigued, she said, "Is lunch on offer? If it is, I'll go with you."

"I'll do my best. But I have no idea what we'll find in the way of likely places to dine."

She considered the warning. "I'll take the risk," she answered finally.

And so it was that at eight on the Saturday morning, he arrived at his sister's house—which had belonged to their parents—and found her dressed for the country and ready to go. As he held the door of the motorcar for her, she said, "The day doesn't look promising."

It was true. Clouds had banked over the city, and as they drove east toward Essex, the clouds seemed to follow at their heels. The brightness far out over the North Sea dimmed, and by the time they were well out into the countryside, the sky was slate gray over their heads and the increasingly marshy landscape was colorless and drab with no features of interest. It wasn't suitable for cultivation or pasturage, and Rutledge decided the people who lived farther out on the hook of land that followed the length of the river must make their living from the sea.

Frances said, "Is this where your curiosity is taking you?"

Rutledge found the turning he was after. "Call it a sudden and irresistible desire to explore. I don't know this part of Essex."

"Then how did you know that turning was there?"

"Ah. As it happens, I was looking at a map."

Just here the river was out of sight beyond the widening stretch of marsh grass and a few wind-stunted trees. But they could see it glinting like pewter from time to time and knew it was there, moving silently and swiftly, the current dark and smooth.

"I'm not sure I like this place," Frances said after a while, gazing out toward the river. "Whatever possessed you to want to come here?"

"Curiosity," he answered. "I told you."

"Yes, well, you must be in desperate need of entertainment. Couldn't we have explored in Surrey? Or perhaps Oxfordshire? There are some lovely restaurants in Surrey. And Oxford, as well."

"I think you'll change your mind before the day is out," he said. But he had a feeling that she wouldn't.

The road had begun to narrow before he saw the gates. He thought there had probably been more traffic here during the war, but now the verges were overgrown and uneven.

The tall stone posts were overgrown as well, a rusted chain stretched between them to bar visitors. A handsome pair of stone pineapples, the symbol of hospitality, capped the posts. A vine had twisted itself around the pineapple on the left, while the one on the right was chipped and white with bird droppings. His first thought was that someone had shot off the top. It had that sort of look to it.

Drawing up in the shallow space before the gates, Rutledge said, "Wait here. Do you mind? I'd like to explore a little."

"I can just see the roof of a house behind those trees. Is that where you're going?"

"Yes."

"I'll come with you," she replied. "I'd rather not sit here alone. I could almost believe eyes are watching our every move. You could hide half a battalion in that grass across the way. I should have thought German spies by the dozens would have found this to be a wonderful landing place. How far is the North Sea, do you think?"

"A few miles. I'm sure this part of Essex was heavily patrolled by the Coastguard for that very reason," he said. "I'm told there was an aerodrome somewhere out here. They'd have been doubly watchful. Are you certain you want to trek through that tangle?"

She smiled. "Of course I don't."

He helped her out of the motorcar and lifted the heavy chain for her to pass under it. They tramped through the high grass and weeds, Rutledge leading the way to break a path for her, and moved up what had once been the drive. Briars caught at her skirts and pulled at the hem of her short jacket.

"Really, Ian!" she said at one point. But they followed the drive for perhaps a quarter of a mile before they reached the trees. Walking through them was easier, but the undergrowth hadn't been cleared for some time, and at one point a fallen tree blocked their way. Helping her over it, he looked beyond where they were standing and realized that he could see the house clearly now.

It was tall, brick built, with peaked roofs, long windows facing him, and an array of chimneys. He could just pick out the swing of the drive before the main door.

The windows were blank gray spaces against a gray, sunless day, giving the house an abandoned look. By the time they reached the broad steps up to the black painted door, it was clear that the house hadn't been lived in for some time.

Looking up at the date incised into a plain scroll set into stone above the door, Frances read, "1809. It's really a rather handsome house, isn't it? What a pity that it's been left to wrack and ruin. I wonder what happened to the family that lived here?"

"The heir probably died in the war."

"Sadly, yes. Very likely."

A pair of unclipped bushy evergreens grew to either side of the steps, and he pushed his way through the scraggly branches of the one to his left in order to peer through the nearest window. "Dust sheets," he reported. "But there's a wide entry, with doors to either side, and a staircase rising just beyond. Elegant ceiling, what I can see of it."

From the condition of the drive and the closed look to the house, it was clear that Wyatt Russell was not living here now. And it was obvious the house hadn't been reopened after the war. Why had he given Essex as his address, if he was currently living in The Marlborough Hotel, not just staying a few days there?

Rejoining Frances, Rutledge added, "Shall we walk round to the water? There may be a bench or two where we can sit and admire the view."

"I'm withholding all expectations," she said dubiously, "but lead on."

A broad terrace faced the river, with long windows looking out to it and large urns marking either side of the steps. Whatever had once been planted in them, they were empty now. From here, across the overgrown lawn running down to the river's edge, the view was spectacular: a broad sweep to marshes on the far side that seemed to come alive with color when the sun broke through the clouds for a moment. On the rotting boards of a landing stage at the bottom of the lawn, a heron stared down at his reflection in the mirrored darkness of the silently moving water. Then in one swift, fluid action, his neck stretched down and came up with a small fish, silvery in his beak. And then the sun went behind the clouds once more, and the view seemed diminished.

But there were neither chairs nor benches.

"What a lovely spot," Frances said, standing beside her brother. "I can imagine sitting here on a summer's evening, watching the water and talking to friends. Did you know the people who lived here? Is that why you came?"

"No."

He turned to look up at the house, scanning the windows. But if there was someone inside on the upper floors, he—or she—couldn't be seen from the terrace below. Heavy drapes had been drawn across the panes on this side of the house, their faded colors somehow sad.

After a time Rutledge turned, and they walked back the way they'd come.

Halfway up the long drive, Frances said, "Ian, I've been meaning to ask you. Have you seen Meredith Channing recently? She appears to have gone away. Only the other day, Maryanne Browning was asking if I'd had any news of her."

Rutledge knew where Meredith Channing had gone. But he shook his head. "Scotland, perhaps?" he said. "There was mention of a brother-in-law there?"

"Yes, that must be it," Frances said, but there was a touch of doubt in her voice.

At the gates he inspected the pillars. The name of the house hadn't been incised here. But he was nearly certain it would have been River's Edge. Unless there was another house ahead?

In the motorcar once more, they drove on.

In another mile or so, a dead tree lifted bare, twisted arms toward the sky, and just beyond, there was a church, a short tower rising from the plain upright brick facade.

Early Victorian, at a guess, Rutledge thought, looking up at the tower. And not a very happy example of village church at that. He wondered what his godfather, the architect David Trevor, would make of it, and he smiled.

The sign between the porch and the road was almost Pre-Raphaelite in its design and would have done justice to an Arthurian legend. It read, in elegant letters set out in gold leaf, THE CHURCH OF ST. EDWARD THE CONFESSOR.

Rutledge regarded that with wry amusement. Very fitting, he thought.

Beneath were the times of services and the name of the pastor: Morrison. Below that was a quotation from the Psalms:

*I will lift mine eyes unto the hills . . .*

"What is it doing out here? In the middle of nowhere?" Frances asked as they drew even with the signboard. "And there's no Rectory. No churchyard. How very odd."

It was not strictly speaking ugly, but there was something about the church that stirred the voice in Rutledge's head. Hamish had been quiet all morning, and now he was a restive presence in the back of Rutledge's mind.

Rutledge tried to ignore him. He said to his sister, "Perhaps the village was moved."

"Yes, that could be, of course. But surely not the churchyard as well?"

He braked, the engine idling. A gust of wind hit the motorcar, shaking it. "It may serve a scattered population."

"It looks as if it's been exiled," she remarked. Then, turning to her brother, she asked, "Ian, what brought you here? And don't tell me again that it's curiosity."

"Actually it was. That much is true. I wanted to have a look at this part of Essex."

"Then it has to do with an inquiry?"

"More a bit of intuition heaped on suspicion and doubt."

Above their heads, wind swirled around the tower, and the clapper touched the mouth of the bell with a sound almost like that of a distant buoy.

The church was in good repair. It appeared that there was a priest who conducted services here. But who were his parishioners? The house they'd passed was too far away, and there was no sign of a village in any direction.

"It makes me sad to look at that church. Is there anything beyond here?"

"Let's find out."

Driving on once more, they traveled at least another three miles before they reached the first outposts of a village. Which, he realized, surely meant that the deserted house they'd seen must indeed be River's Edge.

There were no stragglers. One minute nothing but tall grass sweeping in waves before the wind, and then the first dwelling appeared, square, brick, and squat beneath its roof. Seven more bungalows, and they were in the High Street, where on the left, others were interspersed among the shops. Beyond stood a small two-storey inn, and where the road curved to the north, a large plane tree towered over the cottages nearest to it.

To the right-hand side of the road, other buildings stood with their backs to the river, among them what appeared to be a schoolhouse, and just after the pub he glimpsed the water stairs. On the strand beyond, there were fishing boats drawn up, waiting for the tide to turn. One or two were flatter-bottomed craft used to hunt waterfowl.

Although it was a Saturday afternoon, the village street was deserted, and as they reached the bend in the road, Rutledge recognized the hook of land he'd seen on the map at the Yard.

The wind had continued to pick up, and as they followed the bend that took the road inland, the motorcar swayed with the force of it. Here the village ended with a house or two like afterthoughts, and to the right beyond the last of the houses the road rose a little, telling him that this hook of land was higher than the village and therefore possessed better drainage. In proof of it, he saw farms ahead and counted three of them before the road turned inland again and the marshy ground reappeared in the distance. Which of the farms had been the site of the airfield? There were no derelict buildings to tell him which had been commandeered. And all three offered broad stretches of pasturage and a few fields of corn for livestock that were flat enough for aircraft to take off and land. Ideal, then, for a small squadron of night fighters and Zeppelin patrols. What's more, it was right on the North Sea, with excellent visibility when the sea mists weren't rolling in.

Frances was saying, "Did you notice? There's no church to be seen in the village. And no churchyard. How odd! Where do they bury their dead? And there's no real hotel, is there? Only that tiny inn. It can't have more than six rooms, and most likely only four. And the way people stared at us, they aren't used to strangers, are they? I doubt we'll be dining here after all."

She was right, he thought. There was no welcome in Furnham. He turned the motorcar and drove back to the village. A few weathered sheds stood back above the tide line, beyond where the boats were drawn up, and a track led out to them.

He pulled up the brake and got out. Frances came to join him and quickly put her hand on her hat. Here the sweep of the wind was fierce.

She hurried back to the motorcar, saying, "You aren't walking down to the water, are you? It's about to rain."

"No." He could see all he needed to see from where he stood. The wind-whipped water was frothy, as if seething just below the surface. Looking over his shoulder, he could see that rain was imminent, and with it would come colder air. He stayed for a moment longer, watching the boats rock as the tide toyed with them. Beyond was the narrow estuary, and a line of mild turbulence where the river met the sea. Returning to the motorcar, he drove on.

Behind the pub, he glimpsed a seawall where larger craft were tied up, bobbing at anchor, their masts swaying. Slowing again, he watched as a man in a heavy fisherman's sweater and wool cap came up between two houses, moving briskly along what must be a path. Without looking in their direction, he turned toward the shops and disappeared into one of them.

"I feel overwhelmed by the warmth of our reception," Frances commented wryly. "Are we leaving, do you think?"

"Not just yet," Rutledge answered. He wasn't sure what he'd hoped to find here in Furnham. Whatever it was, he was still unsatisfied.

There were others on the street now, and the feeling that the village must be as deserted as River's Edge lessened. But the air of friendliness often encountered in summer was still missing. Frances was a very attractive young woman, and yet none of the men had even glanced her way. It was almost as if they wished to discourage any excuse for personal contact.

He'd no more than thought that when a short, heavyset man coming their way stopped and said brusquely, "Looking for someone?"

Not "Can I help you?" or "New to Furnham, are you?"

"Actually," Rutledge answered, pulling up, "we were wondering where we might have lunch."

The man considered them. "We don't run to restaurants," he replied. "Not here. You might find something more to your liking back the way you've come."

But there was nothing back the way they'd come. Not for miles.

While over the man's shoulder, Rutledge could see what appeared to be a small shop of no particular distinction perhaps, but most certainly catering to the local people. He thanked the man, who walked on without another word.

Rutledge pulled to the far side of the street, indicating the shop.

"We might try our luck here," he suggested. "Not precisely the *Michelin Guide,* but we could do with a cup of tea, don't you think?"

"Ian," Frances said quietly, "I really feel we ought to take the none-too-subtle hint and be on our way. In fact, I've rather lost any appetite I might have had."

"Quite," he answered but nodded toward the shop as two women stepped out and turned up the street, not looking at them. "All the same, it could be two hours or more before we find a suitable restaurant. Let's take our courage in our hands and go inside. Those women seem to have survived the experience."

Frances laughed. "You are impossibly optimistic."

Coming around to open her door for her, he added, "Surely not everyone in Furnham is churlish. There could even be a friendly smile inside that door."

But as they stepped into what turned out to be a small tearoom-cum-bakery, he caught the quick look the woman behind the counter gave them and watched her mouth turn down, as if she resented their intrusion.

It was cozy enough, inside out of the wind. Pretty blue checkered linen covered the tables, and the chairs were painted white. A large mural along the back wall showed the sea on a sunny day, the water as blue as the sky, and white puffs of cloud sailing along the horizon. A man and a woman sat on the strand, a picnic basket between them, while three children splashed in the water or built sand castles with the aid of a small green bucket and a white shovel. It was unexpectedly good workmanship. A local artist, or someone from the flying field?

The woman was saying, "Sorry, love, we're just closing." In spite of the friendly words, her voice was cold.

The three elderly women sitting in the far corner turned to look in Rutledge's direction, taking in what his sister was wearing, and then turning away, as if they'd lost interest.

"I expect," he said pleasantly, "that you could provide a cup of tea for two travelers who have lost their way." He ushered Frances to a table and stood waiting for the woman to answer.

With poor grace, she said, "A cup of tea then."

Frances was about to protest, saw her brother's expression, and sat down in the chair he was holding for her.

As he joined her at the table to await their tea, Frances said quietly, "This *is* Yard business, isn't it?"

Without denying it, Rutledge looked out the window at the buildings straggling along the riverfront across the way. One, he thought, was indeed a small schoolhouse, and another appeared to be a shoemaker's shop, a third a chandler's. Furnham gave him the impression that it hadn't changed since Queen Victoria's day. And its inhabitants seemed to be intent on keeping it that way.

And yet the airfield must have provided the decent if overgrown road that he had followed out here, keeping to the river most of the way and turning only when it opened into the sea beyond. There would have been officers to house, and the pilots. Had there also been an antiaircraft battery? The crews who kept the aircraft flying, the men who fed all of them, saw to their needs, maintained the fields they used for runways, and kept up the buildings they lived in must, at a guess, have doubled the population of Furnham. They must also have brought with them the breath of an outside world the local people were so intent on shutting out. Yet there was no sign as far as he could tell that the airfield had ever existed. As if on the day the war ended, those who had lived and worked there were as eager to make their escape from this isolation as their neighbors were to be rid of them, and like the Arabs, folded their tents and quietly melted away. He could almost envisage Furnham mustering to a man to tear down and obliterate this thorn in their side.

Their tea was brought on a tray painted with wildflowers tied in a bunch by a pretty ribbon. The woman set down a pot and two cups, spoons, a bowl of sugar and a small jug of milk without a word. As she went back to her counter, Rutledge saw a young couple start to enter the shop, notice the strangers by the window, and turn away.

Frances drank her tea with an air of enjoying it, and Rutledge was amused. He rather thought she was determined to make the shop owner, if that was who she was, suffer their presence for as long as possible. He caught the glint in her eyes as she leisurely accepted a second cup and made light conversation as she drank it. Finally, with no tea left in pot or cup, she smiled at him and thanked him.

"That was lovely, Ian. Not quite the luncheon I was promised, but a very nice interlude indeed," she added sweetly, just loud enough for the woman behind the counter to hear.

He paid for the tea, then escorted his sister from the shop. Outside, she said in a low voice, "I swear there must be at least a dozen daggers in my back. Will you pull them out? If looks could kill, I ought to be dead by now. And you as well."

Laughing, he said, "Thanks for being a good sport."

They were walking back to their car when another man, dressed in corduroy trousers and an old shirt, stopped them and asked, "Looking to find property hereabouts, are you?"

Surprised, Rutledge said, "Why do you think we're interested in property?"

"People like you who come here generally are. Possibilities, that's what they said at the end of the war. Turn Furnham into a holiday town for the East End of London looking to enjoy the seaside. Well, you can see for yourself there's not much in the way of seaside, is there? The river's swift and the marshes run down to it, save for here in Furnham, where we've had boats as long as anyone can remember. We make our living from the river, it's true, but there's not much on offer for strangers wanting to amuse themselves."

"A friend," Rutledge said slowly, "was here during the war. He told me that Furnham was a very unfriendly village. That's not likely to bring holidaymakers rushing to visit here, is it?"

"Yet you came, didn't you?" the man retorted. "In spite of our being unfriendly."

"Yes, well, I thought he might have been mistaken. I was—curious, you see."

The man's eyes narrowed. "Just why did you come, then?" He glanced at Frances, standing to one side, then turned back to Rutledge. "We're at the end of a long road. It wasn't happenstance brought you here."

"I told you. Curiosity."

"Was it the house with the gates? The ones with pineapples on the posts? It's not for sale. Whatever you may have heard. Someone saw you walking there."

"A fine view to the river," Rutledge said, as if agreeing with him. "But I prefer neighbors whose rooftops I can see."

"Then you'll be on your way back to wherever it is you came from. I'll bid you and your lady good day."

And he walked on, leaving them standing there.

Frances said, "Ian, it's not amusing any longer. I'd like to go."

As he walked with her to the motorcar, she added, "What are they hiding? For surely it must be that."

"A murder," he said. "At a guess. But whose and when and why, I don't know."

"Then I was right, there in the shop. It *was* Yard business that brought you here."

He shut her door and went to turn the crank. "I'm not quite sure what made me come here," he said, joining her in the motorcar. "A man walked into my office recently and confessed to a murder. I'm not sure I believe him."

"But why would he confess, if there was no truth to it?"

"A good question. To protect someone else? To cover up another crime? To settle a property dispute? Or just to see what we knew—or didn't know—about someone's death?"

"We're back to curiosity, again. His—and yours."

"Exactly. But the Yard can't investigate a crime just because someone tells us it happened. There's no body, for one thing. Nor proof that it ever existed."

The rain arrived at last with steady lightning and heavy thunder, explosive drops striking the windscreen and blinding him as he concentrated on following the nearly invisible road. They ran out of the storm into a wind-driven downpour that pounded the motorcar, ending any conversation. Eventually that passed as well, leaving behind a steady drizzle that was more manageable. He was glad to be out of the marshes now, low lying and no bulwark against a rising river.

Frances said, replying to what Rutledge had been explaining just as the storm broke, "And yet you drove all the way out here. There must have been something about him that made you wonder."

"He told me he was dying. From the look of him, that part may well be true."

"You think, once he's dead, the thread will be lost? Is that why you are looking into this on your own?"

"I expect I didn't care to be made a fool of. With the truth—or with lies."

"But what have you learned? How did this jaunt help you?"

"I now have a feeling for this part of Essex that I didn't have before. And I was grateful for your company. A man on his own would have drawn far more attention, and the last thing I wanted to suggest was Scotland Yard's interest."

His reply satisfied her. But as he drove on, he wasn't sure he'd satisfied himself.

# 4

Ten days later, Rutledge was in his office finishing reports when Sergeant Gibson knocked at the open door and came in.

Looking up, Rutledge said, "I'll have these ready in another half an hour."

Gibson answered, "It's not the reports, sir. There's a dead man found in the Thames and brought into Gravesend. He didn't drown, and no one's claimed the body. They've sent along a photograph, in the hope that the Yard can help out. It's likely he went into the Thames in London. He's not known in Gravesend, at any rate."

He took a photograph from the folder he was carrying and set it down on Rutledge's desk.

Rutledge's first glance was cursory; he didn't expect to recognize the thin face staring back at him from the photograph. His gaze sharpened. Looking at it a second time, he said, "Is this the man who came to the Yard a fortnight ago? Surely not." He hadn't expected Russell to end his suffering quite so soon.

"It was twelve days, sir. As I remember. Sergeant Hampton spotted the likeness—he was the one brought the man up to see you—and in my view he's usually right about such things. A good memory for faces, has the sergeant. That's why I brought the photograph up to show you. I thought you might want to know. There's a strong resemblance, Sergeant Hampton says, although the water hasn't been kind to him."

"No. What did the postmortem show?"

"He hadn't long to live. An abdominal cancer, inoperable. It could well have been a suicide, given that. Except for the fact that someone shot him in the back of the head."

"Did they indeed?" He studied the photograph. "The man who came to the Yard was dying of cancer. Given this photograph, I should think the body must be his. Who is handling the inquiry in Gravesend?"

"Inspector Adams, sir."

"I've heard of him. A good man. Very thorough." He shuffled the papers in front of him into a folder and set it aside. "These can wait. And it's as well to see the body for myself. To be sure."

Gibson said, "Will you be asking the Chief Superintendent? He's having lunch with the Lord Mayor."

"I'll leave a message. It will be late afternoon before he's back at the Yard." Rutledge took out a sheet of paper, and after a moment's thought, wrote a few lines on it. Capping his pen, he passed the sheet to Sergeant Gibson. Glancing at his watch, he said, "I should be back before they've reached the last course."

As the sergeant left, Rutledge collected his hat and notebook and walked out of his office. Five minutes later he was in his motorcar and threading his way through the busy London traffic as he headed east.

Gravesend was an old town on the south bank of the Thames, set-

tled where a break in a long stretch of marshes provided the only landing stage. For centuries, ferrymen here held the charter to transport
passengers to and from London. If anyone knew the river it was the
people of Gravesend. On the outskirts of the town, Rutledge stopped
for directions at a coaching inn that had been refurbished, then followed the omnipresent Windmill Hill into town, where he found the
police station.

Inspector Adams, a slender man with horn-rimmed glasses
perched on the top of his head, looked up as Rutledge was ushered
into his office.

"Scotland Yard?" he said as Rutledge gave his name. "You're here
about our corpse, I think. It was an educated guess, sending that photograph to London. He's not one of ours, we're fairly certain of that.
And the most likely place he came from was somewhere south of the
Tower."

Rutledge asked, "Any idea how long he'd been in the water?"

"At a guess, a good four and twenty hours."

"And there was nothing in his pockets to help with identification?
A hotel key, medicine bottle, even a handkerchief?" There should at
least have been a key from The Marlborough Hotel.

"Nothing." Adams pulled his glasses down and searched for a
paper in the clutter on his desk. "Here we are. White male, approxi-
mately thirty years of age, fair, five feet eleven inches tall," he said,
reading from the sheet he finally located under a stack of books. "No
distinguishing marks, suffering from terminal stomach tumor that has
metastasized. Pockets empty, shot at close range, most likely with a
service revolver, judging from the caliber. Clothes those of a gentleman. In the water for a day, day and a half." He looked up over the
rims of his glasses. "If his killer had waited a few months more, Nature
would have dispatched our victim for him. Hasty, I should say."

"He admitted that he didn't have long to live."

"You know him then. Does he have a name?"

"As a matter of fact, he does. Wyatt Russell, Furnham Road, Essex. It's the name he gave when he came to the Yard recently to report a crime. At this stage we haven't found any evidence to indicate that his information is true. But we also can't prove that it isn't. The question is, does his murder nearly a fortnight later have any bearing on what he told us? What did he intentionally—or unintentionally—stir up? Who else is involved in this?"

Hamish spoke, his voice jarring in the small office. "Ye ken, ye asked yoursel' that same question, when the man wouldna' gie ye any details about the murder."

Rutledge nearly lost track of Adams's reply. He had to repeat himself.

"What sort of crime was he reporting?"

"A murder."

"Well, there you are. Someone will have taken exception to that."

"Except that my visitor claimed he was the killer."

"Did he, by God!" Adams pushed his glasses back to the top of his head. He sat there for a moment, then asked, "Have you considered the extent of his cancer? He must have been in almost intolerable pain and taking a fair amount of drugs. You have to wonder if he was in his right mind. He could have felt responsible for a man's death and finally convinced himself that he'd actually killed him. Guilt can take many forms."

Rutledge was all too aware of that.

"We'd have to ask a medical man. Russell himself had made some remark about the morphine speaking."

"I'm glad it's your case and not mine. Will you want the body? No one so far has claimed it. Potter's field seems an ignominious end. He must have a family somewhere." He opened his desk drawer and fished out a small packet. "This was around his neck. Whoever killed him missed it when going through his pockets."

He tossed the packet to Rutledge, who caught it deftly and unwrapped the brown paper.

Inside was an oval gold locket on a gold chain. An ornately scrolled
*E* graced the front. The locket itself was either old or worn, possibly
both. Rutledge found the clasp and opened it. Inside were two small
spaces for photographs. The right-hand oval was empty, but on the
left there was a woman's face. Despite the water stains, he could see
that she was pretty, young, the just visible collar of her dress fashionable, her hair drawn softly back into a knot behind her head. It was
impossible to judge her coloring, but he rather thought her hair was a
light brown.

"I wondered if this was hers, and she was dead. That would explain why he's wearing a woman's necklace," Adams said. "A senti-
mental gesture."

"Russell lost his wife in childbirth a little less than a year after they
were married. Neither her Christian name nor her maiden name began
with an *E*."

"So much for sentiment," Adams said dryly.

Still considering the face in the locket, Rutledge said, "He knew he
was dying. That means he'd seen a doctor. Possibly in London. We'll
need to find him and speak to him."

"I thought you told me he lived on the Furnham Road in Essex.
That's on the Hawking, isn't it?"

"The house there is closed. When I met him, he was staying in The
Marlborough Hotel. Someone there should be able to tell us more."
Rutledge frowned. "Are we absolutely certain that Russell didn't fire
that bullet into his own brain? To avoid a worse death?"

"Impossible, according to the doctor. Unless the man was a contor-
tionist. Would you like to see the remains?"

Rutledge accompanied Adams to the hospital where the body had
been taken. Down in the bowels of the building they walked through a
series of passages to where a small morgue had been set up. The other
three bodies had died in the hospital, Adams explained, and were
awaiting the undertaker. In the far corner lay their murder victim.

When Rutledge pulled back the covering over the body, he recognized Russell instantly. The likeness was stronger than that of the photograph, which must have been taken in poor light. "Yes. I'd swear to his identity in the witness box." He moved the dead man's head slightly to look at the entry wound of the bullet. "Your doctor is right, he couldn't have shot himself. Who did you say found the body?"

"A waterman by the name of Acton. He got it into his boat and brought it in. You can speak to him if you like. He should be back in Gravesend in about five hours."

"You have his statement? It's satisfactory?"

"On my desk. And yes, Acton has been on the river for years. No reason to think he had anything to do with Russell's death."

"Then I'll take the statement rather than wait." As he replaced the sheet over the dead man, Rutledge said, "If you learn any more about him—if anyone in Kent comes to you searching for him—let me know. But I rather think you're right about London being the place to begin."

"I've already gone through our list of missing people. No one fits his description, and he'd have been missed by now. Surely someone would have come looking for him."

"What about Tilbury, across the Thames from you?" Rutledge asked as they left the hospital.

"We sent a photograph to the police there at the same time we sent one to the Yard. I followed it up with a telephone call, and my opposite number didn't know him or have him on any lists there. Still, I'll ask again, now that I have a name to give them and I know he once lived in Essex."

Rutledge thanked him, taking with him the locket, a copy of the statement from the ferryman, and the report of the postmortem.

They lay in an envelope on the seat beside him as he drove back to London. And from the rear of the motorcar came the voice he knew as well as his own, and dreaded to hear.

Hamish said, "You didna' believe him. Russell. Ye ken, if ye had, he might well be alive."

"No. He made his choice. He wouldn't tell me what I needed to know. He made a mystery of what he had to say because he didn't want to incriminate himself. Or betray someone else."

There was a derisive chuckle.

Hamish wasn't there. Rutledge had told himself that a thousand times, but it was no comfort. Hamish was dead and buried in France, and that was no comfort either.

The doctors had called it shell shock, this hearing of a voice that was so real Rutledge answered it in his head—or sometimes to his absolute horror, aloud. Corporal Hamish MacLeod had fought beside Rutledge almost from the start, a young Scot, but with a grasp of military tactics well beyond his years. A bond had grown between the two of them, officer and man, because each knew he could trust the other implicitly, and both knew that the care of the men under them was paramount. Watching the maimed and the dying through two years of heavy fighting had taught them that. Green men, facing battle for the first time, had only a slim chance of survival. If their officers could double those odds, it counted for much.

And then on the Somme, in those first bloody weeks of fighting, Hamish MacLeod had put Rutledge in an untenable position: he had refused an order outright, in front of his men. His reasons were sound—he knew going over the top one more time after a well-concealed German machine-gun nest was insane, that more men would die needlessly. And yet HQ had ordered that it be taken out at any cost before the next assault, and Rutledge had had no alternative but to try, for the sake of the hundreds of British soldiers who would be crossing No Man's Land in only a matter of hours. The good of the few—or the good of the many. That was the choice. Hamish had chosen his bleeding and exhausted company.

No amount of argument could sway him. Even when, as an example to other weary and dispirited men, Rutledge had to threaten his corporal with a firing squad, it had not changed his mind. And Rutledge had had to carry out that threat, against his better judgment and against the weight of his own guilt. He had had to deliver the coup de grâce to the dying man, taking out his pistol and firing it point-blank, and watching the anguished eyes go dull.

He hadn't wanted this, he hadn't wanted Hamish MacLeod on his soul. Even his own mind had refused to accept what he had done. The burden of guilt had been insupportable. And in the way of damaged minds, his had created a living Hamish, proof that the young corporal hadn't died. Keeping him alive through two more years of grinding stalemate and death, bringing him home in the only way he could.

Military necessity had been paramount. Rutledge had almost hated Hamish for breaking, for forcing his own hand. But close as he was to breaking himself, he had known that the young corporal was right. Still, Duty was all. Compassion had no place on a battlefield. Obeying orders was the paramount rule.

There had been times when Rutledge himself had wanted to die, to shut out the voice hammering at him. And he couldn't, because when he himself died, Hamish would finally be dead as well. He'd led a charmed life in the trenches those last two years of the war—his men had commented on that again and again. But Rutledge had understood it for what it was. God had not wanted him. A murderer . . .

To put an end to the memories threatening to overwhelm him, Rutledge pulled to the verge and stopped the motorcar. Reaching for the envelope on the seat beside him, he took out the locket. Opening it, he looked down at the face of the woman whose photograph had been so carefully placed inside.

Who was she? Why had she been important in the life of one Wyatt Russell?

The woman staring up at him was silent, and after a moment he closed the locket and returned it to the envelope. Why had the dead man been wearing it?

Perhaps if he knew the answer to that, he told himself, he would know why Wyatt Russell had died.

When he reached London, Rutledge went directly to The Marlborough Hotel, where he and Russell had dined. If Russell's belongings were still in his rooms there, it was possible they could tell him more about the man than he'd wanted to reveal when he was alive.

There was a couple just arrived, and it took several minutes before they had registered and relinquished their luggage to the man waiting to carry it to their room. As they walked away, Rutledge stepped forward and asked to see the register for the date, twelve days ago, when he'd come here with Russell.

The clerk was reluctant at first until Rutledge quietly identified himself as Scotland Yard. And then he insisted on checking the register himself.

After going through the guest book, the clerk shook his head. "I don't find a Mr. Russell for that date or any other close to it," he said. "I'm sorry."

"If you would, go back through it again. He indicated he'd taken a room here. He wasn't well."

The clerk ran his finger down the list of hotel guests, turning the pages slowly.

"No, Inspector, I'm sorry. I don't see that name."

Either Russell had lied about where he was staying—or he had lied about his name.

Rutledge thanked the clerk and left. By the time he'd returned to the Yard, Chief Superintendent Bowles was waiting for him. Gibson gave him a warning, with an I-told-you-so expression on his face.

Knocking on the Chief Superintendent's door, Rutledge stepped inside. "You wished to see me, sir?"

"What's this business about Gravesend and a cadaver?"

"I recognized the photograph they sent to the Yard, and I went to see the body for myself." He gave a brief account of Russell's visit and the information he'd learned in Gravesend. But he said nothing about the lunch with Russell or stopping at the hotel before returning to the Yard.

"And you're sure of this dead man's identity?"

"I'm sure he's the same person who came to my office," Rutledge answered carefully. "I'd like to go to Essex, to verify the information I was given. And there may be people there who can tell me more about Russell."

"Yes, yes, by all means. I don't put much stock in his confession, I suggest that you not waste your time in that direction. It's his death that concerns us." He paused, taking up his pen and rolling it in his fingers, as if it might produce answers for Rutledge if he stared at it long enough. Then he said, "I'm acquainted with Inspector Adams's superior. It wouldn't do to let this matter drag on. If you take my meaning?"

Rutledge did. Bowles was pleased to take over the inquiry, bring it to a swift and certain end, and put his opposite number's nose out of joint.

An hour later, Rutledge was on his way to Essex.

This time he didn't have Frances to keep him company. This time it was Hamish. Although the sun was shining and the day was fair, the journey seemed to drag, and he would have sworn that Furnham was twice as far as it had been earlier.

He'd decided that perhaps the place to begin his inquiries was with the clergyman in charge of the isolated church that he and Frances had seen. It was roughly halfway between the deserted house at River's Edge and the village of Furnham. If anyone knew something about Russell's background, it would likely be the man who had ministered to his family.

As he passed the gates to the estate, he wondered again why Russell had deserted it. Because of his wife's death? Or because he had committed murder there and got away with it? Until someone had found him out and come for him.

An eye for an eye.

Ahead he could just see the peaked roof of the church, standing out like a sentinel in the long reaches of the marshes. The grasses had more color today, varied in texture as well as shade, and the river beyond was intensely blue as it mirrored the sky. And yet the warm late summer's day was chilled by the whispers of the wind through the grasses, setting them to move and rustle, as if hidden among them were crowds of people talking together.

Frances had noted it as well, but alone now, he realized that it was defining this place in a way that he hadn't expected.

*As if I'm being watched,* Frances had said.

It would tend, he thought, to make a man with a guilty conscience nervous. Was that why the house stood empty? The whispers that a man's mind turned to accusation?

He drew up before the church. He had no idea where to look for the Rectory, although there must be one. But with luck, he might find someone inside who could direct him.

The sign announcing that this was the Church of St. Edward the Confessor had a new message today on the hoarding below: *Seek and ye shall find. He will welcome all who come to Him.*

Rutledge hoped that a welcome would prove to be true. It had not in Furnham.

He opened the door, listening to the squeal of rusty hinges as he stepped into the plain, Victorian interior.

"Ye willna' have to seek anyone. Yon caterwauling will bring them running."

And Hamish was right. A door at the rear of the sanctuary opened and a man stepped through.

He was wearing a clerical collar and an anxious expression on his square, sun-browned face. It was difficult to judge his age. He was one of those men who would appear boyish well into their forties. Rutledge found himself thinking that this must be a drawback for a clergyman trying to project an image of experience and wisdom.

He didn't come forward. He merely stopped where he was, seeing a stranger, and asked in a strong voice that belied his anxiety, "Are you lost?"

"Mr. Morrison? I'm from London. Scotland Yard. I'd like to speak to you about one of your parishioners."

"Indeed?" It was a question, not a statement. "We have the usual number of reprobates here, but I can't recall that any of them has lately come to the attention of Scotland Yard."

"Is there somewhere we could talk?" Rutledge asked.

The man gestured to the pews that filled the sanctuary. "There are seats aplenty here. Shall we take one of them?"

Rutledge walked forward, and the other man didn't move until he had come to the last row but one. "Will this do?"

"Yes. Thank you." The man stepped forward and finally held out his hand. "I'm afraid you have the advantage of me."

"Inspector Rutledge."

"Ah. Well, Mr. Rutledge, I must confess that I'm not in the confidence of many of my flock, but I'll do what I can to help."

They sat down on the hard wood of the pew, facing each other. Rutledge reached into his pocket and took out the locket on its delicate chain. Opening it, he held it out, but he already knew the answer to his question before he asked it. "Do you know this woman?"

"Yes. Yes, I did," Morrison replied slowly, reaching for the locket, although it was clear he didn't require a closer look. "She once lived nearby."

"Could you tell me her name?"

"Where did you find this locket? May I ask?"

"In Gravesend," Rutledge answered. When the rector said nothing more, his eyes on the photograph, Rutledge added, "The police found it around the neck of a body taken from the Thames."

"Dear God!" The rector closed the locket with a snap, as if he couldn't bear to look at it any longer. He turned his gaze toward the altar. "Who—has the body been identified?"

"We have reason to believe that it is, was, one Wyatt Russell."

The relief filling in the rector's eyes was almost painful to watch. Rutledge looked away. "Did you know him?" he asked.

"I—yes, I knew him. He lived not far from here."

"At River's Edge, in fact."

"Yes, how did you know?"

"He came to see me shortly before his death. You haven't told me who the woman is."

"Was he a suicide?"

"He was murdered," Rutledge replied shortly. "What is her name, Rector?"

"God rest his soul," Morrison said fervently, crossing himself. "As to the woman in the photograph, her name is Cynthia Farraday. She came to live at River's Edge when her parents died of typhoid. Her father and the late Malcolm Russell were cousins, I believe. She was too young to live on her own, and Mrs. Russell, his widow, was made her guardian. She was alive then. Mrs. Russell, I mean. Wyatt's mother. And then one day in the summer of 1914—August, it was— Mrs. Russell simply disappeared. "

"Were the police called in?"

"Yes, the police from Tilbury. When it was realized that she was missing, there was a frantic search for her by the family and the staff. And then someone was sent posthaste to Tilbury. Men were brought out from Furnham to help, because they knew the marshes so well. But she was never found. The inquest concluded that she had drowned herself, for fear her son would die in the war. She'd lost her husband in the Boer War. Her son remembered that when she was a girl, a gypsy had read her hand and predicted that war would take all she loved from her. Her husband's death convinced her that the prediction was true."

There had been a great deal of speculation that summer, after the Austrian archduke and heir to the Hapsburg throne had been assassinated in Sarajevo. Rutledge remembered it well. Would Austria demand a reckoning with the Serbs? And what would Germany do, if Russia insisted on protecting her fellow Slavs? Would France be drawn in, as an ally of Russia? Governments began to mobilize. And in the end, armies began to march. And Belgium, tiny Belgium with open borders and only a small army, had been overrun by the Kaiser's forces on their way to France, in spite of Britain's pledge to protect her. Britain had had no choice then but to declare war on Germany. And all Europe burst into flame.

No one had believed it would happen. And then everyone had believed that it would all be over by Christmas, that the heads of state would come to their senses.

Instead, the war had dragged on for four bloody years. Mrs. Russell had had every reason to be afraid for her son, although no one could have guessed it at the time.

"Was this a strong enough reason for her to kill herself? Surely further inquiry would uncover a better motive for her disappearance? And I should think that if she had drowned, sooner or later her body would have surfaced?"

"You didn't know her," Morrison said wearily. "Elizabeth Russell was obsessed with the news, reading everything she could find. She had daily newspapers sent down from London by special messenger. She corresponded with a friend who'd married a Frenchman, and a telegram was sent telling her when the Germans had marched. And in spite of everything, her son joined the Army not a fortnight after she vanished." He shrugged. "The local people, in their wisdom, were just as glad she hadn't been found. The stigma of suicide, you see, and where to bury the body. They put up quite a fuss even when Russell wanted to set up a memorial to his mother in the family's mausoleum. I must say, that surprised me. Furnham is not a very religious parish, as a rule."

"You said the local people had helped in the search. Could they have seen to it that her body wasn't discovered?"

"Dear God." He was shocked. "I never thought of that."

"Where is this Furnham mausoleum? Is there a churchyard associated with your parish?"

"Ah. The churchyard. The water table is too high, this near the river. It's the reason there isn't a crypt in this church. There's a turning between here and the village. It doesn't appear to be more than a dusty cart path. It leads to higher ground. The Rectory is there as well."

"Forgive me, Rector, but isn't it odd to have a church this far from a village? And the churchyard in another place?"

"It's a long story," Morrison answered. "And not a very pleasant one. I don't know all of it myself. Suffice it to say, this church was built several years before Victoria ascended the throne. It was felt by the Bishop of that day that one was needed in Furnham parish. But over the years very few people in Furnham have availed themselves of it. I have a handful of elderly farmers' wives, a few young children preparing for their first communion, often a bride and groom, and occasionally those who have nowhere else to turn in their misery but to God. I hadn't expected to serve in a parish like this. It has tried my spirit, I can tell you."

And Morrison had very skillfully directed Rutledge away from his questions about Russell and the woman in the locket.

"When was the last time you saw Russell?"

"I don't believe he came home again once he'd joined the Army. Or if he did, I never saw him. I did learn that he was a major. His name appeared on a list of wounded."

"And Miss Farraday?"

"Without Mrs. Russell there to act as chaperone, Miss Farraday went to London. A sad state of affairs, that. With Russell off to war, she might have stayed in the house without any criticism. But when she came to see me to say good-bye, she told me that the house was haunted."

"Literally?"

"I asked her that question myself. She answered that it was filled with the ghosts of what might have been. It was 'not a happy house,' to use her words."

"I understand that Russell was married."

"Yes, on his last leave before sailing for France. I don't believe he ever brought his bride to River's Edge. I'd have liked to meet her. Later I heard she died from complications of childbirth, and the baby with her."

"Perhaps that was why Miss Farraday chose to leave. Because of the marriage."

Morrison smiled, a sadness in his eyes. "If anything it was the other way around. Russell would have married her on the instant. It was my understanding that she refused him. I feared that he'd married just to provide an heir for River's Edge. If he did, it was not given to him, was it? But I understand he survived the war. So much for his mother's superstitions."

Rutledge reached for the envelope again and brought out the photograph of the dead man, taken in Gravesend. "I need confirmation that this is, indeed, Wyatt Russell. If you have any reservations, I'll be happy to take you to Tilbury for the ferry to Gravesend."

"Let me see the photograph, first."

Rutledge passed it to him. Morrison took it and held it to the faint rays of sunlight coming through the plain glass windows high up in the sanctuary wall.

"But this isn't Russell," he exclaimed. "What led you to believe it was?"

"It's not Russell? You're quite sure of that? You haven't seen him in six years," Rutledge countered, making an effort to conceal his consternation.

"I'd stake my life on it!"

# 5

"Could this be Justin Fowler?" Rutledge asked.

"I'm afraid not."

"Then you knew Fowler too?"

"He was a connection of Mrs. Russell's, although I don't believe she had known his family very well. She told me before he came that she'd lost touch with his mother after she married Mr. Fowler. I had the feeling that Mrs. Russell didn't approve of him. That's to say, of the husband. This was just after the solicitor had come to ask her to take the boy in. She said that God in his wisdom had seen fit to give her only one child. But to make up for it, God had sent her the daughter she'd never have and now a second son. I wondered later if she was as happy as she'd expected to be. They weren't that easy to mother. They weren't *hers,* after all. Then she was gone, and the boys—they were young men by that time—left to join the Army. I don't know if

Justin Fowler survived or not. I drove him in Mrs. Russell's motorcar to meet the train to London, and that was the last time I saw him. A quiet boy, kept to himself. I didn't know him well. But he was afraid of something. I never knew what it was."

"Then who is the man in this photograph?"

Morrison frowned as he considered the face again. "I'm sorry. I don't believe I've ever seen him before. But you said he'd come to call on you at the Yard? The man in this photograph? How did you come to believe he was Major Russell?"

"It was the name he gave me," Rutledge said trenchantly.

"How very odd! And you tell me he was wearing the locket with Miss Farraday's likeness in it when his body was pulled from the river?"

"According to those who found him."

"Then I should think you ought to find her and ask her if she knows this man."

"Before I do, what else can you tell me about the Russell household? Are there any of the staff still living in the vicinity? Perhaps in Furnham."

"There was only a small staff. A housekeeper, of course, and several maids. A cook. An elderly groom. And I believe there was a man who acted as butler when there were guests, but generally drove Mrs. Russell when she went out. The household didn't get on well with the local people and kept to themselves more often than not. The groom died soon after Mrs. Russell disappeared. And the cook went to live with a member of her family, when the house was closed. Mrs. Broadley. I remember how apt her name was. An excellent cook! I don't know what became of the housekeeper, Mrs. Dunner. I was told she found employment in the Midlands. Harold—the chauffeur—stayed on as caretaker in the first few weeks of the war, then was called up. There was no one at River's Edge after that."

"The maids?"

"I'd nearly forgot. Nancy married a farmer's son on the other side of Furnham. Samuel Brothers. The others went their ways."

"Tell me how to find this farm?"

"You must drive through Furnham, and when the road curves to the left, just continue along it. The second farm you come to belongs to Brothers."

Rutledge thanked him and took his leave. Morrison walked with him up the single aisle of the church and to the door, like a good host seeing a guest on his way.

He said as they reached the door, "I hope you can identify that poor man in the photograph. I shall pray for him."

"Thank you, Rector."

And then the door was closed behind him, and the rector's footsteps seemed to echo in the emptiness of the sanctuary as he walked back down the aisle.

"He was in love with the lass. In yon locket," Hamish said as Rutledge crossed the narrow strip of lawn to his motorcar.

"Morrison?"

"Aye, the priest."

Rutledge remembered the sadness in the rector's eyes as he said that Russell would have married Cynthia Farraday. Russell was more her equal than a country parson. It could explain why Morrison had found it difficult to discuss her.

He paused as he reached for the crank, and in the silence he could hear the whispers in the grass. It was easy to imagine people hidden among the reeds, some of them taller than a man. For that matter, it would be hard to find someone even twenty feet away from where one stood. It explained the difficulty in searching for Mrs. Russell.

He left the church, turning toward Furnham.

Who the hell was the man who had come into his office, claiming to be Wyatt Russell and swearing he'd murdered Justin Fowler? More to the point, who had killed that man not a fortnight later? And were the two events related? Or was there something else in the victim's past that had led to his death?

Hamish said, "The lass in the locket will know."

"Yes, very likely." But finding her was going to be another matter.

Making a point to look for the turning Morrison had spoken of, he saw it to his left three-quarters of a mile from the church. He drove on, passing through Furnham and out the other side, turning away from the river's mouth toward the farms and pasturage wrested from the marshes. The farms were not large, but they appeared to be prosperous enough. Dairy herds, mostly, he thought, judging from the cows grazing quietly. With only enough acreage for the corn and hay to feed them. He could just see the green tips of the corn in a field beyond, moving with the light sea breeze.

He found the Brothers farm and took the rutted turning that led to the house. Beyond it stood a weathered barn and several outbuildings.

No one answered his knock, and after a moment he walked round to the kitchen door at the rear. There he found a woman in a black dress that had seen happier days, inside a wire pen scattering feed for the chickens bunched and clucking around her ankles. She looked up as Rutledge came toward her, her eyes wary.

It was an expression he was growing accustomed to, here on the River Hawking.

She said, politely enough, "Can I help you, sir?"

"Good morning. My name is Rutledge. I'm looking for Mrs. Brothers."

"And what would you be wanting with her, when you've found her?"

"I'm trying to locate anyone who knew the family at River's Edge. The rector at St. Edward's, Mr. Morrison, has told me Mrs. Brothers was once a housemaid there."

Nodding, she emptied the bowl she was holding in the crook of her arm and walked out of the pen, latching the gate behind her. "Come into the kitchen, then."

He followed her down the path and over the stepping-stones that led between the beds of herbs, flowers, and vegetables flanking the kitchen entrance. Someone, he noted, took pride in the gardens, for they were weeded and the soil between the rows had recently been hoed.

Inside the kitchen, he saw the same care. The cloth over the table was not only clean but also ironed, and both the sink and the cabinets below it were spotless, as was the floor.

"I'm Nancy Brothers," she said, offering him a chair and going to stand in front of the broad dresser. "Why are you looking for anyone from the house?"

"I'm not precisely sure," Rutledge answered her. "This locket has been found, and I'm trying to trace the woman shown inside." He took it from his pocket and held it out to her by the gold chain. "I was told she might have lived at River's Edge."

Instead of reaching for the locket, Mrs. Brothers asked, "Are you a lawyer, then? Or a policeman?"

He told her the truth. "I'm from Scotland Yard. We don't ordinarily search for the owner of lost property. But in this case, it could help us in another matter of some importance."

Mrs. Brothers took the locket, found the clasp, and opened it. "Oh."

"You recognize her?" Rutledge prompted as she stood there staring at the tiny photograph.

"The locket. It brings back memories," she replied slowly. "I thought I'd put all that behind me."

"What had you put behind you?"

She sighed, and turned her head to look out the window. "In the end it was a troubled house," she said finally. "I'd have left if there had been anywhere to go. It's not as if this was London or even Tilbury, where I could have found another position."

Was she making excuses for staying on, despite her feelings about the house? He wondered whether she was lying to herself or to him.

"How troubled?"

Nancy Brothers took a deep breath. "It's not my place to gossip about my betters."

"I understand. That's commendable, in fact," he told her gently. "But it's not a matter of gossip, you see. In a police inquiry, it's your duty to help the authorities in any way you can. If you know something, you must let us decide if it's important or not."

"Mrs. Russell was wearing this locket the day she disappeared. I know, I helped her put it on, and I saw it at noon that day, when she came in for lunch. She was still wearing it."

"What happened to Mrs. Russell? Did the police find her? Or failing that, her body?"

"That was the odd thing. They never found any trace of her. Her son saw her walking toward the landing stage at two o'clock, but no one knew she was missing until I went up to help her dress for dinner." She turned to set a bowl that had been draining in the sink up on a shelf. "They questioned all of us, the police did. Was she anxious about anything? Was she worried? Was she frightened? Did anyone harbor hard feelings toward her? She could be a trial, sometimes, to tell you the truth, but she was getting older, and crotchety. At least it seemed so to me at the time, young as I was. Sometimes she fussed over her hair until I was fit to be tied, wanting it to be thick and pretty as it was when she was eighteen. Or the ashes hadn't been swept out proper, when I could see they had. But you don't do someone a harm for that, do you?"

"Was this same photograph in the locket when Mrs. Russell wore it last?"

"No, it wasn't. It was her and her late husband. On their wedding day."

"Then how can you be sure this is the same locket?"

"I must have touched it a thousand times. Settling it around her throat, under her hair. Making sure it was hanging proper. She took it off each evening and put it on each morning. Even if she was wearing other jewelry, this was still around her throat." She reached for the kettle and filled it with cold water. "Can you tell me how you came to have it? Does this mean you've found her body? And who put that other photograph in it?"

"We haven't found Mrs. Russell. Someone else was wearing the locket."

"How did *she* come by it?"

"Before I answer your question, will you give me the name of this woman?"

She was measuring tea for the pot, but she lifted the spoon and pointed with it. "That's Cynthia Farraday. She came to live with Mrs. Russell when her own parents died."

"What became of her?"

"She went to live in London after Mrs. Russell disappeared. She said it wasn't fitting to live in the house without a chaperone. Mr. Russell proposed marriage, but she didn't want that. She wanted to be free, she said, to live her own life."

"Who else was in the house—besides the staff?"

"Mr. Justin, of course. He was another cousin come to live at River's Edge. After Miss Cynthia came. They weren't related, those two. She was connected through the Russell side, while Mr. Justin's grandmother and Mrs. Russell's were cousins. I heard it said that Mr. Justin's mother had died of the consumption. Her lungs was bad. I never heard anything about his father."

"What became of Mr. Fowler?"

"He went off to war and as far as I know never come back."

"I see." As the kettle began to whistle, Mrs. Brothers turned to fill the teapot. Watching her, Rutledge said, "And Mr. Russell, himself?"

She stirred the leaves in the pot, peering at them as she spoke. "All I know is, he survived the war. But I don't know that he ever came back to the house. A shame, that was. It was a lovely house. I wish you could have seen it when I was in service there. They had money, the Russells did. I often wondered how it was the family built that house out here, in the marshes. It could have been set down anywhere."

While the tea steeped, Rutledge said, "I have a photograph to show you. It isn't a pleasant photograph, but perhaps you will be able to identify the man in it." He took out the envelope from Gravesend, opened the flap, and passed it to her.

She reached inside tentatively and pulled out the photograph. He saw her grimace as she looked down at it.

"He's dead, isn't he? This man."

"Yes. He was found in the river."

"The Hawking?" She glanced from the photograph to Rutledge's face. "My husband never said anything to me about a body being found."

"It was the Thames. Do you know him?"

"He's changed so much I hardly recognized him at first. He was just a lad when last I saw him, all arms and legs, and polite enough," she said slowly. "I didn't go into Furnham that often, but he came to River's Edge a time or two. From the village. As I remember, his father was a fisherman. I'm sorry I can't put a name to him after all this time." She turned away from the photograph, and Rutledge put it back in the envelope.

"Do you remember anything else about him?" When she hesitated, he added, "Was he a troublemaker? Was there gossip about him?"

"If there was, I don't remember it now," she answered. "But of course we didn't mix all that much with the villagers. The staff at River's Edge." She smiled wryly. "We thought ourselves above them. And here I wound up marrying one of them. You never know, do you? But at the time, Mrs. Russell encouraged us not to go into Furnham. On our days off, every other week, she'd let us go into Tilbury for the day. Let us have the use of the cart, even, as long as Harold Finley drove it. And she cautioned us to stay well away from the docks."

"You are sure this man isn't Major Russell?"

"Oh, no, I'd know Mr. Russell anywhere. Even after all this time. I was a maid in that house for fifteen years, until Mr. Brothers come along. Yes, I'd recognize him even today, for certain."

Throughout the questioning, Hamish had been silent. Now he interjected a comment, catching Rutledge off guard as he was setting the envelope down by the leg of his chair, out of sight. Mrs. Brothers was bringing the teapot to the table, and he glanced up quickly, certain she must have heard the voice as well. But she had turned away to pick up two cups and saucers.

"Ye ken, yon dead man knew the people at River's Edge well enough to accuse the one of killing the ither."

It was an excellent point.

"What was the relationship between Fowler and Russell? Did they get on?"

"They did, well enough, except where Miss Cynthia was concerned. Then it wasn't so friendly, was it? And some of it was her doing, flirting with first one and then the other. It wasn't serious, I'll say that for her. Mind you, I know the difference. She didn't fancy either of them, but she was the sort to like their attentions."

"You didn't care for her?"

"Not to say didn't care for her," Mrs. Brothers replied. "That's too harsh a word, isn't it? But I was not taken in by her ways. She even flirted with Harold Finley. Not in quite the same fashion, but enough to turn his head. That wasn't fair, was it? To lead him on? But he was a fine figure of a man, tall and strong and clever as well. She couldn't resist proving he was under her spell too."

Harold Finley. The driver-cum-butler, when the need arose.

"How did she flirt with him?"

"She'd invent little errands where he was to drive her here and everywhere. To Tilbury to return a book to the lending library in the bookshop. To Furnham, to find a ribbon that matched her hat. Once to London to see a friend. But Mrs. Russell put a stop to London visits. A young girl like that. It wasn't wise, was it?"

London, the den of iniquity? "No, it must not have been," he answered.

"I don't suppose you know how that man came by Mrs. Russell's locket or had Miss Cynthia's photograph in it?"

"No. But when I find Miss Farraday, perhaps she can tell me."

"Yes, and she'll lead you up the garden path, if I know her, unless she's changed." As if she'd said more than she intended, Mrs. Brothers added, "But to be fair, she wasn't wicked, just lively and sometimes trying."

"Did you by any chance keep in touch with her after she left River's Edge?"

"There I can't help you, and I'm that sorry. I never knew just where it was she went to in London. But she could have told me ten times over, and it wouldn't have made any difference. I was never in London, you see. I did hear that the house had belonged to her parents, which isn't much help, as she's likely married by now and living somewhere else."

He finished his tea, retrieved the locket from the table along with the envelope, and prepared to take his leave, thanking her.

"You never told me how you came to have Mrs. Russell's locket."

He owed her the truth.

"The dead man was wearing it when he was pulled from the river."

"If this man," she said after digesting what Rutledge had told her, "had the locket—where did he get it? Did he know what became of Mrs. Russell?"

"I wish I could answer that," Rutledge said. "But he told the police at one time that Russell had killed Fowler."

She shook her head vehemently. "I don't believe a word of that. Now I could see maybe Mr. Russell taking his fists to Mr. Fowler. He had a black temper on him, Mr. Wyatt did. But murder? No."

"But you said that they were jealous of Cynthia Farraday's attentions."

"If every jealous man took to killing his rival, you'd be busier than a beaver in a rainstorm!" she retorted. "What's more, in your shoes, I wouldn't believe someone wearing a dead woman's locket."

From the Brothers farm, Rutledge drove back to Furnham and left his motorcar by The Dragonfly Inn. It was small and for Furnham, rather picturesque, with a cottage garden in front where hollyhocks bloomed among other summer flowers.

The streets were busier now, women going about their marketing, fishermen coming up from the water, workmen standing in front of the ironmonger's, passing the time of day. Beyond the High Street, the river was dappled with sunlight, and the boats riding at anchor were turning with the tide.

Rutledge stopped the first man he encountered. From his rough clothing, he appeared to be a laborer, and there was cement crusted in the cuticles of his fingers.

"My name is Rutledge," he began, already drawing the photograph out of its envelope. "I'm trying to locate the family of this man." He held it out.

The man barely glanced at it. From his flat expression it was impossible to tell what he was thinking. "Don't know him," he said, and brushing the extended photograph aside, he walked on.

Rutledge continued down the street, found another man just coming out of the ironmonger's, a bolt in his hand, staring down at it as if he weren't satisfied with the choice he'd made. He looked up when a shadow fell over his hand.

"Who are you?" he demanded, as if Rutledge had dropped from the moon.

Rutledge recognized him, the man in corduroy trousers and a

workman's shirt who had challenged him earlier as he drove along the street with Frances. He wasn't sure, however, that the man remembered him. He repeated his earlier approach.

The man pushed his extended arm aside. "Never saw him before," he said brusquely as he walked on.

Rutledge tried three more times, and met with the same unfriendly refusal to admit to recognizing the dead man. And there was no way to tell whether they were speaking the truth or whether the man was their long-lost brother or son.

Hamish said, "Speak to a woman."

But Rutledge was reluctant to show the photograph to a woman. He'd done so with Mrs. Brothers because she knew the household at River's Edge and could tell him if she recognized the face.

He had reached the end of the High Street, where the bend in the road turned slightly north toward the farms. Looking back the way he had come, he decided to try the pub. It was on the river side of the street, just before the small harbor cut into the reedy land.

He hadn't chosen to go there first, unwilling to spread word about his search. He knew very well that the men he'd already spoken to might gossip, but he had a feeling they wouldn't. In a pub, where men gossiped as freely as members of the Women's Institute, rumor would fly after he'd gone, and he preferred to watch reactions for himself. Still, he needed to find a name, and Chief Superintendent Bowles would be expecting him to produce it when he'd returned to London. And Bowles didn't care for excuses, however valid. The pub was named—not surprisingly—The Rowing Boat. And the sign above the door, swinging in the light breeze, showed three men pulling for the open sea in their small vessel, backs bent to the oars.

Rutledge stepped inside. In the dim interior, he could see two men playing cribbage at one table. Another man sat hunched over a corner table, eating a thick sandwich and drinking what appeared to be cider. The windows at the far end of the room looked out over the river, and stairs to one side must lead, he thought, down to a cellar and possibly the water as well.

Behind the bar, with its gleaming brass, the wood polished from age and generations of elbows, stood a very tall, thin man with receding gray hair. He straightened when he saw that the newcomer wasn't a regular, and he watched Rutledge stride toward him without a word of welcome. His eyes gave away nothing, but there was a tightening in the muscles around his mouth.

His first words were, "Police, are you?" The men at the two tables turned to stare.

"My name is Rutledge," he began without further identification, and as he passed the photograph across the bar, he repeated what he'd said before, that he was searching for the man's family.

"Coming into money, are they?" the man asked.

"I won't know until I succeed in finding them."

"How did he die, then?"

"He was found in the river."

The barkeep's eyebrows rose, his first sign of interest. "In the Hawking?"

"Nearby," Rutledge replied. After all, the Thames passed Tilbury. That, in terms of distances in this part of Essex, could be called nearby.

"Never seen him before," the man said finally.

"How long have you been barkeep here?"

The question was met with silence.

"My guess is a good ten years," Rutledge continued. "I'm told the dead man once lived here in Furnham. I should think you'd know your custom by face if not by name."

"I have a very poor memory," the barkeep answered him, and lifting his voice, he asked, "You there, at the corner table."

The man had gone back to his sandwich and now looked up, his craggy brows lifted in surprise at being addressed.

"Have I ever called you by name?"

The man at the table hesitated.

"Well, have I?"

"No. Never," the man responded at last, taking his cue from the barkeep's tone of voice.

"There, you see?" he said to Rutledge. "And do I remember," he went on, to the cribbage players, "do I remember your favorite beverage when you come in?"

They shook their heads, eyes wary as they stared from Rutledge to the publican and back again.

"Sorry I can't be of help, Mr. Rutledge or whoever you are. But there it is."

Rutledge said, "Then how could you tell that I was a stranger?"

That caught the man off guard just as he was beginning to grin at his own cleverness.

"You'd have asked what I'd have. Instead you identified me as a policeman."

The barkeep pushed the photograph back across the bar.

"No one here can help you," he retorted. "You'd be better off looking elsewhere, if you take my meaning."

"Scotland Yard doesn't take kindly to threats. I'll have you closed down within the day."

"On what charges?" the man demanded.

"The bar is greasy with spilled beer. The plates you've used to serve those men have leftover food clinging to them. And this floor is so filthy I should think a meal here would send a healthy man to his grave. The Chief Constable will be glad to know of these conditions. And as he isn't likely to trouble himself to travel all the way to Furnham, he'll take my word for what I've seen."

"It's all a lie. You wouldn't dare—"

"Try me," Rutledge said, his voice cold. And he turned toward the door, ignoring the barkeep, who was shouting abuse after him.

Rutledge had almost reached the door, his back to the bar, when Hamish said, "'Ware!"

He turned in time to see the man coming toward him, the heavy wooden club usually kept behind the bar raised in one hand. Rutledge had expected no less.

"Put that down, you fool. Killing me won't stop the Yard, and you know it."

The barkeep hesitated, a flash of uncertainty in his eyes. And then it was gone, and his intent was clear—he would finish what he'd begun.

In the next instant he was bent back over the bar, the club across his throat, and Rutledge was saying through clenched teeth as he put pressure on the length of wood, "If anyone else in this room moves, I'll break his damned neck."

There was a scraping of chair legs against the floor as the other patrons hastily sat down.

"Now," Rutledge said to the red-faced barkeep struggling to breathe, "I will step back, and you will sit down in the nearest chair and conduct yourself with decorum. Do you understand me?"

The man could barely move, but he signaled with his eyes that he understood.

Still holding the club, Rutledge released him, and the man nearly sank to his knees. Catching himself with one arm across the bar, he stood there for a moment, fighting for breath, and then he moved to the nearest chair, sinking into it.

He glared at Rutledge, but the fight had gone out of him.

Rutledge said, "What was worth an attack on me? This photograph? What's your name? And don't tell me you can't remember."

"Barber. Sandy Barber."

"Who is this man in the photograph?"

He waited, and after a moment the barkeep said hoarsely, "It's Willet's son. The old man's youngest boy."

"Who is Willet?"

"Ned Willet. He's a fisherman. It will kill him, seeing his boy dead."

"And who is his boy, when he's at home?"

"That's it, he hasn't been home since before the end of the war. He's in service in Thetford—Ben never wanted to be a fisherman, you see. Abigail sent for him as soon as Ned took a bad turn. But Ben never answered. Well—now we know why, don't we? Look, he's not got long to live, Ned hasn't. Let him think his boy can't leave his post."

"Why doesn't Willet have long to live?" Rutledge asked, thinking about Ben Willet's stomach cancer.

"He got hurt bringing his boat back in a storm. Gear shifted and pinned his foot. It turned septic. They wanted to take his foot off and he wouldn't hear of it. Stubborn old fool. Now there's gangrene, and it's only a matter of time before it takes him. You should see his leg—nearly black it's that purple, and so swollen it doesn't look like part of his body." Gesturing with his chin toward the envelope Rutledge had dropped on the bar, he added, "What happened to Ben, then? You said he came out of the river."

"Someone shot him in the back of the head. Before putting him in the river."

There was consternation in the room. The other men, listening, stirred restlessly.

The barkeep shook his head. "Well. They'll meet on the other side, won't they?" he said after a moment.

"What's Willet to you, that you would have stopped me any way you could?"

"My wife Abigail is his only daughter. Who'd want to kill Ben? We never heard of him making enemies. He could put on airs with the best of them, but no one minded."

"Fishing is a hard way to make a living. Furnham didn't hold it against Ben Willet that he'd escaped to a different life? Possibly a better one?"

"Ned wasn't happy." Barber frowned. "If anyone else felt strongly, I never heard of it."

The older man who had been sitting alone, eating, spoke from the far end of the room. "When he came back on his last leave before sailing to France, showing off his uniform, everyone was glad to see him. I remember. My daughter fancied him. But nothing came of it."

"You said he could put on airs. What did you mean by that?"

"He'd hobnobbed with his betters, hadn't he? He could pass himself off as a duke, he said, if he'd half a mind to do it. He had Abigail in tears one night, she laughed so hard, describing the family he worked for, taking all the parts. It was better than a stage play." As if realizing he was speaking of the dead, Barber added, "Aye, that was Ben."

Rutledge recalled the man who had come to his office, passing himself off as another person, a gentleman. He had done it so well that he'd even fooled an inspector at Scotland Yard. But then he, Rutledge, had had no reason to doubt him. It was unlikely that such a man would come forward to confess to a murder he hadn't committed.

Or had he?

Pulling out the photograph again, Rutledge said, "And you are absolutely certain that this man is Ben Willet?"

"Ask them," the barkeep said, gesturing to the other men in the bar.

And so he did, showing the photograph to each of the three men in turn. He met hard eyes staring up at him, but in them Rutledge read recognition and certainty.

Walking back to the center of the room, Rutledge said, "And what about Wyatt Russell? How many of you know him?"

There was a silence. One of the players finally answered, "Not to say *know* him. He lived at River's Edge before the war."

"How well did Ben Willet know him?"

"I doubt they ever spoke to each other more than a time or two," Barber said. "The Russells wanted no part of us here in Furnham. The family never has." He appeared to be on the point of adding more, then thought better of it.

"I was told the men of Furnham helped the family search for Mrs. Russell when she went missing."

"That was the police set us to scouring the marsh," one of the older men answered. "It wasn't the Russells."

"Justin Fowler, then."

One of the older men stirred in his chair, but when Rutledge turned his way, he said only, "I've heard the name. I doubt I could put a face to it."

"He never had much to do with Furnham either," Barber told Rutledge. "From River's Edge it was easier to go west than turn east. There was nothing here the family needed or wanted."

"Someone sold them fish from time to time," Rutledge said, remembering what Nancy Brothers had told him.

"Ned would take part of his catch to the cook. Mrs. Broadley. And she was the one who paid for it. I doubt he saw Mrs. Russell five times over the years."

"She did come once to thank him," the lone diner put in. "I'll say that for her."

"Do any of you know what became of Wyatt Russell or Justin Fowler?"

After a moment Barber said, "They went off to fight in the war, didn't they? No one opened the house again afterward. Which says they didn't come home."

But Rutledge wasn't sure he was telling the truth. When he turned to look at the other men in the pub, they refused to meet his eyes, staring out at the river at their backs.

He said, "I'd like to speak to Mrs. Barber. She should know more about her brother's years here in Furnham, before he went into service. Where will I find her?"

"Here! You aren't showing that dead man's face to my wife, and him her own brother!" Barber was on his feet. "And how is she to keep the news from her father? I ask you!"

"I'll strike a bargain with you. Find a way for me to speak to Mrs. Barber and I will keep her brother's death out of it. For now."

The barkeep considered him. "I have your word?"

"You do."

Barber turned on his patrons. "I'm leaving. If one word of what happened just now goes beyond this room, you'll have me to answer to. Am I understood?"

There were hasty nods of agreement, and then Barber said to Rutledge, "Come with me."

From The Rowing Boat they went left, and Rutledge soon found himself in a muddy lane that led north from the High Street past a row of elderly cottages. The one at the far end was barely larger than its neighbors, and here Barber turned up the walk.

"You'll remember your word," Barber demanded before reaching out to lift the latch and swing the door wide. Rutledge nodded.

The front room was surprisingly comfortable. The furnishings were old but well polished and upholstered in a faded dark red. A thin carpet with arabesques in deep shades of blue, red, and cream covered the floor. It seemed out of place here, somehow, but gave the room an air of worn elegance, and Rutledge wondered if it had come from River's Edge. Sunlight spilled across it to touch the iron foot of a plant stand where the fronds of a luxuriant fern overhung a dark blue fired clay pot. To Rutledge's eyes, it appeared to be French.

Barber left Rutledge standing there and went to fetch his wife.

After several minutes he returned accompanied by a small, plump woman with a pretty face, although she was pale and there were dark pockets beneath her green eyes, as if she hadn't slept well in a very long time.

"Mr. Rutledge, I've told Abigail that you're trying to find anyone connected with the family that lived at River's Edge."

"I hardly knew them," she said apologetically. "I don't know why you should wish to see me."

"I'm casting at straws," he told her, smiling, and she appeared to relax a little. "Did you know the family? Mr. Russell or his mother?"

"I knew them if I saw them in the shops, 'course I did. But not to speak to. They didn't come into Furnham all that often."

"How would you describe them?" he asked. And when she hesitated, he added, "There's no photograph, as far as I know, of the family members."

"Oh. Not even in River's Edge?" Shyly offering him a seat, she asked, "What is this about, then?"

From behind her shoulder, Sandy Barber sent him a fierce frown.

"Alas, the house is closed." He fell back on his recollection of his father's methods of dealing with clients. John Rutledge had been a very fine solicitor, and his easy manner had belied his sharp mind. "A legal matter," he told her. "To do with a certain piece of personal property that has been recovered. We don't seem to know where to return the item."

Reassured, she said, "Well, then. Mr. Russell was tall and fair. A friendly enough man. He'd touch his hat to us if he encountered my mother and me on the street or in a shop, and say 'Ladies' as he passed by. My mother always said he had good manners. But he wasn't one to stop and ask after the children if one had been ill, or inquire how my father's boat had fared after a high wind. Mrs. Russell, now, she would speak to my mother if she met her in a shop. She knew my father; he sometimes would take a choice bit of fish out to Mrs. Broadley, the cook at River's Edge. 'That was a fine bit of sole,' Mrs. Russell would say. 'Thank Ned for thinking of us.' Sad that she disappeared the way she did."

Rutledge caught Barber's eye. The barkeep had left the impression that the Willet family had had very little to do with the Russell family. "What did local gossip have to say about her disappearance?"

"We thought she'd drowned herself. Well, it was what you'd naturally wonder about, isn't it? Last seen walking down to the water's edge?"

"People don't drown themselves without a reason," he responded quietly. "Was Mrs. Russell—unhappy?"

"Not precisely unhappy," Abigail Barber answered, trying to remember. "I do recall my mother saying that she hadn't seemed like herself in a while, as if something was on her mind. But then the war was coming, wasn't it, and there was her son and Mr. Fowler, of an age to go."

"I understand you had brothers about the age of Mr. Russell. Did they ever spend time together—go off on the river together?"

She laughed, her face flushing a becoming pink. "God love you, Mr. Rutledge, I don't think I'd live long enough to see that day. But Ben had an eye for whatever Mr. Russell was wearing. He longed to be a footman, and someday a gentleman's gentleman. Once or twice he went up to the house with my father, and he'd come back and say, 'I wonder how he gets that polish on his shoes,' or 'He must have dressed in a bit of a hurry today. The back of his coat wasn't properly pressed.' He could mimic their voices too. It came natural to him."

"Did he indeed? Was he hoping to be taken on as a footman in the Russell household?"

"Oh, no, sir, it wasn't at all likely. Ben said he'd be best off where he wasn't known. But what he learned would help him fit in, he said." She glanced over her shoulder at her husband. "He was a fisherman's son here. He said he could be anybody somewhere else."

Ben Willet, so it seemed, was ambitious.

"How did your father take this desire to go into service?"

"He had other sons to go out in the boat with him. That was before the war, of course. Tommy and Joseph never came back from France. But Ben was always his favorite, and I think he was sorry not to have him want to go to sea."

"Did you know Justin Fowler?"

She shook her head. "He was a cousin or some such, wasn't he? But I never saw him, that I know of. He didn't come to Furnham. We put it down to him being more of a snob."

"Was there bad blood between Russell and Fowler?"

"I wouldn't know, sir."

He could hear a weak voice calling from another part of the house.

"My father," she said, rising quickly. "He's not well."

Rutledge rose as well. "One more question. Did Miss Farraday come to the village on occasion?"

Her face hardened. "Oh, yes, I knew who she was. If you want to know, she had an eye for the lads, and no time for the rest of us."

"Any particular lad?" he asked.

"I saw her once or twice speaking to Ben. But he told me later she hadn't."

And then with a hasty excuse, she hurried back to her bedside watch.

Rutledge said, "Thank you. Mrs. Barber was very helpful."

"Was she?" Barber was urging him toward the door. He lowered his voice. "To my way of thinking you're no closer to knowing about Ben than you were before. I told you it was no use speaking to my wife."

"No closer to finding his killer, perhaps."

Barber said, an edge to his voice, "Then what was that all about?"

"Catching you in several lies."

"What lies?"

But Rutledge gave him no answer. And they walked in uneasy silence back to where he'd left his motorcar.

Rutledge had stayed longer than he'd intended in Essex. He set out for London, and driving out of Furnham, he felt a sense of relief as the village disappeared in his mirror, reduced to a tiny rectangle of glass.

In the war, he'd been blessed with a strong sixth sense, which had kept him alive far more times than he'd deserved. And unexpectedly that had stayed with him as he'd resumed his career.

There was something wrong in Furnham. Not just Ben Willet's killing, but something else that seemed to reside in the very bricks and mortar of the village. Frances had felt it and had been made uneasy by what she'd called the whispering of the grasses. If there was such a thing as a communal conscience, he thought, it was laden with guilt.

Barber had been defending his wife and her family, and that was understandable. But the easy shift from surly to murderous was not common. The club Rutledge had taken from the man could have been lethal, and the back windows of the pub looked out over the river, offering a swift passage to the sea for an unwanted body. The narrow estuary, with few shallows to trap a corpse, was at a guess not a quarter of a mile away, the current running strong.

What was appalling was Barber's certainty that his patrons would hold their tongues if he'd killed the interloper in the pub.

Hamish said, "If someone there killed yon victim, ye willna' ever ferret him oot."

And Rutledge believed him.

Whatever had knit that village together so tightly, Ben Willet had escaped it. And Rutledge found it hard to believe that he'd been punished for it so many years later. What then had he done in the past few months that had put him beyond the pale?

But what to make of the fact that the body in Gravesend was not Russell's?

What to make of Ben Willet's passing himself off as another man while confessing to murder?

Was that what had put Willet beyond the pale? Had his conscience driven him to bring a murder to the attention of Scotland Yard in the only way he'd dared?

The next step, then, was to find Major Wyatt Russell and see what he had to say.

# 6

When the gates of River's Edge loomed ahead, the pineapples atop the posts promising a hospitality that was far in the past, late as he was, Rutledge stopped the motorcar and got out.

He had come earlier with a different perspective. The house had belonged to a confessed murderer. Or so he'd been led to believe. And for all he knew—given the reluctance of the man passing himself off as Wyatt Russell to give any details of his crime—the body could still be somewhere here.

With his sister present, he'd been content to look at the house and grounds, noting the marshes across the river and on either side of the acres of once smooth lawn on which the house had been set. And it had seemed all too likely that the house had remained closed because the memories it evoked were disagreeable.

Now as he walked down the long, brush-choked drive and made

his way around to the riverfront, he had a clearer picture in his mind of the people who once had lived in this house.

Standing on the terrace, he gazed out over water dancing in the sunlight with an almost macabre gaiety. On a warm August day when the clouds of war were gathering on the horizon and threatening her son, as another war had taken her husband, Mrs. Russell had gone down these shallow steps and walked to the river's edge.

Had worry for her son really taken her there? And had that worry been strong enough to drive the woman to suicide?

Nevertheless, she'd vanished. The police had been satisfied. Still, it was possible that they had heard what they wanted to hear. And when there was no evidence to the contrary, it was easier to accept the unlikely.

Nor had her son questioned the verdict or appealed to the Chief Constable for Scotland Yard to intervene.

It would be easier to accept a confession by the false Wyatt Russell that he had killed his mother, not Justin Fowler.

That brought up another issue. Would Elizabeth Russell have killed herself and left behind the three children that she had once thanked God for giving her?

There seemed to be no good reason to suspect murder.

Unless, of course, Wyatt Russell had learned almost a year later that Fowler had killed his mother and hidden her body.

If that was the case, how did Ben Willet come to have Mrs. Russell's locket?

Standing there watching the river moving silently toward the North Sea, he found himself wondering why, when Mrs. Russell had disappeared, the family had sent for the police in Tilbury, more than an hour away. And it had been Tilbury who had asked for the help of the villagers, not Wyatt Russell.

On both occasions when he'd been in Furnham, Rutledge had seen neither a police constable walking along the street nor a police station.

He himself hadn't sought out the local man because he was still in the early stages of the inquiry and Willet's murder had occurred in London, not River's Edge. But there must be a constable in the village. Surely—

A woman's angry voice cut into his reverie, and Hamish was warning him to beware.

"What the devil do you think you're doing? This is private property!" She came striding through the French doors at his back, and he knew her as soon as he turned, although the expression of the living face was very different from the one in the locket he had carried with him to Furnham.

"Miss Farraday, I think?" he asked pleasantly and watched her go as still as if she had been carved from marble.

"Who are you?" Her voice was guarded, cold.

"My name is Rutledge," he told her. "And I may ask you the same question. What are you doing here? This property, as far as I know, was not left to you by the previous owner."

It was a shot in the dark, but it struck a spark.

"Are you Wyatt's solicitor?" she snapped.

"At the moment I'm representing him," Rutledge replied.

She was very attractive, with more spirit than he'd expected from her photograph. She had also changed in other ways. There was a maturity about her that wasn't present six years ago. The girl had grown into a very self-assured young woman.

"I'm looking to buy the property. Is it for sale?" she asked. "Is that why you're here?"

"Even in its present sad condition, I doubt that you could afford to buy it and then keep it up."

An angry flush flared in her cheeks. "I have come into my inheritance," she retorted. "You can speak to my own solicitors if you don't believe me."

"How did you arrive here? I didn't see a motorcar or a carriage in the drive."

"I came by boat."

But he hadn't seen a boat by the landing stage either.

"It's a launch, I rented it upriver. It's tied up out of sight." She read the doubt in his face. "There's another place where a boat can tie up."

"The tradesman's entrance?"

To his surprise she laughed. "Yes, as a matter of fact. The Russell who built River's Edge didn't wish to see viands and coal and other goods carried across his hard-won lawn. The path leads directly to the kitchen. What do you do, come here once a fortnight to see that all is well? I noticed, when last I came, that someone had walked up the drive. The grasses were bent over, and even broken here and there."

"How often do you come?"

"When the spirit moves me," she countered.

"How did you get into the house?"

"When I left, no one thought to ask me for my key."

"When did you leave?"

"Before the war," she answered evasively.

"Why did you leave?"

She pondered that, her eyes taking on the expression of someone staring into the long and unforgiving past. "A very good question. I expect it was because I felt it was the right thing to do."

"Indeed?"

"It's a lovely day. Would you care to bring out two chairs? We could sit here and enjoy the afternoon. Sadly there's no one to bring us our tea. Never mind. And I must warn you I promised to have the launch back no later than five o'clock."

He did as she asked, walking into the house for the first time.

The room behind the French doors was spacious, with a marble hearth set across from the long windows. The high ceiling was decorated with plaster roses and swags of floral garlands, while trellises of lemon and peach roses climbed the wallpaper. Several chairs and settees, what he could see of them beneath the shrouding dust sheets, were covered in pale green and soft yellows. The effect was tranquil, an indoor garden, created for a woman's pleasure.

He found two chairs that would do, removed the sheets covering them, and carried them out to the terrace.

Cynthia Farraday was standing where he'd left her, staring out over the river.

She turned as he set a chair down near her, with a clear view across the lawns to the water, and she smiled, sitting down and stretching her booted feet out in front of her.

"Heaven," she said as he took the other chair. "I have always loved this terrace. Aunt Elizabeth—Mrs. Russell—used the garden room more than any other, and I could understand why. The two go together, don't you think? I spent many happy hours there."

"When did you arrive here today?" he asked.

"I came just after noon. In fact, I've missed my luncheon. I didn't think to bring any sandwiches with me."

"How long did you intend to stay?"

"Not this long. But then I didn't have the courage to bring out a chair. It felt somehow—wrong—to disturb the furniture. As if it were all sleeping."

"Did you live here as a child? What do you remember most about it?"

"You're very inquisitive for a solicitor. But since you were gallant enough to bring out our chairs, I'll answer that. I remember being happy, for the most part. Of course in the beginning I missed my parents terribly. Wyatt did his best to amuse me, out of kindness, knowing how I grieved. And not very long afterward, another cousin—Wyatt's, not mine—came here to live, and the three of us passed an agreeable few years together. And then we all grew up, and it was vastly different." Her voice had taken on a sad note.

"What happened to them?"

"You're the solicitor. You tell me."

"Justin never came home from the war. And Russell married but lost his wife and his child at the same time. He was a widower. And he still loved you." That last was a guess, based on what Nancy Brothers had told him, but it clearly found its mark.

Cynthia Farraday stirred uneasily. "You know too much. Have you been prying?"

"Hardly. Just fleshing out the facts. How did you get on with Mrs. Russell?"

"She liked me at first. I was a lost child, in need of mothering, and she treated me like a daughter. I was fond of her, and it was comforting to have a home again. I'd been so frightened when my parents died, and everything changed. They wouldn't let me stay in the London house where I felt safe and everything was familiar. They told me it was for the best to go to strangers."

"They?"

"My father's solicitors. Very officious old men—well, I thought them old at the time—who kept telling me it was what my parents would have wished. But I was just as certain they'd have wished nothing of the sort."

"You said earlier, 'for the most part'?"

"At first the three of us, Wyatt and Justin and I, did everything together. It helped me heal, I think, and I expected it would always be that way. But we grew up, as children tend to do, and Wyatt thought he'd fallen in love with me. Sadly, I wasn't in love with him. Aunt Elizabeth encouraged him. At least so I thought. I was too young at the time to realize that she might truly have liked to keep me in the family. I believed she was pushing us together for his sake, and I'd have none of it. I wasn't a very pleasant child, I expect."

"It's logical, isn't it? She knew you well, you stood to inherit from your parents when you came of age, which meant you were Russell's equal socially and financially, and you were already friends. I should think she was pleased to see River's Edge in good hands for another generation. Her son could have made a worse choice."

She took a deep breath. "In fact, he did. The woman he married was hardly what any of us would have chosen as the future mistress here. She hated the marshes, for one thing. Justin told me that when Wyatt brought her down to see River's Edge, she refused to spend the night. Even though her sister was with her. And she felt it was silly to keep a country house, servants and the like, when they could live in London."

"Then why did Russell marry her?"

"I don't really know. Unless he didn't much care anymore. He wanted an heir, I expect. And she was enthralled with the idea of a military wedding, uniforms and raised swords and a husband going off to fight for King and Country. She told me that it was just too exciting for words. I told Wyatt he could have scoured England and not found anyone quite so selfish."

"That was rather unkind, don't you think?"

She shrugged. "I told him the truth. That his mother would have been appalled. That was the day before he was to be married, and I haven't seen him since."

"Then why should you wish to buy River's Edge?"

"Because it stands empty. I can't bear that. I could live here. There are no ghosts here for me."

But that wasn't what she had told the rector.

"What do you believe happened to Mrs. Russell?"

"I don't know. At the time I thought it was my fault, that I'd disappointed her and she wanted to punish me. I was too young to understand that it probably had nothing to do with me, or Wyatt falling in love with me, or Justin being angry with him for spoiling everything for all three of us. I heard him tell Wyatt that he hated him. But of course he didn't. Not really. I remember telling someone that I'd wished I had been a boy, and then none of this would have ever happened. "

"Someone? Who did you confide in?"

"That's none of your business," she snapped, as if already regretting she'd given so much away.

"Was it by any chance someone from Furnham by the name of Ben Willet?" As he spoke, he was watching her eyes, and he thought that once again he'd found his mark.

But she shook her head. And evaded his question. "I didn't know Furnham very well. A few of the shops, where I could purchase things without having to go all the way to London. Or having them sent out to River's Edge without the pleasure of choosing what I liked."

"Ben Willet went on to become a footman in Thetford. Did you know?"

"Did he? Was he happy there, do you think?"

He smiled inwardly at her answer. *But Willet knew you, my girl, and wore your photograph until the day he died. The question is, how did he come by that locket?*

They sat there in silence for a time as Rutledge considered what she had told him so far. Certainly encountering her here had saved searching London for her. But it had brought him no closer to the truth about what had happened to Ben Willet or, for that matter, Wyatt Russell.

"Do you think it will be possible for me to buy River's Edge?" she asked, looking him straight in the eye. "You must know I'll see to the property. I won't let him down."

"I have no idea how Mr. Russell will feel about that."

"But you will ask?"

"I think it would probably come better from you."

She smiled, but it was twisted, as if the admission hurt her. "There you're wrong."

He rose. She would have to leave soon, and he was overdue in London. "And if he feels that he might wish to sell? How will he find you?"

"Tell him I'll find him."

"He might prefer to contact you himself."

"My life is my own. If he wishes to find me, tell him to speak to my solicitors."

Hamish said into the ensuing silence, "There's the man who let her take the launch."

"Shall I return the chairs to the house? Or do you wish to sit here a little longer?"

"I'll close up," she said, her gaze once more on the river, as if she saw the past there.

"I should ask. What's left in the house that's worth stealing?"

This time the smile was amused. "Don't you trust me?"

"Still—" He left it unfinished.

"Anything of value is gone. Pictures on the wall. Jewelry. Silver in the pantry. Stored somewhere in London, I expect. I wouldn't make my fortune selling what's left. But it's lovely and familiar, and I'd want to keep what's here if I could."

"Whatever happened to the locket that Mrs. Russell wore every day of her life?"

She was very still, her eyes on his. "If they ever find her—or her body—it will be there. I don't know that I ever saw her without it."

He nodded and walked down the broad steps from the terrace to the lawns, making his way around the house to the drive without looking back.

He had let her believe he was a family solicitor. She hadn't realized that he was a policeman. He was of half a mind to go back and correct that impression. But then he decided that this wasn't the time to put her on her guard.

If she had nothing to hide, then no harm done.

# 7

Hamish, who had only spoken once after Miss Farraday had stepped out onto the terrace, was busy now in the back of Rutledge's mind as instead of taking the main road to London, he drove along the headwaters of the River Hawking, searching for any spot where a launch could be rented. There were only three tiny villages along this narrower section of the road, mainly inhabited by families who made their living from the water, and while there were any number of boats drawn up along the shoreline, they were mainly skiffs, rowing boats, and other small craft, hardly resembling a launch that someone like Cynthia Farraday could manage. He persisted, but everywhere he was met with a shake of the head.

Nothing to hire here.

He was ready to concede that she'd lied to him when he followed a rutted lane through high grass and saw his quarry actually stepping out of a sleek launch, greeting a tall man in a white shirt and trousers.

Realizing that this was a private landing stage used by sportsmen—the half-dozen boats here were a far cry from the rough craft he'd seen until now—he pulled up and waited.

It was clear that the man knew Miss Farraday well, for they were laughing about something as he helped her secure the launch and then gestured toward the newly built shed to the left of the landing stage. On the far side of that he could see the bonnets of two motorcars, the late afternoon sun reflecting off the gleaming paint.

He hadn't been spotted, he was sure of that, and when the opportunity presented itself as Miss Farraday followed the man inside the shed, shutting the door, he reversed until he'd reached the main road, such as it was, and considered his situation.

He could hardly approach the man after Miss Farraday had gone, and ask who had borrowed the launch for the afternoon. Whoever he was, he would undoubtedly report Scotland Yard's interest in her as soon as he saw her again.

But it was just possible that if one of the motorcars was hers, he could follow it back to the city through the evening traffic.

There had been a tumbledown barn some distance back the way he'd come, and Rutledge decided it would offer some semblance of shelter. He thought it likely that Miss Farraday hadn't seen his motorcar outside the gates of River's Edge because it wasn't visible from the house. And he was fairly sure she hadn't followed him as far as the gates to make certain he'd left. There was no reason then that she would immediately recognize it, even if he stayed behind her for miles.

He found the barn with no difficulty and was able to drag one of the doors open wide enough to back his motorcar inside, pulling it nearly shut in front of the bonnet. And he stood there in the narrow opening, keeping watch.

The rank smell behind him was a mixture of damp, rotted manure, musty hay, mildewed floorboards, and bird droppings. Smothering a sneeze, he listened to Hamish's voice echoing through the rafters as a startled dove flapped away through a gaping hole in the roof.

He understood what Hamish was saying, that following Cynthia Farraday's motorcar was unlikely to work, that the Yard could find her more readily. But could it? And once lost, the opportunity might not arise again.

It was nearly half an hour before two motorcars came down the road. In the first one he glimpsed Cynthia Farraday's profile, strands of light brown hair whipping around her face. And in the second, he could make out the white shirt of the man who had greeted her at the landing.

He gave them a five-minute head start before going after them. They had already made the turning toward London by the time he reached it, and he had to drive faster than the rough road allowed before he sighted both motorcars in the distance.

It was not easy to keep up with the two of them as traffic increased on the road and an overladen lorry pulled out in front of him. At his next sighting, the man was ahead. He thought they were playing tag, one and then the other taking the lead, which kept them occupied but made it more difficult to follow them.

Hamish said, "It was a foolish notion." His voice was gloating.

But Rutledge was patient, overtaking another lorry as soon as he could. On his left, the River Thames flowed in golden glory as the sun moved lower in the western sky. Ahead he could just begin to see the tower of St. Paul's when the man, with a short blare of his horn, turned off toward the north.

The motorcar driven by Cynthia Farraday continued through the dingy outskirts of London, where industry belched black smoke above their heads. And then she was threading her way through even dingier streets, where barrows and handcarts were a danger to motorcars and themselves. As he watched she narrowly missed a barrow boy who had ignored the warning tap of her horn. He shouted imprecations in her direction, fist raised, then turned to glare at Rutledge as he passed.

He nearly lost her in the swirl of traffic around St. Paul's but then caught up with her again by guessing which direction she might have taken. Finally they were in a maze of streets in the West End, where it was easier to keep her in sight and harder to hide himself behind other vehicles. Houses here were handsome, taller, and grouped around small fenced squares. It was a part of the city Rutledge knew well from his days as a constable with the Metropolitan Police, new to the force and eager to prove himself.

Cynthia Farraday turned left from the main road, and he recognized the square. Belvedere Place, with its tiny rectangular garden surrounded by tall white houses with dark mansard roofs. Spring bulbs had long since given way to perennials in full summer bloom. It was a fashionable address.

He paused some thirty yards from the entrance to the square, waited five minutes, and then drove slowly past Belvedere Place, searching for the Farraday motorcar.

And he saw it, stopped in front of a house at the far end of the square. Number 17, he thought as he kept going.

It took him ten minutes to find a constable. He was patrolling several streets away, but Rutledge was fairly certain the man would know the answer to his question. Showing his identification, Rutledge asked the man if he knew the name of the household at number 17, Belvedere Place.

Constable Prettyman frowned. "Aye, that would be the Raleigh family, sir. Mother, father, four girls. Staff of five. Is there anyone in particular you would be wanting to know about?"

"A Miss Farraday."

"Indeed, sir. I don't believe there's anyone by that name in Belvedere Place. But of course she could be visiting the family, right enough. Shall I make inquiries, sir?"

"No. Thank you." He could hear Hamish in the back of his mind. Nodding to the constable, he drove on, reversing at the first opportunity and returning to Belvedere Place. As he reached the corner, he looked for the Farraday motorcar at the far end of the square.

But it had gone.

Rutledge swore, then found himself laughing.

Cynthia Farraday had outwitted him.

He had no idea when she had discovered that he was following her—he had been damned careful!—but he thought it must have happened shortly before she turned into Belvedere Place, when his was the only motorcar in sight, even though he had stayed well back.

And that, he thought, must mean that she had a reason to cover her tracks.

When he reached the Yard, he set Sergeant Gibson the task of locating Cynthia Farraday and Wyatt Russell.

"I thought Mr. Russell was dead in Gravesend," Gibson reminded him.

"So did I," Rutledge answered grimly. "But it appears the man is actually one Ben Willet."

"But he said—"

"I'm aware of what he said. The question now is, where is the real Mr. Russell? And was Willet even telling the truth about a murder in 1915?"

"It could explain why this man Willet was killed. He'd come to the Yard with what he knew. Even if it was muddled, like."

But from what Rutledge had been able to discover in Furnham, it wasn't clear whether the two men's paths had ever crossed during the war. Then how had Willet learned about what Russell had done? More to the point, why should it matter to him? And why the charade?

"Find Russell, and we could have a few answers."

He thanked Gibson and walked on down the passage to his own office. The Duty Sergeant had already informed him that Chief Superintendent Bowles was not on the premises, "his being called to a murder scene in Camdentown."

It was a reprieve of sorts, offering Rutledge an opportunity to think through the problem before having to present it to his superior. Bowles was not noted either for patience or for understanding. He demanded answers without a thought given to the difficulty involved in finding them. And Rutledge had already had a taste of the man's hasty interpretation of information brought to him.

He sat down at his desk and turned his chair so that he could look out the window, his view blocked by trees in leaf. They cast cool shadows across the pavement as the sun settled in the west.

River's Edge was isolated and had stood empty for upwards of five years. A perfect site for a quiet murder. Perhaps it had already seen one. Mrs. Russell.

He thought again that it would have made more sense if Willet had come to the Yard to confess to murdering her.

The question was, had Ben Willet been killed because of the past— or for something else completely unrelated to his visit to Scotland Yard? He wouldn't have been the first—nor the last—man to have a finger in too many pies.

Hamish said, "D'ye believe the woman, that she wished to purchase yon estate?"

"It was a sound enough reason to explain her trespassing. I'd have said yes, it was the truth—until she played that game in Belvedere Place. If she had nothing on her conscience, she wouldn't have cared whether I discovered where she lived or not. But what does she have to do with a footman from Thetford who washed up in Gravesend?"

He set himself the task of finishing the paperwork waiting on his desk, but his mind kept coming back to the riddle of Ben Willet.

Mrs. Brothers had recognized his face but couldn't put a name to it.

That would say that Willet could have come home to Furnham from time to time, but not often enough for Nancy Brothers to know who he was. And the men in The Rowing Boat had been reluctant to identify Willet in the photograph. True, Barber's father-in-law was dying, and the family had no wish to upset him with the news of his son's death. But was that another convenient lie? One that the man from Scotland Yard could investigate for himself, and then accept at face value? If so, the people in that village held a poor view of the police.

The barkeep at The Rowing Boat had been ready to kill to keep the truth from coming out. But what truth? That Willet was dead? Or that someone in Furnham recognized him?

Hamish said, "Ye ken, verra' likely it's no' the fact that Willet was dead but why he died."

They had come full circle.

Signing the last of the papers in front of him, Rutledge rose and carried them down the passage to hand them over to Constable Benning.

Back in his office once more, he asked aloud, "Where is Wyatt Russell?"

It had been a rhetorical question, but on the other hand, if Ben Willet had felt safe in impersonating the man, it could well mean that Russell too was dead.

"Miss Farraday didna' appear to think he was deid."

Rutledge left his office and went in search of Sergeant Gibson. "If anyone wants me, I'm going back to Essex. I expect to return tomorrow afternoon."

"Where will you be staying, if I should need to reach you?" Gibson asked.

"I doubt there's a telephone within thirty miles of Furnham," Rutledge said.

Hamish said something that he missed as Gibson asked, "Would it be best, then, to speak to the Chief Superintendent before you leave?"

"I think not," Rutledge replied, and walked on.

On the stairs he realized what it was that Hamish had tried to interject.

If there was no way the Yard could reach him while he was in Furnham, then it would be equally impossible for him to reach the Yard in the event there was trouble.

R utledge went home, packed a small valise, and set out for Essex once more. The sun was low on the horizon now, and ahead lay the dark lavender clouds of the North Sea, where evening had already begun to encroach on the day. And it was fully dark and very late when he pulled into yard of The Dragonfly Inn. He had intended to call on Mr. Morrison before he drove on to Furnham, but there had been no lights in the church and looking for the Rectory would have taken more time than he could afford, if he wanted a room for the night.

When he strode into the tiny Reception, there was no one behind the desk, but a bell stood to one side of the register, and he pushed it. It sounded rusty with damp, a grinding noise rather than a ring.

After a moment a man in his shirtsleeves appeared from the rear of the inn, frowning as he realized that here was custom he didn't wish to serve.

"Looking for a room, are you?" he said, his manner surly. "Sorry to say, they're all taken."

"Indeed?" Rutledge answered. Before the man could stop him, he reached out and turned the register around, opening it to where the black ribbon marked the current page. "The last guest appears to have signed this page some ten weeks ago. Are you telling me he's still here?"

"There's no room available. A problem with the roof."

"I'm here to call on Ned Willet."

"Then you're too late. He died not half an hour ago."

Surprised, Rutledge said, "Then I'm here for the funeral."

After a moment the man said grudgingly, "Very well. The room at the top of the stairs. You won't be needing a key."

"On the contrary. I insist on a key."

As Rutledge signed the register the man fished in a drawer, eventually coming up with a key. He passed it across the desk, and Rutledge pocketed it.

"Good night," he said as he turned and took the stairs two at a time. They curved slightly as they climbed, and the first room was in fact just at the top. On either side of his were two more rooms, and across the passage were three others, these overlooking the High Street. At the ends of the passage there were windows, the shades already drawn for the night.

Rutledge opened his door and fumbled for the lamp that must be near it. Finding it, he struck a match and lit the wick. As the flame strengthened, he took in his surroundings. The room wasn't very large, but neither was it small enough to aggravate his claustrophobia. There were two narrow beds, a desk under the window, and a small wardrobe with two doors. Turning the key in the lock, he left it there and set his valise down between the beds. The coverlets were faded, a deep green that was now nearly the color of moss in the shade of a tree. There was a medallion in the center of each, with what appeared to be entwined initials, but they were spotlessly clean and the room smelled faintly of lavender and Pears' Soap.

It had been a long day. Walking to the open window and looking out, he realized that his room was over the kitchen, and just beyond, the kitchen gardens. A lighted window cast a golden glow over the rows of vegetables, and as he watched, someone walked past the beds and came up to the rear door of the inn.

He stood, half concealed by the curtains, and through the open window he could just hear what was being said, even though whoever it was spoke in a low voice.

"Did they tell you? The old man is gone."

"Yes. Molly stopped in on her way home."

There was silence for a moment, and then the first voice said, "How is she?"

"Well enough. Considering. She's still grieving for young Joseph."

"It will be hard on her, losing his dad. Molly and Ned were close."

"Whose motorcar is that I see on the street in front of the inn?"

"Belongs to a fellow by the name of Rutledge."

"Yes, I thought I recognized it. What brings him back so soon?"

"He came for the funeral. He says."

"Damn. How did he know? It just happened."

"I told him there was no room to be had. But he insisted."

"How long does he expect to stay?"

"He didn't tell me."

There was a longer silence. "Hell. We can deal with him if we have to."

"Not in my inn."

"No."

And then it appeared that the man in the shadows outside the kitchen must have left, because the squares of light vanished and the garden was quiet enough that Rutledge could hear the crickets.

He was nearly sure the man outside the kitchen door was Barber, from The Rowing Boat.

Hamish said, startling him, "I wouldna' go wandering in the dark. No' here."

But sleep wouldn't come, and Hamish was fretful in the back of his mind as well. In the end, Rutledge dressed, went quietly down the stairs and out into the night.

The stars were bright in the blackness of the sky, and across the road he could hear the unseen river moving toward the sea. Turning toward his left, he walked to the edge of Furnham and out into the countryside. Ahead he could just see the silhouetted barns that marked the three farms.

He was fairly certain that the airfield hadn't been built at the middle farm, where Nancy Brothers and her husband lived. And if he were choosing, the land nearest the estuary would offer greater clearance for night fighters taking off in a hurry or crippled aircraft looking for an easy landing. It would also afford a better view of Zeppelins moving toward the mouths of the rivers that would point them directly into the heart of London. France was not so very far away, after all, and there would be no problem with navigation over a short stretch of open sea.

Looking over the low fence designed to keep cattle from roaming, he could see the massive black bulk against the stars that would be the house and barn. Far enough away, he thought, that he could do a little exploring without awakening the owner.

The fence was rusted and broken in places, although grasses and vines had mended the wire in their own fashion, running up the posts and making a heavier barrier than the original one. Finding a short gap some twenty feet farther on, he stepped through the tangle of briars and vines and into the field beyond. He kept walking, minding where he went, and soon enough he could see where the airfield had been laid out, including the rough foundations of the buildings that had been put up in haste. Where the actual flying field had been, the texture of the grass and weeds was different. Moving back to explore the ruins again, he tripped over a low-lying pile of stones and swore as he fought for his balance. In the distance a dog began to bark, and he stood still.

But it wasn't chained by the farmhouse, as he'd expected. He could hear the barking growing louder as the animal raced toward him.

Rutledge stayed where he was, and when the dog was fifty feet away, he whistled softly and held out one hand palm down. The dog, large and dark, slowed, legs stiff, tail straight, and the ruff on the back of his neck standing up. Rutledge dropped to his haunches and called, "Come on, there's a good dog," speaking quietly until it approached.

All at once its tail dropped and began to wag, and stretching out its muzzle, the animal sniffed Rutledge's fingers.

It had been a good two years since the airfield had been shut down, but clearly the dog remembered the men posted here and their friend-liness, and soon accepted Rutledge as one of them, letting this new-comer scratch behind its ears.

Together they walked on across the field, and then turned toward the barn. Here Rutledge saw great stacks of wood and brick out behind the building, where the thrifty farmer had retrieved what the Royal Flying Corps had left behind. In another pile were broken pro-pellers, cracked struts, and even torn bits of canvas and metal, where aircraft had crashed or been in a dogfight, and the equally thrifty ground crew had salvaged what they could. He wondered what the farmer intended to do with such bits.

The dog wandered into the farmyard, and Rutledge turned back the way he'd come. Finding the gap in the fence was harder from this side, but after several tries, he came across it.

On the road again, he walked toward the village. He was almost there, the river glinting in the distance, when he heard oars in oar-locks and quiet voices echoing across the water. Then close by, the sound of a boat being dragged up on the rough shale.

He stepped quickly into the shadows of the large plane tree at the bend in the road, well hidden beneath the broad leaves weighing down the branches overhead.

Three men strode up from the water, silent and staying close to one another as they made their way along the side of The Rowing Boat, keeping between the tall shrubs that marked the pub's boundary line and the darker shadows under the roof's overhang. As they reached the High, Rutledge could see that each man carried a haversack slung over his left shoulder, hunching a little under of the weight of it. And under his right arm, each man carried a shotgun, the barrel just catch-ing the starlight and glinting dully.

Smuggling, Rutledge realized, and slid deeper into the shadows until his back touched the smooth bark of the tree. He stood no chance against three shotguns.

The men separated without a word, two hurrying off up the High and the third coming directly toward him.

# 8

There was nothing he could do but stand where he was, his back pressed against the tree trunk, his body braced for whatever he would have to do. There was no time to pull his hat lower to cover the paleness of his face or even to turn away. He carefully ducked his head so that his chin was nearly touching his collar, and waited.

Hamish, his voice a low growl, seemed to be waiting too, just behind his shoulder. But Hamish was not there, and no help if it came down to a fight.

Rutledge watched as the man cut diagonally across the road, grunting as he shifted the haversack a little to ease his shoulder.

Fifty feet. Thirty. Twenty feet and closing.

Near enough now to see him standing there, surely. And the men who had gone the other way were still within hearing. One shout and they'd turn. He could deal with one of them, he even stood a good chance of disarming the man nearest him, given the element of surprise. The other two could bring him down from a distance, and his only hope was to make it out of range before they fired.

Barber had had no qualms about clubbing him to death. These men would shoot first and worry later.

Something in the way the man walked was familiar. Had he seen him before? When he was here with Frances?

Just then, only ten feet away, the man grunted as he shifted the haversack again.

And the haversack was all that stood between them, blocking the man's view of Rutledge there under the tree. He walked on, whistling under his breath.

It also prevented Rutledge from seeing the man's face.

He wouldn't have been able to identify him if his life had depended on it. Not in a courtroom. There was just that instinctive recognition. And it too could be wrong.

A door opened a little farther along on Rutledge's side of the street and then shut again as quietly as possible. By that time it was too late to move away from the tree to see where the other two men had gone.

Hamish said, his voice seeming loud enough to be heard on the far side of the river, "Ye ken, this is why no one is happy to have Scotland Yard come to ask questions."

Had they known anything about Ben Willet's death? Or had they believed that it was only an excuse to look into other matters?

The inn was only a short distance ahead, but Rutledge waited until he was certain there were no watchers guarding the backs of the three men. He was just about to move when someone detached himself from the recessed doorway of The Rowing Boat and turned to jog up the High Street, disappearing into the small village school.

He waited another ten minutes, in case the watcher left the school and went home. Finally, satisfied that he was in the clear, he stepped quietly out of the shadow of the plane tree and walked without haste toward the inn.

Rutledge had seen Barber—or in point of fact, heard him—at the kitchen door of the inn hardly more than an hour ago. Therefore he couldn't have been one of the three coming up from the river. Nor was he the watcher in the pub's doorway, for that man was smaller in stature. Still, Rutledge wouldn't have been surprised to learn that Barber was the force behind the smuggling.

Smuggling wasn't unheard of along the southern coast of England even in this day. Fisherman had long ago learned that they could supplement their meager living from the sea by dropping in at a French port and making quiet arrangements with their opposite numbers. War or peace, men needed to eat, and His Majesty's Excise be damned. But this last war, with submarines as well as Naval vessels and German raiders patrolling the seas, must have curtailed the usual cross-Channel trade, much less fishing. Times would have been hard for villages like Furnham. The question was, why had the village turned its back on the airfield, which could have brought in much-needed revenue to the shops and pub?

He reached The Dragonfly without incident and, as silently as possible, climbed the stairs to his room. The innkeeper was nowhere in sight. And his room was as he'd left it. No one had come in to search it in his absence.

Rutledge wouldn't have put it past the inn's owner.

The next morning, Rutledge was grudgingly served his breakfast in the small dining room overlooking the street. There were five tables, crowded together cheek by jowl, but he was the only guest.

"Tell me about the airfield," he said to the young woman who was serving him.

She was pretty, fair hair tending to curls in spite of rigorous attempts to keep it out of her face, and her eyes were hazel. He wondered if this was the Molly who had brought news of Ned Willet's death.

"I dunno much about it, sir," she said. "I was only twelve when they came to build it, and my mother saw to it that I had nothing to do with the young men who were posted here. She said they'd break my heart by dying, and there was no use to befriend them. And she was right about the dying. We saw three of them go down out over the water, trailing smoke. I was glad I didn't know them then."

"Still, the airfield must have changed the way of life in Furnham. By sheer numbers if nothing else."

She cast a wary glance toward the kitchen door, firmly shut. "It did that. There was a scuffle or two between some fishermen and the men up at the farm. After that, they were ordered to stay behind the fence, and we were left to ourselves. Still, we got to hear things. How they carried on in London on leave, like there was no reckoning tomorrow. How they took up with the girls and ruined them. How they made the younger lads restless and eager to try things they had no business trying. One of my brothers ran away to enlist. He was mad to fly, but he was only fifteen. My father had to go and fetch him home. It was a terrible time, really. The men would roar up the road in their motorcars and motorcycles, and three or four even had boats of their own, and it was hard enough fishing without them stirring up the river. We were that glad when the war ended and they went away."

Someone in the kitchen began to bang pots and pans. She reached for his empty toast rack and hurried toward the kitchen to refill it, putting an end to any conversation. Over the racket he could hear a male voice shouting at her.

Rutledge found himself thinking that to the people of Furnham, isolated and insular, the murder of an unknown archduke in Sarajevo held little importance in the course of their lives. The arrival of strangers in their midst—some of them volatile and living only for today because they couldn't count on tomorrow—was immediate and personal. Furnham hadn't wanted change—or to change. And it was thrust upon them without a by-your-leave.

Finishing his tea, he didn't wait for his toast. But as he walked out of the dining room into Reception, he heard someone crying in a corner behind the stairs. He thought it was very likely the young woman who had served him.

There was nothing he could do, and trying would only have made matters worse.

He went out to his motorcar and drove back to the farm where he had trespassed the night before.

He found the farmer in the milking shed, busy washing down after the morning milking. The man was ruddy-faced and broad in the chest, a little taller than Rutledge. He looked up suspiciously as the stranger walked into the shed, followed by the black dog busy wagging its tail as if it were well acquainted with the newcomer.

"I thought you were here to protect us," he said to the animal, then turned to Rutledge. "And what is it you want?"

Rutledge said easily, "My name is Rutledge. And you are—?"

"Name's Montgomery."

"Good morning, Mr. Montgomery. I understand your farm was taken over during the war for use as an airfield."

Montgomery bristled "I had no choice in the matter. Your lot took my land without a word to me, just walked in and told me that my best pastures and the marshes nearest the sea were now the property of His Majesty's Government. Near enough. And I had to find somewhere else for my cows to graze where those damned aeroplanes wouldn't frighten them into fits. And somewhere else to grow my corn and my hay for the winter. One of the aircraft crashed and caught fire. The blaze nearly touched off my roof. You won't persuade me to anything you could have in mind. So you might as well turn around and walk out of here before I lose my temper."

"I'm sorry. I'm not here to ask anything of you other than information. I'm interested in learning how Furnham felt about the field."

"I don't know why it should matter to you. But the fact was, I was vilified. Threatened. You'd have thought I'd written to the King personally and begged the lot of them to come here. I was damned whichever way I turned. If it hadn't been for Samuel Brothers and the other farms, I'd have lost everything. As it was, it took me nearly a year to clear away the broken glass, uproot the foundations, and turn the landing field back to pasturage. The latrines soured the land, and there was oil and petrol everywhere. I did it myself, and no one volunteered to help me. The rabble-rousers were all for sabotage, but nothing came of that. Still, there were clashes. I'd not have been surprised to see murder done on either side. The fliers called this a hardship post. No one wished to be assigned here. We even had a few American aviators from Thetford, and three of them died here. That upset my wife, I can tell you. When a man burns, the smell doesn't go away for days."

"You mentioned Americans coming in from the field in Thetford. Did you know that Ned Willet's son was in service there?"

"Ben? I can't tell you when I last saw him. It was before the war, I know that. Is he coming down for the funeral? Ned was a decent sort. I was that sorry to hear he'd died."

"Ben Willet himself is dead. He was found floating in the Thames nearly a week ago."

"*Ben?* Now that's sad news." He shook his head. "My wife called him a changeling. Nonsense, of course, but he wasn't like the rest. He came here with his father one summer, needing work. A boy of twelve, mucking out the stables and the like. She lent him books, and I found him once in the loft, reading. He was that upset, thinking I would sack him."

"Did you know Wyatt Russell or Justin Fowler?"

"I knew who Russell was. And his father before him. Who was Fowler?"

"He came to live at River's Edge when he was orphaned."

"I doubt I ever set eyes on him. What do they have to do with young Willet drowning?"

"I don't know. Scotland Yard is looking into his death. That's why I'm here. Before he died, Willet came to the Yard and gave his name as Wyatt Russell, saying that he had information about the murder of Justin Fowler."

"He claimed he was Russell? Now why would he go and do such a thing?"

"We haven't discovered why. Did you often see Cynthia Farraday in Furnham?"

Something in the man's expression altered. "My wife, Mattie, never liked her."

"Why not?"

"She never would say. Except that she brought trouble in her wake."

"And did she, do you think?"

He glanced over Rutledge's shoulder, as if making certain his wife wasn't within hearing. But he didn't answer the question. Instead, he said, "When Mattie's bitch had a litter, Miss Farraday came here asking if she might buy one of them. I was all for letting her have her pick, but my wife wouldn't hear of it. Women do take odd notions sometimes. She said the pups would be better drowned than given to her. I found other homes for them."

It was a harsh judgment.

As if suddenly aware that he'd been led off the subject, Montgomery added, "For Scotland Yard to be interested in Ben Willet's death, it must mean that he was murdered."

"He was. We can't find the connection between him and the Russell family at River's Edge, but there must have been one."

"Here, you didn't tell Ned before he died that his son was murdered! He didn't deserve that. Ned was a hard man but a fair one. And he was proud of that boy."

"I didn't tell him. I don't know if anyone else did."

"Was Ben still in service at Thetford? What was he doing in London?"

"His family thought he was still there. I'll be speaking to his employers. Do you by any chance know their name?"

"I couldn't tell you if I'd ever heard it mentioned. Why did you come here to the farm? It wasn't just the airfield that brought you, was it?"

Rutledge smiled. "I was getting nowhere in Furnham. I thought you might have a different perspective."

"That lot wouldn't help the devil put out the fires of hell. I never knew what Abigail saw in Sandy Barber. But there's no accounting for tastes."

Rutledge thanked Montgomery and walked back to his motorcar, the black dog trailing at his heels.

He went next in search of Sandy Barber and found him scrubbing down the floor of the pub. The man looked up as Rutledge approached, his mouth turning down in a sour scowl. Getting to his feet, he stood there, waiting.

"I kept my part of the bargain," Rutledge said, without greeting. "I said nothing to Ned Willet. As far as I know, he died at peace. Now I want you to tell me what you know about his son, Ben."

Setting his mop to one side, Sandy Barber said, "I know nothing about Ben. Or his death."

"Look. I'm not here to hunt down smugglers—"

"Who have you been talking to?" Barber demanded. "Who told you such a wild tale?"

"I didn't need to be told. Not after you nearly took a club to me. If you hadn't killed Ben Willet, there was only one other reason to be afraid of a policeman. Here on the Hawking, France just across the water? The airfield must have been quite a problem. They'd have been patrolling the river and the estuary. You wouldn't have stood a chance getting past the Coastguard with contraband goods. It follows that someone resumed this business as soon as the airfield was evacuated."

"I don't believe you."

"Suit yourself."

"And as for murdering Ben Willet, what reason would any of us have to go after him? Look in London. Or Thetford. It would make a hell of a lot more sense."

"How often did he write to his sister? Or his father?"

"He hardly ever did. We got a letter after he was demobbed, and he said he would get in touch with us again as soon as he'd settled in Thetford. That was that. Ned tried to say he was too busy, but Abigail thought there could have been a girl he was fond of, and he spent all his free time with her."

"What connection did he have with the Russell family at River's Edge?"

"He didn't. Not so far as I know."

"Then why was he wearing a locket that had belonged to the late Mrs. Russell? With a photograph in it of Cynthia Farraday as a young girl?"

"Good God," Sandy Barber said blankly, staggered by what he'd just been told.

Rutledge took the slender chain from his pocket and passed it to Barber. The man fumbled with the delicate clasp that closed the locket. Finally, when it lay open in his fingers, he stared at the photograph as if half afraid it would vanish before his eyes.

At last he said, "How do you know the locket belonged to Mrs. Russell?"

"I asked someone who knew her well enough to have seen her wear the necklace every day of her life. It was presumed that she was wearing it the day she disappeared."

"But there must be dozens of lockets like this one. How can anyone be sure—not after what? Six years? It was the summer before the war began that she died, if I remember right?"

"So I've been told."

"It makes no sense. How did Ben come by such a thing?"

"Who was in charge of the investigation into her death?"

"The family called in an inspector from Tilbury. None of us think much of Constable Nelson. He's drunk half the time these days and stays in his cottage minding his own business."

"Then why haven't you asked for him to be replaced?"

"You know damned well why. Nelson turns a blind eye because he has a taste for French brandy." There was contempt in his voice. "And better the devil you know . . ."

"Where can I find Constable Nelson?"

"He lives in a cottage half way down Martyr's Lane."

"Can you tell me the name of the family Willet worked for in Thetford?"

"Damned if I know."

Rutledge couldn't judge whether he was telling the truth or deliberately being obstructive.

"I'll speak to Nelson then."

As he turned to leave, he had the feeling that Barber was about to say something more, but the man thought better of it, and Rutledge let it go.

He'd said nothing about witnessing the smuggling run.

Making what appeared to be an educated guess about the resumption of the contraband trade, even on such a small scale, was one thing—having proof that it still went on was another.

Three short lanes ran north from the High Street, away from the river. Barber himself lived on the nearest of these. The last was Martyr's Lane. About halfway down it stood a weathered cottage with a bedraggled front garden surrounded by a wrought iron fence sadly in need of paint.

Hamish said skeptically, "It's no' verra' promising."

Rutledge stopped before the gate for a moment, then reached over, lifted the rusted latch, and made his way up the overgrown path. He knocked several times and finally tried the door.

It wasn't locked, and he opened it, calling, "Constable Nelson?" as he stepped inside.

The hall was dusty but presentable enough. In contrast, the front room of the cottage looked to Rutledge as if the constable had lived in it. Used dishes sat on every flat surface, a quilt had been thrown over one chair in front of the hearth, and the carpet looked as if it hadn't been swept in months. A stained and creased shirt had been thrown on the floor, and a crumpled pair of stockings had been tossed into a corner. The desk, where the constable was expected to conduct official business, was littered with teacups, opened tins of fruit, and several pairs of boots in need of polish.

A thick fug—a combination of cigarette smoke, unwashed clothing, and brandy— made him cough.

The room appeared to be empty, and Rutledge was on the point of trying another when his shod foot collided with an empty bottle, sending it spinning under the nearest table. It was then he saw the constable on the floor behind the divan.

His first thought was that the man was dead.

He strode to the constable's side and knelt to feel for a pulse. Just then Nelson snored raucously, and Rutledge realized that he'd passed out.

The constable lay where he must have fallen, his face turned to the wall, his collar undone, and his tunic unbuttoned. His shirt was stained with food, and his boots appeared not to have been polished for some time, the toes scuffed and dull.

Rutledge rose, and touched the man with the toe of his boot, and none too gently.

"Constable Nelson?"

The man didn't move.

"Constable Nelson!"

It was the voice of command this time, and Nelson's body jerked; his lids fluttered and then revealed a pair of bloodshot eyes that could barely focus.

"Who are you?" he demanded in a hoarse croak.

"Scotland Yard. Get to your feet, man, you're a disgrace to your uniform."

Nelson tried to rise, fell back, and vomited profusely.

Disgusted, Rutledge said, "I'll give you an hour. Clean yourself up and present yourself at The Dragonfly. I'll be waiting."

He turned and walked out, slamming the inner door and then the outer one, knowing full well the shock to Nelson's ears.

But it was easy to see what had happened to the man. Shunted aside by the villagers, paid in contraband to eke out his meager resources and keep him too dulled to interfere, and without the strength to stand up for himself in these circumstances, he had accepted his lot. Someone must have seen to it that he was sober and presentable if or when the need arose, or the Chief Constable would have got wind of his condition and replaced him long since.

The question was, even fully sober, could Nelson still function?

Hamish said, "More to the point, he wouldna' be trusted by the ithers."

There was that as well.

Rather than return directly to the inn to wait, Rutledge made a detour to Barber's house. He could see the black crepe that had been hung over the door, and several neighbors were just leaving, embracing Abigail Barber as they stepped outside. Behind them, the rector was preparing to leave also. As Rutledge approached, he heard Morrison asking a last question about the service for Ned Willet, and from the shadows of the front room someone answered. He could see the outline of a head and broad shoulder, but not the face. It wasn't Barber. He was nearly certain it was the man he had seen twice before, once when he had come to Furnham with Frances, and once when he had tried to find someone willing to identify the photograph of Ben Willet. Whether he had been one of the smugglers coming up from the river in the middle of the night, Rutledge couldn't be sure under oath, but he had a strong feeling he had been.

The rector offered a last word of comfort to a tearful, red-eyed Abigail Barber, touched her briefly on the arm, and with a nod to the man just behind her, walked away. As he reached the lane, he looked up and saw Rutledge waiting.

"Good morning," Morrison said, surprised.

Rutledge said, "I thought you were not welcomed in Furnham." They fell in step, walking to where Morrison had left his bicycle leaning against the nearest tree.

"I thought you had returned to London."

"I still haven't solved the riddle of a dead man."

"I understand." Morrison collected his bicycle and pushed it along with him as they continued toward the High Street. "Ned was one of my parishioners. He was always one to question, but he came to believe that he was safer in the church than out of it."

Rutledge smiled. "A wise man, I think."

"A careful one. Abigail liked to attend services with him, and Sandy tried to put his foot down, but Ned told him to worry about the state of his own soul."

"Who was the man standing behind Mrs. Barber as you were leaving just now?"

Morrison had to think for a moment. "I expect it must have been Timothy Jessup. He's Abigail's uncle. Her mother's brother. Not what you would call the friendliest of souls. The Jessups have always kept to themselves. But for all that, the rest of the village listens to them when they do voice an opinion. I've never quite worked out why, but there you are. Villages have their own hierarchy inherited down the generations, I should think."

Rutledge waited until they had moved out of earshot of several women carrying dishes covered with linen cloths, on their way to the Willet house, then said, "When I left the church yesterday I decided to look in at River's Edge. I expected to find the house closed and empty, as it was before. Instead Miss Farraday was there. She gave me to understand that she was interested in purchasing the house, if Russell intends to put it up for sale."

"Cynthia Farraday?" Morrison turned to stare at him. "I had no idea . . ." He left it there, busy coming to terms with this piece of news. "I had no idea," he said again.

They came to the High Street, and Morrison pulled his bicycle around, preparing to mount it. "You said *Miss Farraday,*" he went on, concentrating on adjusting the band around his trouser legs. "That must mean she never married."

"Apparently not." But he had not asked her name, he had greeted her by it. And she had not contradicted him or used *we* in her subsequent conversation.

"I see." With a nod to Rutledge he pedaled briskly out of Furnham.

Rutledge watched him go. He hadn't told the rector the identity of the face in the photograph. It was up to Barber to find the right opportunity to break the news to his wife first.

Hamish commented. "Yon priest. He's afraid to linger."

And yet he'd ventured into the village to offer comfort to Abigail Barber, and would very likely conduct the service for her father.

Why had he stayed so long in a parish where hope was outpaced by the knowledge that he was not wanted here?

"Like yon constable, he hasna' anywhere else to go."

# 9

Rutledge's ultimatum to Constable Nelson was sixty minutes. It was closer to ninety when he finally walked through the door of the inn and found Rutledge standing in Reception, waiting impatiently.

But the constable had bathed, shaved, changed his shirt, and brushed his tunic and trousers until they were at least presentable. There was nothing he could do about his bloodshot eyes and a face gray from fighting down his nausea. His hands shook as well, and he seemed not to know what to do with them, pressing the palms against his trousers.

He was out of condition, and Rutledge could see that he was running to fat around his middle, for the last button on his tunic was straining across his belly. And yet he was a younger man than Rutledge had thought when he'd seen him lying in a stupor on the floor. Thirty-eight? Forty?

"Constable Nelson reporting, sir," the man said, unable to keep the resentment out of his voice.

"Inspector Rutledge, Scotland Yard. Let's walk, shall we?" They left the inn and turned toward the Hawking. "You were here before the war, were you?"

"Yes, sir, I'm going on my twelfth year in Furnham," Nelson answered uneasily as he tried to see what it was that this man from London wanted of him.

"Good. I'm here to ask questions about one Ben Willet, and also about the former inhabitants of River's Edge."

"What's he done, then, Ben Willet?"

"He was found in the Thames a few days ago. Murdered."

Nelson's eyebrows flew up. "Indeed, sir. Murdered? He was a quiet sort, not one you'd expect to be in trouble, much less murdered. Does Abigail Barber know? She's his sister."

"Barber is waiting for the proper time to tell her."

"She'll take it hard." He paused. "Were you thinking it was someone from River's Edge who killed him? I don't see that being likely, sir."

"Was Ben Willet here in Furnham when Mrs. Russell went missing?"

Nelson frowned. "In fact I believe he was, sir. Now you ask. His mother was taken ill of a sudden, and he got permission to come and see her. He was one of the searchers, as I remember."

"What do you think happened to Mrs. Russell?"

"As to that, I don't really know, sir. Tilbury handled the inquiry. I was asked to leave the matter to them."

"Why?"

"Because there was hard feelings between the family and Furnham. I can't tell you why, only that they wanted no part of me. They spoke to the Chief Constable. Of course he did what he had to do, and called in Tilbury."

"Her body was never found? That's difficult to believe. If she drowned, which seems to be likely, surely it would have washed up somewhere between River's Edge and the sea."

"The current's tricky sometimes. Especially after a storm. There's no telling whether she'd have been found if she'd washed up in the marshes on the other side of the Hawking. There's inroads that the storms have made. A body could lie in one of them for weeks without being discovered."

"Someone must have searched that side of the river!"

"Yes, sir, they did. All the same, no one, not even the likes of Ned Willet, knows all the secrets of those marshes." He stopped at the water's edge, where it lapped gently at the toes of his boots. "Can I ask you what this has to do with Ben Willet's death?"

"It seems that he was carrying a photograph of Miss Farraday in a locket that had once belonged to Mrs. Russell. Apparently she was wearing it on the day she vanished."

"I'll be damned," Nelson said. "Are you sure of that, sir?"

Rutledge took out the locket and held it up. "See for yourself. It's been identified as belonging to Mrs. Russell."

Nelson took it tentatively, as if he had no right to touch it. "As to that, sir, I can't tell you that this belonged to Mrs. Russell."

"Any idea where Wyatt Russell might be? Did he even survive the war?"

"I heard that he had. But that's all."

"I was told that he could very well have killed one Justin Fowler in 1915."

"Mr. Russell, sir?" Nelson shook his head. "I don't see him as a murderer. Who told the police such a thing?"

"It was Ben Willet."

Nelson stared at him. "But how could he know? Willet, I mean? Did you speak to him yourself? How did that come about?"

"Willet came to the Yard a fortnight before his death. Where did he join the Army, do you know? With the men of Furnham, or in Thetford?"

"He was in Thetford when he enlisted. So I was told by Ned Willet. He had friends there and joined with them."

Rutledge said, "I shall have to go to Thetford. But this isn't a good time to ask Mrs. Barber where to find the house."

"If I ever knew, I've forgot," Nelson said, looking away.

They watched a heron lift off from the far side of the river and fly toward the distant mouth in that strangely elegant slow motion that marked their flight. Then the two men turned back toward the High.

"We never really knew Ben, if you take my meaning," Nelson said after a moment. "He wasn't like the rest of them. Eager to go to sea as soon as they could, or if they weren't fishermen, to work the farm or mind the greengrocer's shop. Furnham is set in its ways, you can see that for yourself. It looks to the sea, not to London. At first I didn't understand, I thought they were all benighted. But I came to like the way things were done here. I didn't want to leave."

"Where did you live before?"

"In the Fen country. Not all that different in some ways from the marshes, as far as the land goes. A hundred years different in our way of seeing things."

"But you couldn't be the village constable and still shut your eyes to the smuggling." At the expression of alarm on Nelson's face, Rutledge said, "I saw the brandy bottle on your floor. It's only my business if it has anything to do with the murder of Ben Willet."

Nelson took a deep breath. There was a suggestion of resentment in his voice, overlaid with guilt. "If I'd told London what I suspected about the smuggling, I'd have had to leave Furnham. I knew that from the start. I made my choice."

"It hasn't been much of a life for you."

The constable shrugged. "I was never an ambitious man."

On the surface that was evident. And yet—what had he left behind, what had he turned his back on, that made spending his days and nights in a drunken stupor a better way of life?

They had reached The Dragonfly. Nelson pointed to the sign above the door, creaking on its hinges as the wind picked up. "That was the name of a ship. Did you know?"

"A smugglers' craft?"

"No." He shrugged again. "Not that it matters. What do you want of me, sir? Do you think the murderer is here, in Furnham? Am I to help you search him out?"

"I don't know. I'd hoped you could tell me something about Willet and the Russells that would explain what connected the two men. All I've found is the disappearance of Russell's mother."

"In your place, I'd look in London. Ben Willet was away from Furnham long enough to have made enemies somewhere. There's no one here who wanted him dead."

But Hamish didn't believe him, stirring restlessly and warning Rutledge.

"Perhaps I will." He saw the relief in Nelson's eyes and added, "You'll send for me, if you learn anything to the contrary?"

Nelson promised, but Rutledge knew even as the words were spoken that the constable had no intention of keeping that promise and contacting him. Whatever he might learn. His duty was to Furnham, not to Scotland Yard.

Rutledge nodded and walked on into Reception. Head down, Nelson turned toward his home. Rutledge wondered what repercussions there might be for the constable now that he'd been seen talking to Scotland Yard. Even if he had told London nothing of importance.

The clerk was behind the desk, sorting through papers, and he looked up as Rutledge approached.

"Where's the churchyard?" he asked, and the man stared at him as if he'd asked directions to the moon. There must, he thought, be a shorter way to get there than driving out of the village.

"The churchyard?"

"Presumably you have one? I understand Ned Willet will be buried there tomorrow."

"Ah." Reassured, the clerk said, "If you go down past his daughter's house, there's a road beyond. Well, not much of a road at that. More of a track that has seen better days. Follow it west, and you'll find the churchyard."

Rutledge thanked him and went out to his motorcar.

Hamish said, "What really kept yon constable in Furnham?"

I'd like to know, Rutledge silently replied as he turned the crank. It's as if everyone in this village has a guilty conscience.

He followed directions, driving down the lane past the Barber house, quiet now, the door shut, and saw that just beyond there was indeed a road half hidden by the tall summer grasses.

When he reached it, he realized that to the east it must run past the farm where he'd interviewed Nancy Brothers, eventually circling back into Furnham. From this vantage point, he had a very clear view of the farm beyond hers, where the land was still high enough for good drainage. And the other end of this track must lead to the Rectory before debouching on the London Road, just as Morrison had told him. A loop, as it were, marching in parallel with the High Street.

As he turned toward the west, ahead across the marsh he could just glimpse the tops of yews. And where there were yews there was usually a churchyard. In the far distance, he thought he saw the glint of sun on water. Another river? Or just one of those temporary pools that appeared after a heavy rain and soon vanished? Indeed, the track under his tires was soft from the storm of the other night.

When he reached the churchyard, the graves were, to his surprise, well kept, the grass cropped short, flowers blooming here and there where they had been planted at a headstone. He could also see, as he got out to walk among the graves, that the village had buried its dead here for centuries, for the older stones had settled crookedly, any inscription on them long since covered by lichen or flaked into dust.

At the back of the churchyard, marking the far boundary of graves, he could see a pair of low tumuli. They were long grass-covered mounds, and surely not old enough to be prehistoric.

Hamish said, "Plague victims."

Rutledge thought he was right. It was often the practice to bury the dead quickly in lime-filled trenches. But he couldn't remember having seen any as clearly defined as these.

Walking among the stones, glancing at dates here and there, he read the familiar names. There were any numbers of Willets and Barbers, Brotherses and Montgomerys, going back generations, and among them a score or more of other family surnames. Among the Willets, someone—was there a sexton here?—had dug Ned Willet's grave. Next to his were two memorial stones to his sons lost in the war.

Behind a phalanx of tall yews stood a stone mausoleum. As he approached it, he could read the name incised above the grille that formed the doorway. RUSSELL.

He was more than a little surprised to find it here. He would have thought that the family would have preferred to bury its dead elsewhere. Ornate stone urns, draped in the carved folds of mourning crepe, were set to either side of the doorway. They were empty, and he realized that there was no one to care for them. Certainly not Cynthia Farraday. Did she ever come here? And where was Wyatt Russell?

He stared into the shadowy interior, trying to read the names on the marble squares that marked each interment. But it was too dark, and all he could decipher were the inscriptions on a pair of plaques nearest the grille.

The first was a memorial to Captain Malcolm Arthur George Russell, his dates, and the final inscription, DIED OF WOUNDS RECEIVED IN THE RELIEF OF MAFEKING.

Below it was the memorial to his wife: IN LOVING MEMORY OF EMILY ELIZABETH MARGARET TALBOT RUSSELL, and the dates of her birth and her disappearance.

This was the plaque that Morrison had spoken of, the one villagers had objected to because of the possibility that Mrs. Russell was a suicide.

He walked on, beyond the lilacs that encircled the mausoleum, as if setting it off in death from the village just as the circumstances of their material worth had set the occupants apart in life.

Another ten steps, and he stumbled over what he thought at first was a low stone wall marking the edge of the churchyard and nearly invisible in the thick grass that hadn't been mown here.

But it wasn't that sort of wall. Pushing aside the grass and brambles, he followed it some distance before he reached the end and realized that it turned. Here the stones had been pulled apart and tossed about, one or two with carvings that must have come from around a doorway, others cut and dressed. Many of them were blackened, as if they had been enveloped in flames.

I've found the missing church, Rutledge thought, the much older one that had stood here next to its churchyard. And it would make sense too that the Russell mausoleum, rather than being at the outer fringe of holy ground—as it now appeared to be—had actually stood nearest the church. In its shadow, where the Russells could take their rightful place at the last trump.

He paced the breadth and then the length of the foundation. It had been small, like many early village churches, and over the years after what must have been a disastrous fire, stones must have found their way into byres and walls, for stone was scarce out here, and brick had been the main building material.

Morrison, the rector, had talked about drainage issues, and the church here was far enough from the river in flood stage to survive. Here too a crypt could be dug, and the dead could lie in the earth, not raised tombs.

There was no way to judge how long ago the church had burned—or even when it had been built. Had its fate been decided in the upheaval and dissolution of the monasteries under Henry VIII, or had the long arm of Cromwell reached even Furnham, with his strong Puritan revulsion for anything that smacked of High Church?

Hamish said, "Naught so dramatic. Verra' likely it came down in a storm, and yon village couldna' afford to rebuild it." Rutledge smiled to himself. Depend on Hamish to see the practical, not the fanciful. The staunch Covenanter whose pragmatism had often made sense of the nonsense of war and military decisions.

Walking back to the motorcar, he said aloud, "Furnham hasn't struck me as a godly place."

Hamish retorted, "More than likely they fear the devil."

He continued along this ill-kept track and saw that a mile before it reached the London road, a small cottage stood alone in a clearing, the marsh grass beaten back and a pair of trees as tall as the low roof sheltering it.

Rutledge would never have guessed that this was St. Edward's Rectory—it looked far more like a farm laborer's cottage—if he hadn't noticed the rector, his sleeves rolled to his elbow, working in his garden.

Morrison looked up just then, seemed surprised to see Rutledge in front of his house, then quickly turned to look back the way the Londoner had come.

It was an odd reaction. As if he had expected to see that Rutledge was being followed.

Rutledge didn't stop. With a single wave of his hand, he went on to the crossroads and turned back toward Furnham.

"Hardly a proper house for yon priest," Hamish said.

"At a guess he preferred the cottage to living in Furnham."

Here in the open, the motorcar was being whipped by a rising wind, and looking ahead of him, out over the North Sea, he could see the storm clouds gathering. The rain had held off when he'd come here with Frances, but this time the clouds kept their dark promise. Just as he pulled into the yard of The Dragonfly, the creaking of the inn's sign on its post was drowned out as the rain came down in earnest. At first a few large drops hitting the dust of the street and his bonnet as he got out of the motorcar, and then with a flash of lightning, a deluge swept across Furnham like a gray curtain as he made a dash for the door.

Shaking the rain off his hat, he took the stairs two at a time and went into his room.

He knew at once that someone had searched it.

The photograph of the body of Ben Willet was safely in his motorcar, and the locket that had belonged to Mrs. Russell was still in his pocket.

What else could the intruder have been looking for?

He debated confronting the inn's owner, and decided against it. Standing by one of the windows in the passage, he watched the lightning move up the river, coming from the sea, the thunder loud enough to rattle the sash in front of him. At one point the very air seemed to turn blue around him, and a tree shattered, then went down with a roar he could hear above the thunder that followed. Someone shouted, but he couldn't tell just where the lightning had struck.

Even after the worst of the storm had subsided, rain continued to fall. But toward the east the clouds broke and a faint rainbow arced above the river to the west. Someone began using an axe to clear away the tree, strong, rhythmic blows, and shortly afterward Rutledge could hear the ring of a second axe as well.

It was nearly time for lunch, and he decided not to dine in the inn but to go up the High Street to the same tearoom where he and Frances had stopped.

He could see as he left the inn that a tree had fallen across the road where the bend led toward the outlying farms. Jessup was one of the men with an axe.

The welcome in the shop was no warmer than before, but he was served a sandwich, a cup of tea, and a Banbury bun. There were several women at two of the other tables, and the topic of conversation appeared to be the death of Ned Willet. One of the women was saying, "Do you suppose Ben will come for the funeral? Sandy told me that Abigail had written to him when her father took ill. But there's been no word."

There was a silence, filled only with the strokes of the axe. And then one of her companions said, "Haven't you heard? He was murdered. In London."

"No—oh, no, I hadn't." The woman shook her head. "What a terrible blow. Do they know who killed him? And what's Abigail to do? First Ned, and now Ben. He was the last of those Willet boys. How is she holding up?"

"Sandy hasn't told her yet. She was fond of Ben," the first woman said.

"He didn't return the feeling," the third woman put in. "How many times has he shown his face here? Too good for the likes of us."

"Yes, well, when you're in service, I daresay you do as you're told," the second woman retorted, hurrying to his defense.

"He came home when his mother was so ill," the third woman reminded her companions. "Just goes to show, I say."

Rutledge finished his meal, paid for it, and then walked over to the table where the three women sat.

"You knew Ben Willet?" he asked. "Do you recall where he was in service? The house is in Thetford."

They stared at him, shocked that he would approach them.

"I had intended to ask Abigail Barber but didn't wish to intrude on her grief," he carried on.

The third woman said, "You're the man from London."

"Yes. Scotland Yard."

They glanced at one another, apparently of two minds about helping him. But Rutledge had the feeling that they didn't know the answer themselves. Then the second woman said, "If it will spare Abigail any more grief, I'll tell you. The family's name is Lawson. Ned claimed the house was twice the size of River's Edge."

He thanked her and left.

He drove back toward London until he found the turning to the north, coming up from the ferry in Tilbury. But the roads had suffered in the rain, and it wasn't until well after dinner that he reached the outskirts of Thetford.

It took nearly half an hour more to locate the house he was after. The local police informed him that there was no one by the name of Lawson or Lawlor, but he might try one Alfred Laughton, who owned a fair-size estate some three miles out on the Bury Road.

It was set well back from the main road and difficult to see in the dying light. Contrary to what the woman in the tea shop had told him, it was most likely the same size as River's Edge, possibly even a little smaller.

But in a far better state of repair. The gardens were immaculate, and the fountain in front of the door was splashing audibly in the quiet of the evening. Even the mortar between the bricks was smoothly dressed, without cracks or crevices. There were gas lamps lit by the door, their flames flickering gently. He lifted the brass knocker and let it fall against the plate behind it.

After several minutes a maid answered the door, her uniform crisp and her manner formal.

He identified himself and asked for Mr. Laughton.

"I'll see if he is receiving visitors, sir."

She left him in the spacious hall and returned finally to invite him to step into the library.

He found Mr. Laughton there, a man of perhaps fifty, in evening dress, his right sleeve empty and pinned at the shoulder. He was standing with his back to the open windows at the far end of a richly appointed room, the gilt and leather bindings on the shelves catching the lamplight while comfortable chairs were arranged by the cold hearth.

"Mr. Rutledge," he said in greeting.

"Good evening, sir. I regret the intrusion, but I'm investigating a crime in London. Information has led me here, where I believe you have employed a footman by the name of Benjamin Willet."

"Good God," Laughton said blankly. "Willet? He was employed here before the war. A good man, as I remember. Very conscientious. Like everyone else, he enlisted as soon as he could—giving us a month's notice, mind you. Typical of him."

"And did he come home from the war?"

Laughton took a deep breath. "No. He didn't. That's to say he survived the war, and his place was waiting for him, as we'd told him it would be. But two months after the Armistice, he wrote to us from London to say that he had discovered a new vocation."

"What was it?"

"He didn't say, but his letter was enthusiastic, as if whatever it was strongly appealed to him. And he asked if we would mind keeping the boxes—those he left with us when he went into the Army—until he could send for them. Now that I think about it, I don't believe he ever did."

"And you've had no further correspondence from him?"

"To my knowledge, no. But he might well have written to someone on the staff."

"Would it be possible to speak to them? And to look at the belongings he left here?"

"Tonight?"

"I'm afraid so. It's a pressing inquiry," Rutledge added.

"Well. Let me see if Thompson can help you find them."

He crossed the room to ring the bell by the hearth, saying, "In the war, were you?"

It was a common question, a way of judging a man that hadn't existed before 1914, when position and money determined who or what he was. War, thought Rutledge with irony, was a great leveler.

"Yes, sir. I commanded Scots troops on the Somme. And elsewhere."

"Did you, by God! Bloody work, that." He touched his sleeve. "Left my hand there, and they took my arm in hospital. Ended my war straightaway, I can tell you. But they kept me busy at the War Office for another year. Replacing younger men, freeing them for service." He sighed heavily. "And they all died, you know. Every damned one of them. I felt somehow responsible. Ah. Here's Thompson. Inspector Rutledge is looking into a crime in London. Do you think you could lay hands to those boxes Willet left behind? I don't think anything was ever done with them."

The butler was late middle-aged, his hair graying. "They are still there, sir. We didn't feel it was right to get rid of them. We'd hoped young Willet would come for them one day. Of course the war has been over for two years. Still and all, we thought it best."

"Yes, quite right, Thompson. Can you see to it? And the Inspector would like to speak to the staff as well. Those who remember young Willet."

"Indeed, sir. If you'll come this way, Inspector?"

Rutledge thanked Laughton and was about to follow Thompson to the door when he was stopped.

"I say, you don't believe Willet is in any way involved in this business, whatever it may be?"

To tell the truth would forewarn Thompson and the staff.

Rutledge fell back on standard police formula. "At this stage of the inquiry, I'm not at liberty to say more. I will tell you that there is no danger of Benjamin Willet being taken into custody at any time."

Laughton accepted that at face value.

"Good. Good. I'd hate to think he'd been in any sort of trouble. Good night, then. I wish you luck."

Thompson shut the door and ushered Rutledge to another under the main stairs, where a short flight led down into the kitchen and the servants' hall.

"We'll begin with the staff, if you don't mind, sir. They happen to be available at the moment."

Rutledge could now see that the servants were just clearing away the dinner served in the family dining room upstairs and preparing to eat their own meal.

Thompson explained who this visitor was and why he had come.

Rutledge thanked him, and added, "Did any of you correspond with Willet on a regular basis?"

The woman in the black dress of a housekeeper said, "We all took turns writing to him and to the others who went away. And he'd answer us. Very interesting letters about France and the war and whatever news he might have. When he came home, he mentioned that he wished to try something new, and if it didn't work out, he'd like to know he was still welcome here. But that's the last we've heard. Is he all right? What has young Willet got to do with Scotland Yard?"

"I'm not at liberty to say," he told them once more. "Do you know what it was that he wished to try? And was he expecting to remain in London?"

"I do remember he was staying with a friend," one of the housemaids answered shyly. "I thought perhaps it was someone he'd met in the Army."

"It was nice stationery," the cook added. "We commented on that. Very thick, very expensive."

"A house in Chelsea," the other housemaid added. "He said there was no room in the house in Chelsea for his boxes, and would Mr. Thompson here keep them safe until he could send for them. I thought perhaps he might have been taken on as a valet by one of the officers he'd served under."

Beyond that, they had no more information to offer him.

Thompson thanked them for their cooperation and conducted Rutledge to the servants' stairs. He followed the butler up several flights to the floor where the staff slept. Halfway down the passage a separate staircase led up to a closed door.

Thompson took out a ring of keys and unlocked it.

There were electric lights in the attic, illuminating the rafters and the detritus of generations who had shared the same house. Trunks and boxes, cast-off furniture, outgrown toys cluttered the floor. Two long shelves on either side of the attic housed a collection of oil lamps, candlesticks, and an array of hat boxes.

Thompson led him down the room to an open space under the eaves where several boxes had been stored, well bound with heavy string and marked with the name WILLET in large letters.

"There you are, sir. I thought they might still be here. I doubt anyone has touched them since young Willet left."

"I'd like to open them," Rutledge said. "Can we drag them out into the middle of the floor?"

"Yes, sir. But you will be careful, will you not, Inspector? He may still wish to claim them."

Willet would never claim them. Still, Rutledge respected the butler's concern.

They carried the boxes out to the nearest overhead bulb and set them down. Pulling forward a stool and a chair, Thompson took out his pocketknife and carefully cut the string.

"There you are, sir," he said again.

Rutledge sat in the chair and took out the first layer of items, mostly shoes and clothing that Willet had worn in the course of his duties in the house. Below that were several newspapers, now yellow with age, reporting events leading up to Britain's declaration of war against Germany. There were even half a dozen broadsheets setting out where men could go to enlist.

Replacing the newspapers and then the clothing under Thompson's watchful eye, he set the first box aside and opened the next one. This seemed to include items that were in Willet's room here in the Laughton household, and more clothing, of the sort he might wear on his half day off. There was a photograph of a fishing boat, presumably his father's, framed in tarnished silver plate, and a cutting from a newspaper, also framed, showing a woman standing in front of a display of flowers. The caption beneath it read: MISS CYNTHIA FARRADAY, AND THE PRIZEWINNING ORCHIDS AT THE LONDON FLOWER SHOW.

The date on the newspaper, just visible at the edge of the frame, was April 1914.

She was as young as the face in the locket, smiling for the camera while one hand lifted a spray of orchids so that the photographer could capture it better.

Hamish said, "He knew her. Knew who she was."

Silently agreeing, Rutledge replaced the contents as carefully as he'd lifted them out, and reached for the third box.

Inside it were several books—one was a volume of poetry, the other a one-volume collection of Shakespeare's plays, and the last was a novel by an American writer, Henry James. Beneath these were a stack of copybooks, the sort that children used to practice their penmanship.

"I don't know that you should look at those," Thompson said as Rutledge took one and prepared to open it. "They may be private papers."

But Rutledge had no choice. It was difficult to decipher the handwriting—it was close together and cramped, the better to fit more lines to the page. He thought at first that this was a sort of diary, and then he realized it was not. The heading on the first page he came to was CHAPTER SEVENTEEN, and there followed a paragraph describing a village in France.

It was, in fact, more fanciful than accurate, although the writing was very good. The next paragraph picked up a thread from what was presumably the preceding chapter, for a woman was looking for a particular house. She found it on a side street and stood for a moment in the rain, trying to decide whether to knock at the door or walk on.

Her internal monologue as she debated what to do was extraordinarily good.

Rutledge looked up from his reading. "Did you know about these? Did anyone?"

"Willet had a room to himself—there was only the one footman, you see—and he spent a good deal of his free time there. Especially in the evenings, when the family wasn't entertaining or had gone out to dine. One of the housemaids accused him of being too good to associate with the rest of the staff in the servants' hall, but he told her that he liked to read, and this was his only opportunity."

Rutledge took out another of the copybooks and read a few pages. It was not as good as the work in the first one. Apparently Ben Willet was trying to write a novel, for there were only seventy-five pages here, and the writing broke off with a splatter of ink, as if he had been disgusted and thrown the pen down.

He had begun again in another copybook, and that one also stopped abruptly. His third attempt showed promise, and by the fourth he lacked the experience to tell the tale he had in mind— witness the incorrect description of a French village that was vaguely reminiscent of Essex—but his characters showed depth and maturity.

Thompson was growing restless, clearly eager to go back to his interrupted dinner. Reluctantly Rutledge put the copybooks back in the order in which he'd removed them, and said, "This will do for now. Thank you."

Thompson helped him carry the boxes back to where they'd found them, and the two men left the attic, turning out the light as they reached the stairs.

"Was it a diary, sir?" Thompson asked, clearly worried about what his former footman had seen fit to write about the family and the staff.

"Not precisely," Rutledge replied. "I should leave the copybooks where they are. They will do no harm."

"Thank you, sir." They had reached the kitchen, and Thompson said, "I still have duties requiring my attention. Mary will see you out."

And the same housemaid who had opened the door to him earlier led him back up the stairs, through the servants' door into the hall. She said, as he stepped out into the warm night, "Was it really Ben Willet you came here about?"

"Why do you ask?"

"I saw him in May, the twenty-ninth, it was, when we were in the London house. He didn't see me. I was on an omnibus and he was walking along the street. He looked—ill. I never said anything. It wasn't my place. But I wondered. Was it a war wound, do you think? Or was he drinking himself into oblivion? They'd never take him back here, if that's what it was."

"He was suffering from an illness," he told her.

"Was? Is he better? Dead?" When he didn't answer, she added, "Then he won't be coming back."

"I'm sorry." He meant it.

"We all thought he'd be back, after the war. His things were here, you see. A promise, you might call it. We liked him. He could be very funny, you know. Really, he should have gone on the stage. He was such a gifted mimic." She bit her lip. "I didn't want to believe it, you know. But someone told me—someone he'd known before the war—that he wanted to live in Paris. That he liked France. But he didn't after all, did he? I saw him last May in London. Myself."

"Who told you this?"

"William Neville. He was a footman in the house next but one to ours in London. He met Ben Willet in hospital in the last weeks of the war. They had trench foot, of all things. He said Ben talked about nothing but France, how different it was from what he expected. He said if he had the money to do it, he'd stay there after the war was finished. William told him he was a fool. And Ben said, all right, he'd come back to London and work five years. Then he'd go back to France and find out if he still wanted to live there. William told him that was brilliant. Ben laughed and said, no, it was economic necessity."

"Did you like him?"

"Not so much a liking," she said, considering her feelings. "But he was nice, if you know what I mean. Never any trouble, never any worry. Sometimes on our afternoons off, we'd go into Thetford. It was great fun. Like having a beau for a few hours, then back to ourselves again when we got home."

He could understand that. Service had strict rules. No romances, no marriages, no unbecoming conduct. All the same, the servants were human, and two young people would find in pretense an escape from the tedium of everyday life.

"Thompson told me that he'd spent a good deal of his time in his room."

She looked over her shoulder, then said, "He liked to take books from Mr. Laughton's library. He wasn't supposed to, but he always brought them back. And so I never told anyone. He was very careful with them."

"What sort of books?"

"I have no idea. I do know he borrowed a Bible once. I said to him, 'Don't you have a Testament of your own?' And he said he'd never had one. I thought that was very strange."

There were voices in one of the passages behind her. She said hastily, "I must go." She shut the door firmly and left him there on the steps.

Hamish said, "It wasna' a verra' profitable journey."

"In some ways it was. For instance, was it his illness that brought the man back to England? Or had he been here all this time?"

"How did he live?" Hamish, ever practical, asked.

It was a good question.

By his craft—or had he fallen on hard times and turned to blackmail?

# IO

At the end of the Laughtons' drive, Rutledge debated whether to spend the night in Thetford or go back to Furnham. And then he decided to go directly to London.

There had been no way to reach Sergeant Gibson until now, and with any luck there would be answers to his questions concerning the whereabouts of Wyatt Russell and Cynthia Farraday.

By the time he'd reached the outskirts of London, the first pale rays of the sun were brightening the eastern sky. He was in need of petrol and found a garage a few miles farther along the road. Making his way through the early morning traffic into the city, where street cleaners were busy and men and women were on their way to open shops and offices, he was caught behind a milk van making deliveries, and it was another half an hour before he reached his flat.

Two hours of sleep, a shave and a change of clothes, and he was ready to go to the Yard.

He had to run Sergeant Gibson to earth. A body had been found in St. James's Park, and the sergeant was trying to trace a member of the man's family.

He looked up as Rutledge called to him on the stairs, and said, "The Chief Superintendent has been wanting you."

"Did you tell him I was in Essex and out of reach?"

"Yes, sir. It didn't seem to do much good. By the bye, I've found the information you asked for. It's on my desk. Shall I bring it up when I've finished here?"

He knew better than to tell Gibson that he would find it for himself. They had always had a very uneasy relationship, ever since Rutledge had returned to the Yard. What drew the two men together was a distinct dislike of the Chief Superintendent, and Gibson as a rule would happily spite the man in any way he could. Helping Rutledge was one of the surest ways to do that. But he did so on his own terms.

Rutledge went on to his own office and shut the door. The long night's drive had been tiring, and he stood for a moment, looking down at the street below, not really seeing the activity there as he considered what he'd learned about Ben Willet.

Small wonder he didn't fit into the village where he was born. The position as footman had only been a beginning, a first step.

What had possessed him to decide to be a writer of books? He'd been a great reader, yes. But what had triggered that leap of imagination that said, I can do this too? Had it begun as boredom and quickly become an aspiration? Or like those afternoons off in Thetford, had writing been another means of escape from a life he'd thought he wanted and found was not to his liking?

Was Paris just another escape?

A large colony of writers and poets, musicians and painters, had converged on Paris after the war. Many of them were former soldiers, restless and in need of whatever they couldn't find at home. Or were too lost to try. A good many drank away their dreams, and others sometimes found disillusionment. A few met with success. How had Willet fared?

There was a tap at the door, and Sergeant Gibson entered rather quickly, shutting it quietly behind him.

"Old Bowels is on the warpath," he said. "The body in the park has Connections."

Bowles was always one to sniff out opportunity. A man with no connections of his own, he had an eye for the main chance. And it just as often eluded him, souring his disposition for days afterward.

Gibson held out a sheet a paper. "This is all I could find, given the time I had to pursue the matter."

Rutledge took it and scanned Gibson's dark scrawl.

"Wyatt Russell is in a clinic? War injuries?"

"So I was told by MacDonald at the War Office."

Of all the results that Rutledge had anticipated, this was not one.

He read on. "Ah, Cynthia Farraday. Well done, Gibson." In his mind's eye he could see the newspaper cutting of Miss Farraday at the flower show. A photographer's delight, finding a pretty girl admiring a prizewinning blossom. And she had appeared to enjoy having her photograph taken. Had this been her one excursion into the city with Harold Finley? Finding her ward's photograph in a newspaper would have given Mrs. Russell a very good reason for curtailing such visits.

"I've another task for you. See if you can find out which doctors in London one Benjamin Willet saw in the past six months for a stomach cancer that was inoperable. I'd like to know where he was staying during that time. He was in London at the end of May. And then a matter of a fortnight ago. That's all the information I have."

The sergeant made a note of that. "Anything else?"

"Yes. See what sort of records the Tilbury police can find on the disappearance of Mrs. Elizabeth Russell, August 1914."

"Where will I find you?"

"I'll be in London this morning, and then I'm off to this clinic in Oxfordshire. Then back to Essex, I expect. I've a funeral to attend."

"If you're leaving, now's the time," Gibson warned him. "Else you'll be taken off the Gravesend death and put to work on the St. James's Park murder. Sir."

The man pulled from the Thames had had no Connections, after all. Bowles's only concern had been to put his opposite number's nose out of joint.

"I'll take your good advice," Rutledge said and reached for his hat.

He made it out of the Yard without encountering Bowles, and drove to a street in Chelsea, not far from where Meredith Channing lived. But she was still out of the country, as far as he knew, and he made a point of avoiding her house. The fewer reminders of her the better, he told himself. Out of sight, out of mind.

Hamish snorted derisively. "You tell yoursel' that, but it does no good."

Rutledge ignored the voice. But he knew that Hamish was right. It had been hard these last weeks to know what to feel.

He found the street number. It was a very good address, and the house was handsome, the sort that would suit a woman like Cynthia Farraday. Large enough for comfort, small enough not to require an army of servants to maintain it. He remembered that someone had told him she had inherited it from her dead parents.

He walked up to the door and was amused when he saw the knocker. It was in the shape of an orchid. He let it fall and waited until a maid appeared to ask his business.

"Mr. Rutledge to see Miss Farraday," he said briskly.

Apparently the young woman hadn't been warned to turn him away. Instead she asked him to wait in the hall while she went to see if Miss Farraday was at home.

He did as she asked.

There was a small table to one side of the door, and above it hung a rather good watercolor of the marshes. On the opposite wall, a gilt-framed mirror reflected both. He thought Cynthia Farraday must have been telling the truth when she said she liked the marshes at River's Edge.

Several minutes later, a door opened down the passage and Miss Farraday herself came out to greet him.

"So you found me at last," she said, smiling, amused. "And the house, River's Edge? Is it for sale?"

"I wouldn't know. Inspector Rutledge, Scotland Yard," he informed her. "I don't believe your housemaid heard the title."

She opened her mouth, shut it again, and then said, "We'll be more comfortable in my sitting room." She turned and walked back the way she'd come, not looking to see if he followed or not.

It was a bright room she took him to, done up in lavender and cream and apricot, a very feminine and unusual setting, and it suited her. Closing the door behind him, she gestured to a pair of chairs set before a window overlooking the back garden.

She said, seating herself opposite him, "Scotland Yard. You led me to believe you were Wyatt's solicitor."

"And you led me to believe you were there in the closed house because you wished to purchase it."

"Touché. Why did you follow me to London? I can't think where you were waiting for me. Still, I didn't know whether to be flattered or annoyed."

He was unexpectedly pleased that she knew nothing about his presence at the landing stage where she'd returned the launch. "Your photograph has a way of showing up in surprising places. For one, in the possession of a dead man."

She was very still. "A dead man?" she asked, bracing herself for the answer. "Not Wyatt?"

"No. It was Ben Willet who was found floating in the Thames," he told her baldly.

He could see the blood drain from her face. But she said, "I don't know anyone by that name."

"It's useless to deny it. He knew you. On the wall of his room in Thetford he had a photograph of you taken from a newspaper or magazine."

"I don't recall that my photograph was ever in a newspaper."

"You were admiring an orchid."

Anger flared in her eyes. "That was taken by chance. I didn't pose for it."

"Yet you have an orchid for your door knocker."

"The owner of the prizewinning orchid—the one I was admiring—sent it to me after seeing the photograph."

"I've been looking into Willet's death, and I went to Thetford to the Laughton house, where he was a footman. Did you find that position for him? I can't think of anyone else who might have had the connections or the interest in helping the man."

His intuition had been right.

"That's none of your affair," she snapped.

"And when he was here in London in May, seeing the specialist, did he come and tell you that he was a dying man?"

She blinked, unable to prevent the spontaneous reaction.

"What was your interest in him? Was it a love affair—"

She cut him off, her voice sharp. "Yes, all right. I lent him books. He saw me reading one day, and he asked where I'd got the book."

"Where was this? And when?"

"In 1913, I think. I'd taken one of the boats and rowed down to a little inlet where I could tie up and read. He came up the river, and I nearly frightened him to death, he said. I was asleep in the bottom of the boat, and he thought I was ill. I found that amusing. We talked for a little, and then I gave him the book. It was a novel by an American writer. He seemed pleased. We met several more times, and he would return whatever book I'd let him borrow and tell me what he thought of it. For a young man educated in the village school, he was remarkably clever. I asked what he wished to do with his life, and he told me he wanted to find a position somewhere. I don't think he had the vaguest idea of what was required to be a footman. Still, he took care over how he dressed and how he spoke. So I told him that I'd write to the Laughtons. I'd known Rose Laughton in school and I was certain the family would be kind, whether they took him on or not. Still, I thought it best to present myself as Mrs. Russell when I wrote to ask if they were in need of a footman." She smiled at the memory. "As it happened the last one had died of complications from the measles he'd caught from the Laughton children. I had to swear—as Mrs. Russell, you understand—that Ben had had all the childhood diseases. I didn't know whether he'd had them or not. In any event, they offered him the position. I gave him several books as a going-away gift. I knew he couldn't afford to buy them."

Which explained the volumes packed away in his boxes when Willet went off to war.

"And so he lived happily ever after as a footman."

"Of course not. There was the war. It changed everything for all of us."

"Did you write to him when he was in Thetford? Or when he was in France?"

"I did not. He was my good deed. That was all. I hadn't taken his soul into my keeping."

"When did you see him again?"

"Ah. After the war. Immediately after, in fact. He was just coming out of Victoria Station, and he recognized me at once. I didn't know him. He'd grown, filled out. A man, not a boy in his father's skiff. He even sported a mustache. I took him to a shop for tea, and he told me he wanted to be a writer. And so I gave him fifty pounds and told him to send me a copy of his first publication. He did. A slim volume of his war memoirs. It was not terribly successful, as far as I know. But he was extraordinarily proud of it. The next one was so much better. I was proud of *him,* then." She turned to stare out the window for a moment. Then she asked, "Did he kill himself? Because of the disease? Or was it for some other reason?"

"The truth is, he was murdered."

*"Ben Willet?"* She faced him now, horror in her eyes. "No. There must be some mistake."

"I can show you a photograph of the body, if you like."

She shuddered. "No. Please, no."

"When did you last hear from him?"

She was still trying to come to terms with murder, but she got up and went to the small desk behind where she was sitting. Rummaging in a drawer, she drew out a postal card and brought it to him.

It was a sepia-tone scene in Paris, a street café with carriages passing and several people sitting at the tiny tables set out on the pavement. He turned it over and read the brief message.

*I want to see my father, and then I'm going back to Paris, to finish the last book. It began there. Let it end there. I shan't write to you again, but I'll see to it that you are sent a copy when it's published. Thank you for believing.*

And it was signed, simply, *Willet*.

The stamp and the postmark were not French. The card had been posted in London, not three days before the man was killed. And he had never reached Furnham.

"Did you go to River's Edge to look for him? You've been playing God with his life for years. Did you think he might have gone back home to die? That it was a lie about Paris?"

"Don't be rude. I went to River's Edge for reasons of my own."

"Did you take the launch to where you once used to tie up to the reeds with your books?"

"What if I did? I was nostalgic for another life. But not for him."

"Did you know that some weeks ago, when he was still in London, he called at the Yard? He wanted to report a murder, he said."

"Murder? What are you talking about?" she demanded. "Who *else* was murdered?"

"He told me his name was Wyatt Russell, and that he was dying of cancer. He wanted to clear his conscience by confessing to a murder. I asked him who had been killed, and he told me it was Justin Fowler."

She had not returned to her chair after handing him the postal card, standing by the window instead. Putting a hand to her forehead, she began to pace, clearly agitated.

"Why would he do that? He hardly knew who Justin was. And why pretend he was Wyatt? No, you must be mistaken—or lying."

"It has been suggested that the morphine he'd been given for his pain might have caused hallucinations."

"No. I still refuse to believe you."

"I wasn't sure what to make of his confession, myself. And so I asked him to join me for lunch. We dined at The Marlborough. And I was never shown any reason to doubt that he was Wyatt Russell. He carried off the masquerade to perfection. Now I ask myself why it should be necessary."

"Even if it was true—and I don't for a moment believe that it could be—how did Ben even know that murder had been done? I don't think he ever went back to Essex. He couldn't have been a witness to something. If he had, surely he'd have confided in me. It makes no sense at all."

"You said yourself that you hadn't bothered to correspond with him during the war. Your duty done. Why should he feel compelled to tell you about Russell? Why would he wish to upset you?"

She took a deep breath, making an effort to steady herself and think clearly. "He must have been out of his mind. I knew he was ill, but not that ill. You don't understand. When I first met him, Ben smelled of fish, and there was no future for him but going out in the boats. Wyatt would have seen nothing in him that required more than a polite nod, if that. But I did. And I did something about it too."

"If what he confessed to isn't true, then where is Justin Fowler? If he's alive and well, we can put an end to that part of the inquiry."

She was silent for a time, then said softly, "I wish I knew."

"Did they quarrel? Fowler and Russell?"

"If they were going to quarrel, it would have been before the war."

"Hard feelings don't always go away."

"Well," she said tartly, "the cause of any quarrel went away."

"You were free to go only because Mrs. Russell disappeared."

She shivered. "When I came to live at River's Edge, I was frightened by the marshes. I didn't like the whispering when the wind rustled the dry heads of the grasses. I wouldn't sleep with my window open, for fear that one day I'd be able to hear the whispers clearly, and I'd know they were talking about me. After a few weeks I grew accustomed to the sound and thought no more about it. But when Aunt Elizabeth disappeared, I dreamed that night that the whisperers had come for her. They'd called her out into the river. I've never told anyone that, but it was the main reason I left so abruptly. The other was that I didn't want to be alone in the house with Wyatt and Justin. They were so certain they were in love with me. If there had been other young women in the vicinity of River's Edge, they'd have ignored me. But there weren't. And so I lost my only home for a second time."

"Is it possible Wyatt Russell killed his mother? That her disappearance was his doing?"

"Oh, my God," she said, sitting down as if her limbs refused to support her. "No." She regarded him. "Even for a policeman you have an extraordinarily nasty mind."

He smiled grimly. "As a policeman, I have seen more than one's imagination could invent."

"Yes. I suppose you have."

"I'm surprised, given your years there, that you care so much for River's Edge."

"I loved the house. I'd have married Wyatt just to be mistress of it. But the thought of living with him happily ever after was too much. Even as a price for River's Edge."

"Could money have been involved?" he asked bluntly. "Was that why Russell was so intent on marrying you? And if you spurned him, perhaps he needed his inheritance sooner rather than later."

Frowning, she said, "I was left with a comfortable income. But the Russells didn't need my money. Besides, my inheritance was in trust until I was five and twenty—to protect me from fortune hunters, or so I was told. By five and twenty, I would no doubt be sensible enough not to run off with the dancing master."

He smiled. "And how many dancing masters did you know?"

"Not one. I thought I might do better by going to London. It was said to be awash with dancing masters."

"What became of Justin Fowler, after the war?"

"You're the inspector from Scotland Yard," she retorted, suddenly tired of him or his questions. "I'm sure you will find him without my help." She walked to the door and held it open. "After all, you found me."

He stood as well.

"You know your way. Good day, Inspector."

Leaving the house, he wasn't sure what to make of Cynthia Farraday. She reminded him of quicksilver. Just when one thought one had it within one's grasp, it was gone, elusive and tantalizing.

"And deadly?" Hamish reminded him.

# II

It was after six o'clock when he reached the little village of St. Margaret's, in Oxfordshire.

The church tower rose above the surrounding houses and shops, a sharp tower, as if to remind people of their duty to God. The clinic, he discovered by stopping at the tiny post office, was on the far side of town. It had once been a graceful country house, with a Dower House across from the main gates. Easily found, the postmistress had assured him.

And it was.

The Dower House was a mellow pink brick, and the late afternoon sun gilded the windows. Faced with white stone, it was set back from the road in a stand of trees, gardens following the short drive up to the door.

Across the road, the contrast was pointed. The gates to the main house were open, and he drove through what had once been a well-landscaped park. Now the rhododendrons were overgrown and dead boughs showed through the leathery leaves like the gray ghosts of other summers. The house too had seen better days, the gardens no longer luxuriant, the window shades uneven, giving the impression that no one had noticed how snaggletoothed this might appear to a visitor.

On the lawns were stone benches scattered here and there, some in the sun, others well shaded. None of them was occupied at present.

He left the motorcar to one side of the door and saw that it, like the gates, stood open.

Hamish said, "They're no' afraid that anyone will escape."

A table stood just inside, in what had been the hall, and a middle-aged woman in a nurse's uniform sat there, sorting charts and patient folders.

She looked up as he came in, and smiled. "Good afternoon. Have you come to visit any particular patient?"

"I'd like to speak to Matron, if I may. Ian Rutledge."

"She's just gone into her office. I'll show you."

And she led him down the passage. At one time the spacious rooms had been divided into wards, but the thin partitions had been removed. Only the pale lines on the scratched and scuffed parquet floors marked where they had been.

Matron's office had been a morning room at one time. Now it was filled with filing cabinets while books crowded one another on a shelf. The desk was utilitarian and well used. An older woman with graying hair was seated behind it, and she looked up as he was shown in, then rose as the nursing sister gave his name.

"Mr. Rutledge," she said, pleasantly. "I don't believe I've had the pleasure of seeing you here before."

"I've come to visit a patient of yours, one Wyatt Russell. But before I go in to him, I was hoping you could tell me something about his condition."

"Are you a relative, Mr. Rutledge?"

He could see that she was reluctant to divulge any information.

"I'm from Scotland Yard, Matron." He took out his identification and passed it across the desk to her.

"Do sit down, Mr. Rutledge." She sat as well, then examined his identification before handing it back to him. "I should like to hear why you are calling on Major Russell. Have you come to ask for his assistance? Or is he accused of something?"

"I don't know how to answer you, Matron. The inquiry is in its early stages. There was a man found dead in the Thames." He gave her the date when Ben Willet had been pulled from the river. He knew, from the twitch of a muscle at the corner of her eyes, that he had touched a nerve. "The problem was, earlier on, this man had given Scotland Yard his name in another matter—but it was false. The name he gave was Wyatt Russell."

"I see. But why should he do that? Had he ever met Major Russell, do you know?"

"I can't tell you how well they knew each other. Slightly, at a guess. But they both lived in Essex, within a few miles of each other. They most certainly were aware of each other's existence."

He remembered suddenly something that he should have spoken to Miss Farraday about. "As it happens, this man was one of the search party trying to find Mrs. Russell, the Major's mother, when she disappeared in 1914."

"Ah. I see." She set the file she had been working on as he entered to one side of her desk and folded her hands. "Major Russell," she began, seeming to choose her words with care, "has a problem with his memory. It is—to put it bluntly—imperfect."

"Shell shock?" he asked, hearing Hamish loud in his mind.

*Please, dear God,* he prayed. *Let it not be that.*

And his prayer was heard.

"Not shell shock, no. He was severely wounded. And while he

can function in so many ways that we consider normal—button his clothes, tie his shoelaces, comb his hair, count his money, carry on a seemingly intelligent conversation—he has difficulty with the past. He recalls it in very irregular and sometimes inaccurate ways. For instance, he told me two days ago that he was being called up again, that his train was to leave in a quarter of an hour, and he couldn't find his uniform. He was quite upset, as you can imagine. And he wouldn't believe us that the war had ended two years earlier. Another example of his confusion—he was allowed a leave, actually a test of his ability to cope in strange surroundings. This was two months ago, you understand. We sent someone with him to oversee his care. A valet, if you will, or a batman. Actually, this person was a trained orderly, and it was his duty to keep an eye on the Major for us." She picked up a pen, looked at it, then put it down on the desktop again. "For the first week, he was a model patient. We were greatly encouraged. And then he came home late from a walk in such a state that we brought him back."

"And he hasn't been away from the clinic since that time?"

She reached for the pen again, her eyes hidden from him. "We have not sent him out to live on his own since then. No."

But the door to the clinic stood open, and the gates as well. Would Matron call in the local police if Major Russell—or one of her other patients for that matter—went missing?

Not, he thought, unless they were on a regimen of medicines and their health was put at risk. Or they posed a danger to themselves or to society.

He thanked her for seeing him, and asked again if he could interview Major Russell.

She told him that he could, and rang a little bell on her desk. There was a tap at the door, and a young nursing sister asked, "Yes, Matron?"

"Take Mr. Rutledge to visit Major Russell, if you please."

And then he was in the passage following the young sister.

They entered a room that had once, he thought, been the billiard room. But there were chairs and small tables set about it now, and men were engaged in board games or cards. A few simply stared into space, their hands dangling over the arms of their chairs, their minds disengaged from the present.

Hamish said, "Ye see yoursel' still in their faces."

He did. And the clinic where he'd been kept until his sister had intervened and had him transferred to the care of Dr. Fleming. In that first clinic men who were shell-shocked screamed at night and sat staring at nothing all through the long day. Dr. Fleming had taken a different approach, dragging out of unwilling patients the reasons for their withdrawal from themselves and the world. Rutledge had had to be pulled off the doctor after he had confessed to the death of Corporal Hamish MacLeod, ready to kill the man who had made him face his demons.

In spite of the warmth of the summer day that filled this familiar setting, he felt cold.

The sister went across to one man, broad-shouldered, fair-haired, in every way seemingly normal, and touched him lightly on the arm. "Major Russell? You have a visitor, sir." He raised empty eyes to her face. She turned and smiled at Rutledge. "If he becomes tired or anxious, you'll let one of the staff know?"

"Yes, of course. Thank you, Sister. " He pulled an empty chair nearer to where Russell was sitting. "Good afternoon, Major. My name is Rutledge."

# 12

Russell turned a little, to see him better. It was then that Rutledge realized that one side of the man's head was slightly misshapen, as if the skull had been damaged. His hair nearly concealed the difference.

"Do I know you?" he asked, frowning as he studied Rutledge's face. With a nod, the sister walked away.

"I don't believe we've met. I was on the Somme." He gave his rank and regiment.

"Were you? Patient here, are you?"

"No. I'm presently an Inspector at Scotland Yard. Someone came to my office not long ago, and I believe he knew you. Ben Willet, lately of Furnham, Essex."

"Cynthia's pet. What did he want?"

"He was concerned about Justin Fowler. In fact, he rather thought that Fowler was dead."

"He is. Died during the war as I remember. What about it?"

"Do you have any recollection of where he died?"

"I'm not in my dotage," Russell snapped irritably. "In 1915 or thereabouts."

"In France?"

"How do I know? I was busy as hell trying to keep myself alive, and my men."

"There was some mention of the fact that he might have been murdered."

"Wouldn't surprise me. He was a self-centered bastard. Probably shot in the back by one of his own men. I never cared for him, you know."

"I understand you were married just before you went to France."

"I was. She died in childbirth. My son with her." He shook his head. "Do you know, I can hardly remember her face. I try sometimes. There's a photograph in my room, but I don't know if it's my wife or someone else."

Rutledge reached into his pocket and drew out the locket. "I believe this may have belonged to your mother?"

Major Russell put out his hand and touched the locket dangling from its gold chain. But he didn't take it or open it. "Never saw it before. Are you sure?"

"The maid, Nancy, appears to think so."

"Nancy. The quiet one. I can't quite bring back her face either."

"How recently were you in London?"

"Last week? No, it must have been earlier than that." He tried to think, his brow furrowed. "I'm sorry. I'm sometimes confused about dates."

"Do you remember walking along the Thames?"

"No, I don't. But that doesn't mean I didn't. Or that I did."

"Perhaps you were walking east of the Tower, rather than nearer Westminster Bridge?" It was east of the Tower that the watermen believed Willet had gone into the river.

"Yes, thank you, I remember now. There was an accident on Tower Bridge. It was blocked by a lorry that had overturned, spilling marrows all across the road. I remember the blood. The driver was bleeding. You couldn't see his face for the blood. I walked away. I'd watched enough men die."

"Was Willet there as well?"

"Ben Willet? No, he was waiting for me on the other side of the bridge. I didn't want to watch him die, either."

"Why should he be dying? Was he involved in the accident?"

"Damn it, I told you he was on the far side of the bridge, waiting."

"Did you have your service revolver with you?"

"I always carry it with me. Every officer does."

"But the war is over."

"Damn it, are you calling me a liar?"

"Not at all. I'm trying to establish a clear picture of events. It's my duty, although I grant you it can be tiresome at times. You had your service revolver with you, then. Did you use it that night?"

"I'd have liked to shoot that wretched lorry driver and put him out of his misery. His head was bleeding, all down his face. I know what that means. Doesn't stand a chance, poor bastard. They drilled holes in my skull. Did they tell you? Because the brain was swelling."

"Ben Willet was suffering from a cancer," Rutledge went on, trying to bring Russell back to that night on the bridge.

"That's right. He didn't want a slow death. But he couldn't bring himself to finish it. His father was strict, you see. A religious man."

"He wanted you to help him die?"

It wasn't an answer Rutledge had considered.

"Yes, didn't I tell you? I was to meet him that night. On the far side of the bridge. I'd run into him in Piccadilly, he was on his way somewhere, someone was waiting. But he asked if I would mind having dinner with him. There was something he wished to ask me. I had to rid myself of my minder—"

Only half aware of what he was doing, Russell's fingers had been fiddling with the locket, which was still dangling from Rutledge's outstretched hand.

And then it opened without warning, swinging around to face him. He stared at it for a moment, then looked up at Rutledge.

"What the hell are you doing with her photograph? You've been lying to me all along, haven't you? My mother's locket be damned." His face was suffused, rage flashing in his eyes, turning the blue almost incandescent.

Surging to his feet, he overturned his chair. The crash startled the others in the room, and they looked up in alarm.

"I thought this talk of London and Willet was nothing but a trick. You stay away from her, do you hear me? She's worth ten of you." And before Rutledge could stop him, he'd flung the locket across the room and strode swiftly out the door.

One of the card players was on his feet as well, shouting at Rutledge.

As he listened to Russell's boots pounding down the uncarpeted passage, Rutledge managed to find the locket where it had fallen among a collection of canes in a porcelain stand. He reached the door just as the nursing sister came rushing in, almost colliding with him.

"What did you do?" she demanded, and behind her Matron was saying, "I heard someone running."

Rutledge pushed them aside. "It's Russell. I think he left the house."

Several other nursing sisters were coming from other parts of the clinic, and he had to dodge them as he ran.

Someone had thought to ring a bell somewhere, the clanging almost earsplitting. Reaching the door, he glanced up to see the bell hanging in a window above the door, and there was an orderly vigorously pulling on the rope.

"That way!" he shouted down to Rutledge, pointing toward the trees of the park.

Rutledge followed the direction he indicated, almost certain that he could hear someone crashing about in the straggling undergrowth. But he reached the road without finding the Major.

Hamish said, "He's gone to ground."

Rutledge swore. He hadn't opened the necklace on purpose. It had been a fluke that it had clicked open at all.

He could hear Matron giving orders as the bell stopped clanging.

Rutledge crossed the road and went into the garden of the Dower House. He circled the house, then looked into the sheds behind the kitchen, swinging the doors wide, before turning back to the road.

"He couldna' have got far on foot," Hamish said.

"I should have been prepared." But he knew, even as he said it, that there had been no warning. Whatever had stirred in the dark recesses of the Major's mind, it had exploded into violent action.

"Ye ken, he mentioned the lass's name earlier, and nothing happened."

*Cynthia's pet . . .*

But a name was very different from a photograph in the hands of another man.

They searched until the sunset colors faded into lavender, purple, and then deep blue, and there was no light to see under the trees. Matron, standing in the doorway, said, "I warned you that his mental state was uncertain."

Rutledge said, "I take full responsibility. But he's done this before, hasn't he? And you failed to warn me of that."

She said nothing, watching the last of the searchers trudging wearily back to the house.

One of the men said as he came close enough to be heard, "I think we should search the house again. In case he doubled back."

But Rutledge didn't think he had. Still, the staff and those of the patients who were ambulatory set about going from room to room.

"When did he disappear the last time?" he asked as Matron stood listening to the search going on over her head. "You can't protect him now."

"Yes, all right. A month ago. He was gone for three weeks. We searched for him, looked everywhere we could think of that he might have gone. I didn't wish to ask the police to help. After all, he'd done nothing wrong, he wasn't dangerous. And my faith was rewarded. One morning he was standing here at the door when we came down. Disheveled, hungry, in need of a bath, but he knew who he was and where he was, and he apologized for worrying us."

"He gave no reason for leaving?"

"He told me he needed to think, that he couldn't here. He needed to be alone."

"Does he have access to his service revolver?"

"No, most certainly not. There are no weapons here, I assure you."

"But he does have a house in London? Where he and his wife lived? Is it by any chance there?"

She hesitated. "The orderly saw to it that the revolver was put away. It was his first responsibility when they arrived in London."

Although she was reluctant to give it, he got the direction of the London house.

"But it's closed now," she protested. "It generally is, when he's in residence here."

He thanked her and left. Then, as he was driving out the gates, a constable came peddling furiously up the road. Rutledge stopped the motorcar and asked, "What is it?"

He had to identify himself before the constable would speak to him.

"There's been trouble in the village," he said. "It must have been someone from here. He struck down George Hiller and took his Trusty."

The Trusty Triumph had been the workhorse of the war. Dispatch riders found the motorcycle the best and fastest way to reach the Front and keep sectors in touch with HQ. They took weather, the shelling, and the rough and treacherous terrain in stride, and the silhouette of the goggled figure, head down and hunched over his machine, was a familiar one.

"Tell Matron, if you please. I'll see if I can find him."

Rutledge didn't wait for an answer. He drove as fast as he dared, given the state of the roads, but he knew—as Hamish was busy telling him—that the Triumph had a head start and would reach London long before it could be overtaken.

But what had triggered Major Russell's outburst?

Rutledge had assumed that it was the photograph of Cynthia Farraday. But what had he said next? *Be damned to my mother's locket.* Had he recognized it earlier, even though he'd said he didn't know it?

Or—was it the locket with Cynthia Farraday's photograph in it? Had Russell thought then that she had had something to do with his mother's death?

Was she in any danger?

He had to find Russell and George Hiller's Trusty before the Major reached the Farraday house in Chelsea.

# 13

Rutledge scanned the distance, searching for some sign that he was closing the gap with the Triumph, but it was wishful thinking, and Hamish relentlessly pointed that out.

Whatever he'd set in motion, he had to stop it.

And still there was nothing ahead, no small red light to guide him.

Russell, he thought, was driving recklessly, his anger goading him.

His own concentration was intense, passing through countryside, avoiding a horse cart moving slowly or a gaggle of geese waddling toward a pond, then through one village after the other with lamplight marking the street in tidy squares. Back into the countryside once more, before finding himself in a fair-size town where people were strolling in the warm summer evening. His eyes readjusting as he returned to the pitch-dark of farms and woods once more. Even Hamish was shut out, and the silence was unsettling.

Had Russell turned off? Taken a different route from the one Rutledge had expected him to take? It was becoming more and more likely, and without a moon, it was impossible to push the motorcar any harder on unfamiliar roads.

And then six miles outside London, he caught up with his quarry.

He nearly missed it, all his attention on negotiating an unexpectedly sharp bend in the road.

The Triumph lay in a ditch, front wheel twisted, and it was the brief flash of the headlamps on metal that caught Rutledge's eye.

Braking hard, slewing the motorcar halfway across the road, nearly sliding into the ditch on the far side himself, he came to a rocking halt, thanking God no one had been coming from the other direction.

He got out quickly and ran to examine the wreckage, shining his torch across it, expecting to find Major Russell there in its beam, dead or dying, entangled in the ruins of the machine. Cursing himself and Russell in the same breath.

George Hiller's Trusty had suffered from the great flaw of its kind, the front fork spring that could take only so much rough handling before breaking. In France, where the roads were even rougher than here in England, a leather strap had often been added for extra support, allowing the rider to cut cross-country when conditions made it necessary.

But the Major wasn't there. Not beside the motorcycle. Not under it.

Dropping to one knee, Rutledge shone the torch over the machine and the bruised grass beneath it, trying to comprehend how Russell could have escaped unscathed. It would have taken a miracle, he told himself. And then he saw the blood.

He got to his feet and looked around. There was a house just on the far side of the bend, and a light shone from the front window. Stopping only to move his motorcar to a safer place than the middle of the road, he went quickly to knock on the door.

A tall, slim woman with iron gray hair opened it. He was struck by her eyes, dark and intelligent—and red rimmed with weeping.

"My name is Rutledge. Inspector Rutledge, Scotland Yard. Did you by any chance see the accident with that motorcycle in the ditch?"

She stared at him for a moment, then said, "You'd better come in."

He walked into the very handsome parlor and sat down on the dark blue couch that she indicated. "May I ask your name?"

"Marilyn Furman."

"And did you see the accident?" he asked again.

"I was just coming home, I hadn't even opened my door when I heard the cyclist coming around the bend at great speed. And then something happened, I don't know what it was. It was as if the front balked, like a horse at a fence. I heard the rider cry out, and then he was flying over the handlebars. The next thing I knew, he was in the ditch, and the motorcycle was coming straight toward him as it slid in the dust." She turned away. "It was quite terrible. I heard him cry out a second time. And then nothing. I was afraid to go across to him. I didn't even want to think about what I might see. But I took my torch and made myself do it, and to my astonishment, he was alive. People from down the road had heard the noise too and came running. I sent them for an ambulance and stayed with him. I couldn't see his face for the blood. I asked him his name, but he couldn't tell me." She turned back to Rutledge. "I thought someone should know it, you see. In the event they came to look for him and saw the wreckage of the Triumph. And the hospital ought to know as well. But he couldn't tell me."

Her eyes filled with tears, and she reached for her handkerchief. He gave her time to collect herself, then asked, "Was he still alive when the ambulance got to him?"

"Oh, yes. They couldn't understand how he missed being killed."

"Do you know where the ambulance men took him?"

But she was still locked in the horror of all she'd witnessed. "They were so long in arriving. I thought they would never come. There was a young couple who appeared from somewhere and sat with me. They wanted to put him in their motorcar, but I was afraid to try to move him. He was in pain, moaning. I couldn't even offer him a little water. I felt so useless, and then the ambulance was there, and it was all right."

"Do you know where I can find him?" he asked again.

"I believe he was taken to St. Anne's. It's about seven miles down the road. I was too distressed to ask. And so relieved to have help for him finally." She took a deep breath, struggling against the tide of memory.

"Do you have any idea of the extent of his injuries?"

"I asked the ambulance men to tell me what was wrong. So that I could reassure whoever came looking for him. They couldn't be certain, they told me. The cut on his forehead was bleeding profusely, and it was possible that he had sustained internal injuries, even broken ribs. Then they were shutting the doors and driving away. I just stood there, watching them go, too dazed to think what to do next."

"Is there anyone here who could take a message to Oxfordshire?"

"Is that where the cyclist is from? There's the man who sees to my gardens for me. He won't mind going, he has friends in Oxford. A head gardener at one of the colleges and his family. I'll give him the day off tomorrow."

"I have the name of the Triumph's owner. He will be glad to come and take it away." He took out his notebook and wrote the direction, tearing away the sheet and passing it to her.

"But Scotland Yard—what had he done? This man—were you following him? Is that why you know all this?" She indicated the sheet of paper in her hand.

"I was following him to London," Rutledge replied. That was true as far as it went. "Are you all right? Is there someone who could come and sit with you?"

"I'm just a little shaken still, but I'll be fine," she said, collecting herself. "It was just—seeing him fly through the air like that. It happened so quickly, I couldn't even cry out. And then the Triumph following, as if it were intent on crushing him. I don't think I've ever seen anything quite so horrible."

He sat there for a few minutes more, talking to her until she was calmer, and then said, "I must go."

"Would you mind terribly? Would you send word to me so that I'll know if he lived or not? It would be kind. I really don't want to spend the rest of my life wondering."

"I'll see to it. The doctors may not know anything at first. They'll have to examine the man and determine the extent of his injuries. You won't hear straightaway. But that will be good news, actually."

"Yes, I understand. I won't worry. But it would be comforting to think I could put that terrible picture out of my mind, no harm done."

He left then, still concerned for her, and went back to look at the Triumph.

And then he started his motorcar and drove directly to St. Anne's.

It was unexpectedly difficult to find. A small hospital in one of the larger villages that had all but been swallowed up by London's growth, it was tucked away out of sight. He had turned around at the outskirts and driven through the village a second time, when he saw the Catholic Church down a side street. A signboard identified it as St. Anne's, and just beyond it was a square building that was set back from the road in what appeared to be a park. He thought it might have been a small manor house at one time, or perhaps a rectory.

Leaving his motorcar by the steps, he went inside.

The nurses were nuns in white habits, and he wondered if this had originally been a lying-in hospital for difficult maternity cases. There was a small casualty ward in the back.

The sister in charge came to meet him, prepared to make a decision on where he was to be sent, but he said, after she asked what his problem might be, "I'm here in regard to the accident case just brought to you. A man on a motorcycle."

"Are you a relative?" she asked, pursing her lips, as if about to tell him he couldn't go into the ward itself.

"Scotland Yard," he told her. "I was looking for this man to help us with our inquiries."

"Indeed. Well, then, you're out of luck."

# 14

H e's dead?" Rutledge asked, unprepared for this news.
"No, he is not. But he ought to be. He may yet be. Bruises
and scrapes all over him. But somehow he just missed breaking his
head or another bone. And he left, refusing further treatment or a few
hours of observation. He said his wife would be worried about him if
he didn't come home before midnight."

But Major Russell had no wife that Rutledge knew of.

"Was he able to give you his name or tell you where he lived?"

"Not at first, but then he did tell the sister in charge that he was Mr.
Fowler, Justin Fowler. From London. Later on he asked if he could
take an omnibus from here to London, most particularly one that
would stop somewhere near Kensington Palace."

*Damn the man!* "And did he find an omnibus that would carry him
to Kensington?"

"He must have done. He asked one of the orderlies which to watch for, and I was looking out the window when he left."

"Thank you, Sister."

"If you please, tell him he must rest. In the event there are more serious injuries than we knew of. Even a concussion. It was very foolish to go rushing off like that."

"I will warn him," Rutledge answered, and took his leave, his mind already dealing with the problem of Major Russell's intentions.

For Kensington Palace was within walking distance of Chelsea, where Cynthia Farraday lived. It was also where he could find another omnibus to carry him to Victoria Station and a train to Tilbury.

Hamish said, "He'll go for the lass. And then to Tilbury, and on to River's Edge."

Rutledge was already turning the crank on the motorcar. "We'll try Chelsea first. Just in case." As he made his way out of the village and found the London road again, he added, "He still has a head start. But the omnibus will be slow. At least we have a fairly good idea where to look. And if he isn't in Chelsea, there's the house in London, and after that, Essex. He knows Matron will send someone to the house, but he may think there's time enough to clean himself up and change his clothes."

London traffic was unexpectedly heavy for this time of night. Lorries filled with produce, motorcars, barrows, and carts vied with omnibuses and even a few larger horse-drawn vehicles, and while there were not that many of them all told, he found it difficult to make good time. The only consolation was that a lumbering omnibus would find it even harder to overtake them.

A summer's dawn was breaking in the east when he finally reached Kensington.

A wagon laden with early cabbages was stopped stock-still in the middle of the road while the driver haggled with a woman shopkeeper over the price of his wares. Impatient, Rutledge left his motorcar in the queue and went forward to speak to the pair.

They turned as one, glaring at him as he said, "How much are your cabbages?"

The driver looked him up and down as the woman said, "Here, I was first!" Ignoring her, the man gave Rutledge a price.

It was outrageous, but without comment, Rutledge paid him for ten, handed them to the woman, and then pointed to the high seat of the cart. "Drive on. You've made your first sale of the day."

Grinning, the man clambered up with alacrity and lifted his reins, calling to the horses.

But the woman said, "Here, I wished to choose my own."

He gave her his best smile. "Madam, you have ten fine cabbages that didn't cost you a farthing. Be grateful."

And he walked back to his own vehicle before she could think of a response.

The rest of the way to Chelsea was uneventful, but Rutledge fretted over the delay as he threaded his way through the streets where milk vans stopped and started with no regard to others. He had a very bad feeling about what he'd find at Cynthia Farraday's house and hoped that her maid would have the good sense not to open the door to a bruised and bleeding stranger.

But when he pulled up in front of Miss Farraday's house and walked quickly to the door, he found it off the latch. Opening it only a little, he stood there for several precious seconds, listening for any sounds of argument or trouble, any intimation as to where he was needed.

The house was quiet.

He pushed the door wider, prepared for an attack if Russell had seen his motorcar on the street. But none came, and he stepped inside.

The ticking of the long clock in another room could be heard clearly.

The house was unnaturally quiet.

Rutledge began to make his way from room to room on the ground floor, listening to the quality of the silence as he went. Each one was empty, and nowhere was there any sign of a struggle.

A door closing behind him creaked, and he stood still, waiting. But no one came or called out.

Worried now, he went quickly down to the servants' hall and found no one there. Miss Farraday's cook should have been feeding the banked fire in the cooker and preparing for breakfast. And the door to the back stairs was firmly shut. Returning to the hall, he cast caution to the winds and took the main stairs two at a time. In the passage at the top, he paused. There were several doors, all of them closed, and no way to judge which one was the master bedroom. He went to the one at the top of the stairs and opened it.

He wasn't sure what he'd expected. What he found was a tidy and very feminine bedroom done up in peach and pale green, with windows overlooking the back garden. A great maple shielded them, the leaves moving gently in the early morning breeze.

Nothing was out of place, neither the chair nor the octagonal Turkish carpet in the center of the room. A large wardrobe stood against one wall, and a door beside it led to what must be a dressing room.

He started across the room to open it, and as he did, he heard a sound just behind him. Prepared for anything, he spun around. But it was only the bedroom door swinging shut.

In the quiet room it sounded as loud as a gunshot.

From the wardrobe came a whimper, cut short.

He turned toward it and reached out for the handles of the two doors.

This time Hamish warned him with a soft "'Ware!" just as Rutledge's fingers touched the gilt knobs.

He stepped back at once, and in that same instant, one of the doors was flung wide from inside and a figure hurled itself at him. He recognized Cynthia Farraday just as he caught sight of the sharp, pointed scissors in her right hand.

He was only just able to dodge the blades as they slashed viciously within inches of his eyes, and he caught her hand before she could try again.

"Steady!" he said as she cried out and began to pummel him with her other hand. And then she blinked as she recognized him and broke away.

"What are *you* doing here?" she demanded, her voice overloud from anxiety.

"The outer door was open. I thought I ought to find out why."

Struggling to regain her composure, she said, "I thought he'd come back. I could hear someone walking downstairs. Didn't you even think to call out? Warn me that you were here?"

"It seemed wiser not to. The house was quiet. I didn't know what to expect."

"Yes, well, you gave me the fright of my life." Her hair had fallen down around her face, and she brushed it back impatiently.

It was then he saw the pink mark on one cheek.

"Who slapped you?"

"If you must know, it was Wyatt Russell. I told you. He was just here, and he was very angry."

"Where is your maid? I couldn't find her or anyone else."

"She and my cook went to Hammersmith to attend a funeral. They won't be back until midmorning. I couldn't sleep, I'd been sitting downstairs reading when someone knocked. I shouldn't have opened the door, yes, I know that now. But I did, and Wyatt was the last person on earth I expected to find standing there. I thought he was in a clinic somewhere."

"He was, until late yesterday afternoon. What did he want? Why did he come here?"

"There was blood all over his face, and his clothes were stained. I asked what had happened, and he said he'd been in an accident and was feeling light-headed. And so I asked him to come in. But he couldn't settle, pacing the floor. He wanted to know if I'd been to River's Edge recently."

"What did you say?"

"I thought it best to say that I hadn't. I offered to bring a basin of water to him, to help him wash off the blood. He thanked me and asked if I'd bring water to drink as well. But when I came back with the basin and some towels, he drank the glass of water and said that the rest could wait. That's when he asked me if I knew a man called Rutledge. I told him I did. I was surprised, I didn't think you and he had met. Next he asked me if I'd given you my photograph, and I told him I most certainly had not. He called me a liar, he said he'd seen it for himself. I told him he was wrong. And he slapped me. I was so shocked. And I think he was as well, because we just stood there, looking at each other. He threw the empty glass in the hearth, shattering it, and then he turned and walked away."

"What did you do then?"

"I cleared away the broken glass, then put away the basin and towels. I was in the kitchen when I heard something upstairs. A door creaking, I thought, and then footsteps. I believed that he'd come back again. I couldn't remember whether I'd shut the door, much less locked it. I was afraid to go and see. I took the back stairs and shut myself in my room, hoping Mary would come soon. But of course it was far too early. When I heard someone coming up the staircase, I knew he was looking for me, and there was nowhere I could go. I took the scissors out of my sewing box and got into the wardrobe. If he opened that door, I'd know he was hunting me."

But her attack on him had been far more serious than a response to a slap. Rutledge wondered if there was more to the account than she'd told him.

Tears started in her eyes, and she brushed them away irritably, going to stand by the window. And then, before he could speak, she whirled around and said fiercely, "Why are we standing here? I'm not accustomed to entertaining anyone in my bedroom."

She crossed to the door, leaving him there, and he followed her down the stairs. When they reached the sitting room, she said, "What did you say to him that made him come for me? You must have found him, you must have said something, done something." She was angry with him now. "And what photograph do you have of me? Not that silly one with the orchids?"

A motorcar backfired in the street outside, and she jumped, her eyes flying to the door before she realized what the sound was.

"She's verra' frightened," Hamish said.

His appearance alone— Rutledge began.

Cynthia Farraday was staring at him. "What do you hear?" she asked, and the question shocked him.

Had she heard Hamish? *Actually heard him?*

And then he realized that he was gazing toward the window, distracted, unaware of where he was looking.

"A motorcar," he said. "It didn't stop, there's nothing to fear." It was all he could muster.

"The photograph? Well?" she reminded him,

He struggled to think. The photograph. He'd never shown her the locket.

"Sit down," he said. "I want you to look at something."

"You haven't answered me. You do have a photograph, don't you? When did you take it? Why?"

He took out the locket and handed it to her.

But she wouldn't touch it, staring at it as if it could bite her.

"Where did you find that?" she whispered, sitting down quickly, as if her knees had failed to support her. "My God, did you show this to Wyatt? No wonder he was so upset!"

"You recognize it?" he asked.

"Of course I do. It's Aunt Elizabeth's. I don't think she ever took it off. *Where did you find it?*" she asked again, and then, her lips trembling, she said, "You've found *her*, haven't you?"

"No. But someone must have done. Ben Willet was wearing it when he was taken out of the river. The locket was given to me by Inspector Adams in Gravesend."

He thought she was going to faint. The color went out of her face, and she leaned back in her chair.

"No. No, Ben would never have done such a thing. He was one of the searchers."

"It's possible he found it when he was searching. It's gold, quite valuable."

"But he kept it, didn't he—I mean to say, if that's true, he never returned it to the family or sold it."

As if, Hamish was pointing out, keeping the locket made any difference.

"He put it to another use." Rutledge took the locket between his fingers and opened it. "This is what was inside."

Cynthia leaned forward reluctantly, as if half afraid of what she might see.

"Oh," she said, drawing back. "My photograph. I thought—she told me that her wedding photographs were inside."

"According to Nancy Brothers, they were. She was surprised to see that they'd been removed."

"This is what Wyatt saw yesterday? Before he came here? This is the photograph he claimed I'd given you? How could you be so heartless as to let him believe such a thing?"

"I didn't. He jumped to conclusions and told me that a policeman was not good enough for you. He left the clinic, and while we were wasting time hunting him, he got a head start. I had the devil's own time catching him up. And then he slipped away again. I was afraid he might be coming here."

"But was there an accident? As he'd claimed? He was so bloody, one of his hands badly bruised, and I couldn't be sure, but it appeared he was limping. You—the two of you didn't come to blows? I thought that was why he was so angry."

He told her about the stolen Trusty, and that Russell had refused treatment at St. Anne's.

"I expect I should have been grateful he only slapped me. I was so frightened. I couldn't know, could I, what had set it off or why."

"He has a temper?"

"That was the problem. I'd never seen him so livid. At least not before the war. I've had very little contact with him since then. He hasn't encouraged visitors at the clinic."

"It would seem that he's still in love with you."

"He has an odd way of showing it," she retorted with a semblance of her old spirit. "And for all I know, he could have believed that I'd killed his mother."

R utledge had intended to leave as soon as possible and go after Major Russell, but Cynthia Farraday was still uneasy. He went down to the kitchen and made tea for her, then waited with her until Mary, her maid, and the cook returned later in the morning.

He saw the alarm in her eyes when she heard someone coming through the servants' door into the hall, and then as she recognized Mary's footsteps, the alarm faded.

When Mary reached the sitting room, Miss Farraday said, "Ah. Mary. Mr. Rutledge is just leaving." And turning to Rutledge, she said coolly, "Thank you so much for coming to my rescue."

And then as he was about to follow Mary out, she added quickly, "Will you try to find Wyatt?"

"I have no choice," he answered her.

"And you'll keep me informed? I should like very much to know more about that locket."

He thought, as he left her house, that she had been embarrassed by her own weakness. The danger passed, no longer alone, her natural resilience had returned, and she was determined to show him that it had.

Driving to Scotland Yard he reviewed part of a conversation he and

Cynthia Farraday had had earlier. She hadn't wanted to be left alone, and so she had gone with him to make the tea. To distract her as they sat together in the tidy kitchen, he had said, "Tell me about coming to live at River's Edge."

She made a face. "It was River's Edge or a boarding school for girls. Young as I was, I told our solicitors that I would run away if sent to one. I couldn't bear it. I wanted so badly to stay at home. Instead they wrote to Elizabeth Russell and asked if she would consider becoming my guardian. She replied that she would, and she came herself to fetch me, which I thought was very kind. I didn't meet Wyatt until I arrived at the house. He was a few months older, but we got on well together until I was seventeen and he decided he was desperately in love with me. I told him not to be silly."

"Did he listen to you?"

"I thought he had. But when he came down from Cambridge, he informed me that while he would say no more about it, I must understand that his feelings hadn't changed. You have no idea how that confused my comfortable and safe world. When I went to Aunt Elizabeth and asked her what to do, she told me that I was far too young to think about love, and she didn't expect to see me married until I was past my twentieth birthday. It was such a relief. But I could tell she was pleased that Wyatt cared, and as I told you once, I didn't know how to interpret that. When she disappeared, I wasn't eager to live under Wyatt's roof without her. Still, I told everyone that I longed for the excitement of London and convinced my solicitors to open the house here. It made leaving easier for all of us."

He said, "You had no feelings for him?"

"As a cousin and a friend, of course I did. I just wasn't in love with him. Yes, he was handsome, he wasn't a dancing master, and he was great fun. I wanted everything to stay the way it had always been."

He smiled at her reference to the dancing master. "How did you feel later when he announced his engagement to be married?"

"Happy for him. Relieved, as well. And perhaps just a tiny bit jealous." She made a face. "So much for his vows of undying love."

"He needed an heir for River's Edge, in the event he was killed."

"I wondered once or twice if he was happy. Content, perhaps, but not outrageously, gloriously happy."

Rutledge couldn't help but think how that had described his engagement to Jean. Only he hadn't recognized it then or even later. Only with time.

"And what about Justin Fowler?"

Her face didn't change, but there was something in her stillness that was different. And then in spite of herself, she said, "I think I could have loved him. I knew he liked me. But he was so—so remote. I never knew why."

And by her admission, she had just unwittingly given Wyatt Russell a motive for murdering Fowler, and possibly even Ben Willet as well.

I t was too late to overtake Major Russell before he reached Essex. If that was where he was going. Rutledge made a detour to drive by the house Russell had inherited from his late wife, and even knocked at the door. As he listened to the sound echoing in the hall beyond, he knew that the house was empty.

It was possible too that after his encounter with Cynthia Farraday, Russell had realized what he had done and returned to the clinic of his own volition.

Given George Hiller's affection for the Trusty, the man would be out for his blood. If word of the accident had even reached him by now. Russell would have to face his anger as well as Matron's.

He decided to make a telephone call to the clinic from the Yard and establish whether or not Russell was there, before making the long drive to the River Hawking.

Rutledge found a place to leave the motorcar and walked the short distance to the Yard, his mind still on Russell.

Stepping through the door, he felt the change in atmosphere almost as a physical blow.

The sergeant at the desk was grim-faced, his greeting a curt nod. And as Rutledge climbed the stairs, he heard the silence.

The Yard was never quiet, with men going in and out of offices, doors opening and closing, telephones ringing, typewriters clicking, footsteps loud on the bare floorboards, voices in the corridors. Sounds that Rutledge had become so accustomed to that he hardly noticed them. Except now, when they were missing.

He was on the point of entering his own office when he saw Sergeant Gibson step out of another room down the passage, closing the door quietly behind him.

Rutledge stopped, his hand on the knob, waiting for Gibson. He couldn't read the Sergeant's face. For once it was blank, without expression.

"What is it?" Rutledge asked. "What has happened?"

"You haven't heard, then?"

"No," Rutledge answered, Hamish's voice sounding a warning in his mind.

"It's Chief Superintendent Bowles. He's in hospital. A heart attack."

Rutledge was stunned. "Bowles?"

He'd thought the man was indestructible.

"What's the outlook?"

"Grim," Sergeant Gibson replied. "Sir. We're to go on about our duties as if he were here and in charge. Meanwhile, upstairs they're making a decision about his temporary replacement."

As long as it wasn't Mickelson, Rutledge was comfortable with whatever choice his superiors made. Not that the man had the seniority for such a promotion. Still, stranger things had happened. And he and Mickelson had a long history, none of it pleasant.

He thanked Gibson and went into his office.

Trying to imagine the Yard without Bowles was impossible, Rutledge thought as he sat down at his desk. The man had been his nemesis almost from the day he arrived here, jealous of the new wave of men replacing those who had risen from the ranks. Rutledge himself had done his duty as a constable, and walked the streets in fair weather or foul. But he came from very different roots, and what's more he'd been well educated. Bowles appeared to believe from the start that Rutledge had an eye to his position, true or not, and had done everything in his power to prevent it. Consequently Rutledge had been passed over for promotion more than once. The reasons for denial had been true, as far as they went, but couched in terms that reflected on Rutledge's ability.

Rutledge also had a feeling that Bowles had used his authority as a Chief Superintendant to search his background for any flaws. And he had wondered more than once if Bowles had somehow discovered just where his newly returned Inspector had been from the day of the Armistice in 1918 to the date of his official return to the Yard, 1 June 1919.

Indeed, his very first inquiry after the war was one where the chief witness was a shell-shocked man. And Bowles had not told Rutledge that. He'd had to discover it for himself when he reached Warwickshire.

If Rutledge's shell shock became public knowledge, his position at the Yard would be untenable. He knew that. And as for Hamish MacLeod—it was unthinkable that anyone should learn about him. The shame would be unbearable.

Rutledge went cold at the thought.

Hamish said, "Aye, but Dr. Fleming is no' one to talk."

But there had been others in the clinic, nurses, orderlies—visitors.

Unable to stand the close confines of his office, he glanced through the papers awaiting his attention, dealt with them swiftly, and remembered his promise to the woman who had seen the Triumph crash.

He wrote a brief note indicating that against all odds, the cyclist had survived the accident without serious injury and had been released from St. Anne's hospital in a matter of hours.

It would do. It was all she needed to know.

Sealing the envelope, he set it to one side for the constable who came round to collect letters for the post, then thought better of it. Pocketing it, he walked out of the building. No one stopped him or asked where he was going.

He found a postbox on a corner just beyond where he'd left his motorcar and then continued to The Marlborough Hotel, where he could use a telephone.

The clinic, he was told by an operator's disembodied voice, did indeed have a telephone, and he was put through after several minutes.

When Matron came on the line, he knew at once that Russell hadn't returned.

Giving her a brief account of events, including the whereabouts of the Trusty, he added that he was still searching for the Major.

She listened to him, then said, "A moment, please, Inspector."

When she returned to the telephone, she said, "I'm so sorry. But a man has just come. He has already spoken to Mr. Hiller, he tells me. I appreciate your message, Inspector."

"Have you looked for Russell at his house in London?"

"I have. That's to say, I asked one of our former orderlies who is now at St. John's to go round and see if anyone was there. That was at ten o'clock this morning. The house appeared to be empty. What's more, a neighbor confirmed that he hadn't seen the Major for some time. I think we can safely say he isn't there. The question is, where do we look now? Should I have Jacobson look at hotels?"

"I'm on my way to Essex," he told her. "I shan't be able to reach you, but I have a feeling that Russell is returning to River's Edge."

"My understanding is that the house is closed, the staff dismissed," she said, doubt in her voice.

"That's true. But given his present state of mind, he may not care."

"Yes, of course. Thank you, Inspector. I shall look forward to hearing from you again."

"And should he turn up meanwhile, will you call Sergeant Gibson at the Yard and leave a message for me?"

She promised, and he rang off.

After a brief stop at his flat, he drove out of London. It would be dark well before he reached his destination, and given his lack of sleep the night before, he ought to wait until morning. But in Essex, he would also be out of reach of recall.

"He doesna' have his revolver with him," Hamish said some time later. "If he didna' go to yon house."

"Not unless he stopped at the London house before he went to see Miss Farraday. But I don't think he would risk that. Not before he spoke to her. The question is, what weapons are in the Essex house?"

"Ye ken, his father was in the Boer War."

"He was buried in South Africa. There's no way of knowing whether his service revolver was sent home in his trunk."

"Or if he kens where it is."

"It's too bad that Willet—when he was confessing to the murder of Justin Fowler in Russell's place—didn't tell me how the victim was killed."

Some miles outside London Rutledge stopped for petrol, and then realizing that he hadn't eaten for nearly two days, he drove on to a pub overlooking the Thames and ordered his dinner. It was slow in coming.

Darkness was falling by the time he was on the road again, the sun a deep red ball behind him, the last of its rays reflected in the Thames, flickering on the current. Ahead, over the North Sea, the sky was a luminous purple.

Hamish said, "It's best to wait until daylight."

"But safer in the dark," Rutledge answered aloud. "He won't see me coming."

He stopped briefly for a cup of strong tea when the food he'd eaten made him drowsy. Then he drove on, the night air warm in the motorcar and adding to his drowsiness. At length he picked up the pitted road that followed the Hawking east toward Furnham, where there was only starlight to guide him, and his headlamps tunneled through the darkness, marking his way. The wheel bucking under his hands was enough to bring him fully awake again.

The gates of River's Edge were ghostly as the glare of his head-lamps picked them up just ahead, alternately white and shadowed.

He drove past them some little distance, and then stopped the motorcar, turning off the headlamps. Taking out his torch but not flicking it on, he walked down the middle of the road as far as the house gates, guarding his night vision.

Reaching the gates, he stood for a moment, listening to the night. The marsh grasses whispered to themselves, and he could hear scurrying as small creatures hunted and were hunted. Insects sang in the warm darkness, or perhaps they were frogs of some sort.

But there was no sound of a man moving on the overgrown drive. It wasn't likely that Russell was just ahead of him, but there was no way of knowing how successful the Major had been finding transportation. Rutledge knew he couldn't afford to be careless.

He used the mental map from his previous visits to guide him now. Up the drive, striving to keep to the flattened paths that he'd made before, he took his time. If Russell wasn't here now, he would surely come at some point, and there was no need to make him unduly nervous.

The night felt empty, like a house where no one was at home— indeed, like Russell's house in London. But he still took no chances. Alert, slowly feeling his way, keeping to the shadows, he finally came within sight of the house rearing up before him.

No lights, he thought, scanning this front. But he would have to step into the open to reach the house from where he stood. Casting about for a better approach, he heard the soft flutter of feathers, and without warning an owl soared out of the trees directly over his head, swooping downward to scoop up its prey. A sharp squeak, broken off, and then the same flutter of feathers as the owl lifted off again and came back to his roost.

It had had all the earmarks of an ambush, and Rutledge felt the rush of adrenaline through his veins, setting his heart to pounding. He stayed where he was for several minutes until it had slowed.

Staying within the shadows as much as he could, he reached the corner of the house and then, bending low, crept across the open ground, keeping his silhouette short and as inconspicuous as possible. If there were guns in there, would Russell use them? Or had his anger burned out?

Rutledge stayed in the shadow of the house for all of five minutes. But nothing happened, and keeping as close to the walls as he could, he worked his way toward the terrace. He was nearly sure that Cynthia Farraday had either been able to force one of the French doors or had left it unlocked for future visits. She had spoken of a key, but he wasn't certain he could believe her.

The terrace was empty. He got as far as the doors and waited again for any sign that he'd been spotted. Five minutes later, he tried the French doors and found that one of them was unlocked, as he'd expected.

He stepped inside and stood waiting again, before beginning a silent and methodical search of the house.

He walked from room to room, sometimes caught off guard by a dust sheet that was unexpectedly as tall as a man or a board that squeaked loud enough to echo.

In the study he found the gun case. In the dimness, he used his hands to identify the contents. Standing upright were four shotguns for hunting the ducks and geese that wintered here on the river. They were well oiled and cared for. In the case below were two revolvers, one a service revolver and the other a smaller caliber that could have been a souvenir. They too were clean and oiled. To one side of the case were several daggers mounted on the wall, the sort a military man might collect on his travels.

When he had made a full circuit of the ground floor with no sign of an intruder, Rutledge started up the stairs, careful not to step on the center of the tread but to stay as close to the wall as he could. At the top he waited and listened before going on. It was late enough that a weary Russell might be sleeping in one of the beds.

But the first floor yielded nothing either. Mattresses had been rolled on the beds to discourage mice, most of the drapes had been drawn, and there was nothing to indicate that a man, tired from a long journey, had tried to rest here.

Still, he went from room to room, as a rule standing in the doorway and listening before going inside to search.

He had reached the master bedroom, which faced the river, with long windows overlooking the lawns and the water. This too offered nothing, and he went into the dressing rooms on either side, before turning to go.

Hamish said, "The kitchen quarters."

In the hope of finding a tin of tea and a kettle as well as a hob to heat it on, Russell could have fallen asleep at the servants' table, unwilling to climb the stairs to find a more comfortable place to rest. It was worth taking the time to have a look.

Afterward he was never quite sure why he decided to go to one of the windows. He had already reached the doorway, his hand on the knob, on the point of shutting it behind him. Instead, he turned and crossed the room a second time, lifting an edge of the drapes to peer out into the night.

The ambient starlight seemed brighter than it had before, as if the moon was about to rise, just touching the horizon. The shadows on the lawn were dark as pitch by comparison, and the reeds and salt grass along the water's edge were nearly as black. But the water itself was bright in contrast, a pewter ribbon making its way to the sea beyond.

He thought at first that his eyes were playing tricks on him. And then he realized that someone was standing on the landing stage, his silhouette blending with the boards, irregular and almost undetectable.

He couldn't tell if there was a boat tied up below, out of his line of sight, or if the man had walked there from the house itself.

Was it Russell? It was impossible to judge height or shape. The only thing he could be certain of was that the figure was not that of a woman. Whoever it was, he was wearing trousers.

Rutledge stood there, watching him for several minutes, and then, as if the man felt his gaze, he turned and looked toward the house, staring up at it intently. The light touched his upturned face, and his eyes were black holes in the paleness.

# 15

Rutledge stayed very still, certain that he had been spotted. That something, some inadvertent movement, had given him away. Then, finally, the man turned back to his contemplation of the water.

Even now he couldn't be sure. Was it Russell standing there? Or someone from the village?

He let the edge of the heavy drapes fall gently back into place and was across the room in swift long strides, shutting the door and making his way to the staircase. It had taken him fewer than two minutes to go down the stairs and reach the room overlooking the terrace.

But when he looked out, he saw no one on the landing stage or on the lawns.

Whoever had been there was gone.

And he had no idea where.

He searched the landings, the grounds, and the park for nearly three-quarters of an hour, but if Russell had come to River's Edge, he'd disappeared.

There was still the chance that he'd seen someone from the village, but Rutledge was unconvinced. What would possibly bring them out this far at this hour of the night?

There had been no indication that the house had or was being used to store contraband, although it wouldn't have surprised him to find that it had been on occasion.

An empty house on the water was always a great temptation. A boat could easily come up this far on a dark night, put in at the landing long enough for the goods in bulk to be unloaded and carried up to the terrace doors. A fairly decent livelihood. But this gift had been handed to them at the same time that crossing the channel had become impossible. The villagers must have cursed their luck. And if the smuggling that he had witnessed was any example, they hadn't reestablished their contacts or else they were unable to afford more than three men could carry.

Hamish said, "They're a suspicious lot at best. They wouldna' trust strangers in France any more than strangers in yon village."

Rutledge had to agree with him.

He gave up the search finally. Whoever had been here had gone, either by boat or on foot. Quietly and without being seen. Walking down the choked drive to his motorcar, Rutledge was glad he'd left it some distance from the stone gates.

All the same, he was relieved to find it just as he'd left it, motor and tires intact. He had no taste for walking all the way to Furnham.

The Dragonfly Inn was dark, but when Rutledge tried the door, it opened. A small lamp burned in the little room behind Reception, and he called to the man who was usually there. No one answered. He wondered how the inn made enough money to stay open, given the owner's aversion to strangers.

And then he realized the answer to that.

Ordinarily this was where the contraband was brought—except when a man from Scotland Yard had stubbornly taken up residence. It could be sorted and passed on at leisure but more importantly controlled by the chosen few involved. The three men in the run he'd witnessed had had to make other arrangements, no doubt cursing the intruder from London every step of the way.

He grinned in the lamplight, amused.

Turning the register around, he saw that one other person had stayed here in his absence, one Frederick Marshall. A single night. A fisherman? Or someone who had once served at the airfield? Rutledge couldn't imagine a sudden attack of nostalgia bringing one of the airmen or their crews back to Furnham.

He signed his name, put down the number of the room he'd been given before, and went up the stairs. In his absence, it had been cleaned and the bed newly made, fresh towels on the rack by the washstand.

Without bothering to turn on a light Rutledge undressed and went to bed, but it was some time before he actually fell asleep.

Hamish was awake and busy in the back of his mind, and Rutledge found himself mulling over the night's events.

Who had been standing on the landing stage? And where had he gone?

Rutledge didn't believe in coincidences. It had to be Russell, and it was very likely that he'd borrowed or taken a boat to make the long journey down the Hawking, reaching the house by river rather than over the road. Why he hadn't stayed was anyone's guess. At least for the night, late as it was. Bruised and tired as he must have been. Or had this simply been reconnaissance—to be sure, before he brought in supplies and prepared to stay, that no one was waiting for him here?

Because there was no other place, really, where Russell could go.

Sleep overtook Rutledge then, and the first rays of dawn were coming in the window when he awoke. The man behind the desk—clerk or owner, Rutledge had never been sure—was startled to find Rutledge coming down the stairs as he arrived the next morning.

It took several minutes of explanation and exclamation before the clerk would accept the fact that Rutledge intended to stay at the inn and wanted his breakfast. When it finally came, it consisted of overcooked eggs, burned toast and tea strong enough to walk back to London on its own. There was no sign of Molly, and he wondered if she was called in only when there were guests to serve.

As he was finishing his meal, he asked the man about the visitor in his absence, Frederick Marshall.

"Here, you're not to be reading the register. It's none of your affair!" the clerk told him, angry.

Rutledge said, "It's done. Who is he?"

"He came to see if there was any good sport fishing here," the clerk said, clearly against his will. "The other rivers in this part of Essex have a fair amount of it, and he thought the Hawking might as well. He was of a mind to buy land and set up a yacht club, if it was promising."

"And is it promising?"

"I sent him over to the pub. He was told that the war had put paid to any good fishing, what with the Zeppelins and the fighters at the airfield, and the Coastguard mining the mouth of the river."

"I should think Furnham would prosper with more contact with the rest of the country. It would mean some changes, but they're inevitable."

"And that's what we don't need," the clerk said, goaded. "What will we do with ourselves when Furnham is overrun with strangers and there's not a spot we can call our own? What we saw in the war will last us a lifetime. Prying, taking us for fools who didn't know our elbow from our nose, cheating us where they could, laughing at us behind their hands. I saw it for myself, the way they lorded it over the rest of us. Loud and brash and not taking no for an answer when it was something they wanted." He was incensed now. "It was a trial of the spirit, the four years they was here. If it hadn't been for the war, we'd have run them off in the first six months. I wasn't the only one went off to fight the war, not knowing if my wife would be mine when I got back, if this inn would still be standing after one of their wild parties. Betwixt the Coastguard and the airmen, it was four years of hell." He turned and walked out of the dining room, leaving Rutledge sitting there.

He rose and left as well, but the clerk was nowhere in sight when he walked through Reception and went out to his motorcar.

This wasn't the only village that war had disrupted and overrun. But for people more or less left to their own devices for hundreds of years, it was harsh reality with no respite, and for some of them, it was impossible to go back to the past.

Hard as Furnham was trying, he didn't think the village would win. Men like Frederick Marshall were always looking to the main chance, and in the end, the villages along rivers like the Blackwater and the Crouch and the Hawking would succumb. Thanks to the motorcar they were too close to London now to survive for very long.

He walked down to the water and stood looking toward the sea. The day was fair and already warmer than usual. Far out in the North Sea he could just make out a ship steaming by, the smoke of its funnels a thick gray line above a hull that was nearly invisible from here.

Barber spoke just behind him, and Rutledge turned quickly. He hadn't heard him walk down to the water's edge. The lapping of the river on the strand had covered the sound of his footsteps.

"What brings you back to our fair village?" he asked.

"Ned Willet's funeral," Rutledge said, keeping his voice light. "When is it to be?"

"It was yesterday. You missed it," the man replied, with some satisfaction.

"I'm sorry."

"We're not." Barber reached down and picked up something from the strand. It was a flat stone, and he sent it skimming across the water. "Not bad. Seven skips," Barber went on. Then he turned back to Rutledge. "You'll be leaving then?"

There was nothing to keep him here. Except for the search for Russell. And yet the man's eagerness to see the last of him aroused his suspicions.

He took a chance. "Making another run to France, are you? Before the moon is full?"

Barber's face was a picture of dismay and anger, then wariness. "I don't know what you're talking about."

Rutledge picked up a stone just by the toe of his boot and sent it skimming across the river. It skipped nine times. "Hypothetically, of course."

Weighing the word, Barber stared at Rutledge, then looked out to sea as Rutledge himself had done earlier. But not before Rutledge had caught the doubt in his eyes.

He had pushed far enough. After a moment Rutledge added, "My only interest is what happened to Ben Willet. I've told you. Help me there, and I'll be on my way."

"I don't know who killed him."

"Nor do I. Was it you, because when he came home from France he was different, no longer a villager, prepared to keep village secrets? Or was it Major Russell, perhaps out of jealousy? Or because Willet knew too much about the death of Justin Fowler? Miss Farraday, because Willet presumed on her friendship?"

Barber picked up another stone, looked at it, and let it drop to the strand again. He was silent so long that Rutledge thought he wasn't going to answer at all.

Finally he said, "The answer could lie in France. Have you thought about that? He wouldn't be the first one to want to stay, hanging about with that useless lot in Paris, drinking and whoring and posturing with the rest of them, rather than coming home and doing right by his family. It would have killed the old man."

Rutledge turned to look up the river so that Barber couldn't read his face.

On the postal card Willet had sent to Cynthia Farraday a few days before his murder, he'd told her he was intending to visit his father and then return to Paris and finish his last book. But Abigail claimed he hadn't come home since the war. And if he hadn't, why did Sandy Barber suspect his brother-in-law had chosen to stay in Paris after 1918?

A footman from Thetford, son of a fisherman in Furnham, would have been eager to return to the Laughton house where his former position was awaiting him.

"Why should you think that Ben Willet would be one of them?" he asked, his eyes on a shorebird flitting here and there after whatever the current had on offer.

Barber lifted a shoulder in irritation. "I don't know. Someone— Jessup, I believe it was—said something after—" He cleared his throat. "He said better men than Ben had been tempted to stay on."

What had Barber been about to say before he'd caught himself? *After one of his runs to France for contraband? After meeting Ben Willet in London or Tilbury or on the road to Furnham?*

"That was an odd remark," Rutledge said, facing him. "Did he know Ben so well?"

Barber flushed. "I don't know what the hell possessed him to make it. It doesn't matter, does it? The point being that once Ben was free from Furnham, he never looked back, not really. Too good for the likes of us, I expect. In his cast-off clothes and his airs, he made fun of the household in Thetford. And most likely he kept the kitchen staff in Thetford rolling on the floor with his imitations of us." There was an intensity of bitterness in his voice that was unexpected.

He loved his wife, Rutledge thought, and was angry for her sake. But this was a new intensity.

*What did he know?*

And as if he knew he'd already said too much, Barber turned on his heel and walked away without a word.

Tales of the wild bohemian ways of Paris, painted in lurid detail, had come home from France with returning soldiers. Most of them had never seen Paris, but most knew someone who had, and those who had were not above embellishing for greater effect. For Ned Willet's son to prefer that world to the staid life of service in a respectable household was unimaginable to someone who had rarely left this backwater of Essex.

Rutledge turned to follow him. "Will you let me speak to your wife?"

Barber shook his head. "She can't help you. And besides, she's still cut up about her father's death and Ben not making it back here in time. She told me this morning that she couldn't understand why he hadn't written. What am I to do? Tell her that he's dead as well? She even asked me to go to Thetford and see if he's all right. What's more, the whispers have already started. Someone talked to his wife, despite my warning. And when I find out who, I'll kill him myself."

Rutledge said, "She'll have to know the truth sometime."

"Let her heal a little first. When will they release his body?"

"I can give the order tomorrow."

"That's too soon."

With a nod Barber turned and walked away again. Rutledge let him go this time.

Hamish said, "There's more to him than meets the eye."

"I agree." Then Rutledge added thoughtfully, "He would kill Ben Willet himself, if he thought Willet was going to hurt Abigail. But there's nothing he can do. The man is already dead. And that's grief he has to carry."

"It's verra' possible that he did kill him. Gie him a little rope . . ."

"Meanwhile, I have to find Major Russell."

And that meant returning to River's Edge.

Halfway to his motorcar in the inn yard, Rutledge saw Nancy Brothers coming toward him, a market basket over one arm. She hesitated, and he thought perhaps she didn't wish it to be known that he had come to the farm to interview her. But after that brief moment she walked on, ducked her head in a diffident nod, and passed him without a word. He touched his hat, but didn't speak, in accordance with her unexpressed wish.

It was a measure, he thought, of the village attitude toward him. Indeed, he'd been surprised that Sandy Barber had sought him out. Hamish reminded him that Barber was a force to be reckoned with in Furnham and made up his own rules. But Rutledge had a feeling that the encounter had gone beyond curiosity. A fishing expedition, then?

He was just stepping into the motorcar when the inn's clerk came to the door.

"Are you leaving, then?" he asked hopefully. "I'll fetch your valise for you."

Rutledge shook his head and drove off toward River's Edge, leaving the clerk looking after him with frustration writ large on his face.

As far as he could tell, after he'd left the motorcar and walked up to the gate, nothing had changed there. The chain was still looped between the pillars, and the high grass showed his passage but not, he thought, that of someone else.

Unless someone had walked in his tracks.

He made his way up the drive to the house, remembering last night and his care not to be seen until he was ready to show himself. And that had been wise, given the weapons he'd found in the study. Now he went boldly toward the house across the open ground, and around to the terrace. It was one thing to shoot an intruder in the dark, and quite another to fire on him in the light of day.

Instead of mounting the steps, he scanned the river for any sign of watchers. Where, for instance, had Cynthia Farraday met Ben Willet?

"Ye canna' tell. You do na' know the coves and inlets. Ye'd require field glasses to be sure."

Rutledge turned to study the margins of the lawns, that line where the cultivated grass ended and the marsh began. How much draining had it taken to rip this estate out of the marsh's grip? Or had this been a naturally higher stretch of land? He could see for himself that there were half a dozen places that might be the beginning of a track through the reeds, but striking out into one of them would be foolish at best, unless one knew what he was about. And how often did the tracks shift? Would Russell have been able to find his way after all this time? Rutledge was reminded, in fact, of a maze, with its artificial twists and turns intentionally leading the unwary down blind alleys.

There was the river, of course, to help keep one's bearings, but as the ground rose in hummocky patches and dipped into small wet pockets, even that guide could disappear.

He was beginning to understand how Mrs. Russell could vanish so easily. But was she alive—or dead—when she did?

Turning to climb the steps to the terrace, he debated whether or not to go inside. If Russell was there, walking in uninvited could be considered trespass. And laying siege, in the hope to see him come out of his own accord, was wasting time.

What was the man's state now? He'd left the house in Chelsea after slapping Cynthia. Not hard, but enough to shock both of them. His body was battered from the motorcycle accident, and he knew he was being hunted. Did he see himself as a man with a damaged mind who had burned his bridges?

There was a good chance that Russell had never intended to stay here, and every intention of dying here by his own hand.

Rutledge crossed to the door and tried it. It was still unlocked, just as he'd left it. But when he swung it wide, the morning sun fell across a muddy footprint on the floorboards just inside.

He hadn't risked turning on his torch, and there was no way of knowing if it had been there last night before he'd seen the man out by the landing, or not. Squatting beside it, he touched the rim of mud. It was hard, dry. And the shape didn't match his own boots; it was longer and wider. He cast about for any indication that the wearer of the shoe had gone out again.

Two or three crumbles of mud were caught in the threads of the carpet a stride away, but after that he could find nothing.

Straightening, he called, "Russell? Major Russell, are you here?"

The words seemed to echo through the house, loud enough to be heard by anyone inside, but even though he called again, no one answered.

Hamish was reminding him that he was here, where the Yard couldn't reach him if new developments occurred in London. Or, for that matter, if something happened to him out here on the Hawking.

But he took his chances and walked into the garden room, taking care not to destroy the footprint or add his own.

He went directly to the study, to look at the gun case. If Russell was here and armed, he wanted to know it before encountering the man.

He opened the glass door. The shotguns were just what he'd expected, used for hunting. Below were the revolvers. And he would have sworn last night that there were only two in the case.

Now there were three.

# 16

He stood there for a moment, thinking. Remembering how the cold metal had felt as he touched the handguns in the dark.

Yes, just the two last night, he was sure of it. He couldn't be mistaken. Not with weapons.

The third was a service revolver, and it was the same caliber as the one that had been used to kill Ben Willet. It appeared to have been cleaned recently, no way of knowing when it had last been fired. The science that could tell him was in its infancy, and not always trustworthy.

Taking out his handkerchief, he examined the other revolver. Fired, but not cleaned since then.

He set it back where he'd found it.

More to the point, how had this third handgun magically appeared in less than twenty-four hours?

Did it mean Russell had finally come home?

What did this have to do with the man he'd seen last night? He'd been upstairs in the master bedroom, after searching the ground floor and then the first floor. Could the man have come in and set the revolver in the gun case? The house was large enough that neither man would necessarily have heard the other's movements. What had taken him to the water's edge before he left? Did he think he was safe enough that he could take his time about leaving? Or was he looking for signs of a boat along the riverbank? If the tide was out, there could have been a rowboat riding low in the water.

No answers to any of his questions.

Rutledge listened to the house. The maker of that footprint could still be here, and for all he knew, the revolver could have been used here.

He remembered that Timothy Jessup had mentioned seeing him at River's Edge, and asked if he intended to buy the property. But Rutledge, as aware of his surroundings as any man of his experience could be, had not seen Jessup.

Frances was right. One could conceal a battalion out there in the grass.

There was nothing for it but to search the house again, and then the grounds.

But they yielded nothing. Save for the footprint and the revolver, he would have been prepared to swear that he'd been the only living soul inside River's Edge last night.

Closing the terrace door behind him, he walked down to the water's edge. No sign of a boat here, but at the second landing, while he couldn't find any proof that anyone had come in here, he found the faint imprint of a man's boot in the damp earth just above the high-water mark.

He squatted there, studying it. It appeared to belong to the same foot as the one in the house, but the soft earth hadn't preserved it as well as the hard surface of the wooden floor.

Standing again, he looked back at the house, beyond the kitchen gardens and the few outbuildings, and felt a rising frustration with Major Russell. Where the hell was the man?

Halfway back to Furnham, just beyond the turning that led to the Rectory and the churchyard, Rutledge saw Constable Nelson pedaling toward him on his bicycle. Rutledge slowed.

"Looking for me?" he asked.

Nelson stopped. Rutledge could see that he was sober, although haggard, as if he had finished the last of his stock. "No, sir. But I will ask. Did you see a loose mare back the way you've just come?"

"A mare? No, I haven't."

"One of the villages upstream reported her missing. Jumped the pasture fence. She's a valuable beast, and I was asked to keep an eye out for her."

"When did she go missing?" Rutledge asked quickly.

"The owner's not sure. He went to St. Albans for a few days, and when he came back, she was gone. He doesn't believe she got this far, but he sent word by the ironmonger's son, who went to the dentist in Tilbury." He gestured to the dusty, unmade surface of the road. "No tracks that the boy could pick up on his way home, and none I've seen so far. But I said I'd look."

A pretense of doing his duty? Or was there more to this? Had he been asked to look for Russell? Rutledge was nearly certain that Matron wouldn't have contacted the police, but the owner of the Trusty might well have wanted his pound of flesh. It was even possible Nelson was keeping a watch on the troublesome Londoner's movements for someone.

Testing the waters, Rutledge said, "How well do you know Timothy Jessup? He was Ben Willet's uncle, I'm told."

"Jessup? You don't want to tangle with that one," Nelson said, alarm in his face. "A nasty piece of work. Never in any trouble with the law, you understand, and I thank God for that. All the same, nobody ever crosses him."

Rutledge heard overtones in the man's voice that made him wonder if Jessup and not Sandy Barber was the leader of the smugglers.

"How well did he get on with Ben?"

"I wouldn't say they were close. Abigail has always been Jessup's favorite. And he was against Ben going into service in Thetford. I overheard them quarreling once. Ben was trying to explain that he wasn't cut out to be a fisherman. Jessup wanted to know if he thought he was better than his father, and Ben said it wasn't that. He'd rather blacken another man's boots in a city than gut fish here in Furnham. Jessup knocked him down then and told him to stop daydreaming and get on with the life he was born to lead. And Ben said, 'You don't want anyone to leave, that's all. For fear he'll talk about things he shouldn't.'"

"What things?"

Nelson said uneasily, "It was just talk. A boy's talk. And he'd been up to River's Edge a time or two. He'd seen a different way of life."

"The smuggling," Hamish said. "Yon uncle was afraid the lad would tell someone."

But was it only that? Had Furnham corrupted its only officer of the law just to protect a few bottles of brandy, a little tobacco, and whatever other small luxuries these men had brought in on their backs? The entire village seemed to be involved in the secret, not just a handful of rogue fishermen.

Constable Nelson was preparing to mount his bicycle again. "Someone told me last year that Ned Willet had written a book and it was published in France. I doubt Ned could put two words together on a page, much less a book. But I didn't believe that. Not for a minute."

"Why not?" Rutledge asked, curious.

"I never knew anyone who wrote a book. And I'm not likely to. Not anyone from Furnham."

And he was gone, pedaling along the road, seemingly the model of a village constable. Sober and responsible until the next bottle of French brandy was left outside his door. It was easy to see where his loyalties might lie.

France.

Rutledge was letting out the clutch, preparing to drive on, when the single word stopped him.

Ned Willet.

What was Ben Willet's full name?

Was it possible that on one of the runs to France, someone had asked Jessup if the old man had written a book? Jessup would have found that as amusing as the constable had. And on his next run, had the Frenchman produced such a book, to have the last laugh?

He reversed and turned into the road leading to the Rectory. How much did the rector know about what was happening in his own parish? Or was he as much Jessup's creature as Constable Nelson was?

Mr. Morrison was sitting in his study-cum-parlor when Rutledge stopped in the short drive. He got up and met his visitor at the door before he could knock.

"Come in, Inspector. I'm sick of my own company."

The parlor was simply furnished, but a lovely old desk took pride of place, and Morrison saw Rutledge looking at it.

"My father's," he said. "The only thing of his that I possess, actually. I was trying to think of a suitable subject for my next sermon." He gestured to a shelf behind the desk. Rutledge could see that there were at least twenty collections of sermons there, bound in leather. He wondered if these were a relic of Morrison's father as well. "One would think," he went on, "that every possible permutation of religious topics had been covered already. But one soldiers on, searching for inspiration."

Rutledge smiled. "In point of fact, it's a book that's brought me here."

"Sermons?" Morrison asked blankly, staring from the shelf to Rutledge's face.

"Actually, no. Do you have the old christening records for the church?"

"St. Edward's? As a matter of fact, we do, going back to the early 1800s. I can search for whatever you need to know. But it will take time. In some cases the ink is faded or the writing is illegible. My predecessors were not always thinking about posterity when they made their notations."

"What I'm after isn't that old. I'd like to know Ben Willet's full name. Abigail Barber hasn't been told yet that he's dead. And I don't care to distress her at this stage."

"Ben's name? I can answer your question without consulting the records. Edward Benjamin Stephen Willet. He was named for his father, his grandfather, and an uncle. He was called Ben to prevent any confusion." Morrison smiled ruefully. "I was entering Ned's death, and looked up Ben while I was about it. He'd have been twenty-eight in September."

"Edward Willet. Yes, he'd have used that name. Honoring himself and his father," Rutledge said after a moment.

"You're releasing the body? Is that why you're interested? For the—er—forms?"

"Actually I was wondering what name Willet would have used if he'd published a book in France."

"Willet? Good God, no, you're mistaken on that score. I heard the story going round about Ned. I'm not sure who started it. Jessup, perhaps, or one of the others. I don't often hear gossip, but there was talk in one of the shops one day. They were laughing, they had forgot I was there."

"You don't have a copy of the book they spoke of?"

"Hardly. It doesn't exist. Or at least I don't believe it does."

"Then how did such a tale start?" When Morrison looked away, as if trying to choose his words, Rutledge added, "You needn't worry. I know about the smuggling. It's not what brought me here, and if it has no bearing on murder, I intend to ignore it."

"Very wise of you," Morrison agreed. "I shut my eyes as well. One can't help but notice that Constable Nelson drinks himself into a stupor on brandy one can't purchase at The Rowing Boat. Poor man, he isn't cut out to be a policeman. He came here just now, asking if I'd seen a lost horse. I never know whether these forays of his into duty are real or a way of salving his conscience. There was a band of Gypsies said to be camping out in the marshes, and before that a stolen bicycle. Um. Where was I?"

"Smuggling."

"Yes, I was going to add that the veil Abigail wore at her wedding was French lace, handed down from her mother. And Ned, God rest his soul, Ned used to do the runs to France before the war. He took Ben with him once or twice when the boy was fifteen. While I sat with Ned after he injured his leg, he told me the story. How Ben was seasick when a storm blew up and they had to put into a different French port. He was so ill he was taken in by a French family, didn't know a word they were saying to him, but he walked about in a daze for weeks afterward, enamored of the daughter of the house. He got over it, of course, at that age boys generally do."

But had he?

Rutledge remembered the copybook in a box in the Laughtons' attic, the description of the woman in CHAPTER SEVENTEEN. Was she based on the girl Ben believed he'd fallen in love with as a boy?

"Did the French ever produce the book they talked about? On another run, perhaps?"

"I shouldn't think so. If they did, no one showed it to me. And Ned would have, he loved a good joke. Why is it so important?"

"Because it's possible the book does exist. And that the author's name was Edward Willet. But not the father, of course. The son."

"I still don't see why this matters. What could it have to do with young Willet's death? For all we know it could be an entirely different branch of the family. Ned told me once that there are Willets in Derbyshire and Norfolk."

"Nor do I see the connection. At the moment."

Morrison shook his head. "How many books do you think the people of Furnham read in the course of a year? The Bible, perhaps. They've always lived hard lives, these villagers. They don't have the luxury of reading, nor the time or the money to buy books. The children go to school until they're old enough to help earn their keep. The war was particularly hard, with the sea cut off."

"I understand."

"Is there any other matter I can help you with? Other than Ben's full name?"

Rutledge said, "I have a puzzle on my hands. Three deaths, with seemingly no link between them. Mrs. Russell in 1914, Justin Fowler in 1915, and now Ben Willet's. You know these people better than I ever shall. Do you see a pattern that I have missed?"

Morrison frowned. "We don't know what happened to Mrs. Russell, do we? She may well have been in great distress over the coming war, as her family suggested. If that's true, I bear some of the blame for not seeing her need in time. As for Fowler, why should you think he's dead? Simply because he has cut his ties with the people who used to be close to him? A troubled man sometimes prefers to turn to strangers, rather than risk the pity of those he cares about. As for Ben, I'm afraid that in the end we'll discover that his death is more related to London than it is to Furnham."

"You present a very reasonable case. I wish I could believe in it. When you've been a policeman as long as I have, there's a sixth sense about murder. The locket around Ben Willet's throat connects him to River's Edge, if nothing else does."

"Ah yes, the locket. But that too has a reasonable explanation, doesn't it? I'm afraid Miss Farraday has left a trail of broken hearts behind her. I shouldn't be surprised if Ben was one of them. She was kind to him, after all."

"It explains the photograph. Not the locket itself."

"Are you so certain that it isn't the only one of its kind?"

"With Mrs. Russell's initial engraved on the face?

"There must be thousands of Englishwomen named Elizabeth, Emily, Eleanor, Eugenia—have you considered that?"

"I don't like coincidence."

Morrison smiled. "I'm afraid I can't help you there. My business is to save souls, not to hunt killers."

As Rutledge rose to take his leave, Morrison added, "If you find that Willet's book exists, I should like to know about it. In fact, I'd like to read it myself."

"I'll be sure to tell you."

They had walked as far as the door when Rutledge said, "This man Jessup. Is he dangerous, do you think?"

"Timothy? He's a hard man to know. And he doesn't care to be thwarted. By Ben going into service instead of to sea, or by an airfield being built in this parish. He nearly killed a man, coming to blows with him, after he discovered he'd come here to weigh the possibility of Furnham becoming a seaside town. I shouldn't like to cross him."

An unwitting echo of Constable Nelson's words. And Morrison's comment explained why he and Frances had been challenged by the man.

After leaving the Rectory, Rutledge spent three-quarters of an hour looking for any sign of a runaway horse. There was always the chance that Russell had taken it to speed him on his way to Furnham. But he had no more luck that Constable Nelson had. Someone had been along the road with horse and cart, that was clear enough, but a single horse—no.

He continued to London, his mind occupied with the problem of

the three victims. While Morrison might believe there was no connection, he had a feeling there must be. It was one of the reasons he'd
come looking for Russell.

He expected, when he reached Cynthia Farraday's house, that she
would refuse to receive him. But the maid, Mary, admitted him and
led him to the small sitting room, where Miss Farraday was writing a
letter.

"If you've come to see if I'm well, you've wasted a trip," she said as
he walked through the door. "I'm angry now. At Wyatt and at myself
for being frightened of him."

"I'm happy to see you fully recovered," he countered, then asked,
"Do you by chance still have a copy of the book Ben Willet is said to
have written?"

"Said?" she asked. "I told you he'd had two volumes published. He
was working on a third. I don't suppose he finished that before he was
killed. But there it is." Rising from the desk, she went to the bookshelf
under the window and retrieved two books. "Here. See for yourself."

He thanked her and took the books. He looked at the name on the
cover—Edward Willet. As he'd expected. Then he opened the first of
the two books at random, reading a page here and there.

It was a war memoir as she had told him earlier. The title was *A
Long Road Home*.

Beginning when Willet went to enlist, it was filled with stories of
the men he'd trained with and then fought with. They were well realized and very human. And it brought the war back all too vividly.

"Have you read this?" he asked, looking up.

"The earlier part. I found the rest too disturbing. How awful it
must have been to have these men come into one's life, to get to know
them, and watch as they are shot or blown up or grievously wounded
by shrapnel. There was another Corporal he came to know very well,
another young man in service in Thetford, and a month before the Armistice, the man was shot and died in his arms." She shook her head,
as if to clear it of the image she'd invoked. "I couldn't bear it."

He said, fighting to keep his voice even, "It was what we knew."
Still skimming, he stopped at the top of a page and read on.

*I hadn't heard from home for some weeks, and then I saw an of-
ficer I recognized. He lived near my village. His shoulder was in
a bad way, and he was being sent to England for further treatment. I asked if he would find out if my father and my sister were
all right. I'd heard that one of my brothers had been killed, the
one here in France, but there had been no news about the one in
the Navy. Captain F— told me he intended to go to Essex as soon
as he was well enough, and he promised to send me word. But he
never did. I expect he must have died of his wounds, because as
far as I know, he never came back to France. I'd asked around,
hoping he was all right and they hadn't had to take off his arm.
All of us fear amputation more than death. My sister did write
finally, and told me that Joseph was dead as well, and she begged
me to come home safe. It was with heavy heart that I went back
into the line that day, and I think I killed a good many Germans
in Joseph's name . . .*

Rutledge was about to ask Miss Farraday if she'd read the chapter
and if she thought Captain F— was a reference to Justin Fowler. He remembered in time that she had told him she could have loved Fowler.
Instead he looked for the date of that passage, and it was in the spring
of 1915. And as far as he could judge, reading on into September,
there was no other reference to Captain F—. He'd have to read the
book from cover to cover, to be sure of that.

"Have you found something of interest?" she said, watching him
as he read.

"It brings back memories," he said, evading her question.

She nodded. "I expect it would."

He turned to the second book, thicker by far, and this time, fiction.
The title was simply, *Marianne.*

It was set in Paris during the war, and the chief character, Browning Warden, was searching for a woman he'd met before the war while smuggling along the French coast.

Hamish said, "Ye ken, it wouldna' make his family verra' happy."

Which was probably why Willet hadn't told them about the books. Or perhaps he felt that he wasn't ready to share this next part of his life, given the trouble he'd had over becoming a footman.

Rutledge said to Cynthia Farraday, "Have you read this one?"

"Yes, I thought it quite good."

But had she known how much truth had gone into the story?

Skimming again, he looked for a chapter similar to the one he'd read in Thetford, and he found it. The description of the war-torn French village was astonishingly real now, unlike the poorly imagined village in the copybook. The odd thing was, the woman in the earlier version had been dark haired, dark eyed, the girl Willet must have recalled from his boyhood. In this version, she had light brown hair and sounded very much like Cynthia Farraday. Had she recognized herself?

The early pages, describing where Browning Warden lived, evoked Furnham, although Willet had renamed it and the river. The isolation, the marshes, the dark river where he learned to sail, the crossing to France, all spoke of firsthand knowledge. The first meeting with the girl he would seek during the war, her search later for the wounded soldier who had deserted to marry her, shadowed a fulfillment of the promise glimpsed in the Thetford notebooks.

Realizing that he'd been reading for some minutes, he set the book aside. "You're right. Willet was quite a fine writer. Do you by any chance know what the third book was to be about?"

"Pure evil," she replied. "That's what he said once, that it was a study in man's depravity. But I can't tell you what story he was telling. I'm sorry. He didn't want to talk about it very much. He said it was a reflection of what he'd seen in the war and what he knew of heroism and cruelty. Ambitious, that was his word for it. And Gertrude Stein, whoever she may be, thought what she'd read was splendid."

"These first two books had roots in Willet's life. His experiences in the war, this love for a girl he could never marry, based on the smuggling he knew so much about. I wonder if the third book did the same."

"Are you saying that there actually was smuggling going on? In *Furnham*? That Ben was a part of it?" She shook her head. "You must be mistaken. He liked the way the past shaped the future. Nothing to do with reality."

And he had lied to her. To protect her? Or to protect the people of Furnham?

There was nothing here, with the possible exception of the reference to Captain F— , to cause a man's death. Or to support Willet's claim that Russell had killed Justin Fowler.

With regret he set the books aside.

Cynthia Farraday was saying, "I'm not in a position to judge, not really, I know so little about writing. But I think the second book is much more mature than anything he'd written before the war. He'd seen the world. He understood far better what he was trying to say. The money I gave him was well repaid. Can you imagine what Paris must have been like after Furnham, or even Thetford for that matter?"

"You lived at River's Edge. Did you feel that the village in the second novel was Furnham?"

"Well, of course it was. I mean to say, he didn't use real names, but I recognized a few of the residents. Those I knew. There are probably more."

"Reading these, I keep asking myself why he came to Scotland Yard and posed as Wyatt Russell. Was that the only lie he told me? Or have I been chasing shadows?"

"I don't know. You haven't told me if you'd found Wyatt. Are you saving bad news for the last?"

"I can't find him. I thought he'd be in Essex, there was nowhere else to go. And I was wrong. Why did you tell me you wished to buy River's Edge, if it were for sale?"

Color rose in her face. "To find the girl I once was, I suppose. Don't you ever wish you could go back? It's heartbreaking to see it standing empty. And I have a feeling Wyatt won't ever live there again. He sees the ghosts that walk. I don't."

"Not even the ghost of Justin Fowler?"

"Justin was handsome, he loved sports—we had croquet and lawn tennis and the like, horses to ride, a boat. But he was—there was something about him, a darkness, I thought at the time, having read too many novels. Still, it was there. I thought at first he missed his parents. They were dead, like mine, but he never talked about them. Never, 'My father and I did this,' or 'My mother loved roses.' I wondered afterward if perhaps he wanted to forget them."

"Why?"

She looked across at the window. "Perhaps it was too painful to remember. My parents died on holiday. There was a typhoid outbreak in Spain, while they were in Córdoba. They were there—and then they weren't. Horrible for me, but I'd said good-bye when they went away, and when their luggage was returned, there were presents for me, ribbons and a cut-glass bottle for scent, some lace, and a collection of photographs they'd bought in famous places. I knew they'd been thinking about me, and I found it comforting. I don't know how his died. Perhaps they were ill and had been suffering for some time. The sort of thing one tries to put behind one."

It was an interesting possibility.

He thanked her and was preparing to leave when she said, "Wyatt didn't come back. Not even to apologize. Do you think he ever will?"

For her sake, he lied once more. "I'm sure he will."


Stopping at The Marlborough Hotel, he used their telephone to put in a call to the Yard.

It was some time before Gibson could be found, and he sounded harassed when he finally answered.

"Sir? Where are you?" was his first question, after Rutledge had identified himself.

"What news do you have of the Chief Superintendent?" Rutledge countered.

"In hospital, sir, and the report is not good. Where are you?"

"Traveling," Rutledge replied. "Have you learned anything about Justin Fowler? Or Benjamin Willet?"

"Nothing about Fowler. As for the other man, he had rooms in Bloomsbury but gave them up to return to France." There was no real connection then with The Marlborough Hotel. Willet had lied when he claimed he had rooms there.

Gibson was saying, "Constable Burton, who located his lodgings, is very thorough. We also found the doctor who treated this man Willet. " He gave Rutledge the address in Harley Street. "Dr. Baker."

"Good work. And keep trying with Fowler, if you will."

"Sir, I'll try. We're at sixes and sevens with the Chief Superintendent in hospital."

Rutledge noticed that Gibson had used Bowles's title rather than what he and the rank and file called him: Old Bowels. It was not a good sign. Nor was the fact that it appeared that no one had yet been asked to fill in either temporarily or permanently. Much as he himself disliked the man, it was hard to picture the Yard without him.

"Someone's been looking for the file on the MacGuire trial. By any chance, do you know where that is?"

"I sent it along to the Chief Superintendent. Look there. If it isn't in his box, it may have been given to someone else."

"Yes, sir, I'll do that. And the Weatherly case?"

Rutledge felt a twinge of conscience. "On my desk. The constable who discovered the body hasn't finished his report."

"I'll get on that, then." Gibson paused, then added quietly, "There's been some question about what to do. One rumor says Chief Inspector Cummins might be called back."

That meant that there had been some discussion in the upper echelons after all, and no one's view had prevailed. In point of fact, the Chief Superintendent would be hard to replace for the simple reason that he had never groomed a successor for fear of being overshadowed—or shown lacking.

Rutledge rang off and stood there for a moment in the telephone closet. He ought to go back to the Yard. But the last thing he wished to do was enter into the speculation and carping that must be going on, much less the ruthless undercurrents as some tried to benefit from Bowles's crisis. He'd become a policeman for very sound reasons, and political intrigue was not one of them. He'd been pleased when Cummins, who had retired earlier in the summer, had suggested that he be promoted as his replacement. It had been a measure of Cummins's respect for a junior officer.

But subsequent events had left a bitter taste in Rutledge's mouth. He'd realized that promotion would leave him vulnerable to attack where he could least afford to tell the real truth about the war. He'd been decorated for bravery, but the stigma of shell shock—regarded as cowardice—would negate that.

He realized that someone was standing outside the door, waiting to use the telephone, and he left the hotel with every intention of going back to Essex. But he actually went to his flat and paced the floor for over an hour, Hamish loud in the back of his mind, his temporary exile from the Yard and the inquiry at hand driving him to physical action.

There was something missing in the case, and he didn't know what it was. Yet.

Why had Ben Willet, facing his own death, come to Scotland Yard to accuse Wyatt Russell of a murder committed during the war? The only connection between Willet and Russell, besides the river that connected River's Edge and the village of Furnham, had been Cynthia Farraday. Had Willet known how she felt about Fowler and as a last gift tried to end her uncertainty over what had become of the man?

He could just as easily have been trying to protect her from the police by pointing them elsewhere. But if the police knew nothing about Fowler's death to start with, why bring it to their attention?

And who had found it necessary to kill Ben Willet when he was already dying? Or had the killer known that? Major Russell had said that Willet wanted to be killed rather than face the indignity and excruciating pain of waiting for the end. But this didn't smack of a mercy killing. Shooting him hadn't been enough—his body had been stripped of identification and shoved into the Thames for good measure. It should have disappeared for good or else have been so badly disfigured by the water, the fish, and the passing ships that any identification would be impossible. But luck had not been on the killer's side.

A third possibility was that someone had discovered that Willet had come to the Yard—or he had actually told someone what he'd done. But why bring up Justin Fowler's death in the first place? What had driven Willet to make such a claim? He had seemed to have no place in either the village or River's Edge, no one but a sister to mourn his loss, no one but that same sister waiting eagerly for news of him or for the closure that finding his killer could bring to those who had survived him.

And what about Willet's writing? What role had that played?

Waiting for Gibson to find out what he needed to know could take days. It was better to drive to Colchester and see what he could discover for himself. That had been where Fowler's parents had lived and died.

Hamish said, "There's the room in Furnham."

"They'll be relieved when I don't return," Rutledge retorted, packing a valise.

But before he left London, Rutledge went to call on Dr. Baker.

He was an older man, his hair nearly white, his eyes a sharp gray.

"Murdered, you say? Willet? That's startling news, indeed." He regarded Rutledge for a moment. "But you're here about his illness, not his murder. There was nothing I could do. We could have tried surgery, of course, but the cancer had spread too far, and Willet knew that."

"What did he take for the pain?"

"I gave him morphine, but I don't believe he took it very often. He said he had something to do before he died, and he wanted a clear mind."

"Why should he come to Scotland Yard, give another man's name, and in that man's name, confess to a murder?"

"Willet did that? I'll be damned. Medically, I can't account for it."

"How did he receive his diagnosis?"

"Quietly. He didn't appear to be particularly religious, but I over-heard him comment as he was dressing again that God was punishing him. He didn't tell me how he'd incurred the Almighty's displeasure. Perhaps I should have asked, but he wasn't speaking to me, and I respected his privacy. Have you considered that his charade was intended to push the Yard into action? As he appears to have done?"

"It's possible," Rutledge answered neutrally. "Would Willet have paid someone to cut short his suffering? Rather than contemplate suicide?"

"I think not. Unless he'd finished whatever it was that drove him to eschew taking something for his pain, and it was growing unbearable. As it would have done. I'm sorry I can't give you a more satisfying answer. I knew very little about his personal life, except for the fact that he'd recently lived in Paris and had come home to be seen by a doctor."

Hamish reminded him of a last question.

Rutledge said, "You examined him, of course. Was he by any chance wearing a gold locket?" He took it from his pocket, holding it out to Dr. Baker.

"Quite pretty, isn't it? And quite old, as well. But no, I've never seen it before."

Rutledge thanked him and was about to walk out the door when Baker said suddenly, "I just remembered. He asked if I had any information on the plague. I gave him a book to read, and he brought it back on his last visit. He said he had found it very interesting. I asked him why he should want to study the subject, and he said that it was a hobby of his."

"A hobby?"

"He must have seen my reaction—very much like yours, I'm sure—and he smiled and said, 'The Spanish flu was a plague, was it not, killing thousands?' I told him the effects might have been the same, the way it ravaged country after country, but that the pathology was quite different. It wasn't spread by rats or fleas. And he said, 'Yes, but you see, it's the only comparison I can make.' "

Colchester had once been a Roman camp, the capital of Roman Britain until Queen Boudicca burned it to the ground during the Iceni revolt. It had also been a prosperous woolen center in the Middle Ages. It was very late when Rutledge reached his destination. The town was dark, quiet, only a few vehicles and fewer pedestrians on the streets as he made his way to the Town Hall with its handsome tower and then found the police station. Lights were on inside, but he knew that only a small night staff would be there. Tomorrow morning would suffice. There was a room available at the ancient hostelry, The Rose and Crown, and he fell asleep almost as soon as his head touched the pillow. Hamish had been busy in the back of his mind from the time he'd left London, and he was glad to shut out the soft Scots voice.

After breakfast the next morning in one of the small half-timbered rooms off the main dining room, Rutledge left his motorcar in the inn's yard and walked to the police station. The streets were busy, men hurrying to their work, women walking small children to school while older boys laughed as they took turns kicking a stone down the road.

Shopkeepers were only just opening their doors, and the greengrocer was setting boxes of vegetables on racks in front of his window. He nodded as Rutledge passed, and then spoke to a woman just behind him, calling her by name and wishing her a good day. Rutledge could feel the warmth of the sun on his back and smell the summer dust stirred up by passing motorcars, the motes gleaming in the sunlight.

Not a day to speak of murder, he thought as he opened the door to the police station and stepped into the dim interior.

The sergeant at the desk looked up as he entered, and asked his business. Rutledge explained what he was after—any information that the local constabulary had on the family of one Justin Fowler, formerly of Colchester before moving to Essex.

He saw the expression in the man's eyes change, although he gave nothing away.

"Scotland Yard?" he repeated. "It might be best, sir, if you speak to Inspector Robinson. I'll find out if he can see you now."

Robinson could, taking Rutledge back to his office and offering him a chair. The man's desk was piled high with paperwork, but the room was tidy otherwise and Robinson himself was spare, neatly dressed, and curious to know why Rutledge had come.

He explained himself as well as he could, given the sparseness of information at his disposal, beginning with a report that had come to the attention of the Yard claiming that one Justin Fowler had been murdered during the war. His body had never been found, but because of another murder closely associated with that case, the Yard was interested in learning more about Fowler's background.

Robinson considered him as he spoke.

"Fowler is dead, you say?"

"We can't be sure. The man who told us about the murder has since died violently. We find ourselves wondering if the two events are connected."

"Hmmm. Yes. What do you know about Fowler's family?"

"Only that his parents died when he was eleven or twelve, and shortly afterward he was given into the guardianship of Mrs. Elizabeth Russell, of River's Edge. Mrs. Russell is dead as well, and her son was gravely injured in the war. We've had no other information."

"I see." Robinson shifted papers on his desk, then looked up and said, "Then you may not know that Fowler's parents were murdered."

# 17

Robinson had been watching Rutledge's face as he spoke, judging the impact of his words.

"I see that that's news."

"I didn't think they had died on the same day. I went to Somerset House."

"They didn't. Fowler's father died at the scene, and his mother two days later. Young Fowler himself was in hospital for six months, first with stab wounds, and then with infection. He passed his next birthday there. When he was about to be released, the Fowler family solicitors contacted Mrs. Russell, and she agreed to take him. A number of people were willing to give him a home, he was that well liked, but the doctors believed that it would be best if he left Colchester altogether. Too many reminders, and so on."

"And you never found the person who was responsible?"

"There was very little evidence to guide us," Robinson answered, his tone defensive. "Mrs. Fowler died without regaining consciousness. When we could, we questioned Justin, but he was asleep when the murders were committed, and he woke up in the dark to find a figure standing by his bed. And then he himself was stabbed and left for dead. It was the housemaid, bringing up morning tea, who discovered his parents, and she ran down to the kitchen in hysterics. The housekeeper went up to see for herself, sent one of the other maids for the doctor and the police, and only then had the presence of mind to look in on the boy."

"The staff was cleared of any involvement?"

"Yes, we felt fairly confident that they weren't to blame. The housekeeper was fifty, the three maids in their early forties, the cook nearing sixty. All of them had been with the family for twenty years or more. And we found a window in the dining room broken, a bloody handprint on the post at the bottom of the drive, and signs that someone had been sick just there. We questioned the staff, but they knew of no one who had a reason to kill Mr. or Mrs. Fowler. He was a solicitor. We spoke to his partner, and we were assured that there was no evidence that the murders were related to his work. Mostly wills, conveyances, and the like. The partner himself had been attending a funeral in Suffolk, and there must be twenty witnesses to that." It was clear that Robinson was not happy admitting to Scotland Yard that the murders had gone unsolved. And it was just as clear that with two dead and one severely injured, no suspects and no answers, the local constabulary had chosen not to call in the Yard. Why?

"Who was in charge of the inquiry?" he asked Robinson.

"Inspector Eaton. I was a constable at the time. I had no voice in decisions. But I can tell you that I saw the bodies. Repeatedly stabbed. As bloody a sight as I'd ever seen, until the war."

"Is Eaton still here?"

"He died in the influenza epidemic. Overworked, if you want my opinion. Policeman, confessor, nurse, he tried to do it all."

"There was no possibility that Justin Fowler killed his parents and then stabbed himself?"

"Good God, no. For one thing, we never found a weapon, even though we searched his room, the ground under his windows, and every inch of the house wall in between. And only his bedding was bloody. There was no blood at all on the floor, and considering his wounds, there most certainly would have been if he'd stabbed himself, thrown away the weapon, and returned to his bed. What's more, he said he'd been too frightened to move. He thought the killer was still in the room, and soon afterward, he fainted from pain and loss of blood."

"And neither parent could have committed the crimes?"

"Not from the evidence. We also looked into that very carefully."

"The inquest?"

"Person or persons unknown. We spent six months investigating every possibility, even a botched housebreaking, and we discovered nothing new in all that time."

"What became of the staff?"

"They stayed in the house until Justin Fowler's future was decided. And then the house was sold, the staff pensioned off according to Mrs. Fowler's will—she survived her husband, you see, but the provisions were very much the same in both cases. There was the usual gift to the church fund, and to a charity school in London that Mr. Fowler had made gifts to over the years. Nothing of a size to suggest that they were killed for what anyone expected to inherit."

"And no disgruntled servant, client, or other person with a grudge against Fowler or his family?"

"None at all. We looked into that as well."

"Had the elder Fowler always lived in Colchester?"

"Indeed, except for a brief time in London—three years when he was a very young man. As I recall, he was a junior in a firm of solicitors there, before coming here and setting up his own chambers."

Rutledge remembered what Nancy Brothers had said, that Mrs. Russell had lost touch with her cousin after she'd married Fowler. That Mrs. Russell hadn't cared for him.

"Was there anything in Fowler's background that was in any way irregular?"

"Irregular?"

"Unusual, a source of concern for the family, skeletons in the closet."

"We never discovered any. He was some years older than his wife, as I remember, a pillar of the church, impeccable reputation here in Colchester. I heard one of the other constables, an older man, say that Fowler was too dull to look for trouble, much less to find it. His wife was a lovely woman. My mother cried when she heard what had happened."

"Perhaps a case of mistaken identity? The wrong people singled out and killed?"

"We considered that as well. And nothing pointed to that possibility."

Then why had someone come into a house in the night, stabbed three people in two different rooms without disturbing the servants in their beds, leaving the victims for dead and disappearing as quietly as he'd come?

What's more, neither Cynthia Farraday nor Wyatt Russell appeared to have had any inkling of Justin Fowler's past. Nor had Nancy Brothers. Whatever Mrs. Russell had been told by the Fowler family solicitor had not been passed on to anyone else. And Justin himself had kept his secret. Small wonder everyone felt he was quiet and preferred his own company. He'd suffered a shocking end to his childhood.

But what connection did this have with Ben Willet's confession, that Wyatt Russell had killed Fowler? Even when Rutledge had questioned him, Willet had refused to say why or how the murder had been committed. Because he didn't know any other details?

He thanked Robinson for the information he'd been given. The Inspector rose to see Rutledge out and said as they reached the door to the station, "You'll be sure to let me know if you find anything that might shed light on our case?"

"I shall. I don't see any chance of that at present, but then inquiries have a way of moving in directions we haven't foreseen."

"Yes. I've had my own experiences of that. Good hunting."

And then Rutledge was out in the street, walking back to where he'd left his motorcar.

Hamish said, "Ye ken, the lad was only eleven. He couldna' overpower both parents, even if they were asleep when he came into the room."

"That's very likely. No, I think we can absolve Justin of any blame."

But it was important to consider one other possibility. That during the war, Major Russell learned about Justin Fowler's past and blamed him for Mrs. Russell's disappearance. He could have jumped to the conclusion that if Fowler had already killed twice, and his own parents at that, he would likely kill again. And how could Ben Willet have discovered that?

Halfway to the Rose and Crown, he stopped, retraced his steps to the police station, and asked the name of the Fowler solicitor. Robinson was reluctant to give it to him, unwilling to hand the Yard his own pet case, but Rutledge said blandly, "It's possible there are other family members I could speak to."

"We asked. There are none."

"Still—"

Robinson hadn't needed to look it up.

With that information in hand, he tracked down the firm of Biddle, Harrison and Bailey.

Their chambers were in a Victorian building with a view of the castle, and the senior clerk informed Rutledge that it was Mr. Harrison who had dealt with the affairs of the Fowler family.

Harrison's hair was white, but his face was smooth, as if age had treated him well. His grip was firm when the two men shook hands, and then Harrison said, "I understand from my clerk that you've come about the Fowler murders. Is there any new information?"

"Sadly, no. But I have been searching for Justin Fowler. I understand he survived the war. Did you handle his affairs as well?"

"He wrote to us when he was about to go into the Army. He wished to draw up his will—as so many young men did at that time. It was the first correspondence we'd had from him since he went to live with Mrs. Russell. As he was underage, she had handled his affairs for him. The trust fund that his father had set up for the boy had paid him an allowance, but the principal wasn't his until he reached the age of twenty-five. He left everything to Miss Cynthia Farraday. In 1917, when he should have reached his majority, we heard nothing from him. But the war was still on, and we thought perhaps he wished to wait until that was over before taking charge of his inheritance. It was quite sizable, in fact, but as one of our junior partners said at the time, there was very little need for great sums of money in the trenches."

"And did he contact you when the war was over?"

"We wrote to him at River's Edge, but the letter was returned. We made an effort to contact Major Russell, to discover if Justin Fowler had survived the war, but he could tell us nothing. Their paths hadn't crossed in the years of fighting. And the War Office listed him as missing in action."

That was news.

"And so Miss Farraday inherited the Fowler estate?"

Mr. Harrison's dark brows, in such sharp contrast to his white hair, rose. "I'm afraid we're a rather conventional firm, Mr. Rutledge. Missing does not necessarily mean dead. We chose not to act precipitously, but to wait and see if any new information might help us to learn Mr. Fowler's fate. We were left in charge of his estate, and it's our duty to be certain that he is dead before disbursing such sums."

"Yes, I quite understand. Did you contact Miss Farraday?"

"No. Not directly. We did make inquiries, and we discovered that she was living in London and was still unmarried. That is to say, her name hadn't changed with marriage. As she made no attempt to contact us, we felt it best not to contact her prematurely, as it were."

"You said that Fowler was missing in action. When was this?"

"It was early in 1915. There was a later report that he was wounded and sent home to England to recover. We tried to verify it and were unable to do so."

"I'd like to know more about the elder Fowler. I was told by one of the maids who was in service at River's Edge that Mrs. Russell had not cared for her cousin's choice of husband. Do you know why that may have been?"

"He was some ten years Mrs. Fowler's senior, but it was a love match, I can tell you that. I saw them a number of times socially, and it was very clear that they were a happy couple."

"Perhaps there was something in Mr. Fowler's background that Mrs. Russell disapproved of?"

"I understood that he was married when he was very young. He'd just come down from university and he was—gullible, shall I say? She was someone he met in London and married without his parents' knowledge or consent. When this woman discovered that he was to be cut off without a farthing, she told him that she already had a husband and walked out the door. That was the last he saw of her, and the marriage was quietly annulled on those grounds. Fowler left London and returned to Colchester. He admitted this freely to his fiancée before he married Mrs. Fowler. At our urging."

"And what became of the first Mrs. Fowler?"

"She died some years later of consumption. She wrote to Mr. Fowler before she died—this was even before he'd met the second Mrs. Fowler—but he refused to meet her. She wanted forgiveness, and he couldn't find it in himself to forgive."

So much, Rutledge thought, for the man who was too dull to know what trouble was, and who wouldn't know what to do with it if he did find it. Small wonder he had led a staid life in his second marriage.

"He paid for her care, through our good offices, and we received notification from the sanitarium when she died. He paid for her burial. It was generous of him. And we never spoke of this matter again."

"Nor did you tell the police about his first disastrous marriage."

"We considered speaking to them. But the woman was dead, and we had actually verified that fact. There was no reason to resurrect the past."

"But she had a husband somewhere, didn't she? Or was he a lie as well?"

"He was in prison. He died there. Before the murders."

"And that also is certain?"

"Yes. His Majesty's Prisons don't make mistakes of that sort."

A dead end.

Which led him back to the River Hawking.

He thanked Mr. Harrison for his time, then asked one more question.

"This woman. What was her name?"

"She's dead. Let her rest in peace."

"I intend to. But I should like to know her name. For completeness."

That was something the solicitor understood.

"Indeed. Her name was Gladys Mitchell. She's buried in the cemetery of St. Agnes, the church associated with the nursing clinic where she died. At the end, she told the sanitarium staff that her father had been a clergyman. They felt that this was an attempt to gloss over her—somewhat irregular—past. She had initially told one of the staff that he was a solicitor."

"What was he?"

"I don't know. We weren't her solicitors. The truth was not something we had need of."

"She had no children?"

"According to Mr. Fowler, she was not pregnant when she left him."

"And no family?"

"A sister. I'm afraid I don't know her name. She was with Gladys Mitchell when she died. It was she who arranged the burial."

"Do you know where she is now?"

"If I'm not mistaken, she died in 1910."

"Thank you."

The senior clerk appeared like magic to escort Rutledge to the street door, deferentially bidding him farewell.

Hamish said, "Yon sister couldna' ha' murdered the family."

"We've come to a dead end. Just as the original inquiry into the Fowlers' deaths had done."

He collected his valise from The Rose and Crown, settled his account, and drove out of Colchester for the road south.

The first call Rutledge made when he reached Furnham was on Nancy Brothers.

She was preparing dinner when he knocked at her door. Wiping her hands on her apron, she hesitated, then let him into the house.

"My husband will be coming in from the pasture where he was repairing a broken fence, and he'll be wanting his dinner," she told him anxiously.

"I just have two questions for you," he told her. "I won't keep you from your work. I'd like to know if Mrs. Russell ever told you what had happened to Justin Fowler's parents?"

"She told me he'd lost his just as Miss Cynthia had lost hers. I took that to mean they died of an illness. I thought Mr. Justin consumptive, for that matter, he was so pale and thin when he first came to River's Edge. I said something to Mrs. Russell, but she told me he was grieving. And it must have been true because he filled out that summer."

"And did Mrs. Russell ever tell you why she didn't approve of her cousin marrying Mr. Fowler?"

"She never said, not directly, but I heard her tell Mr. Wyatt that he was too old."

All of which corroborated what he'd learned in Colchester.

He thanked her and left the farm just as Brothers was walking in from the pasture, his shoulders stooped with fatigue and his face red with sweat and smeared with dust. He saw Rutledge turning out of the gate and lifted a hand in greeting.

Nancy Brothers had done well for herself.

He was just turning around to go back to the farmhouse, a thought tickling at the back of his mind, when he saw Constable Nelson coming toward him on his bicycle.

"Found the missing mare?" he asked.

"We did. T'other side of River's Edge, some five miles down the road. I notified the owners. No, I've come to find you. Abigail Barber is that upset. She wrote to her brother in care of that family in Thetford, to tell Ben that his father was ill. And then again to tell Ben that his father died. Now a letter's come from them saying they haven't seen Ben since the start of the war. Sandy Barber is beside himself, trying to think what to say to her."

"The truth would be best," Rutledge said. "It wouldn't have been possible to keep the news from her for very much longer. Others have seen the photograph I brought with me."

"Yes, well, Barber wants you to come and tell her."

And explain as well why no one had told her before this.

He followed Nelson into Furnham and went alone to the Barber house.

Abigail was sitting in the front room when he knocked and then opened the door.

"Mrs. Barber?" he called from the entry, and when she replied, he joined her. Constable Nelson had been right. Her eyes were red-

rimmed, her face blotched by tears. There was a crumpled handkerchief in one hand.

"They've sent Scotland Yard to me?" she asked, looking at him as
he took the chair she offered. "He said you were an Inspector. Sandy.
It can't be good news." Her voice was thick, husky.

"I'm afraid not. But first I think it best to tell you what I know
about your brother. He didn't go back to Thetford after the war. He
was afraid to tell his father what he really wanted to do. And apparently, from what I've learned from Miss Farraday—"

"Oh, Miss Farraday is it?" She looked up at him, anger in her eyes.
"It was Miss Farraday that put ideas into his head about going into
service. He never would have left Furnham if she hadn't. He would
have gone to sea like his father and grandfather, and never got notions about leaving his family. She and that driver of hers, sweeping
into Furnham like the Queen come to call, was like a thorn in my side
every time I saw her. As if she was gloating over taking Ben from us.
What did she persuade my brother to do this time?"

"You didn't like her driver?" He was surprised. Nancy Brothers had left the impression that Finley was dependable and helpful.
Indeed, he'd been left in charge of River's Edge until he himself had
been called up.

"He was a servant, wasn't he? No better than Ben was. But you'd
have thought he was the Lord High Somebody. Standing stiff as a
poker by that motorcar and not a word to say to anyone."

"I don't believe Miss Farraday was responsible for your brother's
decision," he said, thinking of the copybooks he'd seen in Thetford.
Still, she'd made it financially possible for him to return to France.
"He was trying to establish himself as a writer."

"He never showed any interest in such a thing when he was growing up."

"Nevertheless, he was actively trying to write while he was a
footman. I don't know what he did during the war, but it must have

shown him a different sort of life, and he decided to stay in Paris and work."

"He's still there? In Paris? Is that what Sandy wanted you to tell me? I've been so worried, thinking something must have happened to him. I'm glad my father never knew. He wouldn't have cared for that. He never liked the French very much. Boastful people, he said, and thinking they know more than anyone else."

"Ben wrote two books that were published in France. They were quite well written, by the way. He used the name Edward Willet. His father's name as well as his own. And then this spring he came back to England to see a doctor. He was diagnosed with stomach cancer. There was not much the doctors could do."

She said slowly, as if she found it difficult to hear what must be coming, "He was dying of it?"

"I'm sorry. Yes."

"But why doesn't he come home then, and let us take care of him?"

"We don't know the answer to that, Mrs. Barber. It's one of the questions we're still asking."

"Where is he? I'll ask Sandy to take me to him. In hospital?"

"I'm afraid he's dead."

She stared at him, and then her face crumpled. "And nobody was there with him? None of his family around him?"

Rutledge took a deep breath. This was the part of his duty that he found the most difficult. "He was found in the Thames, Mrs. Barber. Someone had shot him."

"He—did he kill himself? Because of the cancer?

"No. He couldn't have taken his own life."

Nodding, she said, "Then you're saying that this was murder?"

"Yes. If it's any consolation, he was intending to come home to see his family before returning to France to die. But he was killed before he could." There was nothing else he could say. A silence fell, and he gave her time to recover from the blow.

Finally she said, "I want to see him. Will you take me to see him?"

"I—don't believe it would be wise, Mrs. Barber. I don't know that he would wish you to see him like this."

"I'm his sister. There's no one else. I want to see my brother."

He considered offering to show her the photograph and then thought better of it. "Will you let your husband take you? I'll see to the arrangements."

"Not Sandy. I don't want to go with him. But I'll go with you, if you'll be so kind."

"Now?"

"Yes, please. I'll just fetch my shawl." And she rose, leaving him there in the room. Five minutes later she was back. He thought she'd splashed cool water on her face, for it seemed less flushed. But her jaw was tightly clenched, and he could tell that she was trying to steel herself for the ordeal to come.

"Is there anyone you'd care to take with you? Another woman, perhaps? Molly?"

"No. I'll go alone. He'd have wanted it that way."

And so he led her out to the motorcar, settling her into the seat. His mind busy planning his route, he chose to take the lane that led past the churchyard rather than to go through Furnham. She looked up as they were approaching it, and he cursed himself for his thoughtlessness, because both of them could see the raw hump of a grave near the east wall.

But she said only, "I'm glad my father didn't know. It's for the best. And if there's any truth to what Rector was telling me, they've already met, haven't they?"

He said, "I'm sure they have." Remembering his conversation with Dr. Baker, he asked, "I saw those barrow-like graves in the back. They're unusual. Plague victims?"

She stared at him, her eyes wide, then said, "I wouldn't know."

But he thought she did.

* * *

It was a long and silent drive to Tilbury, where they took the ferry across to Gravesend. He found a cab to convey them to the hospital and sent a message to Inspector Adams as well.

By the time they had found someone to escort them down to the cellar, Inspector Adams came in, frowning as he saw Rutledge with Abigail Barber.

"Your note asked me to meet you here?"

"Thank you for coming. Mrs. Barber, this is Inspector Adams. He had made every effort to learn the identity of the man brought in by the Thames boatmen. Otherwise we would have had no way of knowing that he was your brother."

"Mrs. Barber," Adams said in acknowledgment, then added, "Are you sure you wish to go through with this? It can be an unsettling experience."

"Did he suffer?" It was a question she hadn't asked Rutledge.

"According to the doctor who examined the—your brother, he did not. He wouldn't have known what had happened."

"Well, then, I expect it was better than dying of that tumor."

They took her back then. Rutledge had already asked an orderly to see that the body was presentable and that no other corpses were in the room.

As the door opened, he watched as Abigail Barber squared her shoulders, as if bracing herself as she followed Inspector Adams into the morgue. It was chilly and the light was glaring pools in the dimness, but she walked resolutely to the table where a body lay under a freshly ironed sheet.

Inspector Adams asked, "Are you ready, Mrs. Barber?"

"Yes," she answered stoically. But Rutledge put a hand on her shoulder, as comfort.

Adams pulled back the sheet. She flinched. "It's Ben," she said, and then tentatively reached out to touch her brother's face, drawing back quickly at the coldness of the flesh. "He's a man, isn't he? He was a boy when he left us to go to Thetford. Now he looks very much like Joseph." After a moment, she leaned down, as if to whisper in his ear. Adams turned aside to offer her a little privacy. And then she straightened.

"I want to take him home," she said.

Adams glanced over her head at Rutledge, who nodded once.

"Yes, all right, I shall see that the paperwork is completed. There's a good man here in Gravesend. The—undertaker. He'll take care of the rest."

"Thank you." Before they could move, she reached out and drew the sheet back over her brother's face, her hands gentle. And then she was walking quickly out of the room, as if she couldn't bear it any longer.

Rutledge thanked Adams and followed her out of the hospital and half a block down the street. She stopped there suddenly, as if she couldn't go any farther, and broke down, crying inconsolably. He put a hand again on her shoulder, but she shrugged it off.

When she lifted her head finally, to his shock her eyes were blazing with anger.

"If you know where Cynthia Farraday lives, you tell her for me. If she ever shows her face in Furnham again—if she even thinks of coming to the service for my brother—I'll kill her myself."

He summoned a cab, and without a word she got into it.

It was very late when he delivered Mrs. Barber to her home in Furnham. Her husband, peering anxiously out the window, saw them arrive and hurried out to open the motorcar door for her. He was about to demand where she had been when he caught the look that Rutledge gave him. Instead he said, as if it had been what he intended in the first place, "Come in, love, there's tea waiting."

Rutledge didn't get out. But he waited until the Barbers had walked into their house and shut the door.

Driving on, he cursed whoever had killed Ben Willet.

"And it willna' do you any guid to damn him."

Still, he went to the Rectory to find Mr. Morrison, to tell him what had transpired, and to ask him to call on Abigail Willet. But the Rectory was dark and silent. No one answered his knock. At the church then? At this hour?

He came to the junction in the road and soon after saw the church just ahead. It was dark except for a dim light in the nave, just visible through the plain glass of the high windows.

Stopping the motorcar at the verge of the road but leaving it running, he crossed to the church door and quietly began to open it so as not to disturb the rector if he was at his prayers.

He had not swung it more than two inches wide when the sound of voices came to him, echoing in the empty church. He couldn't see anything but the opposite wall without pushing the door wider. But he knew the voices and could put a name to both of them.

That was the rector, saying, "What is it you wish to confess, my son?"

And the response came from Major Russell.

# 18

His voice was hoarse, but still recognizable. "Damn it, Morrison, there's nothing to confess. I just need to talk to someone. The police are after me, I've left the clinic again, and I don't know where to turn. River's Edge is closed, there's no refuge there. The house in London has very likely already been searched."

There was a long pause. And then Morrison said, "Why do the police want you, Major?"

"I took a man's motorcycle. Well, it was the only way I could get out of that clinic and reach London. Then I frightened Cynthia, which I didn't mean to do. I just wanted to know—never mind that. I sometimes muddle things. It's getting better, I think, but then there are days of torment, pure hell, when I can barely remember who I am."

"They've come to Furnham. The police. I've been told that Ben Willet has been murdered. And possibly Justin Fowler as well. I don't know what to think. And there's your mother's disappearance. Is River's Edge cursed? Or is it Furnham? I grew up in a quiet village where murder was unheard of. I have no answers to give you."

"They aren't connected, if that's what you're afraid of. There's no madman out there picking us off every year or two. It's the war, people are different. The England I nearly died for is gone. I don't recognize anything." There was despair in his voice. "For that matter, I'm not the same either."

"We must have faith that God in his wisdom—"

"I don't know that I believe in God any longer. He damned well wasn't there in the trenches when we needed him. Did you know that Willet has written a book? A novel? I saw something about it in a newspaper a year ago."

"So it's true, then. Gossip had it that the French believed it was his father who'd written a book. It caused a great deal of hilarity, I can tell you, among Ned's friends. Were these books something he was ashamed of? Is that why Ben never told his family about them?"

"I have no idea. Apparently one's all about smugglers in Essex before the war. I suppose I should have read it. But I wasn't ready to revisit Furnham. Or River's End."

Morrison was still concentrating on the books. "It's just as well everyone thought it was a good joke. Otherwise it could have got him killed. Jessup hadn't forgiven Ben Willet for becoming a footman. Putting Furnham into a book would have angered everyone."

"I doubt it would have led to murder. I saw Willet in London quite recently. Twice, as it happens. The last time there was a crash on Tower Bridge, and I couldn't get through."

"What did you talk about?"

"I didn't recognize him at first. But he knew who I was and spoke. He asked how I was faring, and I asked why he looked so ill. We commiserated on our war, and I told him I'd seen a mention of his book, asked him if he was still writing. He said he was just finishing another manuscript. And then he told me he wished once it was finished that someone would shoot him and put him out of his agony. I told him not to be a fool. I thought he was asking if I'd do it, and I wouldn't. I couldn't understand why he believed I could do such a thing. I hardly knew the man."

"Then why were you meeting him a second time?"

"He told me there was something he must tell me. Before he died." Wyatt took a deep breath. "I didn't come here to talk about Willet. Will you risk it, Rector? Taking me in? I can't ask Nancy to do any more than she has done. She must be afraid her husband will find her out. I had trouble enough persuading her to bring me food in the old church ruins."

There was another silence.

Russell said irritably, "If you're afraid I'll murder you in your bed, I'll find somewhere else to go."

"It isn't that," Morrison began, then before Russell could speak, he added, "there's hardly enough room for one in the Rectory. Much less two."

"I'll sleep in a chair if I have to."

But he must have read something in the other man's face, because without waiting for an answer, Russell went on, "Yes, all right, I understand. I think there's a bicycle in one of the outbuildings. It was used by the servants. I can manage. At least let me clean up a little. I've slept rough too long and I can't very well bathe in the river in plain sight of anyone coming upstream."

Rutledge eased the door closed, careful not to let the latch click to, and went back to his motorcar, driving off as soon as he was behind the wheel. Without turning on his headlamps he continued down the dark road until he was certain that neither the rector nor the Major could see his rear light.

Hamish said, "Ye didna' think to search yon ruins."

It was an accusation. But there was barely cover enough to conceal a human being. He hadn't expected it to hide a stray sheep, much less a grown man.

"More to the point, how did he get there?"

"Ye must ask him."

"I intend to."

He drove for more than a mile past the gates of River's Edge, then left the motorcar at the verge, as far into the heavy grass as he dared. Walking back toward the house, he considered where best to set his ambush.

Just past the gates?

But then if Russell knew a shorter way across the marshes—and Rutledge was fairly sure now there must be one—closer to the house would be wiser.

He chose his spot under the windows at the side of the house, leaned against the wall under the drawing room windows, and waited. How long would it take a man to bathe and shave, perhaps drink a cup of tea? An hour then, before Russell appeared.

But an hour passed. And then another.

Had Morrison taken pity on Russell after all, and allowed him to stay the night in the Rectory?

He'd been certain that Morrison wouldn't change his mind.

Hamish said, "Ye could ha' confronted him in yon kirk."

"If Russell had put up a fight, Morrison would have had every reason to raise the question of sanctuary. No, it was better to wait for him here, alone."

By half past two, it was clear that Russell wasn't coming.

A wild-goose chase.

"Then go to yon Rectory now and ye'll have him."

It was the only option left to him. By morning Russell could be miles away from this part of Essex. The roads were rutted but flat, and a bicycle could make good time, given an early start.

It was a long dark walk back to his motorcar.

But when he reached the Rectory, there were no lights, and no one came to the door.

After an early breakfast the next morning, Rutledge drove to the Brothers farm. He found Nancy cutting flowers for the house, a basket over her arm and secateurs in her hand.

She looked up as she heard the motorcar come up the farm lane, straightening to stare warily at Rutledge as he got out and walked across to the garden. He was beginning to understand why she had been eager to see him go yesterday before her husband had come in from the fields. She was afraid her husband might learn that she was harboring the son of her late mistress, a man wanted by the police. And yet out of her feelings for the family she had served so long, she'd taken the risk.

"Good morning. I've come to ask you about Major Russell."

She set the basket of zinnias and marigolds to one side, trying to decide whether he knew the truth or was merely looking for information. He could read the uncertainty in her eyes.

Rutledge said, "I've learned you've been taking food to him at the old church. Did your husband know?"

Flushing, she said, "Who told you?"

"You did. Looking back, I should have guessed you were hiding something. Or in this case, someone."

She made no attempt to deny the truth. "He doesn't know— Samuel. He was glad the house at River's Edge was closing just as I was marrying him. That was my old life, he said, and this was the new. He didn't want me keeping up any acquaintance with the others. Mrs. Broadley, the cook, and I were friendly, and Mrs. Dunner, the housekeeper, helped me sew my wedding gown. They told me they wouldn't mind hearing from me from time to time. But Samuel told me he'd rather I didn't. They were in service still, you see, and I was a farmer's wife now. And so I never wrote to them. When the Major came, I hardly recognized him. I couldn't turn him away, could I? And I couldn't take him in, neither. I didn't know what Samuel would have to say about it. Instead I agreed to feed him. I'd take sandwiches and fruit and a jug of tea to him, whatever I could spare that wouldn't be missed."

"That was rough living for a man like the Major."

"Don't I know that? But he said he'd learned to do without while in the trenches. That he'd be all right. And I couldn't go as far as River's Edge without taking the cart."

He could see her quandary.

"Was this the first time you'd seen him since the war?"

"Since my wedding, in fact. He gave me away. I was that grateful. I couldn't turn him away, could I?" she asked again.

"What did he tell you? How did he get out here to Furnham?"

"He came with the van from Tilbury that brings the meat to the butcher's shop. It comes twice a week. He'd remembered that."

"Didn't you wonder why a Russell would be reduced to traveling in the butcher's van? He owns a motorcar, I'm told."

"I did wonder, but he told me that the doctors wanted him to stay in hospital, and he'd left instead. He said it would be all right, they'd stop looking and he could go his own way. I believed him. Why should I not? He's not one to lie. I never remember him telling a lie to anyone at the house."

"It's true. What he told you. As far as it goes."

"He's not done anything wrong. He just didn't want to be found and made to go back to hospital. He said he'd heal better on his own, if they'd leave him to it. I could understand that."

"Did you ever see Russell come to blows with Justin Fowler?"

"Mr. Justin?" She was surprised at the shift in subject. "They weren't as close as Mrs. Russell had hoped. But there was never any hard feelings between them. There was a time when Mr. Wyatt was jealous over Miss Cynthia, and all that. But it was silly nonsense. Like two cockerels discovering the new hen. I've seen it happen before and since."

"Did Russell blame Fowler for his mother's death?"

She stared at him. "What did Mr. Justin have to do with that?"

"I must depend on you to tell me."

Shaking her head, she said, "I never heard any such thing."

"Then what happened to Mrs. Russell?"

"You asked me that before, when you showed me the locket. The good Lord knows. I don't. Samuel said once there must be a murderer in that house, but that's nonsense. I don't believe it for a minute. Who could do a thing like that?"

"Yet she disappeared."

"I know. It troubled all of us. The Major most especially, as you'd expect. I never knew a suicide before that. But it was the most likely thing."

She glanced over her shoulder, and Rutledge knew she was anxious that her husband not see her speaking to the man from Scotland Yard. Then, looking back at him, she said, "I thought you came here about Ben Willet's death. Not about the Major. Unless you're looking to take him back to hospital."

"I'm more concerned about his welfare than returning him to hospital."

"Then you should know he wasn't there when I went to the church this morning early. I didn't know what to make of it, unless he decided that he'd be better off going back. He hadn't said anything last evening about leaving. He just said he'd give much for hot water and a razor. I asked if he wished me to buy a razor for him, and he said, best not."

He thanked her and left, intending to go directly to the Rectory now. Instead as he came through Furnham, he was hailed by a furious Sandy Barber, standing outside the door to The Rowing Boat. He looked haggard and out of patience.

Reluctant to take the time to soothe Barber's ruffled feathers, Rutledge weighed putting him off, then decided against it. Until now they had maintained a workable truce, and that had to be considered. He pulled up in front of the inn and got out. Barber said almost as soon as he was in hearing, "Why the hell did you take my wife to see her brother's body?"

"She asked to be taken. I tried to persuade her not to go, but she was adamant. When we got there, I saw to it that the body was presentable and there were no other corpses in the room."

"Yes, well, that's as may be, but she couldn't sleep last night. She sat in the parlor and cried. There was no comforting her. I went to find Morrison, finally, but he wasn't at the Rectory. I came back home and sat up with her. First her father and then her brother. I wish to hell she'd never found out about him."

"She has asked to have the body brought to Furnham. I've given permission for it to be released for burial."

Barber swore. "Another funeral. We've not got over the first."

He paced away from where Rutledge was standing and stared out to the mouth of the river, then paced back again. "Are you any nearer to finding out who killed Ben?"

"No. The question is, did his killer know Willet was dying? Would it have made any difference?"

"Why wasn't he in Thetford where he belonged? Why was he wandering about in London? Abigail just told me some faradiddle about Ben wanting to be a writer of books."

"Apparently he'd lived in Paris after the war. He wrote a book about a man who smuggled goods between England and France. This man met a girl on one of his journeys, and he went to look for her during the war. The book was published in France."

"I'll be damned. Abigail never told me that. And there *was* a girl he mooned over for weeks." Another thought struck him. "Here, was it Furnham he wrote about?"

"I haven't read the book."

"Does Jessup know about this yet? He'd be spitting mad."

"Will he indeed?"

Barber paced away and back again. "When Ben went to be a footman, Jessup asked Ned if he thought the boy could keep his mouth shut, and Ned said he would. Jessup said the last thing we needed was for Furnham to become notorious. He said people would come just out of curiosity, and if one or two of us was hanged, even better."

"I hardly think Furnham would become notorious over a few bottles of brandy and the like. Still, do you think Jessup could have killed Willet?"

"God, no. I'm not suggesting that. Look, you've stirred up feelings here that we thought had ended with the war, when they dismantled the flying field. That's all. The Blackwater and the Crouch are drawing holidaymakers from London. We've seen what that does to a village. We don't want it to happen here."

"Then help me find Ben Willet's killer. You do want him found, don't you? The dead man isn't a stranger, he's your wife's brother."

It was clear that Barber simply wished that the whole matter would go away. But he said, "Yes, all right, I do. For Abigail's sake. And her father's. I liked the old man."

"Was the killer one of your merry band of smugglers?"

Barber grimaced. "We can get the things we need easier from France than from London. What's so wrong with that? We don't pay the tax on them, but we don't go about with a barrow selling them in the streets either, do we? A bit of tobacco, a few bottles of spirits, some lace or a length of cloth. Where's the harm?"

"The men go armed."

Barber's face changed. "You've seen them?"

"'Ware!" Hamish said in the back of Rutledge's mind. "Ye canna' tell them."

And Rutledge himself saw the danger he stood in. "Don't they always? Swords, muskets, shotguns. It doesn't matter. Men in that line of work know the risks."

The tension in Barber's face eased. "True enough. You don't always know what you'll be dealing with at either end. Back to Ben Willet. If I knew who had killed him, I'd tell you. But I don't." And with that he walked off.

Rutledge watched him go as Hamish said, "D'ye believe him?"

I don't know, Rutledge responded silently. I haven't forgot the club.

"Aye, and it's no' wise to forget."

Anxious now that Barber had also been unable to raise the rector, Rutledge considered his next step. Russell hadn't come to River's Edge last night. And Nancy Brothers had looked in vain for him in the church rubble. Morrison, in spite of his vows, had been uneasy about giving the man houseroom. Where was he now? More to the point, what had become of the rector?

The question was, how well had Nancy Brothers looked in the ruins?

They were on his way, and it would take no more than ten minutes to be sure. He drove there, got out, and made his way through the tumble of stones in the thick grass, a snare for unwary feet. He had to keep his mind on what he was doing, but he reached a slight depression where two of the larger stones formed a sort of wedge. He hadn't come this far in his earlier exploration, and it was a place he would have chosen if sleeping rough. Well protected without being a trap. The nights were warm enough, and the weather had been dry. Russell had been lucky on that score. Squatting, he looked at the flattened stems. And watched an ant busily dragging away a tiny crumb of bread. Just outside he saw the pit of a plum, where it had been cast aside.

Satisfied, he rose and scanned the terrain. Then he walked back the way he'd come, to the road.

He found Jessup leaning against the wing of his motorcar, arms crossed.

"What's so interesting about yon ruin?" he asked, his voice neutral.

"A habit of mine, looking at ruins," Rutledge said easily. "My godfather happens to be an architect."

"Is he, now?" Jessup asked, insolently measuring Rutledge with his eyes.

"When did the church burn?"

"When it was struck by lightning."

"How old was it?"

"Old enough for the timbers to be dry."

And that, Rutledge thought, must be true.

He walked past Jessup and bent down to turn the crank.

"On your way back to London, are you?"

"Not until I find the man who killed Ben Willet and tossed his body into the Thames." He straightened and went around to open the driver's door.

"He was killed in London. Not here. You should be looking there."

Rutledge corrected him. "He was put into the river in London. But is that where he was killed?"

"Ben hasn't been in Furnham since the war. You can ask his sister."

"Perhaps he tried to come and was waylaid. When was the last time you were in London?"

Jessup's eyes narrowed. "None of your business."

"I can make it my business," Rutledge told him, his voice harsh now. "And before you make a decision to take me on, speak to Sandy Barber. He'll tell you it isn't worth your while."

He got into the motorcar, and Jessup put his hand on the other door, then thought better of it. He stepped away, and Rutledge drove on.

"A dangerous man," Hamish said, echoing Morrison. "He likes playing the bully."

"Because no one ever had the courage to face him down."

At the Rectory, Rutledge stopped and pounded on the door. There was no answer. The door was unlocked and he looked inside, but there was no sign of a struggle, and the remains of breakfast for one still sat on a table in the corner facing the back garden.

Where, then, was the rector? Called to a sickbed? And what had become of Russell? Frowning, he stood outside for a moment. It would be hard to explain another disappearance in Furnham. Whatever the police had concluded in 1914.

Hamish said, "Were ye' o'er hasty last night? Did he come later than expected?"

It was possible. Possible too that after his own breakfast, Morrison had taken one to the house for Russell, since it was too far for Nancy Brothers to venture.

He had just reached the Furnham road when he saw the rector bicycling furiously toward him from the direction of River's Edge. Morrison hailed him frantically, and Rutledge waited at the crossroads for him to come within speaking distance of the motorcar.

"I can't find the Major," he called. "Do you have him in custody? Or has he gone away? Back to London?"

"I haven't arrested him. Or anyone else. When did you see him last?" Rutledge waited, giving the rector time to catch his breath and interested to see how he would explain himself without admitting to speaking to Russell in the church last night. But Morrison answered without prevaricating, indicating no confession had taken place after all.

"He came to the church last evening, quite catching me by surprise, and we talked. Why didn't you tell me he was in Furnham?" Without waiting for an answer, Morrison went on. "He was in a shocking state, and I didn't know who he was at first—the scratches on his face, all the blood on his clothing—he looked like a scarecrow. But he explained about the motorcycle and why the police were hunting for him. He also told me about the clinic. To tell you the truth, I can't see that it's doing him any good."

"Where did he go when he left the church?"

"I took him to the Rectory. He needed a bath, a shave, and a night's sleep. But he couldn't sleep. After pacing for an hour or more, he came to my room and asked if I'd bring him some food this morning to the house. I didn't think it was a very good idea for him to leave in the middle of the night, and I told him so. He promised to reconsider. But five minutes later, I heard the door open and close. I got up and looked out the window, and he had set out on foot—to River's Edge, or so I thought. But he's not there. And I'm worried."

"What time of night was it when he left?"

"I don't know. A little after one o'clock, I suspect?"

But Rutledge had waited until well after two.

"How long would it take Russell to reach the house, if he took a shortcut through the marshes?"

"I'm not sure. At a guess, no more than half an hour? I'm really not very familiar with the marshes. Walking around in all that tall grass makes me claustrophobic. Forty-five minutes if he went by the road. What ought we to do?"

"Leave your bicycle here. I'll drive."

Morrison hesitated, then set the bicycle by the side of the road before joining Rutledge in the motorcar.

"Which door did you try?"

"He told me to come around to the terrace overlooking the water. He'd be waiting for me there. But he wasn't. The door was ajar, I thought he was inside, that tired as he was, he might still be asleep. I called several times, and then went to look for him. I disliked walking in unannounced, I can tell you. Still, I searched, and there was no indication that he'd slept in a bed. I left as quickly as I could, to find you."

They drove in silence until they had reached the gates. Rutledge said, "We'll leave the motorcar outside."

It was easy to see that Morrison had been here this morning. A new path had been beaten through the undergrowth. But then the rector hadn't been concerned with being seen.

Rutledge led the way, and when they reached the terrace, he pointed to the edge of the lawns. "If you've searched the house, then we should begin with any shortcut the Major could have taken."

"That looks promising. See over to the left of that stunted tree? I should think you could make your way in just there."

They walked to the stunted tree. "Ah—someone has been through here, and fairly recently. Those broken stems haven't withered in the morning sun." Rutledge touched one of them.

"Haven't they? No, you're right. Although I should think it was a dog that came through, not a man."

"Let's see how far in it goes."

"Perhaps I should wait out here. In the event you can't find your way out again."

Rutledge stepped into the thick grasses that quickly yielded to reeds. He was a tall man, but the fronds moving in the light breeze were chest-high in places, and several times brushed his face. For a while he believed he was following where someone had walked before him, and then twice lost the trail and had to cast about to find it again.

Morrison called anxiously, "Anything?"

"Nothing."

"Perhaps he decided to go back to the church ruins. It was closer. And he was used to it."

"I was just there. So was Jessup. But not the Major."

He moved on, using his sense of direction to guide him toward the road he couldn't see, keeping the water on his right.

He'd gone perhaps three hundred yards into the grass when he realized that the track no longer led anywhere. Stopping, he looked about.

"I've been following a false trail," he said aloud, irritated. "There must be another way in."

Hamish answered him. "Nearer to the drive?"

"Yes, very likely."

Morrison called, "What have you found? Who are you talking to?"

Rutledge shook his head and began to make his way back, trying to follow the bent grass stems that had marked his progress. A hare broke cover just in front of him, tearing off in a zigzag before darting into a thicker clump of reeds and disappearing.

He changed his mind after some ten yards, and cut toward the water, where he thought it might be less confining. Once more he had to force his way through, but he did find that a muddy water line where the river lapped into the weeds provided damp but easier going. It turned out to be better than the original track he'd taken. Once back at the lawns, he could start again.

Coming to a thin stream, drainage that fed into the river, he saw that just beyond was a larger inlet where the river had eroded the land. Swearing, he realized that to ford it, he would have to wade. There was nothing for it but to strike out inland once more. He quickly discovered that he would be wiser to follow the inlet a short distance or fight his way through a thicker stand of reeds.

The print of a boot in the soft earth warned him that he wasn't the first to come this way recently. It was very like the one he'd seen on the floor of the garden room, but not sharp enough to be definitive.

Casting about for more, he found the Major some ten paces farther on.

Russell was lying on his side, curled into a fetal position, as if he had been in great pain, and Rutledge could see the spread of a blood-stain on the back of his coat.

He shouted to Morrison and bent over the body. It was cold to the touch as he reached out to roll the Major onto his back. And then Russell groaned, without opening his eyes.

"My God, is he alive?" Morrison asked, starting toward Rutledge.

"Go to one of the sheds. Find something we can use to bring him out. He's bleeding and in a bad way. Be quick about it!"

Rutledge was already ripping open the man's shirt to get a better look at his wound. And it was a gunshot wound to the chest. High enough not to kill straightaway, to the side where the ribs might not have protected the lung. There was a chance. Slim, but they had to hurry.

There was no doctor in Furnham, and Rutledge doubted that Tilbury could deal with such a wound. London, then. If Russell could be kept alive that long. And that appeared to be very doubtful.

Morrison came finally with a heavy horse blanket, struggling through the marsh grass, losing his way once but grimly persevering. His face was flushed and set from the effort. They got Russell onto it and managed between them to carry him as far as the lawns.

Bent over, his hands on his knees as he fought for breath, Morrison said, "We'll never make it to your motorcar. Just the two of us?"

"We have to try," Rutledge said bleakly, and they lifted the corners of the blanket again. The overgrown lawn was easier, but the drive was daunting.

Russell wasn't a light man. They were both breathing hard and sweating heavily by the time they reached the gates, their coats left where they dropped them, shirtsleeves rolled to the elbow. The grass and thick undergrowth of the drive seemed to be diabolically intent on making every step twice as difficult as it should have been.

Collecting himself, Morrison said, "We've probably killed him. I'm afraid to look."

"Out there where I found him, he'd have died regardless. This is the only chance he has." Rutledge hesitated, conscious of Hamish's firm grip on the rear seat, and then he said, "In the back with him. Are you coming? I can't make good time without you."

"Yes, of course."

It took precious minutes and an energy they no longer possessed, but in the end Russell was settled in the motorcar, supported by Morrison.

Rutledge ran back to retrieve their coats and then they set out for London.

Miraculously, Russell was still alive—and still unconscious—by the time they had reached the nearest hospital of any size on the outskirts of the city.

Hamish was saying, "Ye ken, the first time he wasna' hurt. This time . . ."

His voice faded as Rutledge sprinted into Casualty and brought nurses and a wheeled examining table back with him.

As the medical staff took over, Morrison sank into the nearest chair. "My God," he said. "I don't know when I've been so completely exhausted. Do you think he'll pull through? Or at least wake up long enough to be questioned?"

Rutledge, pacing the floor, said, "I'd give much to find out who shot the man."

"Don't ask me," Morrison said. "You're the policeman."

"He's been lying there for hours. Possibly since the middle of the night. Or else someone came to the house this morning. From the look of the wound, my guess is last night. The blood in his clothing had dried a little."

"I didn't hear a shot fired."

"You wouldn't, indoors, if the wind was the other way." Nor had he, Rutledge thought, which meant that it must have been fired after he'd left River's Edge.

"Yes, I suppose you're right—" Morrison broke off as a doctor came through the door where Russell had been taken, glanced around, and then spoke to Rutledge.

"You're the man who brought in the gunshot victim?"

"Inspector Rutledge. Scotland Yard. Yes."

"Dr. Wade. It's not as bad as it could have been. Dehydration. Loss of blood. Damage to the ribs, the left lung nicked. Somehow the bullet missed the major arteries, and he's got a fair chance of surviving. What happened?" He looked the two men up and down. Rutledge realized that he and Morrison were in a sorry state.

"We don't know yet. We found him in the marshes up the River Hawking. I'd like to speak to him. Is he awake?"

"We've already given him a sedative to help with the pain. I'm sorry."

"You didn't find the bullet?"

"No, it went straight through. But judging from the wound, my guess is that it was a .45 caliber. An inch either way, and he'd be dead. What's more, he was shot in the back. Cowardly thing to do."

Rutledge said, "It was dark. And a warm night. He was wearing his coat, unbuttoned—it was that way when I found him. In the high grass he'd have made a very poor target at any distance. How long ago? Could you tell us roughly when he was shot?"

"From the clotting around the wound, I'd guess around three in the morning. Give or take an hour. He was cut and scraped as well. An earlier accident, was it? Or a drunken brawl?"

"He ran a Triumph into a ditch."

"Yes, that fits."

"Major Russell also suffered a head wound in the war. He's sometimes confused."

"I noticed that as well. He's lived a charmed life, the Major has. I don't think he'll be riding his Triumph again anytime soon. With that head wound, he really shouldn't be riding one at all."

Rutledge indicated Morrison. "This man is the Major's priest. I should like to leave him here, in the event that Russell comes to his senses and can describe his attacker. Will you see to it that Mr. Morrison is allowed to stay with him at all times?"

Morrison was on his feet, about to protest. "I'm needed—Mrs. Barber—"

"In good time," Rutledge finished for him. "I have to leave, but I'll be back by late afternoon." He turned back to Dr. Wade. "Is there anything else you can tell me?"

"Sorry, no. Not at this time. It's a watching brief at the moment, with surgery a possibility if those ribs press into the lung or there's more internal bleeding. He's lost enough blood that I'd rather not risk costing him more. We'll see."

Rutledge thanked him and left. Morrison, resigned, walked with him to the door.

"Should I ask for a constable to come in and sit with Russell? Or bring in a sister to hear whatever he has to say?"

"He's not confessing, Rector. Either he can identify his assailant or he can't. If he dies, we're back to where we began. If he names someone and then dies, you're a reliable witness."

"Yes, I see. I must admit," he said wryly, "I'm still a little shaken. Seminary doesn't prepare one for police duties."

Rutledge smiled. He cranked the motorcar and got in as Morrison hurried back into Casualty to begin his watch.

But he sat there for fully five minutes after the rector had closed the door behind him.

There hadn't been time to go back into the house and look at the contents of the gun case.

There was also the fact that Jessup had been waiting for him at the ruins of the old church. Had he discovered that Russell had been hiding there? And had he come to gloat, because he knew that Russell was now lying in the marsh near River's Edge? It would fit. But why should he wish to shoot Russell?

It was Hamish who answered that. "Ye ken, in the dark, he thought the Major was you."

Rutledge let out the clutch and drove on to his flat to change his torn and bloody clothes.

He went to The Marlborough Hotel and put in a call to the Yard, asking for Sergeant Gibson.

Gibson was not at present in the building, he was told.

So much for the information that Rutledge needed.

He rang off, left the hotel, and drove back through London to the hospital where he'd taken Major Russell.

When he found his way to the ward where the patient had been transferred, he saw Morrison sitting next to the Major's bed. Rutledge thought the rector was asleep in his chair, but as he came down the aisle, Morrison looked up. He waited until Rutledge was standing by his side to say quietly, "He was awake. Briefly. I don't think he knew where he was or why."

"It could be that he will recall more details later. How is he?"

"The doctors are worried about infection. Where he was lying was not helpful on that score. Damp, marshy land, and God knows what festering in it. Otherwise the wound appears to be clean enough. And they don't believe there's as much internal bleeding as they feared in the beginning. He has a fair chance of making it."

"He's lucky his assailant was a poor shot. Or possibly he came up on Russell sooner than he'd expected—" He broke off as he saw Russell's eyelids fluttering.

And then he was fully awake, grimacing in pain. Recognizing Rutledge, his gaze swung around the room, eyes wide with alarm. Then he made a sudden movement, as if to sit up, and sucked in a breath between teeth clenched in a grimace as he fought the fire that seemed to explode in his shoulder. Sweat broke out on his forehead, and he lowered himself gently onto the pillows again.

"Lie still," Rutledge admonished him. "The doctors are worried enough, and so am I."

"The motorcycle?" Russell asked, his voice rough and without much force. It was clear that he had lost track of everything since going into the ditch with the Triumph.

"You survived that well enough. Someone tried to kill you at River's Edge. You're in a London hospital where you were brought from there. Do you remember anything at all about going to the house?"

The Major struggled to assimilate that bit of information. Finally he managed to say, his gaze on Rutledge's face, "Shot?" as if it was as alien as the fact that he didn't recognize his surroundings. "When?"

"Last night. Do you remember sleeping in the church ruins outside Furnham? Being brought your meals by Nancy Brothers?" It took some time to take Russell step-by-step from the crash of the Trusty to leaving the Rectory in the middle of the night. Finally Rutledge asked, "Who shot you? Do you know?"

He shook his head slightly, as if afraid the movement would bring back the fierce pain. "He—betrayed me," he said, his gaze moving on to Morrison's face.

"In point of fact, he probably saved your life. He came for me when he couldn't find you this morning."

"Told me—he told me he couldn't lie if you asked—if you asked where I was."

"If we hadn't found you in the marsh, you'd be dead by now. As it was, it was a close run thing."

One hand lifted vaguely in the direction of his chest. "Dying?"

"Probably not. But we need to know who shot you. Do you remember anything?"

"Nothing."

"If there's anything on your conscience, I'd advise you to clear it. Morrison will hear your confession, if you like."

Russell closed his eyes. "Hurts. The very devil."

He asked Morrison to summon one of the nursing sisters. When he was out of earshot, Rutledge said in a low voice, "Before I go, I must ask you. It's my duty. Did you kill Justin Fowler?"

"God, no."

"Did you kill Ben Willet?"

"Told you. No. Refused."

Hamish said, "Do you believe him?"

Rutledge didn't answer him. Morrison was coming back with the sister, and she carried a tray with water and a small medicine cup.

Russell's good hand tried to clutch at Rutledge's arm, his fingers grasping at air.

"As I fell. Silhouette. I remember now." He paused, and when the sister was about to hold the water to his lips, Russell shook his head, still watching Rutledge's face. "Am I—will they send me back to St. Margaret's?"

"Speak to Dr. Wade. He will have to work that out."

Yet Rutledge understood how the Major felt about the clinic. He himself had left Fleming's clinic a month before the doctor felt he was ready. And the doctor, as it turned out, was right, he hadn't been prepared for Warwickshire.

Russell leaned back, taking the medicine the sister had brought. Rutledge waited until he had swallowed it, and then he left, promising Morrison to drive him back to Essex as soon as possible.

As he walked back to where he had left his motorcar, he debated his next move. And he came to a conclusion. He drove back to the center of London and once more availed himself of The Marlborough Hotel's telephone, reluctantly shutting himself into the tiny closet and putting in a call to someone he knew in the War Office.

George Munro listened to what Rutledge had to say, then replied, "Do you know what you're asking?"

"I do. A great deal of time and work. My present inquiry revolves around finding the answer. "

He could hear the sigh down the line. "I know. I owe you, Ian. I'll do it."

"Thank you." He put up the receiver.

George Munro had been a fellow officer during the third battle of the Somme. The bullet that tore through the femoral artery in his leg should have killed him. But Rutledge had managed to stop the bleeding and drag him back to his own lines, sending him to a forward dressing station where a doctor named MacPherson and three nursing sisters had saved Munro's life—and more important than that to Munro, his leg. He walked with a permanent limp thereafter and had complained bitterly when he was sent to the War Office after his release from hospital rather than back to the front lines. In the end, he'd stayed in the Army and at the War Office, glad of the decision that had taken him where his knowledge of strategy and tactics had seen him promoted.

Meanwhile, his wife had named their first son Ian MacPherson, in gratitude for her husband's life.

He had been absent from the Yard long enough. Reluctantly Rutledge left his motorcar in the street and climbed the stairs to his office.

No one seemed to have noticed his absence. Gibson had come in and taken several of the files on his desk, replacing them at some point with several more. He sat down and scanned them, added his signature to two, and noted that two others were ready to be filed.

Someone tapped at his door, and Sergeant Gibson came in.

"Sir. Constable Greene told me he thought he'd seen you."

"What news is there of Chief Superintendent Bowles?"

"Resting comfortably. It was a near run thing. It appears now that he'll live. But whether he'll come back to the Yard—or when—is uncertain at best."

"What do the Yard punters have to say?"

Gibson grinned sheepishly. "As to that, sir, it's currently five to one against his returning. Much of that may be wishful thinking."

Rutledge smiled.

"Superintendent Williamson has taken over as of this morning, and Chief Superintendent Bowles has been placed on medical leave for the present."

Rutledge had not had many dealings with Williamson. The jury was out on whether he was a good man kept on a short leash by Bowles, or whether he was a weaker imitation of Bowles.

"At any rate," Gibson was saying, "we're to go on as we were. Any questions, his door is open. Otherwise, he expects us to do our duty as if the Chief Superintendent is here."

Rather trusting of him, Rutledge thought, but said nothing. The Yard as a whole was professional and responsible. And Williamson was wise not to appear too eager to step into his predecessor's empty boots.

It was clear that Gibson was waiting for him to comment.

"Good man," he said, then asked, "Any progress on the requests I've put in?"

Gibson frowned. "I've not been able to find this Justin Fowler. He appears to have dropped out of sight. Last known address as far as I can judge was River's Edge, the Furnham Road, Essex."

And that would fit with what Rutledge had been told, that Justin Fowler had been the last to leave the house, save for Finley, the driver. Had he felt obliged to go so that the house could be closed, the servants released from their duties?

"Where did he go when on leave?" Hamish asked.

His family home in Colchester had been sold, the money put in trust for him. And it was doubtful that he would have wished to return there, given the memories of his parents' deaths in the house. Unless he'd taken a flat or bought a house in London, River's Edge was his home.

Was that why he had gone there while on leave in 1915? Because he needed to remember a happier time before the war? He couldn't have stayed there, but he could have spent a few hours on the grounds or in the house, if he still had a key.

And that brought up another problem Rutledge hadn't considered until now. How had Fowler reached the River Hawkins?

Aware that Sergeant Gibson was still talking, Rutledge said, "Sorry! I was fitting together pieces of the puzzle. Go on."

Gibson said, "Have you spoken to Miss Farraday or Major Russell? I should think they ought to know where Fowler is."

"They've been less than helpful. If he's alive, where is Fowler now? If he's dead, why hasn't it been reported?"

"In my view, sir—for what it's worth—you must assume the worst."

Twenty minutes later, Rutledge set the last of the folders in the basket for filing. There had been no telephone call from Munro, although he'd given the man more than an hour. Not a good sign, as Hamish was pointing out.

There was one other person he needed to speak to before he went back to the hospital and from there to Essex.

Miss Farraday was at home. She said, when he was shown into her sitting room, "I've had enough unpleasant news. I hope you aren't here to add to that."

"Where did Justin Fowler live, after the house at River's Edge was closed?"

"He went into the Army in late September, I think it was, and on his first leave he took rooms at the Prince Frederick Hotel. He invited me to dinner one night, and we talked. Mostly about the Army and about our years at River's Edge. I asked if he'd like me to write to him, and he said he thought it would be better if I didn't. He was still quite upset about Aunt Elizabeth's disappearance. I think one of the reasons he stayed on at the house after Wyatt and I left was the hope she might come back and someone ought to be there if she did."

"And after that?"

"The Prince Frederick was flattened in one of the Zeppelin raids, worst luck, because in my opinion, the hotel restaurant was the best in London. I don't know where he stayed after that or even if he came to London at all. If he did, he never got in touch with me. His name never appeared on the lists of killed, wounded, and missing. I've heard since that not all of the missing and dead were ever accounted for." She looked away. "Perhaps he found someone he liked and spent every minute of any leaves with her."

He detected the faintest note of jealousy.

"His solicitors have had no word of him. I've spoken to them."

There was a sadness in her voice that she couldn't quite conceal.

"Justin went his own way, and Wyatt has been damaged by the war. Ben is dead. It makes me aware of how fleeting life is. How little we can hold on to anyone or anything. I wish I could understand why he'd been the way he was. What the shadows were in his life."

It wasn't his place to tell her about Justin Fowler's past. But he said, "Something happened before he came to River's Edge. The shadows were there before you knew him."

She nodded. "Thank you for telling me that. It helps. I always had the feeling that he was waiting. For something to happen or someone to come. It was one of the reasons he didn't go into Furnham. He liked the isolation of River's Edge. He told Aunt Elizabeth once that he felt safe there. I know, because I happened to overhear him."

He thought about the boy Justin Fowler had been. His parents had been murdered, he himself had nearly been killed. Was he afraid that the unknown killer would come for him one day and finish what he'd begun? It was a dreadful burden for a child to bear.

"If he went to River's Edge on one of his leaves, how would he have got there?"

"Aunt Elizabeth's motorcar. Harold Finley brought it to London when he enlisted and stored it in the mews behind Wyatt's house. All of us used it from time to time. Mostly it just sat there, of course. But I drove it to Dover once, and another time to Cornwall for a friend's wedding."

"Do you remember who used it in the summer of 1915?"

"No, of course not. Not now. I can tell you that the few times I wished to borrow it, it was always there in the mews."

As he rose to leave, she said, "There's something I just remembered. The first warm weather we had, after he'd come to River's Edge, we went swimming in the river. I saw Justin's chest. It was horribly scarred. I asked him what caused them. He said he'd been in hospital for a long time. I thought he meant he'd had some sort of surgery. It explained how pale and thin he was. I was young, easily put off.

But I realize now the scars were not the sort that come from surgery. I helped with the wounded during the war—reading to them, writing letters, keeping their minds off their suffering. It never occurred to me at the time—those scars of his were *wounds*."

He said nothing.

"Did his parents—were *they* responsible?"

"Not his parents," Rutledge replied. "A stranger."

"Dear God. I wish someone had told me. I wish I'd *known*."

"I don't think Mrs. Russell wanted you to know. She understood that it was important to forget."

"But did she tell Wyatt?"

"Probably not. For the same reason."

She took a deep breath. "If you find him, will you let me know—if he's all right?"

"If that's what he wants me to do."

And she had to be satisfied with that.

# 19

The first person Rutledge met as he walked into the hospital was a nursing sister he had dealt with earlier. As they walked together to the ward where the Major was being kept under observation, he asked if there had been any change in his condition.

She reported, "He's been rather restless, and the doctors are quite concerned about a fever. That would mean infection. He needs sleep, but he keeps trying to remember what happened to him." She paused, then said diplomatically, "It might be best if the rector left for a time. There would be less temptation to talk."

Russell had in fact dropped into a light sleep when Rutledge walked into the ward. Morrison was not there, and so Rutledge took the empty chair by the bed.

He himself had left River's Edge at a little after two the previous night. And he had seen no one, had heard no shots. Morrison had told him that the Major had left the Rectory after one o'clock. Where had he been between half past one and half past two? Or to look at this problem another way, who had encountered Russell on the road—or in the marshes? Was it a planned meeting—or simply opportune?

Who came to the house at night, who kept those terrace doors unlocked for easy access to the guns in the study? Who stood by the landing stage and stared out over the river to the far side, as if lord of all he surveyed?

The only people who were usually abroad late at night were the smugglers.

And while they wouldn't brook any interference in their business, it seemed unlikely that they would go out of their way to stalk Major Russell through the marshes.

Although Timothy Jessup might well have his own reasons for seeing that River's Edge remained closed. Hadn't he asked if Rutledge was interested in the property? On that first encounter when he was here with Frances?

Perhaps it was time to find out who would inherit River's Edge if the last of the Russells died. Rutledge realized he knew very little about the Major's father, who had been killed in the Boer War. Cynthia Farraday was distantly related to him. Who else might be? Surely not Jessup. But stranger things had happened. Men sometimes committed indiscretions in their youth—witness Justin Fowler's father—that they kept firmly locked away in their past.

Dr. Wade, Rutledge thought, was right. The Major seemed to live a charmed life. The war wound, the motorcycle crash, and now this gunshot. Any one of them should have killed him.

Hamish said, "He willna' escape the hangman."

"We must prove he killed Fowler first."

He was suddenly aware that the Major was awake and staring up at him. His first thought was that he'd answered Hamish aloud, without thinking.

Russell said after a moment, "Have you come back—or have you never left?"

"I was at the Yard. Where is Morrison?"

"He went to the canteen. He wanted a cup of tea."

"Just as well. Do you feel like talking?"

"Not particularly."

"If you had died of this gunshot wound, who stands to inherit River's Edge?"

"I made a will leaving it to my wife. After she died, I left everything to Cynthia. Why?"

"Are there any other cousins?"

"I don't know. I don't remember much about my father. Or his side of the family for that matter. A grandmother, I think, when I was very young. She read to me, and I remember her voice, not her face."

"Do you know where Justin Fowler stayed, when he was on leave during the war?"

"There was a hotel in London he liked. A little out of the way for my tastes, but it suited him, he said. Cynthia went there to dine with him, I think. But don't trust that memory. I was jealous and could have imagined it."

"I'm told the hotel was destroyed in a Zeppelin raid."

"Was it?"

"Did he go back to River's Edge, after it was closed?"

"I ran into him in France and he told me he'd gone down to Essex a last time before being sent over with his regiment. That it was all right. I'd heard that one of the raids had taken out a windmill and some houses, but he told me that that was on the Blackwater. Or maybe the Crouch. I don't remember."

"When was this?"

"Early in 1915, I think. He'd seen some fighting, and I was in the relief column. He told me he'd borrowed my motorcar and driven out to Essex."

"Did he stay at the house? Or just spend a few hours there?"

"He built a fire in my mother's sitting room, he said. It was damned cold, the house had been shut up for months. He'd brought tea in a Thermos and a packet of sandwiches, and he ate them by the fire rather than on the terrace as he'd planned. I asked if the chimneys were all right—I didn't relish the idea of the house burning down. But he'd checked them first, he said, and made certain the fire was out before leaving."

"When next did you see or hear from him?"

"Someone told me he'd been wounded. Late May? It earned him a ticket home, I expect. He wrote once from hospital. He'd heard that we were expecting a child, my wife and I. They'd done surgery on his knee and he was hoping to be released for duty by late August. He told me he might drive down to Essex again, if he could manage it." Russell lay still, closing his eyes. "I never heard from him again as far as I recall. But letters get lost."

"Do you know if he survived the war?"

"You must ask Cynthia that. She kept track of both of us and Harold Finley as well. Why the interest in Justin? You don't think *he* shot me, do you?" He had opened his eyes, his gaze fixed on Rutledge. "Why on earth should he do that?"

It was clear that he'd forgot what Rutledge had told him about Willet's confession.

"I'm still investigating Willet's death. Were you in England during that summer of 1915?"

"I was in France. No, that's not true. I was sent home on compassionate leave when my wife died."

"Did you go down to River's Edge? Or look up Fowler in hospital?"

"I don't think so. It was—I don't remember much about that time." He grimaced. "I was ridden by guilt. I hadn't loved her. She died because of me. I didn't think I'd made her happy." He turned his head aside. "Go away. Leave me alone."

Rutledge was on the point of saying something more when Morrison came back.

"There you are," he said, stepping in. "Is he asleep?"

Rutledge answered, "Yes, I think so. The nurse warned me not to disturb his rest. We should leave."

He rose and got Morrison out of the room. Walking to the motorcar, Morrison asked, "Could you talk to him? Did he tell you anything else?"

"Only that he doesn't know what happened to Fowler. It may be that he will never be able to remember. If he's guilty of murdering him, Russell could well go free."

Morrison digested that, then said, "You don't intend to take him into custody?"

"Suspicion isn't truth. I need facts."

Morrison cranked the motorcar for Rutledge and then got in. "How, I wonder, did Ben learn about Fowler's death and Russell's role in it?"

"I don't know. But the fact that he did tells me that whatever happened, happened in River's Edge. Or somewhere along the Hawking. Not in London or Dover or Portsmouth. I told you before I don't believe in coincidence. And it would have been difficult to kill someone and get rid of the body where hundreds of men are collecting and boarding their transports. But the River Hawking is rather isolated. If it swallowed up Mrs. Russell, it could swallow Fowler just as easily."

"Then why wasn't Willet killed in Essex as well?"

"I haven't worked that out yet. Perhaps someone didn't want him to reach Essex."

"We don't know he was intending to go there."

"I've discovered that he was."

That silenced Morrison. After a time, he said, "I'm tired. I'll shut my eyes for a bit, if you don't mind." He leaned his head against the window strut.

Rutledge was grateful for the chance to think. With his eyes on the road, he let his mind review everything he knew.

Hamish said, "There's no answer."

"Exactly. And there's only one reason I can think of to explain that. Somewhere is a piece of the puzzle we haven't found. Not yet. And I'm not sure where to look."

"Aye. Ye must start at the beginning."

By the time he'd passed the gates of River's Edge and made the turning to the Rectory, Morrison was awake and complaining of being stiff.

He said, preparing to get out of the motorcar, "I never thought he would live."

"Nor did I. But if he had died, the inquiry on Justin Fowler would have to be closed. Without Willet and without Russell, there is no case."

Morrison shook his head. "I watched you question a man who was in great pain. How do you live with the fact that the person you take into custody will be tried and judged and very likely hanged? Do you never feel merciful?"

"It's not a question of mercy. I don't judge people. I leave that to the courts. It's my task to collect the facts that will help them arrive at the truth."

"That's very self-righteous, don't you think?"

And then he was gone, shutting the Rectory door behind him.

Rutledge continued into Furnham, realized he'd eaten nothing since breakfast, and stopped by the tea shop-cum-bakery. But it was already closed, and he went on to the inn.

The clerk told him that he hadn't asked for dinner, and so there was none to be had. But when Rutledge offered to pay him well for a meal, he agreed to prepare something. When the tray was brought to his room, Rutledge found under the cloth covering several sandwiches, a dish of fruit, and a square of cheese with rather stale biscuits.

He ate his meal sitting by the window, where the cool evening air made him drowsy. Setting the empty dishes outside his door, he went to bed.

But the drowsiness seemed to evaporate as soon as he blew out the lamp and got into bed.

Instead, his mind went over and over what he knew about the three murders and the attack on Russell. And he didn't like what he was beginning to conclude.

Cynthia Farraday had wanted River's Edge, but not its owner. It would have been easy for her to murder the unsuspecting Mrs. Russell. But despite his protestation of his love, Wyatt Russell married someone else for the sake of an heir. If that was her motive, it didn't make sense for her to kill Fowler or Ben Willet.

Wyatt Russell had the best motive—jealousy. He could have killed the men he perceived to be his rivals. But why kill his own mother?

Jessup, for reasons of his own, could have killed Mrs. Russell, her son, and his own nephew. But why murder Fowler?

And if the person who killed Fowler's parents intended to return one day and murder the son as well, why had it been necessary to kill the Russells and Ben Willet?

Was it possible that there were two people at work here?

He was close to the answer when sleep overtook him.

And then he was back in France, the sound of the guns loud in his ears, the screams of the wounded and the dying all around him while the machine gunners whittled away the numbers coming toward them until only Rutledge was left on his feet, and struggling through the mud toward the gunners, his revolver in his hand and determination giving him the strength to keep going despite the bullets plowing into his body. But when he reached the nest, there was only one gunner, nothing but bones grinning at him from behind the gun sight. And Hamish's voice at his ear was shouting to him, trying to make him understand that he too was dead.

"Fall down and let it be over," the Scots voice cried. "For God's sake, let it be over!"

Rutledge fought against it, clinging to life, struggling against the darkness that was overwhelming him, reaching out for a handhold and unable to find it. For he could see that the River Somme was filled with blood, and he would drown in it, in spite of all he could do.

With a shock he came wide awake, wrestling the bedclothes, crying out in the darkness.

He could feel the cold sweat drying on his body, and his chest was heaving as he tried to breathe again.

In the quiet room, unseen, Hamish said, "It will never go away. Not even when ye die. The dead dream too."

He got out of bed and thrust his head out the window, letting the night air blow away the last remnants of the night terror.

Finally he dressed and went out to walk until the sun brightened the horizon, not caring if the smugglers had made a run in the night. It wasn't until he could see his hand clearly before his face that he went back to his room and, without undressing, fell into a deep sleep.

In the morning he went to see Nancy Brothers, spending half an hour in her pleasant kitchen, and when he had the information he wanted, he thanked her and left.

And then, because he didn't think he could spend another night in the room at The Dragonfly Inn, he packed his valise and drove out of Furnham.

When he finally reached London, he went directly to Somerset House and began his search.

The first name on his list was Mrs. Broadley, the cook at River's Edge. According to Nancy Brothers, she had gone to live with her sister when the house was closed.

He hadn't expected to encounter quite so many Broadleys, but it appeared to be a fairly common name in some counties. Finally he found the one he was after.

She had died in a village north of Derby during the influenza epidemic of 1918.

He turned next to Mrs. Dunner, who had taken another post in the Midlands.

There was no record of her death. And he had the address that Mrs. Brothers had given him.

The last name on his list was the young chauffeur, Harold Finley.

There was no record of his death.

It had taken him two hours, but he felt satisfied with the results.

On a whim, he also looked for Gladys Mitchell, Fowler's first wife. Her death was recorded here, and he jotted down in his notebook the name of the sanitarium.

He found the name of her husband in the marriage records and looked at his death date.

He had died in prison, just as the solicitor in Colchester had said.

If there was a child, he couldn't find it.

Satisfied, he thanked the clerk who had been assisting him and left.

At the Yard, he went to a telephone, and after some effort on the part of the operator, he found the house in the Midlands where Mrs. Dunner had taken up another position. When he was put through to the number, a butler answered, and Rutledge identified himself before asking for Mrs. Dunner.

"I'm sorry, Inspector. Mrs. Dunner is no longer housekeeper here. She is now the housekeeper for Mr. and Mrs. Linton's daughter, who lives in London."

"Is she indeed?" Rutledge asked, relieved to be spared the long drive north. "I should like her direction, if you please."

The butler told him, then inquired, "Is there any problem concerning Mrs. Dunner? She's always been an exemplary employee."

"Not at all. We are looking for information about a family she once worked for in Essex. We're hoping she can help us locate other members of the staff at that time."

The butler thanked him and rang off.

Rutledge looked at the address in his hand. Belvedere Place.

Cynthia Farraday hadn't chosen a house at random when she was intent on eluding him. She had chosen the residence where Mrs. Dunner was employed. It was not surprising that the constable he'd spoken to hadn't recognized Miss Farraday's name. She didn't live there and she wasn't a regular visitor to the Linton family. Hamish was echoing his own thinking: Miss Farraday was too clever by far.

By the time he'd reached Belvedere Place, it was nearly the dinner hour, but he lifted the elegant knocker, and when a maid in a starched black uniform opened the door, he stated his business.

She hesitated, repeating "Inspector Rutledge? Of Scotland Yard? To see Mrs. Dunner?"

He was tired and felt an urge to ask if any of the silver had gone missing, but resisted the temptation. Instead he repeated what he'd told the butler in the Midlands.

"The family has only just gone in to dinner." She looked over her shoulder, then said, "If you'll come this way?"

She led him through to the servants' quarters, and tapped on the door of the housekeeper's small room. Mrs. Dunner was just finishing her accounts, and she looked up as the maid came in. She was tall and slim, her dark hair only beginning to show gray, although he thought she must be well into her fifties.

"What is it, Daisy?"

"An Inspector Rutledge from Scotland Yard to speak to you, Mrs. Dunner."

"Thank you, Daisy. They will be looking for you in the kitchen, I think."

The maid nodded and went away as Mrs. Dunner invited Rutledge into her room and shut the door behind him. "What has brought you to Belvedere Place, Inspector? Is there a problem with one of our staff?"

"Not at all," he assured her. "It's about the staff at River's End. I've spoken to Nancy Brothers, and now to you."

"How is Nancy?" she asked. "I had hoped to hear from her from time to time, but she's never written to me."

"I expect she's been busy."

"Yes, I'm sure. Does she have any children, do you know?"

"I don't believe she has."

"A pity. And now you have found me as well. What is it you need to know about River's Edge? I believe the house has been closed since the war began. What interest does Scotland Yard have in it?"

But he thought she knew what he was about to ask her.

"You were there when Mrs. Russell disappeared?"

"I was. It was a terrible day. I don't think I shall ever forget it."

"What do you believe happened to her?"

"The most obvious conclusion was suicide, of course. But I could never reconcile myself to that. I found it hard to believe in murder, as well. Still, it seemed to be the most logical explanation."

"Why murder?"

"Because Mrs. Russell wouldn't have deserted her children. Yes, I know what was said about her belief that her son would die in the war that was coming. And I can tell you it was very distressing for her. She'd lost her husband. The thought of losing Mr. Wyatt as well was insupportable. There was no question but that he would join the Army once war was declared. He was his father's son. She couldn't forbid it. She was trying to make peace with her fears."

"Did you tell the police what you believed?"

"I didn't feel it was my place to stir up more trouble for the family."

"If you were willing to consider murder, there must have been someone you believed was capable of it. Who could have wished her dead?"

There were tears in her eyes as she answered him. "That's just it, you see. I couldn't imagine it. Not one of the staff, certainly. All of us had been with her for years. Everyone that is but Harold Finley, but he was a quiet, responsible young man. And as for the people in Furnham, why should they want to harm her?"

"What about the family?"

He could see a shocked expression in her eyes.

"Justin Fowler, for one," he suggested.

"Oh, no, not Mr. Justin."

"Why not?"

"Poor child, he had nightmares when he first came to us. Mrs. Russell would go in and wake him up, then comfort him. It was terrible. My room was just over his, and I could hear his screams. Some nights she got no sleep."

"Did her son or Miss Farraday know about this? Were they jealous, do you think?"

"How could they be? Mrs. Russell had put him in a room nearest hers, so they wouldn't be disturbed."

"What if they came looking for her, and she wasn't in her room?"

"I doubt that ever happened. Mr. Wyatt was a deep sleeper. As for Miss Farraday, she never was one to need pampering. An independent little thing from the first time I saw her. I was told she was accustomed to her parents going away and leaving her with the servants."

"Did you like her?" he asked, hearing an undertone in her voice.

"Not to say didn't like her. She was such a pretty child, everyone liked her. Still, she wasn't one to come down to the kitchen and beg a treat, or ask me to sew her ribbons on for her. Little things, but they endear a child to you. She lacked that quality."

"Why did Justin Fowler have nightmares?"

"I asked Mrs. Russell, and she told me that he had been ill in hospital and I was not to worry, it would pass when he regained his health. But I always wondered, you know, if his father beat him. He had such fearsome scars. Not to speak out of place—but Mrs. Russell told me she was pleased that he had more of his mother in him than his father. I had the feeling Mr. Fowler had a dark past."

"What sort of past?"

"She never said as much outright, but I gathered Mr. Fowler had been involved with a woman of the streets. It was a reflection on his character."

"Did he marry this woman? Or live with her?"

"He couldn't have married her, could he? She already had a hus-band and a child. It didn't stop him from taking up with her."

It was the first he'd heard of a child. Harrison, the solicitor, had as-sured him there was no issue in the bigamist marriage.

"A child of his? Or by her husband?"

"I should think her husband's. Which made it all the more shock-ing that Mr. Fowler should have anything to do with her."

"A boy or a girl?"

"I don't think Mrs. Russell knew. You must understand, Mrs. Rus-sell never confided in me, but sometimes she'd be distracted and say things, and I had eyes, I could see some things for myself. When Miss Cynthia showed a partiality for Mr. Justin, she worried that he might break her heart. Then he was off to university, and it all blew over. But sometimes the seed doesn't fall far from the tree, as they say."

He was reminded of something. Something Inspector Robinson had said while reviewing the terms of the Fowler wills.

It came back to him then. That Mr. Fowler had supported a charity school in London over the years. An odd choice of interest for a young bachelor reading law.

"Did you keep in touch with the family after the house was closed?"

"Mr. Russell wrote to me once or twice, and Mr. Justin wrote to me before he was sent to France. They were young men, I wasn't sur-prised that there were no more letters after that."

"Did you know Mrs. Broadly was dead?"

"Yes, sadly, her sister wrote to me."

"Did Harold Finley survive the war?"

"I don't believe he did. He wrote to me quite a few times. Very pleasant letters they were too. He came to see me in early summer, 1915. He'd been wounded— when the caisson he was in charge of was blown up, it crashed into his leg, breaking it. I thought he looked tired and still in pain, with a nasty limp. He said he was eager to get back to

France. I wished him well. That was the last I heard from him." She picked up her pen and put it down again. "I was very fond of him. If I'd been blessed with a son, I would have wished to have one just like Harold."

"Where did he come from?"

"He was from Norwich, I believe. You haven't told me why you are reopening the inquiry into Mrs. Russell's disappearance. Or why Scotland Yard should take an interest in it."

He decided to tell her the truth, about Ben Willet and his visit to the Yard as Wyatt Russell.

"That's Ned Willet's boy, isn't it? The fisherman. But why should he do such a thing? I can't believe it."

"He was found dead a fortnight later, and he was wearing this." He handed her the locket.

After looking at it, she raised her eyes to his. "It's Mrs. Russell's. But that's not the photograph she kept in it." She was silent, then she said, "He couldn't have killed her. He was only a *boy*."

"A gold necklace must have been tempting even to a boy, when his family was struggling to keep food on the table."

"But he kept it, didn't he, he didn't buy bread with it."

When Rutledge said nothing, she added, "If he'd killed her, then Mr. Wyatt or Mr. Justin would have killed *him*, if they discovered it. What I don't understand is, if it was one of them—Mr. Wyatt or Mr. Justin—why did they leave this locket on his body when they knew how much it meant to her?"

Hamish spoke for the first time. "Because," he said, his voice so clear in Rutledge's mind that it seemed to come from just behind his shoulder, where the young Scot had stood so often during the long watches in the night, "he knew the police would gie it back to him."

## 20

Calling on Mrs. Dunner had been profitable. Rutledge drove to his flat, unpacked his valise, and sat by a window, watching the moths dance futilely around the lamp on the table at his elbow.

He could feel another storm building, and it suited his mood.

The housekeeper's words echoed in his mind.

*What I don't understand is, if it was one of them—Mr. Wyatt or Mr. Justin—why did they leave this locket on his body when they knew how much it meant to her?*

There was another possibility, that the body had gone into the Thames before the locket could be removed. Someone could have come along just after the killer had emptied the dead man's pockets, and the only choice was to let the locket go.

Had Justin Fowler accused Willet of the murder? If so, Willet had had to kill him. And then he had attempted to clear his own name before dying of his cancer by putting the blame squarely on Wyatt Russell.

That at least would go a long way toward explaining the false confession.

*Cynthia's pet...*

Wyatt Russell's words. Was Willet cold-blooded enough to kill Cynthia Farraday's foster mother as well as the man she had grown up with, and still faced himself in the mirror after all Miss Farraday had done for him?

Hamish said, his voice almost inaudible in the rumble of distant thunder, "Sandy Barber killed him to spare his father and sister."

It could be true, if Willet had changed so very much. Kill him before he could come home to Furnham and reveal his true character.

That begged the question of who had tried to kill Wyatt Russell.

Perhaps it wasn't Sandy Barber who had killed Willet. Jessup was fond enough of Abigail to have done the deed to spare her. He too was in a position to intercept any message from the prodigal son. And he could have known more about the book published in France than he'd told anyone.

Whichever way he turned what he knew, Rutledge found that one piece always failed to fit into the puzzle.

Hamish said, "If Willet's murder was blamed on Wyatt, then someone wanted revenge."

And that made sense.

But Rutledge wasn't satisfied.

He watched the storm break over London, watched trees along the street bend before the sudden wind as lightning shattered the darkness and thunder rolled like cannon fire.

There was enough evidence to make an arrest, and Superintendent Bowles would argue that it was the role of the court to sort it all out.

Rutledge had always seen justice differently, that it was the policeman whose duty it was to sift the evidence and bring in the guilty party, while the courts judged whether or not the facts as presented supported punishment according to the law or the release of the accused without prejudice. A test, as it were, of truth. The rector hadn't understood that. Even Mrs. Channing had once questioned why he had chosen the police over following in his father's footsteps in the firm of solicitors.

Old standards died hard. Many people still expected a policeman to come to the servants' entrance where he belonged. But that was the view of a generation ago, and it was changing.

Hamish said, breaking into his thoughts, "You must decide. Which man took the law into his ain hands?"

Jessup? Who had always believed that Ben Willet had made the wrong choice when he left his family and his village? Or Sandy Barber, who loved his wife and would protect her at any price?

There was still no answer.

The next morning Rutledge set out early, driving through rain-washed streets to stop briefly in the Yard. There he put in a telephone call to Mr. Harrison, the solicitor handling the affairs of the late Mr. and Mrs. Fowler.

When Mr. Harrison was brought to the telephone, Rutledge asked what charitable school for boys the Fowlers had supported.

"It's the Jamison Baldridge School," he replied. "Before seeing to the disbursement of the bequest, I took the opportunity to inquire about them. Mr. Baldridge was an MP and close friend of William Gladstone, who encouraged the childless Baldridge to donate large sums to a charity school in London. It's soundly funded and responsibly managed. And so we carried out the elder Mr. Fowler's wishes."

"What was Fowler's interest in it?"

"I'm afraid he never told me. He had begun supporting it before he returned to Colchester."

"What sort of school is it?"

"It is for poor boys without reference to religion, only need and ability. It has a high scholastic standard, and most of the boys have gone on to do well in life. Several have served in the Metropolitan Police, a number went to the Army, there's a clergyman or two, many became teachers, and a few have even gone into service."

"Into service?" Rutledge was surprised.

"One was a valet to a cabinet minister. Another became an estate manager in Scotland."

"And their failures?" Rutledge asked.

"I was led to believe that they did very well too," Harrison replied dryly.

"None in prison, then?"

"If there were, the headmaster never saw fit to mention them."

Rutledge thanked Mr. Harrison for his information and went to find the Jamison Baldridge Charity School for Boys.

It was in a respectable street near St. Paul's Cathedral and had grown considerably since its founder's day. The Victorian brick building was several stores high, with an arched stone doorway resembling a bishop's palace, but rather than saints, the reliefs set into the stone ledge that ran across the front featured classical figures. As he rang the bell, Rutledge recognized Plato and Homer above his head.

A young man dressed in much the same fashion as a student at Harrow or Eton opened the door to him and politely asked his business.

"The Headmaster, if you please. My name is Rutledge."

He was invited into a wide hall, the floor a checkerboard of white and black marble, and the young man excused himself. After several minutes, an older man with the look of a don greeted him and asked his business with Mr. Letherington.

"Scotland Yard. I'm here to inquire about a former student."

"Indeed, Mr. Rutledge. My name is Waring. I can help you with that. Will you come this way?"

He was led down a quiet passage to a small office filled with bookshelves and rows of ledgers.

Waring offered him a chair. "I should like first to ask you why you are inquiring about one of our boys."

"As I understand it, his mother died of consumption and his father died in prison. I don't know that he was ever at the school, but there is circumstantial evidence that he was. We are attempting to find him because he may have been a witness to a crime some years ago. Whatever information he can provide will help us in our inquiries."

Waring gestured to the array of ledgers. "If you will tell me the name of the boy and when he might have been in our school, I'll be happy to look for him."

"I have his mother's name. Gladys Mitchell. And an approximate date. What leads me to Baldridge School is the fact that a man with a possible association to this boy was also a benefactor of your school. His name was Fowler."

Mr. Waring's face reflected his recognition of the name, but he said only, "And the possible dates?"

Rutledge had made his calculations.

There were only two ways that Gladys Mitchell could have claimed that her son had been fathered by Fowler. He had been conceived after a brief affair with Fowler that had been resumed at a later date. Or he had been conceived just after the relationship had ended. There was a space of ten years between Fowler's relationship with Gladys Mitchell and his marriage to Justin's mother. The murders occurred when Julian was short of his twelfth birthday. The boy—if it was indeed a male child—could have been as young as twenty-two or as old as twenty-four at the time. Add another twelve years since then, and the killer could be as young as thirty-four today. Which would make him close to Harold Finley's age. Or even thirty-five or thirty-six. He gave Waring the possible dates.

"Was he in the war, do you think?"

If it was Finley, the answer was yes.

"Possibly."

"In our small chapel we have an honor roll of boys who died in the war. His name may be there. But first let's have a look at"—he ran his finger along the spines of the tall ledgers on the third shelf—"this one, I should think. Mitchell, you said?"

"Yes." And then as an afterthought, "It could be Finley."

Half an hour later, Waring closed the ledger and shook his head. "I'm afraid you must have been mistaken. I don't find him at all."

"Could it possibly be Fowler?"

Waring looked up at him sharply. "Are you saying this boy could have been Mr. Fowler's son?"

"He was not, to my knowledge. But the boy's mother could have used the name. Er—to honor him for services to the family."

"There wasn't a Fowler, either, I would have noticed."

There was nothing more to say. Rutledge had used every variation he could think of. There was one other, but he didn't know the woman's name. She was Gladys Mitchell's sister. And he would have to return to Somerset House to ferret her out. Or speak again to Mr. Harrison.

He thanked Waring for his assistance, and he rather thought the man was glad that the search had drawn a blank. For the sake of the school if not his own.

At the Yard, Rutledge put in a call again to Mr. Harrison, only to be told that the solicitors had no record of Mrs. Mitchell's sister's name.

"I recall that you told me she had arranged the services."

"Indeed she did. However, we were billed directly by the undertaker. We had no correspondence with the sister."

In short, the solicitors had not thought it advisable to trust Mrs. Mitchell's sister with any sums, although Harrison had not directly said so.

"And this was true of care at the sanitarium as well as a headstone for the grave?"

"Precisely."

Rutledge had just put up the receiver when Sergeant Gibson walked by.

"What news do you have of the Chief Superintendent?"

"He's been allowed to sit in a chair for the first time. But it's a long road ahead for the Chief Superintendent, and he's not one to be idle."

Rutledge agreed with him. But there had been a subtle difference in the Yard since Bowles's heart attack. A quieter mood, men going about their business with an air of uncertainty about what the future held. Inspector Mickelson, sent to Northumberland to investigate a murder, had made a point of staying out of sight. Rutledge wondered if the man's head would roll if Bowles was forced to leave for medical reasons. Mickelson had stepped on more toes than he could reasonably count, knowing he was protected by Bowles. The question was, would Bowles see to it that his successor also protected the man?

As far as Rutledge was concerned, Mickelson's absence was a respite.

He went back to his office and made an effort to concentrate on a folder that Gibson had brought up earlier that morning. But his mind kept wandering to his dilemma.

Mrs. Dunner's remark about the locket rang true.

And there was still the riddle of the charity school.

The elder Fowler's support of it from such an early age must have some connection with his first disastrous liaison. Had he bought Gladys Mitchell's silence about their annulled marriage by seeing to it that her son was properly educated? It wouldn't have done for her to appear in a year or two with blackmail on her mind just as he was preparing to take another wife. The education of her son—but not his—would be the surest way of protecting his future. And a gift to the school, with the promise of more to come, as the boy's education progressed, would keep him there.

But what did this have to do with murder?

It could be the connection that he had so far failed to find.

A bitter and forgotten child might look for revenge, if it had been fostered in him by a bitter and dying mother. First to kill the Fowlers. And when Justin survived, to look for him and destroy his new family.

Hamish said derisively, "Willet was no' a member of the family."

Rutledge took a deep breath. "He had the necklace. That somehow brings him into the circle."

"They were all there the day Mrs. Russell disappeared. He could ha' killed them all. And finished wi' the past then and there."

"He would have been hunted down."

"He was no' hunted down when the Fowlers were killed."

Unable to sit still, Rutledge left the Yard, walked over the bridge to the far side of the Thames, then turned and walked back again. The exercise didn't help.

Rutledge went to his motorcar and drove to the hospital where Major Russell was recovering, and found him propped up in a bed in the men's ward.

"You've made progress," Rutledge said, taking the chair beside him. "First, the Casualty ward. Now with the rest of the sufferers."

Major Russell grimaced. "They snore like the very devil. I couldn't sleep last night for it."

"You probably wouldn't have slept well anyway."

"No. It's hard to breathe. That keeps me awake. What do you want? Are you here to ask more questions? If I could answer any of them, the bastard would be in irons by this time."

"I've come to ask you about Harold Finley. Mrs. Dunner regarded him as the son she never had. Cynthia Farraday cajoled him into taking her to London against your mother's wishes. Your mother hired him to drive her. It's how three women saw him. I want to know how he struck you."

"Finley? I never gave him much thought. The groom usually drove my mother wherever she needed to go, until she bought the motorcar. She didn't like it, she called it the contraption. And he couldn't manage it. She advertised for a chauffeur who could work in the house if needed. The agency sent three or four men to be interviewed. She chose Finley. He worked out very well. Cynthia flirted with him outrageously, but she was a child, and he treated her like one, much to her chagrin. My mother was pleased with that. He dealt with Justin and with me just as easily. I took him for granted, I suppose, the way I took Mrs. Broadly and Mrs. Dunner and Nancy and the others. They were *there*."

"Did he strike you as a man who was angry beneath the politeness of a servant?"

"I don't think I ever saw him lose his temper."

"Was he different when you were alone with him? When Mrs. Russell wasn't present and he could be himself?"

"Not to my knowledge. He knew his place and he kept to it. What is it you want me say?"

"I don't. This man came to an isolated household of women and children. Do you think he was hiding anything? His past? His name?"

"God, you've got a twisted imagination. No. Finley was Finley. That was all."

"It seems to me that he could have found work anywhere. Why choose the marshes, and only Tilbury for any social interaction on his free afternoons?"

"He actually seemed to like the marshes. He took me out in the boat once, and we sat for an hour or more watching the marsh birds. I'd never really noticed the birds before. He fashioned a penny whistle for Justin, and none of us could play it, but we tried, and Cynthia laughed until she cried."

Rutledge could see that he was getting nowhere, and he said, "Did strangers come to River's End very often?"

"If they did, I never saw them. What are you getting at?"

"I expect I'm chasing ghosts."

There was a moment of silence, then Russell said, "I expect there's no chance Cynthia will take pity on me and visit?"

"I don't know. She was shaken by your last encounter."

"Yes, I've no doubt of that," he said ruefully. "I always seem to get off on the wrong footing with her. I have a knack for that."

"Is there anything you need?"

"Patience," he said.

Rutledge left soon after and returned to the Yard. Constable Henry saw him walking down the corridor and called to him.

"Sir? There's a message on your desk. A George Munro returning your call."

"Thank you. I'll take care of it."

Ten minutes later, he had reached Munro, and he said, "You have something for me?"

"Yes, I do. But I don't think it will help you very much."

"You found the information about Justin Fowler and Harold Finley?"

"Mind you, it took me hours, because I was looking in the wrong place. Finally, as a last resort, I tried another direction, and that's when I found both of them."

"Let me take out my notebook."

"You won't need it, Ian. It's very straightforward."

"All right. Go ahead."

"I looked at the rolls of the dead and then searched the missing. They weren't there. I went to the list of deserters. And I found both their names on it. The Army would very much like to find both of them. The war is over, but the Army is still of a mind to shoot them."

"When did they desert?"

"In the summer of 1915."

# 21

Rutledge sat there with the receiver to his ear.

After a time Munro said, "Are you there, Rutledge?"

"I'm still here."

"How did you come across these names? I should very much like to know."

"They came up in a murder inquiry I've been conducting. Neither man had contacted anyone since the Armistice. What month did they desert?"

"Both men had been wounded but at different times and neither wound was self-inflicted for a free ticket home. Finley failed to report to France in July. Fowler's wound was more serious, but he didn't return to duty in September. What's more, he missed a medical examination to update his recovery. That was in August. From my end, the two cases don't appear to be related. I'd like to hear what you see at your end."

"It shoots my own theory full of holes."

"Yes, I expect it does. All right, the shoe is on the other foot now. You owe me, rather than the other way around. Give my love to Frances, will you? Joan was asking about her just the other day."

"I'll be sure to."

With that Munro was gone, and the line went dead. Rutledge realized he was still holding the receiver when the operator asked if he cared to place another call.

It was late when Rutledge got home, having had to interview a possible suspect in someone else's case. The air in the flat was hot and oppressive, and he opened several windows to let in what little breeze there was. London had had a particularly long spell of warm dry weather, punctuated by a few storms that hadn't seemed to bring in cooler temperatures.

He was all too aware that he was back at the beginning in the Willet case. And the more he learned, the more unlikely it was that the disappearance of Mrs. Russell had anything to do with Willet's murder. If he'd found the locket in the marshes while searching for her, then put a photograph of Cynthia Farraday in the place of the wedding pair, Willet was guilty of theft, not murder. And it was more and more likely now that he had posed as Wyatt Russell because his mind was confused by the drugs he'd been taking.

Yet he had carried that imposture off flawlessly.

Which brought Rutledge back to the likelihood that Major Russell had been shot because coming through the reeds along the riverbed, he'd been mistaken for the man from Scotland Yard. It would be easy to rid themselves of him in the middle of the night with no witnesses, and the reason why Ben Willet had had to die would be safe.

Even if the Yard knew to look for him here, a dozen inspectors sent out in his place would have no better luck finding a body than earlier searchers had had looking for Mrs. Russell.

"He didna' come to see if you were dead."

"No, that would have left footprints. If I hadn't been found in a few days, whoever it was could safely put me in the river."

Hamish said, "The house is his."

"He must come there often enough to feel it is. And if he isn't Jessup, I'll wager Jessup knows who he is."

"Aye, it's verra' likely true."

Which mean a confrontation with Jessup looming. He didn't altogether regret it.

Rutledge left the window and went to bed shortly after that, but he lay there for a time, thinking about Cynthia Farraday and trying to decide what it was that made her so attractive to so many men.

No great wisdom arrived with the morning.

On the way to the Yard, he considered placing a request in the Personals of the *Times*, asking either Justin Fowler or Harold Finley to contact Scotland Yard. Both men were considered deserters by the Army, and the risk for them was too great to expect them to yield to curiosity. That avenue was effectively closed to him.

There must be another.

In his office, refusing to admit defeat, he played with the wording of such a request.

Hamish said, "Ye ken, Fowler hasna' used a farthing of his ain money. He's deid. It's the reason why he's shown as a deserter."

"Then where was his body hidden?"

"There's the river. The same reason Mrs. Russell's body has no' been found."

"Then Major Russell's body should have been put into the river as well." But he knew the answer to that. There hadn't been time to bring a boat up to River's Edge and take the body aboard. Morrison's concern and his own search of the high grass had seen to that.

An idea was taking shape.

Galvanized, Rutledge worked feverishly for three-quarters of an hour, crumpling sheets of paper as he made false starts and was faced

with unexpected hurdles. Finally, satisfied, he went to find Sergeant
Gibson.

"Read this. I'd like to see it in tomorrow morning's *Times*."

Gibson scanned the sheet of paper, then looked up at Rutledge.
"Sir? Is this true?"

"Only half of it. Russell is alive but badly wounded. It's possible
that the person who shot him also shot Benjamin Willet. I need to
draw him out before he kills again."

"You believe he will?"

"If he discovers that Russell is alive, he will bide his time and try
again."

Gibson read the paragraph more carefully.

*Major Wyatt Russell was shot three days ago on the lawn of his
house on the Furnham Road, Essex, and taken to a London hospital where he was expected to recover and name his assailant.
This morning at six o'clock, he succumbed to severe blood loss
and infection. Scotland Yard is treating this death as a case of
murder by person or persons unknown. Anyone with information
that could help the police with their inquiries is asked to contact
Sergeant Gibson at Scotland Yard. All replies will be held in the
strictest confidence.*

"I'll see to it," Gibson told him, but there was doubt in his voice.
"You've told the Major?"

"I'm on my way now."

At the hospital he caught Dr. Wade just coming out of surgery.
They retired to an empty office and Rutledge explained his plan.

"I don't care for it," Dr. Wade said flatly. "The danger of infection
hasn't passed."

"I understand that risk. But if Major Russell survives this wound,
whoever shot him will still be out there waiting."

"You can't be sure of that. Can you?"

"I'm not willing to find out."

"Yes, there's that. But where are you taking him? He needs care, he can't fend for himself."

Rutledge had considered the possible answers to that on his way to the hospital. His first choice had been the rector, Mr. Morrison. But the cottage was small, and if there were any changes in the Major's condition, medical care was too far away. And the cottage was far too close to Furnham. Morrison would be no match for an angry Jessup.

The second choice was the clinic in Oxfordshire, but he was fairly certain the Major would have no part of that. And a careful killer just might think to look for him there, to see if the *Times* article was true.

The third option was to take the Major to Cynthia Farraday. That too had its risks.

Which left him with no alternative but to offer his own flat, with a nursing sister in charge of Russell's care. And yet he had rejected that for personal reasons. His flat was his sanctuary, his dark corner where he could scream in the night when the war came back again. Here Hamish was at his most vocal, and his presence was a living thing.

His rational mind told him that the Major and the nursing sister would find nothing there to betray his connection with Hamish MacLeod. And yet the part of his mind that Hamish inhabited recoiled in terror and refused even to contemplate such an idea, even when Rutledge himself would not be in the house at all.

The rest of the journey had seen a battle with himself. But now he said to Dr. Wade, "My flat in London."

And for the next half hour together Rutledge and Wade hammered out every possible detail until both were satisfied.

Dr. Wade said, "I'm still not convinced that this is necessary."

"It's important to try."

In the ward, he found the Major sitting up against pillows and drinking a glass of water.

"I'm surprised to see you again," he said as Rutledge took the chair by his bed. "I thought our business was concluded until you found my assailant. I've told you all I know."

"I've come to arrange for you to die."

"I'm damned if you are."

He handed Russell a copy of the sheet that he'd given Sergeant Gibson. Setting aside his glass, Russell read the words written there and then read them a second time.

"Yes, I see what you're driving at. All right, how do I go about dying? And where will you take me? Not to Oxfordshire or I'll refuse to help you."

"That was a bit of a problem, but we've found a solution. I'll find a way to make it happen. You must play your part and call for the nursing sister in half an hour, then let her examine you and cover your face. Someone will come and remove the—er—body."

"When you've got what you want, will you retract the death notice?"

"As soon as I can. Yes." He took the sheet of paper and returned it to his pocket. Then he said, "Did you know that Justin Fowler is listed by the Army as a deserter?"

"Justin? You can't be serious! Yes, you are, aren't you." He lay there for a time, then said, "That's odd. Because Justin said something I've never understood. He told me that the war was too bloody for him, that it gave him nightmares again."

Rutledge leaned closer, to make certain his voice didn't carry, but a patient was coughing heavily behind him, covering his words. He said, "Did you know that Justin Fowler's parents were brutally murdered, and he himself repeatedly stabbed and left for dead?"

"Good God. No. Is that true? Justin? Did they catch whoever did it? No?" He whistled softly. "Did my mother know? She never said a word to me. But that explains the scars on his body. Something was mentioned—surgery, I think." After a moment he added wryly, "I was a boy, I didn't believe her. I was envious because I thought he'd done something daring. And so I asked him. Do you know what he said? *I have no scars.* I thought he'd been sworn to secrecy, and it was rather exciting."

Rutledge said, "It's time we got started. I must go."

Russell stopped him.

"I remembered something last night as I was falling asleep. When I ran into Ben Willet in London, he asked me if I'd see that Cynthia got boxes that he's left for her in his lodgings in Bloomsbury. He was in love with her. I could see it as plain as the nose on his face. But he didn't want her to see him, ill as he was. I asked why the boxes shouldn't go to his family in Furnham. Willet said they wouldn't have any use for them. But I was jealous, I didn't do anything about them. As far as I know they're still there. My conscience pricked all night. It was wrong of me. There's no one else, Morrison hasn't come back. I'd like to ask you to make certain they're kept until I can deal with it myself."

"What sort of boxes?"

"I don't know. I wasn't curious enough to ask."

Rutledge thanked him and left.

He waited out of sight in one of the other wards until the transfer was over, watching the nursing sister he'd dealt with before hurrying out of the ward, summoning Dr. Wade, and then a few minutes later, the body of Major Russell was taken away on a stretcher under Matron's grim, watchful eye. Finally the undertaker arrived, and Rutledge went out to his motorcar and left.

It was at a lay-by some two miles away that the transfer was made, the nursing sister settling the Major into the rear of Rutledge's vehicle. It was painful work, but the Major took it stoically. Rutledge thanked the driver of the undertaker's van, and an hour later, the Major was in Rutledge's flat, lying exhausted in the bed while the sister took his vital signs.

Rutledge quickly packed a valise of whatever he would need for the duration and stowed it in the boot of his motorcar, then warned the nursing sister not to open the door unless she could see him through the window beside it.

And then he left, driving to Bloomsbury, and after asking a man walking a handsome English setter, he tracked down the lodging house where Ben Willet had stayed in London.

It was a small, well cared for, with a neat sign by the door advertising a vacancy. The woman who answered his knock was tall, with graying red-brown hair and a lined face, and when she spoke, he realized she was Irish.

"Hello, my dear, I'm that sad to tell you that despite that sign, we have no rooms to let just now. I've not had the time to change it. But I'll give you the name of a friend one street away who does."

"I'm actually here to collect Ben Willet's boxes." He smiled. "He seems to make a habit of leaving them behind. I hope you still have them?"

"Oh yes, of course I do, Major. He told me you'd be here sooner or later. Did he reach France safely? I was so afraid, you know, that ill as he was, he'd collapse on the journey."

"I should think all is well. But I haven't heard myself. What sort of lodger was he?"

"Neat as a pin, and such a gentleman. He's a lovely man, and he could make me laugh until my sides ached, you know. Such a grand mimic, he was. What a pity that he took ill so sudden. I thought my heart would break. But there you are, we shouldn't be questioning the Lord's way, should we? All the same, I can't help but think how his family must feel."

"Did his sister or her husband come to visit him?"

"He didn't want her to know, you see. I thought it wrong, myself, she sounded like such a lovely girl. He wrote to her, and I posted it for him myself. It was sent in care of someone else, to be given to her after he'd passed on. And then the man came to see him, and they left together."

This was unexpected. "When was this?"

"It was the night he was to meet you at Tower Bridge. He said to me as they were walking out the door, 'Good-bye, Mrs. Hurley. If the friend I was to meet comes looking for me, tell him I've gone ahead and will be there as promised.' When Mr. Willet came back he told me there was a terrible accident on the bridge, and no one could come across. The next evening he left for Dover, and that was that. I held his room for a few days, just to be sure."

"You're very kind. Do you remember the man who came to see him?"

"I was in the dining room serving dinner and only caught a glimpse of him. It was Mr. Willet who told me why he'd be missing his dinner, and here I'd made his favorites. But I saved him a plate, in case, and when he got home he sat there in the kitchen with me and ate it."

"Could you describe this visitor?" "

"I had no reason to remember him, did I? I was only glad for Mr. Willet's sake that he'd come, hoping he might persuade Mr. Willet to go home and see his father and his sister after all. I tell you I cried when he walked out the door that last time. I was that upset."

"The other man didn't come back with Willet?"

"Oh, no, he was alone. He told me the visit hadn't gone as he'd expected, and I was sorry for that. But here I've kept you standing at the door. Come in, Major, my dear, and we'll find those boxes."

He followed her inside, and she led him to a tiny box room in the back of the house where there were odds and ends piled neatly to allow access, and to one side were two boxes marked with Willet's name.

"In a way I'm that sad to see them go," Mrs. Hurley told Rutledge. "As long as they were here, I'd hoped for a miracle, and that he'd come back the way he was before the sickness came on him. I couldn't bear to hand them over to that constable who came for them. I was told to pass them to no one but the Major, and I keep my word when it's given."

And he was grateful for her insistence.

"There. I've said good-bye," she said as he lifted them to carry them to his motorcar. And she turned and walked swiftly back into the house, shutting the door, so that Rutledge wouldn't see her cry.

The Major was in Rutledge's flat, so he took the boxes to his sister's house. When he walked in carrying the first of them, Frances said, "Are you moving in?"

"Not precisely. I need to leave this and its mate with you after I open them. The study?"

"Yes, that will do very well."

When he'd brought both boxes in, Rutledge set about opening each one.

Both contained sheets of paper neatly typed, and then others written in longhand.

"I wonder what became of his luggage?" he mused. "But I suppose it went into the Thames with him. I'd have done the same in his shoes."

"Whose luggage? Whose shoes?" Frances asked.

"If I knew the answer to that I'd be ahead of the game."

"Does this have to do with that awful village where you took me for tea? I still haven't forgiven you for that."

"Furnham? Yes, that was rather dreadful, wasn't it? In hindsight, I shouldn't have taken you there." He lifted the first hundred or so pages out of the box.

But the pages he held were drafts of Willet's first two books, and he set them aside, disappointed. And yet he knew that to the dead man, these had been precious.

When he reached the bottom of the first box he retied the cords and set it aside.

It was in the second box that he found what must have been a draft of the unfinished third book. He took it out, sorted through the hand-written pages, and then came to the typed sheets.

A title had been written by hand above the first paragraph: *The Sinners.*

He began to read, sitting in a chair by the open window, his sister leaning her elbow on the back beside his head.

After half an hour she turned away.

"It's Furnham he's talking about, isn't it? And it must be true. The inn is called The Dragonfly."

"I'm afraid so."

"I wish you'd never taken me there," she said, crossing the room, as if to put as much space as possible between herself and the pages in his hand. Rearranging a bowl of flowers, she said, "It was done, wasn't it? Luring ships into rocks and the like, bringing them aground so that they could be plundered. In Cornwall, they were called the wreckers."

"I expect the people along the shore had done well when ships wrecked themselves in a storm or on a foggy night. And then someone had a clever suggestion. 'If we could bring in more wrecks, not waiting on natural causes, we could prosper."

They had had to kill the survivors, or else what had happened would quickly reach the ears of the authorities.

Furnham had no rocks on which to beach ships. Only a sandbar at the outer edge of the estuary's mouth that sometimes shifted in storms and caught an unwary pilot by surprise. As a rule ships were able to refloat with the next tide.

And so Furnham's story was very different from Cornwall's. They hadn't lured *The Dragonfly* ashore. It had struck the sandbar in the night and was still there at first light. One of the fishermen had noticed something odd about her, and several men decided to board her and ask what was wrong.

They found the ship empty. No crew. No passengers. It was decided to take whatever was useful on board, and then refloat her, jam the rudder, and let her break up elsewhere.

There were chests of goods in the hold, trunks of clothing, and barrels of provisions, leaving the impression that the passengers had been traveling as far as the New World. There was a box of Bibles, another of hymnals, and the log indicated that she had sailed out of Newcastle-on-Tyne, stopped briefly in Holland, and was expecting to put a few passengers ashore in Plymouth and then take on another half dozen for the remainder of their journey. Their destination was New England.

The man who discovered the log had read the final pages, and he quietly tossed it overboard through a stern window in the captain's small cabin.

It required close to four days to empty the ship of all that was useful. Men had stayed aboard, guarding the goods, and others came and went with the fishing boats and rowing boats from the village.

This was the background of a plot revolving around the rector, who told the fishermen and their cohorts from the village that the ship had been sailing on God's business and that everything taken from her belonged to the men who had funded the voyage.

He had railed against their greed and their covetousness, but no one listened. Every household had benefited from *The Dragonfly,* and no one wanted to return his share.

There was salt, flour, pork, tea, a cage of live chickens, and even a cow for milking. They'd had to build a sling to get her ashore. Boxes of nails and hammers and other tools, bolts of cloth, chests of bedding, wood for construction of huts until houses could be built—the list went on. It could all be put to good use.

The rector, in frustration, told his parishioners that they were doing the devil's work, and that the devil would exact his price.

*Hear me. There is a curse on these comforts that have come to you.*

And not even a fortnight had passed before the first of the men who had stayed on board for four days came down with the plague.

Rutledge put the pages aside. He'd asked about the mass burials, assuming that they must be plague victims, and no one had answered his question.

"Why is he writing such a story? This Edward Willet?" Frances asked.

"I don't know. His first two books were personal. One of them his war memoirs, and the other an account of a girl he'd seen once when his father took him to France and that he'd searched for during the war. It's not surprising that his third effort would be something in the past of his village. How much is true I don't know. But so far the facts are there. The name of the inn, the barrows I'd seen in the churchyard that were mass graves for plague victims. It takes place in the mid-1700s. Almost two hundred years ago."

"I wish you would take it away," she said, gesturing to the box. "I feel uncomfortable even knowing it's here."

He smiled apologetically. "I'd forgot. I shall have to stay here for several days. Would you mind terribly?"

R utledge spent the day at the Yard, then stopped by the flat to be sure that all was well. The nursing sister welcomed him, and he saw that she had been reading to Russell from one of the books on the shelf across from the bed.

The Major had more color this afternoon but no fever. Sister Grey told Rutledge he was a difficult patient, and Russell had smiled.

Rutledge said, "What do you know about a ship named *The Dragonfly*?"

"It's on a sign above the inn in Furnham."

"Nothing more? No one from the village ever told you the story?"

"I didn't know anyone from the village well enough to talk about legends and the like," Russell replied. "I don't believe Mother did. She never mentioned it."

"It went aground on a sandbar by the mouth of the river. When the village men went out to see why there was no activity on board, they found the ship abandoned. The cargo was rich enough to salve their consciences. One of the villagers who could read saw what was written in the ship's log, then deliberately tossed it overboard. Then plague erupted in the village, and it must have run through it fairly quickly. I've seen the mounds in the back of the churchyard."

"I've seen those as well. Many villages lost three-quarters of their population to some of the plagues. I don't think it's that unusual. "

"Here it was considered a curse from God for taking the ship's goods."

"Where did you discover all this? In Furnham?"

"Willet was writing a novel about what happened. I collected those boxes of his from his lodgings. They were filled with manuscripts. I expect that's why they were intended for Cynthia Farraday."

"Good God. That history will set the cats among the pigeons, if it ever comes to light."

"He told Miss Farraday that his next book would be a story of pure evil. I expect he was right. Tell me, how are you faring? Do you have everything you need?"

"I'm well enough. Sister Grey tells me I'm healing. It doesn't feel like it. My chest still hurts like the very devil."

"I expect it does."

"Does Cynthia know where I am? It's not all that far to Chelsea," he said hopefully.

"Only Dr. Wade, Matron, and Sister Grey know you're alive. Only Dr. Wade was told where I was taking you."

"Foolishness. I'd have been safe in the hospital."

"I'm sure you would have been. On the other hand, are you willing to risk another attempt on your life? I'm using you as bait to draw out a murderer. The Yard would take a dim view of your dying while in our charge."

"Yes, all right." He closed his eyes. "Good hunting."

Rutledge left him to rest and went to Frances's house. She had gone for the day with friends, and so he shut himself in the study and took out the manuscript.

It was close to eleven o'clock when she came through the door.

"Here you are. I saw your motorcar, but when I called you didn't hear me. Have you had dinner? I think there's a bit of cold chicken in the pantry. Shall I make you a sandwich?"

"I'd forgot the time," he told her. "I'll come with you."

"I see you've been reading more of that manuscript. I hope it's better than the part I saw."

"It's not as interesting as I'd hoped," he answered her. "I'm continuing from a sense of duty rather than pleasure."

It was a lie. He didn't want his sister to know the truth about Furnham.

"I'm sorry. You'd said he appeared to be a talented writer." And she began to tell him about her evening as she went to find a plate for him and bring in the cold chicken.

After he'd eaten, he went to bed so that Frances would also go up. And then when he was certain she was asleep, he quietly returned to the study and finished the manuscript.

Setting it aside, he considered what Ben Willet had done.

Was he exorcising ghosts—first the war, the French girl he looked for but couldn't find, and the past that still hung over the village where he'd lived most of his life? Was it what had made him want to leave Furnham in the first place?

Would his next work have been the story of Wyatt Russell's murder of Justin Fowler, out of jealousy?

Rutledge understood now why Jessup and Barber and others had not wanted the airfield to be brought to Furnham, for fear someone— bored, or clever, or simply looking to annoy the villagers in his turn— would stumble on a history no one wished to remember. It wasn't so

much change they feared, but that the more people who came, the
more likely it would be for Furnham, now only a backwater village of
no importance, to find itself famous for the wrong reasons. What had
Barber said? That Jessup didn't want Furnham to become notorious.

Did Jessup want that badly enough to kill Willet before the book
could be published? Or had he thought he'd been in time? For all
anyone knew, judging from these typed sheets, *The Sinners* was ready
for publication, barring a final revision before it went to the printer's.
Willet's arrival in France was all that was needed to carry on.

In light of what he'd been reading, Rutledge suddenly realized that
the manuscript explained the missing luggage.

Whoever had come to see Willet at the lodging house must have
known—or guessed—what Willet was carrying to France with him.
The finished work. The man had to die so that he couldn't re-create
what he'd written, and the manuscript couldn't survive him to be sent
to Paris posthumously.

Was that what had happened?

Gathering up the pages he'd read, Rutledge set them carefully
back into the box they'd come from, and rummaging in what had
been his father's desk, he found a roll of twine with which to bind it
shut. That done, he carried the two boxes into the attic and left them
there until he could decide whether they were evidence or Willet's
personal property, to be handed over to Cynthia Farraday as the man
had wished.

Back in his room, he lay on the bed, staring at the ceiling.

Most of the facts had been there, and he'd failed to see them. Still,
the few that had been missing made a whole of the story, and without
them he had been unable to understand what was wrong with the village of Furnham-on-Hawking.

It was a fisherman named Jessup who had tossed the logbook overboard so that no one else would realize that this was a plague ship.
The last survivor on board had written there,

*All dead but me. I still don't know who brought the plague
aboard. I do fear we stayed too long in Rotterdam. I watched
them die, and now I find I can't face such an end alone and without comfort. If you find this, whoever you are, know that I chose
self-destruction. I pray God will forgive me. But if I'm damned
for it, then the devil must look for me in the sea.*

So many more dying in Furnham all because of one man's greed.
But it was what the villagers did next that was unthinkable.

The rector had gathered all the plague victims in the tiny church
and was nursing them there, setting the dead outside on the porch,
trying to contain the sickness as best he could, dependent on food and
fresh water brought to him by villagers and left in the churchyard. The
man had worked day and night to save as many souls as possible.

And outside, by the harbor, the man who had destroyed the logbook harangued the remaining people of the village, telling them
that the only way to stop the spread of the plague was to burn it out.
In the end, they collected wood and torches, blocked the exits from
the church, and set it afire. The rector and the victims inside had
screamed for mercy, but there was none. The church burned to the
ground.

No one knew whether it was God or the devil who answered their
prayers as the church burned, prayers that the plague would end and
everyone else would be spared.

There were no more victims.

But Jessup, watching his own wife burn alive, hanged himself
within a year on a tree near the harbor, in plain sight of the villagers. A
pact was made then never again to speak of what had happened. It was
Jessup's defiant son who had renamed the inn for the doomed ship. No
one had dared to change it again.

# 22

After breakfast with his sister, Rutledge went to the Yard. She had commented as she poured his tea that he looked tired and asked if he'd slept well.

He had lain awake most of the night for fear he would have a nightmare and start up screaming, frightening Frances. But he smiled and said, "Chief Superintendent Bowles has had a heart attack. The Yard is tense, waiting to see if he'll return when he's stronger or if we'll have a new Chief Superintendent. We all feel it."

"I'm sure that's true. You and he never got on, did you? Well, I hope the new man, if there is going to be one, is more sympathetic."

When he walked into his office there was a message on his desk from Gibson, and attached to it was a cutting of the request for information from the *Times*.

Rutledge read it again, then set it aside. He wasn't sure now what sort of response there would be. He doubted that anyone in Furnham read the *Times,* and he would have to take a copy to them. With what he knew now, he hoped he could finally clear up the murder of Ben Willet. He had a motive now and clear suspects. As for the attack on Russell, it would most certainly no longer be an inquiry for the Yard. It would be turned over to the Tilbury police, now that the Major had survived. The other deaths—if there were others—would have to remain unsolved.

Hamish said, "It willna' be resolved."

True enough, Rutledge thought. Tilbury had never solved the disappearance of Mrs. Russell, just as Colchester had never solved the murders of Justin Fowler's parents.

Still, even though he couldn't quarrel with the evidence before him, he was not satisfied.

Another question was what Cynthia Farraday would do when Willet's new novel failed to arrive, even though he'd promised her a copy. Would she raise the matter with his Paris publishers?

He had no more than formulated the thought when there was a tap at his door and Constable Henry stuck his head in.

"A Miss Farraday to see you, sir. And she appears to be very upset."

He wasn't surprised. He hadn't told her about the fabricated article, just in case Fowler tried to contact her.

She came in, her face flushed with anger, and he thought too that she had been crying.

"You didn't have the courtesy to come and tell me," she said at once. "I was left to read the news in the *Times*. I would have gone to him, I would have been with him when he died."

"I sorry. There has been no opportunity to tell you."

"Did he suffer? Who shot him? When? Where? I don't know anything!"

He had been standing when she came in, and he offered her a chair. "Sit down. Let me tell you what I know."

She did as he asked, but her eyes were still blazing with her fury, and he felt a surge of regret for what he was about to do.

He told her how he had finally learned that Russell had gone to Essex. "And I left the church before they could find me there listening. I went on to River's Edge and waited for him to come. But he didn't, and I believed that Morrison had relented and let him spend the night at the Rectory. The next morning I spoke to Nancy Brothers, who told me he hadn't come back to the church ruins, and I went myself to be sure. From there I drove to the Rectory. But neither Morrison nor Russell came to the door. I was just turning toward River's Edge when I saw Morrison coming from that direction. He'd been looking for Russell as well, and together we went back to the house to search more carefully."

He glossed over discovering what he'd thought was Russell's dead body and the difficulty of carrying the wounded man to the motorcar. He said only, "We found him on one of the marsh tracks. We managed to get him to a London hospital, Morrison and I. I don't believe he ever regained consciousness."

"And you don't know who shot him—or why?"

"We've had very little luck. That's why we asked the public for assistance."

"And you think anyone in Furnham has even *seen* this article?" She shook her head in disbelief. "First Ben. And now Wyatt." She angrily brushed away a tear. "And so far you've done nothing to stop it. Nothing at all. Scotland Yard, for heaven's sake! And no better than that poor drunken constable in Furnham. Do you realize that I'm alone now? They're all gone. Aunt Elizabeth. Justin. Ben. My parents. It's a frightening feeling, I can tell you. And you didn't have the courage or the decency to come to me and break the news yourself."

She began to cry then. He handed her his handkerchief as she fumbled for her own. She rejected it, as if to take it would be to forgive him.

"I can only say how sorry I am."

"Would you have come at all?" she asked finally.

"I was hoping to reach you before you'd seen the *Times*."

"I don't believe you." She rose to go. "Where do I find the undertaker who took Wyatt's body? I shall deal with the arrangements myself."

It was the one thing he hadn't planned for.

"The hospital is sending that information to us. I'll see that you get it."

"Just as you saw to it that I was informed before the *Times* arrived this morning?"

"No, Miss Farraday. I'll see that you know in good time. If I must send Constable Henry to you with the information."

Turning toward the door, she said, "You've brought me only unhappiness. When I thought you were Wyatt's solicitor, I liked you. And then you tried to follow me home, and I was frightened. Since then, nothing has gone the way it should. I hold you accountable."

He walked with her as far as the street in front of the Yard. "Shall I take you home? My motorcar is just there."

"I'd rather walk," she told him, and turned toward Trafalgar Square, leaving him standing on the pavement.

He drove to Essex, feeling the guilt of the liar. Telling himself that what he had done was necessary. But it didn't help.

On the way he stopped and bought a copy of the newspaper.

Arriving in Furnham, he took the paper, already turned to the proper page, into the cool morning dimness of The Rowing Boat.

Barber was there, and Jessup as well, with four or five others. Rutledge realized that he'd just walked into a planning meeting for the next run to France.

They stared at him with animosity, and he told himself grimly that it was only to get worse.

He put the newspaper down on the bar in front of Barber. "I don't imagine you've seen this," he said.

With a glance at the others, Barber picked up the newspaper, found the article that Rutledge had referred to, and began to read it. Then he stopped and began again, reading it aloud this time.

There was silence in the room as he put it down. "What's this got to do with us?" He nodded to the others.

"I should think you'd be interested in helping find his killer. Even if you had no interest in finding Ben Willet's."

"Perhaps it was suicide," Barber said after a moment. "Did you think of that?"

"I should think he would have found it difficult to shoot himself in the back and then walk as far as the house, leave the revolver where he'd found it, and return to the marshes to collapse."

As he stood there, waiting for them to answer, he found himself wondering if any of the shotguns the runners had carried had come from the gun case at River's Edge. Something in the faces turned toward him told him they knew the gun case as well as Rutledge did.

Jessup said into the silence, "Why should one of us wish to kill Russell? We hardly knew him. He wasn't one to come to The Rowing Boat of an evening and drink with us."

"There have been too many deaths at River's Edge. Beginning with Mrs. Russell and including Justin Fowler. Bodies don't disappear in the river, not without a little help."

Jessup stirred. "Don't be a fool," he said after a moment.

"What reason did we have?" another of the men asked.

"I was hoping you would tell me. There is something wrong at River's Edge. I haven't found out what it was, but I will." He gestured to the newspaper as he picked it up. "As this says, any information will be treated with strictest confidentiality. So don't be afraid to speak up. I should think Miss Farraday will be offering a reward as well."

He turned, walking out the door, feeling a tightness between his shoulder blades until he had swung the door shut behind him.

At the Rectory, he saw Morrison trimming a hedge that ran along the back of his property. Getting out, he walked past the house and said, when he was in earshot, "I think you'll want to read this." Holding up the newspaper, he waited until Morrison had put down the wooden-handled hedge trimmers and joined him by the kitchen door.

"What's that? It can wait, I'm thirsty. Would you care for a lemonade?"

Rutledge went into the small but tidy kitchen and took the chair Morrison indicated. An oiled cloth in a rather garish shade of green covered the table, and the hutch and the cabinets were old. After a moment he came back with a heavy pitcher in his hands.

"It's not terribly cold," the rector said apologetically. "It's hard to come by ice out here. I've taken to keeping the jug in the root cellar." He poured a glass and handed it to Rutledge. "Now. What is it I ought to read?"

Rutledge thanked him and pointed to the top of the page.

"Dear God," he said after he'd finished it. "He's dead? But I thought— Dr. Wade gave him a very good chance of living."

"I was there yesterday. Just before his fever shot up. I've shown this to Barber and Jessup and a few of the others. And as you can see, I've kept your name out of it. I thought it best."

"Thank you very much. I can do without any other quarrel with my parishioners. But this is sad news. After all our efforts to get him to a Casualty Ward. Did he ever remember anything more?"

"Apparently not."

"Well, that will just make your task harder, I should think. Much as I hate to say it, it must have been one of the villagers." Morrison shook his head. "But there's no motive. He hadn't been here for years. Why shoot him?"

"Perhaps because he'd seen Ben Willet the night before he was killed. With someone from Furnham."

Morrison's eyebrows shot up. "Are you sure? In London? That's a long journey for someone from Furnham. None of us has the luxury of your motorcar."

"There are vans that come to the butcher's shop and the green-grocer's shop. Someone must come for the milk out at the farms. There are ways."

"Yes, I suppose that's true. Well, then, it should be easy enough for you to find out. Still—I know these people, Rutledge. Which one have I failed to understand?"

"You told me that Jessup was dangerous."

"Yes, that's true, he is. He will hammer you within an inch of your life if you cross him. His fists are his weapon of choice."

"Nevertheless, one of your flock shot Russell."

"All right, yes. I just don't want to think that men I've known and argued with and cajoled into coming to a service or letting a son or daughter be baptized are killers. Is it possible that someone from London followed him here? There was that business of the loose mare."

"Probably very slim at best." Rutledge could appreciate Morrison's concern for the souls in his keeping, whether they wanted his keeping or not.

Finishing his lemonade, he asked, "Did you know the history of the church that preceded yours?"

Morrison roused himself from whatever he was thinking about the men of Furnham. "I was told it was struck by lightning and burned. Flat as it is out here, a steeple is the tallest point around. Not surpris-ing."

"Jessup told me the same story."

"It's one of the reasons why the new church, St. Edward's, has a truncated tower. I suspect the beams were ancient and as dry as several hundreds of years could make them. They'd burn in a flash. I asked if it had been a Sunday, if anyone had been trapped in it. But ap-parently not, it was in the evening."

Rutledge left it at that. Picking up the newspaper, he said, "I'm going to River's Edge. It's possible that in our concern for Russell we overlooked something."

"I can't imagine what. Do you want me to go with you? Two pairs of eyes and all that."

"It's just as well if I go alone. And then I'll carry on straight to London."

"Will you tell me when the funeral will be? I'll take the service, if Cynthia—Miss Farraday—wishes me to."

He was prepared this time. "The body won't be released straight-away."

"Yes, I understand. But you'll pass along my offer, I hope."

Rutledge promised, thanked him for the lemonade, and left.

"Are ye going to River's Edge? Ye'll be a target, if ye do, and no one to help."

He answered Hamish aloud. "If it's someone from Furnham, he'll follow me to London. And there I won't see him coming."

"Aye. But watch your back."

Rutledge stopped at the gates of River's Edge, walked up the drive and around to the terrace. And although he stood there for nearly three-quarters of an hour, he saw no one. No one took a shot at him.

All the same, he could feel eyes watching him. From the high grass? Among the reeds across the river? Or concealed in the dozens of inlets and coves barely deep enough for a small boat?

He hadn't thought to bring his field glasses. And he cursed himself for that.

Debating the wisdom of spending the night in the empty house, he decided against it.

Hamish said, "Yon Major was shot after dark."

"If I'm to be shot and killed, it won't matter if I see who it is in broad daylight."

"Aye, there's that."

"When next I come, I'll bring Constable Greene with me."

The drive to London lay ahead. Reluctantly he walked back to the motorcar. He wouldn't have been surprised to find his tires slashed. But they were not, the crank turned and the motor caught, and nothing at all happened.

He didn't feel reassured by that.

I t was too late to return to the Yard by the time Rutledge reached London. But he stopped at his flat to look in on Russell. He was sleeping, and Sister Grey, who had been nodding in her chair by the bed, assured Rutledge that there were no changes in his condition.

He found Frances waiting for him.

"I didn't know if you were coming here again tonight. What did you do with the boxes? Take them with you this morning?"

"They're evidence. I put them in the attic for safekeeping."

"I'm glad they're out of sight. I'm starving. Will you take me to dinner? I'm afraid you still owe me a lunch."

At the restaurant, they met several friends, but sat at a table for two. Rutledge was just as glad. The four people they had spoken with as they came in often included Meredith Channing in their dinner plans. He couldn't sit there and listen to speculation about where she might be or why she was away so long. He'd told himself a hundred times to put her out of his mind. But it was harder to do than he'd ever imagined. The wound was still too raw.

Hamish's voice, without warning, spoke from just behind him. "You willna' walk away. It's safer to love someone ye canna' have. You willna' have to tell her about me."

Frances said, "A penny for your thoughts." Stretching out her hand, she put a copper penny in front of his plate.

Collecting himself, he recognized the profile of Edward VII staring up at him and managed a smile. To gain time, he handed it back to her. "What else is there to think about? The Yard."

She made a face. "Put it aside for tonight. Listen, the orchestra is starting to play. Talk to me, or I shall make a fuss until you dance with me."

Laughing because she expected it, he cleared his mind of everything except for the ever-present Hamish and tried to pretend it was before the war and the golden summer of 1914 had lasted forever.

The next morning he went to the Yard early and found an envelope on his desk. Sergeant Gibson's name was on the front, in care of the Yard. There was no return address.

Rutledge took out the single sheet of paper.

*I saw the request for information in the newspaper. Will you meet me? Just by St. Martin-in-the-Fields will do. 2:00?*

It was unsigned.

The hunt was beginning. And he had a feeling he was the prey. But who was the hunter?

He walked out of the Yard at one-thirty and made his way to Trafalgar Square. He stood there for a quarter of an hour, surveying the people coming and going, trying to spot anyone looking for him as well.

At five minutes before two o'clock, he walked to the west door of St. Martin-in-the-Fields, its white facade bright in the afternoon sun.

He stood there until well after two o'clock, and no one came.

Giving it up, he turned and walked back toward the Yard. He was waiting at the corner to cross the street when someone came up behind him and said quietly, "Don't turn around. You aren't Sergeant Gibson. Who are you?"

"Inspector Rutledge. I put that request in the *Times*. Sergeant Gibson was merely the contact. What's your name?"

"No, I told you, don't turn. In exchange for what I know, I want one thing. Immunity from prosecution for desertion. Can you arrange that?"

A break in the traffic was coming, but Rutledge stayed where he was.

"I don't have the authority to make such an arrangement."

"Then you don't need to speak to me."

"Wait!" Rutledge said quickly. "I'll do what I can. Give me twenty-four hours."

"I'll give you until dark. Come back alone. I know what you look like now. If you try to see me, it's finished."

"Very well."

Another break in the traffic came.

"Go," urged the voice behind him. And Rutledge crossed the street with six or eight other people hurrying on their way. Even before he reached the far side, he knew he was alone.

The encounter had yielded several pieces of information. He had met a deserter, for one. And he was absolutely certain the Army wouldn't offer immunity in exchange for information that would bring a murder inquiry to an end. And finally, he hadn't recognized the voice at his back.

Was it a trick? A deserter seizing the opportunity to help himself? The man claimed he knew Sergeant Gibson. Or had someone actually come forward and been clever enough to ensure he himself wasn't tricked?

Rutledge tried to replay the voice in his mind. Low, but not deep. Most certainly male. It reminded him of Ben Willet's, the same timbre, the same cultured overtones. Willet was a good mimic, the voice of a gentleman coming naturally to him. But he was also dead, and his sister had identified the body.

Rutledge sent a message round to his sister's house to say that he would be late. And then he went to see Major Russell.

"Someone contacted me," he said as he came into the bedroom. "It wasn't such a wild idea after all."

Russell said quickly, "Who was it?"

Handing him the envelope, Rutledge said, "Do you recognize the handwriting?"

After studying it for a moment, Russell said, "I don't think I've seen it before."

"Would you know Findley's hand? Or Fowler's?"

"I don't know that I've ever seen anything in Finley's handwriting. And it isn't Justin's. His had more of a slant to it."

Rutledge told him what had transpired, ending with, "He asked for immunity from prosecution for desertion."

"Good luck to him," Russell said. "The Army will never agree to that. I wouldn't be surprised to learn it's someone from Furnham. You did see to it that they knew about the *Times*? All right then. I've dealt with soldiers from isolated villages. Some of them were so homesick they would have deserted if they hadn't been too afraid to try."

Rutledge himself had dealt with raw troops facing battle for the first time. "Or it's a trap?" he said slowly. "I'm to meet him again when it's dark."

"What would he have done," Russell asked, "if this man Gibson had met him? He'd have been prepared to put him off, wouldn't he, and make certain that you would come."

It was an interesting point.

"Take someone with you," Russell added. "That's my advice."

"I'll ask Constable Greene. I can't risk taking Gibson with me."

"No need to frighten him off. Have a service revolver, do you? The clinic took mine away. Carry it with you."

"Good advice." But policemen were not expected to go armed.

Later when Rutledge asked Constable Greene to accompany him to the meeting, the man said, "It's my wife's birthday, sir. I don't think she'd forgive either of us."

Constable Henry had already left for the day, and Sergeant Gibson was closeted with the Acting Chief Superintendent.

Rutledge left the Yard on his own, walking through the quiet streets back to St. Martin-in-the-Fields.

He wasn't sure what he was facing. Still, he hadn't brought his revolver. He would take his chances without it.

Arriving at the church, the first thing he saw was a white square of paper pinned to the door.

Taking it down, he walked to the pool of light cast by a streetlamp, unfolded the half sheet, and tried to read what was written there.

The words were a black scrawl. Not at all the neat writing on the first message. He thought, this must be the man's true hand. Or else he's apprehensive, afraid of a trap.

With Hamish uttering a warning in his mind, Rutledge finally deciphered the tangle of words.

*Walk another quarter mile north, and I'll find you.*

Whoever it was, he was being very careful. But then the price for desertion was death.

Rutledge continued north, out of the square, coming finally to a dark street where trees blocked the light of streetlamps, casting long black shadows across the road. Half seen beneath one of the trees stood a tall slim man in country clothing, a cap pulled down over his eyes.

He was suddenly reminded of Furnham, when he had waited under another tree, this one by the bend of the road until three men with sacks over their shoulders had come up from the river. He'd been alone, tense, prepared for trouble, then had watched it walk directly toward him and knew that he stood no chance if he was caught there.

Rutledge understood what the other man was experiencing, knew the price he'd paid to come to this meeting. Stopping some ten feet from him, Rutledge waited for him to speak. All he could see was the pale glimmer of a face beneath the cap but no distinguishing features.

"They aren't offering me anything, are they?" the man said after a moment, resignation in his quiet voice.

"I'm sorry. No." He could see a faint lift of his shoulders as the man accepted the bald truth.

"Well. I'll have to take my chances, won't I?"

"I'll do what I can. But I make no promises. Still, I need whatever information you can give me. I can't find a killer without it."

There was a pause, as if the man was considering how to begin. Finally he said, "All right. My name is Harold Finley. I worked at River's Edge until it was closed and stayed on as caretaker until I was called up."

Rutledge stayed where he was, waiting for an errant breeze to shift the leaves a little and show him the man's face. It had nearly happened once already.

"I came back to the house twice after that. When my training was finished and I was given leave. And later in the summer of 1915, when I'd recovered from my wounds. I knew Justin Fowler was already in England, so I wasn't surprised to find the terrace doors open. There was no one inside, and I decided to walk down to the water, and I stood there for a while. I was beginning to wonder where Fowler had got to, and just in case he'd brought in supplies at the kitchen landing, I thought I might go along and help him carry boxes up to the house. Do you know where it is, this landing?"

"I do."

"Fowler was there, stretched out on the ground. I thought he was dead, and I couldn't believe it. I didn't want to find out it was suicide, but he wouldn't have been the first to fall into despair at the prospect of returning to France. I got to him and discovered he'd been shot in the back of his head. That was a shock, I can tell you. What's more, when I touched him, the body was still warm. I tore open his tunic to listen to his heart, hoping I could save him. It occurred to me that whoever had done this must still be nearby, that I could be shot as well, but I found a faint, irregular pulse. I couldn't leave him."

As he relived the event, his words tumbled over one another. And there was the ring of truth in his voice, echoes of the shock and fear and desperation he'd felt.

"Any idea who could have shot him? Why they should still be nearby?"

"It had to be someone from Furnham. Who else?" Something had changed in his voice now.

"But with the war on, there was no smuggling. Nothing to store at River's Edge. Why Furnham?"

"I couldn't think clearly, I tell you." He turned away. "I didn't want him to die. And just then someone spoke, and I wheeled, thinking—but it was Fowler. I could barely make out what he was saying, even though I put my ear to his lips. And what he said made no sense. No sense at all. And he died while I was holding him."

"What did he say?"

"Brother. He said it twice. *Brother*." Finley hesitated. "All I could think of was Major Russell. And that was impossible. They weren't actually brothers, were they?" He leaned forward, waiting for an answer.

"Wyatt Russell was an only child. As was Justin Fowler." He paused. "It's possible that there is someone who believed that he was Fowler's older brother. It isn't true. But as a child he must have been led to think of himself as the elder Fowler's son. And it's also possible that this man—if he exists—killed Fowler and murdered both of his parents. Perhaps that's why the police have never found the person responsible. The family's solicitors never told them about this man."

"Gentle God." There was a long pause. Rutledge wished he could see Finley's face. "Is that true?" he asked finally. "Can you be certain of it?"

"I believe it to be true. I've tried to find this man. But I don't have his name. For a time, I thought he might be you, coming to work for the Russell family in order to finish what had been started in Colchester."

"You thought I'd killed Fowler—and now Russell?" Even in the darkness, his surprise was evident.

"There's no one else, is there? You were the only outsider at River's Edge."

Pacing back and forth in the shadows, the man said, "Yes, all right. But if I'd killed them, why would I come to you now? Just to bargain with the Army?"

"Why did you desert? Why not go to the police? Were you afraid they would suspect you?"

"I couldn't go back to France. Even in the artillery—" Shaking his head, he couldn't continue.

"The rest of us had the courage to go back."

"It wasn't a matter of courage. Damn it, I'm as brave as the next man." Taking a deep breath, he said more calmly, "I didn't come here to defend myself. Fowler told me it was his brother. When I read the Yard's request in the *Times,* it occurred to me that perhaps he'd been mistaken. Both men had been killed at River's Edge, and I was afraid—the wrong person might be blamed."

Rutledge realized that Finley had come to protect Cynthia Farraday.

"What did you do with Fowler's body? Did you leave it there, where you'd found it?"

"I didn't know what else to do."

And that was a lie, his voice betraying him once more.

"Then why was it never found? Even the bones?"

"It was never found? Fowler's body?" There was genuine consternation now.

"Mrs. Russell also died at River's Edge. Who killed her?"

"I wish I knew. We searched until we were stumbling over our feet, and still we kept looking, and there was no sign of her. I've had a long time to think about it since then. I knew she had to be dead. They whispered suicide, but she wouldn't have killed herself. It had to be murder. Was it the same person?" The tension in his voice was mirrored in the way he waited for the answer.

"It could very well be. If he'd taken Fowler's first family from him, why not the second? But we won't have an answer, will we, until we've found him."

"Then he's killed all of us, hasn't he? Except for Cynthia. Except for Miss Farraday," he corrected himself. "That's all I can give you. It's all I know. Just—find him. For the love of God, find him." He waited, expecting something from Rutledge. When it didn't come, he simply walked away.

Rutledge let him go. But when he was nearly across the road and just into the shadows of the trees on the far side, yet still within hearing, Rutledge called in a normal voice, "Fowler?"

And before he could stop himself, the man began to turn. He said quickly, "My name is Finley. I told you."

"I think not."

"I didn't kill them—" he protested angrily, taking a few steps forward. The whites of his eyes were stark beneath the bill of his cap.

"I'm arresting you for the murder of the people who gave you shelter and love when you were a victim yourself. Did you kill Mrs. Russell and her son?"

"No. You can't—I'll be hanged—it's not true," he began, not ten feet away, and Rutledge felt himself tense as he moved even closer. "My name is Finley." He broke off as an older couple came out of one of the houses behind them, and turned to go the other way.

Rutledge waited until they were out of earshot.

"I suspect Harold Finley is dead. And you survived because he was."

"You're wrong. I didn't have to come, I didn't have to meet you. I did it for the Major's sake."

"You aren't a very good liar, Fowler. What really happened at River's Edge?"

The sudden shift in his weight betrayed him, and Rutledge said sharply, "If you run, I'll find you. No matter how long it takes. And when I do, I'll hand you over to the Army."

"I didn't want them to die," the man cried. "Dear God, do you think—it's why I ran. So that it would stop. But it didn't, did it? Whoever is doing this finally came for Wyatt too, didn't he? And I couldn't let Miss Farraday be the next victim."

"If that's the truth, come with me, we'll find somewhere to talk. I give you my word I won't arrest you, if in turn you'll give me the truth."

Rutledge expected Fowler to refuse. And then he changed his mind, almost against his will, a part of him needing relief from the burden he'd carried too long.

Finally, to Rutledge's surprise, he said, "Where?"

Russell was in his flat. And Frances was at the house. "Let me take you to Miss Farraday's house. It isn't public. You can leave anytime you like."

"No. Anywhere but there."

"Then name a place."

"There's a pub some distance from here."

"Too public."

"I expect you're right."

"My motorcar is not far from the Yard. We can sit in it."

Fowler considered the risks and finally said, "Yes, all right. But I need another guarantee, that you won't ask the name I now live under."

"Very well."

Hamish was already questioning whether Fowler would make it that far. Before they reached the motorcar there would be a dozen opportunities to disappear.

But the man followed without a word, and under the brighter lamps by Trafalgar Square, Rutledge could see his haggard face and haunted eyes.

Before they reached the motorcar, Fowler said, "How did I betray myself?"

"You weren't shocked when I told you about the murders of your parents. No one else knew. Mrs. Russell had kept it a secret from the other two children. It wasn't likely she would confide in her driver. And you said, 'He's killed all of us.' Not all of them."

Fowler swore softly. "I thought I could carry it off."

They reached the motorcar, and when Fowler stepped in and shut the door, he put his head back against the seat. "I'm so very tired," he said, his eyes closed. "I thought it would never end."

"Where did you start lying?" Rutledge asked after giving him some time to collect himself.

"It's true. Most of what I told you. Only it was I who arrived early that morning to find Finley dying down by the water's edge. He'd been shot in the back of the head. I wasn't sure what he said to me—it could just as well have been a gurgle of pain. But it sounded very much like *brother*. I didn't know if Finley had any brothers. And then I remembered that Wyatt had been a little jealous of me. We were the same height and build, Harold and I. A split second later, I knew."

"Knew what?"

"There's something I never told anyone. Not even Mrs. Russell or the police. While I was in hospital recovering from the stab wounds, there were messages from my parents' friends, our neighbors, clients, general well-wishers. All of it very kind. The police and my solicitors opened them at first, to be sure they wouldn't be upsetting. After the first weeks, realizing that the messages were actually comforting, they just let me open them as they arrived. A week before I was released, there was one with just two lines on the page." He stopped, trying to steady his voice.

"What did it say?"

A constable came toward the motorcar, and Fowler tensed. But the man walked on by and went inside the Yard.

" 'He was my father and the woman with him was a whore, and you're my bastard half-brother. I'm not finished. Wherever you are, I will find you.' "

"No signature?"

"Nothing. I knew one day he'd come for me. That it was only a matter of time. And so I stayed close to River's Edge. But I never expected him to attack the others. By the time Aunt Elizabeth went missing, I'd been to Cambridge, and I'd convinced myself that it had been a vicious prank by someone, because you see, nothing ever happened. It had been an empty threat from the start. A hoax that had haunted me, shaped my life. I didn't *want* to believe he'd killed Aunt Elizabeth."

"Go back to the day you found Finley's body."

"I did the unthinkable. I stripped Finley, put my uniform on his body, and shoved him into the river. I expected him to float down to where the fishermen would find him and report me dead. I started walking, and I didn't stop until I was too exhausted to go any farther. That's why I realized I couldn't return to France when my leave ended. If I did, I'd have to explain about Finley and how he came to be wearing my uniform and carrying my papers. On the other hand, if I simply disappeared, by the time Finley was spotted in the river, he'd be unrecognizable. And whoever was out there, stalking us, would think it was finished. There's be no point, would there, in killing Wyatt and Cynthia if I wasn't alive. And I was right. Nothing happened to them. When I saw that column in the newspaper, I had to do something. It had started again, you see."

"Why do you think it stopped for five years? The killing?"

"I expect whoever he is, he was satisfied. And Wyatt stayed away. There was no temptation. No opportunity."

"Did you know that Cynthia Farraday often went out to River's Edge for the day? She was there fairly often, I expect, and a perfect target."

But he remembered—she borrowed a launch. There was no telltale motorcar outside the gates. Still, there could have been an encounter—it was only a matter of luck that she hadn't been seen by whoever watched the house.

"Dear God." Fowler seemed to fold into himself, hunched over, almost as if he were in physical pain.

"Why didn't you tell the police what you suspected when Mrs. Russell vanished?"

Fowler roused himself to stare at Rutledge. "I told you. I hoped it was all my imagination. Besides, the Tilbury police didn't know about my past. I was afraid that if I told them, they'd think I'd run mad. The Colchester police were suspicious enough. In the beginning, if they could have shown that I'd killed my parents, they would have been very pleased. I was young, but not so young that I didn't understand where their questions were leading. If I'd reported a body at River's Edge, what do you think would have happened? I'd have been the chief suspect. I decided to let the fishermen report him for me. Four people dead, Rutledge, and I was present each time. What's more, I don't think Tilbury would have any better luck finding the killer than Colchester had done."

"But they never reported a body."

"Are you sure? Did you ask that man Nelson? The constable? They should have found him in the shallows. I'd emptied my pockets and put everything in his. I was in such a funk I forgot and left the pounds he was carrying and my own in the wallet."

"How much money was there?"

"I don't know. I had almost fifty pounds with me because I was expecting to stay in a hotel in London for a few days. He could have had twenty or so. I cursed myself, I can tell you. That money would have made my disappearance a lot smoother. I dared not touch my inheritance."

Had Jessup found the corpse—and just as his ancestor had done aboard *The Dragonfly,* had he taken the pounds and left the body in the water?

Jessup had much to answer for.

"You gave no thought to Finley's family?"

"He had none. That's why he went into service. But he was a decent chap, and I thought long and hard about what I was doing. He was still serving us, in a way. And if after the war, Wyatt reopened the house, he'd be all right. Safe."

Rutledge remembered the man he'd seen at the landing. Looking. Waiting.

After a time he said, "Is there anyone—anyone at all—who could have been stalking your family before they were killed? Anyone you felt the slightest suspicion of?"

"I was eleven."

"Sometimes children see more clearly."

"Do you think he would have taken that risk? That he'd be among the people the police interviewed?"

"I'll have to look through the statements the Colchester police took at the time. Meanwhile, what will you do? Where will you go? Is there a way to contact you?"

"I've made a life of sorts for myself. Perhaps not what I'd have wanted, if none of this had happened. But I was content. You can imagine what I felt when I read about Wyatt in the *Times.* My God, that was a shock, I can tell you. I had to make a choice then. I had to come forward."

Hamish spoke suddenly in the stillness of the motorcar. "Do ye trust him?"

And Rutledge, weighing all the evidence, wasn't sure.

"I shall go to Colchester tomorrow and look for the statements. Meanwhile, there's something you should know."

He told Fowler about Willet's visit to the Yard, the accusation he'd made, and his subsequent death.

"He said Wyatt had killed me? But how did he even know I was dead? You said my—the body was never found."

"A good question." Had Willet heard something, believed it, and later tried to do the right thing without involving his family? A fisherman's son, he had a strong connection to the men who lived by the water. He could have heard whispers.

"What are you going to do about me?" Fowler asked after a silence.

"If I ask you to testify, the Army will take you into custody."

"Yes. I know."

"Give me a way of reaching you. If I find something, I may need to contact you."

"If you sent a letter to the Pipes Tobacco shop in Chester, addressed to Finley, it will eventually reach me."

"Fair enough. It's late. I'll take you to a train if you like."

"Thanks. I'd rather walk." He got out, thanked Rutledge again, and then said, "I've never dealt with such hatred as this. Such evil. You must find him. You know that."

Rutledge said, thinking about a burning church and the screaming victims inside, "Evil is always there. If we look for it."

With a nod Fowler walked on. Rutledge watched him go, wondering if he'd done the right thing. Or if he'd made the worst mistake of his career.

In the end, as he started the motorcar, preparing to drive to his sister's house, he rather thought that he had done the only thing possible in the circumstances.

If he could ignore small-scale smuggling, he could ignore a case of desertion.

But he was still not certain about Fowler, even when he let himself into his sister's house and climbed the stairs to the room that had once been his.

Hamish said, "Ye didna' face murder when ye were eleven."

Rutledge, hanging his clothes in the wardrobe and preparing for bed, tried to put himself in Fowler's shoes. How would he have felt if he'd been awakened in the night by a murderer, and then barely surviving himself, learned the next morning that his parents had already been killed with the same knife?

It didn't bear thinking about.

# 23

When Rutledge walked into the police station in Colchester, he found that Inspector Robinson was elsewhere investigating a housebreaking. The constable who had been summoned in the inspector's place didn't remember the Fowler case—he had come from Suffolk—and spent over an hour searching for it in the cellar archives.

"And you're quite certain, sir, that the Inspector is willing to allow you to read the file in his absence?"

"He's knows of Scotland Yard's interest in these murders."

He directed Rutledge to a small interview room and ten minutes later reluctantly turned over the box containing the statements taken when Fowler's parents were killed.

It took Rutledge two hours to sort through the statements. Everyone had been interviewed. The staff in the house, Fowler's partner, the neighbors, Mr. Harrison, who represented the family, anyone who made deliveries to the house, from the milk van driver to the man who brought the post. Anyone who had worked on the grounds or in the house, from gardeners to painters to the chimney sweep and the coal man.

No one had seen or heard anything. No one knew of any trouble touching the family. The killer had come quietly, finished his work, and left, taking nothing, leaving nothing but death behind.

Hamish said, "If the wife had screamed, and one of the servants had come running, there would ha' been another murder."

"Very likely. But I don't think the killer wanted that."

He replaced the statements in the box and sorted quickly through the other pieces of evidence in the file. The postmortem report that graphically described the number and placement of the knife wounds in the bodies of Mr. and Mrs. Fowler, indicating the savagery of the attack and commenting that Mrs. Fowler's survival for even a few hours after it had been nothing short of miraculous, although she hadn't regained consciousness. That was followed by a statement from the doctor who had treated Justin Fowler, describing the severity of his wounds and expressing concern about telling the boy that his parents were dead, suggesting that the police wait until he was out of danger.

A sergeant had meticulously made a list of all the personal correspondence found in Fowler's desk in the six months before the murders, and another had been compiled of clients he'd dealt with in the past six months. The police had been meticulous, even to keeping a list of those who had called at the hospital in the first few days after Justin had been rushed to Casualty.

And there it was.

A name he recognized.

Rutledge sat back in the chair, telling himself it had to be a coincidence. A faint echo of memory awoke, something that Inspector Robinson had told him. What's more, it explained why Mr. Waring hadn't been able to find the right name when he'd been questioned at the school. Another discordant fact had fit well into the whole now.

And other odd pieces began to fall into place, making a pattern.

He just might have found the connection after all.

Armed with this new knowledge, Rutledge asked to use the station's telephone and put in three calls to London.

When the last of these calls had been returned, Rutledge whistled under his breath.

Gladys Mitchell's son had been adopted when he was barely a year old—just about the time she met the young man who would later become the father of Justin Fowler. Ridding herself of an encumbrance in the hope of impressing a rich man? But it hadn't worked out the way she had planned. Meanwhile, the boy's new parents hadn't wanted to give him up. Still, they had sent him to the Charity School in London because he had had a scholarship there. They were too poor to do otherwise.

That much Rutledge had already worked out, but for the details.

What he had had no way of knowing was that Gladys Mitchell had become a matron at that same school, using the name Grace Fowler. Had the solicitor, Harrison, been aware of that? It was most certainly when she'd poisoned her son's mind against the elder Fowler and his family. The boy grew up to follow in his adoptive father's footsteps as a shoemaker, but he hadn't prospered. His adoptive mother—Gladys's sister—died soon after, followed within a year by her husband, and the boy, now a grown man, was penniless, unhappy, and in search of a new life. He had found it in an unexpected place.

Sitting down again at the table, Rutledge stared at the box of evidence in front of him. Hardly able to take it all in.

"Dear God," he said aloud.

Behind him, Inspector Robinson replied, "He's not available, but I am. What have you found?" When Rutledge didn't answer straightaway, he said harshly, "It's my case. I remind you of that. The Yard hasn't charged you with this inquiry. You have your own."

Rutledge turned as he collected the rest of the file and added it to the box. "Quite. I can't connect my murder to yours. I don't know why your killer should have shot my victim." He rose and handed the box to Robinson. "I might add that your predecessor was a careful and thorough man. If anyone should have found this murderer, it was he. The only problem is, we aren't omniscient, are we? It's what gives the criminal an edge."

Taking the box, Inspector Robinson said, "I don't appreciate your examining this file without speaking to me. What were you looking for?"

"Any tangible evidence that could be useful. A name, a coincidence, an irregularity, anything out of order."

"If an answer comes of what you've discovered, I want to know."

"There's no real proof, Robinson. Only a faint hope." He was on his way to the door. "What I'm afraid of, if you want the truth, is that if I'm not careful, they will hang the wrong man. And even if I'm careful, that could still happen."

Inspector Robinson was a zealot when it came to this particular crime, and there had to be some way of proving what he, Rutledge, suspected, without involving Justin Fowler or having him taken up for desertion. Rutledge didn't approve of what the man had done, refusing to go back to France. But that was a matter for Fowler's conscience.

He left then, faced with the dilemma of what to do with the information he had.

Wyatt Russell could probably tell him what he needed to know. But Russell hadn't seen his assailant. And Rutledge wasn't eager to put words in his mouth.

Who could answer his question?

Nancy Brothers?

When he came to the junction with the road to the Hawking River, he took it.

But halfway to Furnham, he changed his mind. Leave Nancy Brothers out of it. Go straight to Constable Nelson.

The rector was wheeling his bicycle along the road, on his way from Furnham to the Rectory. Rutledge slowed to keep pace with him.

"Back again, are you?" Morrison asked.

"I'm afraid so. Willet's death is still a mystery."

"I thought you'd all but settled on Jessup."

"In truth, I've yet to place him in London. But all in good time."

They had reached the Rectory drive. Morrison went ahead and leaned his bicycle against the side of the cottage. "Come in. I'm making a pot of tea."

Rutledge followed him inside and walked to the window to look out as Morrison brought down the teapot and filled it with cold water.

"I need more information. I considered speaking to Nancy Brothers or Constable Nelson. It's possible you can help me as well."

"If I can."

"When did you take up the living at St. Edward's? Were you here before Cynthia Farraday came to live at River's Edge?"

"I don't believe there was a priest here then. There hadn't been since 1902, I think it was. I refused the living twice myself before my bishop convinced me it was my duty to bring God back to this benighted place. Or words to that effect. He's dead now. I often wonder what he would have to say about my dealings with the people of Furnham. I'm not the most successful shepherd, I grant you, but this is not the general run of flock."

Rutledge laughed. "What about Nelson? When did he come to Furnham?"

"About five years before the war, I should think. 1908? 1909? But you were asking me about Cynthia Farraday. I've told you most everything I can think of. Is there anything in particular?"

"I've spoken to her a number of times, and I've begun to think that she's still in love with Justin Fowler. She refuses to believe he's dead. She feels he must be among the missing. What she doesn't know—I didn't care to be the one to tell her—is that he's been listed as a deserter by the Army."

Morrison's surprise was genuine. "Has he been, by God?"

Rutledge finished his tea. "Now I must beard Jessup in his den. Do you know where he lives?

"The house just past the bend in the road. On the right."

But when Rutledge stopped in front of that cottage, he changed his mind. Reversing, he went instead to The Rowing Boat. It appeared to be closed, but he knocked at the door. There was no answer.

From there he drove to Abigail Barber's house. She came to the door, and as soon as she recognized him, she said, "My father and my brothers are dead. There's no more bad news to bring to me."

"My apologies, Mrs. Barber. I need to ask you again. You had no word from your brother for months?"

"That's true. I expect he didn't want to tell us he was dying." Her eyes filled at the memory. "He was so thin, lying there under that sheet. It broke my heart to see him."

"Someone paid him a visit in London. The night before he died. He'd written a letter, and the visit must have been prompted by that."

"He couldn't have written. Sandy would have told me. Nor would he have gone to London without me. Not if it was Ben he was seeing. He wouldn't have gone to London without me!"

"Your father was ill," he reminded her.

"He would have taken me to see Ben. I'd have found someone to sit with my father. It would have been all right."

He reminded her of the date again. "Was your husband away at that time?"

"No, of course he wasn't. Besides, there's the pub. He doesn't trust anyone else to manage it."

"Your uncle, then." When she hesitated, he added, "I know about France. It's not important."

Her face wasn't good at hiding what was going through her mind. He had his answer. Jessup had been away. But where?

Mind reading couldn't put Jessup in London, and it was clear that Abigail Barber had no idea where her uncle had gone.

"He was in France," she said finally. "He goes, sometimes."

He thanked her and left.

"Now ye must ask the man himsel'," Hamish warned him. "Before yon lass asks him."

"I'd have preferred not to. He's spoiling for a fight, and I'm not."

"Aye, he is that."

This time Rutledge walked up the path to Jessup's door. Before he could knock, Jessup opened it in his face.

"I saw you before, trying to gather your courage. I won't ask you in. It's my house, and I'm rather particular about who I invite to step across my threshold."

"Yes, I rather thought you might be," Rutledge said easily. "Where would you prefer to go instead? The strand there, where everyone in Furnham can watch you being taken into custody for obstructing the police in the course of their duties? Or shall we retire to the church-yard, where only the dead will be disturbed by your humiliation?"

Jessup measured his chances. They were nearly of a height, Rut-ledge slightly taller, while he himself was running to fat around the middle and could give Rutledge at least a stone.

Rutledge said, "You're wasting my time, Jessup."

"Talk."

"What did Ben Willet tell you in his last letter? That he was writ-ing a book about *The Dragonfly*? About the plague and the burning of the church with a hundred souls inside? Is that why you went to London and killed him?"

Rutledge had prepared for any reaction. What he got was a frown-ing stare.

"What last letter? What do you mean, he was writing a book about *The Dragonfly*? God, if I'd known that I'd have killed him myself. Bloody coward. Are you sure? Damn it, he swore to me and to his father. He swore he would say nothing." He was furiously angry, striking the frame of the door hard with the edge of his fist. "Is that why he was afraid to come home before Ned died? Did Abigail know this?"

"She did not. I don't know why he never told her about his books."

"He's the one they were talking about in France," Jessup said suddenly. "Not Ned. I thought they were putting us on. Georges and his son. They're bastards, but they get what we want. How did they know when we didn't? Besides, I thought they said the book was about smuggling."

"They knew because the books were published in France under the name Edward Willet. Smuggling was in his second work. *Dragonfly* would have been his third."

"If you're lying to me, I'll kill you."

"Someone knew. Someone met him in London. There's a witness to the fact that he wrote that letter. The same witness can swear to the fact he met someone the night before he died."

"I got no letter. He'd write to Sandy, not me. Or to Abigail." His gaze moved toward the pub.

Looking up the street Rutledge saw Sandy Barber in the doorway of The Rowing Boat, watching them. He said, "Who found Mrs. Russell's body?"

"Found—she was never found."

"But the locket was, wasn't it. Her locket." He watched the man's eyes, and they gave Jessup away. "And who found Justin Fowler floating in the river and never reported it?"

Jessup looked toward Barber again. "Nobody."

"You didn't want the police asking questions. That's why you didn't report the locket. Or Fowler's body. Who killed them, Jessup? Your merry band of smugglers? Or someone else?"

"Get the hell out of Furnham," Jessup said through clenched teeth. "I'm warning you."

"You've intimidated Constable Nelson, but you can't intimidate Scotland Yard. I will have a dozen men here to search every house and question every person in this village. We'll drag the river as well and tear every boat apart. The London newspapers will be kept abreast of our efforts, and when we're finished, Furnham will be changed forever. And your name will be synonymous with the evil your ancestor did. *I read the manuscript, Jessup.*"

He knew that he'd pushed too far. If the shotgun had been to hand, Jessup would have used it.

Hamish warned him, and he realized that while he'd been speaking, Sandy Barber had come up behind him. He moved slightly so that he could watch both men, waiting for whatever would happen next. But he'd been angry with the intransigence of these men, the obstruction at every turn. And it was time to end it.

Into the hostile silence, Barber said, "If we tell you, will you leave us in peace?"

"No!" Jessup said explosively.

"We're making a spectacle of ourselves." Barber shouted at him in his turn. "There's no one in The Boat. We'll settle it there."

Barber waited, and Rutledge held his tongue.

Jessup was struggling to get himself under control. He seemed to realize through the haze of fury that villagers going in and out of the shops were staring at the confrontation on his doorstep.

Rutledge could almost read the thoughts passing though the man's mind, that this was too public a place to do murder.

Finally he nodded curtly, shoved Rutledge to one side, and walked off toward the pub. He didn't look to see if anyone was following him.

When he was out of earshot, Barber snapped, "Why did you make him so angry? He could have killed you."

"He could have tried," Rutledge said, and strode to the pub in his turn, with Barber hastily falling in beside him.

"Was the book that explicit?" he asked. "God, I never—he went to be a *footman*. That's all Ben wanted. What happened?"

"I expect it was going to France that changed him. The war. He

must have kept a diary. He wrote a memoir after it was over, and someone in Paris published it."

"Damn the war," Barber said as Rutledge opened the door into the
pub. "And damn the French while we're about it."

Jessup was waiting. He said to Barber, "What are we going to do
with him? He has to be stopped."

"You fool, do you want to hang? They know where he is. The Yard
does. If he goes missing, he's right, they'll come down on us and tear
Furnham apart. Tell him what he wants to know. Tell him, or I will.
Then make him promise."

The flush on Jessup's face was a measure of his rage. "They won't
know what he knows. They can't."

"There are the boxes Willet left behind. The manuscripts are
in them," Rutledge said. "You'll be taken up for the murder of Benjamin Willet when they come to light. What's more, the murder of
Justin Fowler and the attack on Wyatt Russell happened here, not in
London. You have that to answer for as well."

"You selfish bastard," Barber said. "You've got us into this. Get us
out of it."

There was a long silence as Jessup weighed alternatives.

Rutledge saw the man glance once at the windows that looked
down on the river. Then he shook his head as if to rid it of the thought.
Instead, he grappled with the realization that he had no choice at all.

"All right," he said finally. "We found Fowler floating, already
dead. We thought at first he was a German spy come to grief on the
river. But it wasn't all that long after the old woman vanished, and we
didn't want the police here again. We towed him to the mouth of the
river and turned him loose."

"Who told Willet that Wyatt Russell had killed him?"

"It must have been Ned," Barber said. "I can't think who else could
have told him."

Jessup cut across his words. "It wasn't Ned. I wrote to him in

France and mentioned there'd been a falling-out between Russell and Fowler, and we'd heard a gunshot. Just in case the body washed up somewhere else. He wanted to know if they'd quarreled over Miss Farraday, and I answered that it was likely."

"You told him—damn it, you never told *me*," Barber said angrily.

"It was to cover us. I thought it best."

Rutledge said, "Willet believed you. That's why I was drawn into this inquiry in the first place. He came to the Yard and told me that Wyatt Russell had killed Fowler. Willet knew he was dying. My guess is he wanted Miss Farraday to learn what had become of Fowler, and he could hardly tell her himself. He must have known how she felt about the man, and it was a way to repay all she'd done for Willet himself." He smiled grimly. "You brought your own house crashing down around your ears, Jessup."

"Willet wasn't dead," Jessup said. "Not when you came to Furnham that first time."

"I was curious," Rutledge countered. "Who killed Mrs. Russell?"

"I don't know. Ned found her locket. He wanted to show it to the police. But I told him not to. I told him to keep it and give it to Abigail. But Ben saw it on his last leave and asked for it. He wanted to put his likeness in it and give it to a girl."

To Cynthia Farraday? Would it have saved three lives if he had? Or would Ben Willet have been hanged for a murder he hadn't committed? Rutledge shook his head.

Jessup mistook the shake to mean he wasn't believed. "He couldn't give it to Abigail. I can see now it would have got all of us into trouble if he had. But what would a girl in Thetford know about Mrs. Russell? Ben could tell her the locket was his mother's, and who would think otherwise?"

They were scoundrels, all of them. Living by their wits, doing what they had to in order to survive.

"Do ye believe him?" Hamish asked.

Rutledge found he did. It was probably not the whole truth, but when did the whole truth ever exist?

"Which brings me back to Willet's letter. He wrote it. He posted it. That much we know. He was leaving for France, he wanted to die there, and at a guess, it told whoever it was to break the news gently to Abigail and her father. What else did it say? And who came to London that last night of his life?"

"It wasn't me," Jessup said. "I was in Tilbury, getting a part for my boat."

"He didn't write to me," Barber said. "It must have been to Ned."

"Ned was too ill to travel to London." But Rutledge had found his connection now. It was the last piece of the puzzle. "How would he have managed to keep such a letter from his daughter?"

"He was a sly old fox," Barber said. "He'd have burned it in the cooker. He wouldn't have wanted Abigail to learn any more bad news."

And Ned Willet was dead. No one could ask him. Or prove what he'd done.

Jessup said, "He'd have told the priest. By God, he'd have sent the priest to London to persuade Ben to come home to his father."

"Make sense, Jessup. The priest wouldn't have killed him," Barber retorted.

"Why not? They were all of them in love with that Farraday woman. I wouldn't be surprised to find out the priest loved her too."

"No. He saw the locket," Rutledge said. "Morrison killed Mrs. Russell. He believed that Ben Willet knew what had happened to her. And a dying man often wants to unburden his soul. Morrison couldn't take that risk."

"Have you run mad?" Barber asked. "The priest? He's like Constable Nelson, he's afraid of his shadow."

"Is he? He came into a house in Colchester one night and butchered Justin Fowler's mother and father, and stabbed Fowler himself so severely he spent six months in hospital."

"*Morrison?*" Barber exclaimed. "I sent for him to comfort my *wife.*"

"You look at the evil your ancestors did, but here is an equal evil right under your nose, and you thought because you could bully the man that he was nothing."

"Did he have a reason for killing them?" Jessup demanded.

"He believed lies he'd been told by his mother. He thought he was owed a different sort of life. His real father was in prison, but he'd been led to look upon Justin Fowler's father as his. He saw himself as the rejected son."

"And you're sure he killed Ben?"

"It was either you or Morrison. I thought you were angry enough with him that you'd killed him."

Without warning, Jessup came straight for him as Barber shouted, "Here!" But Jessup shoved Rutledge aside and was out the door before either man could stop him.

"He'll tell Abigail, she dotes on Rector," Barber said, and was through the door before Rutledge could reach it.

But Jessup wasn't heading in the direction of the Barber house. With long, determined, angry strides he went toward his own house.

Rutledge was halfway there when he realized what Jessup was intending to do. It wasn't the shotgun in his house that he was after, it was the motorcar sitting in front of it.

He turned the crank with the vigor of his anger, got in, and was already gunning the motor before Rutledge reached him. As his hand gripped the door, Jessup used his fist to pound it, and when he couldn't break Rutledge's hold, he drove off, throwing Rutledge backward, twisting his arm and then slamming it against the side of the motorcar. Careening as he fought for control of the wheel, Jessup nearly collided with Barber, who was yelling at him to wait. The motor sputtered, caught again, and then Jessup was gone.

"He'll kill him!" Barber exclaimed. "He's that angry."

Rutledge looked up the street. A grocer's van was stopped in front of the tea shop, its motor running, and he sprinted for it, Barber at his heels.

Rutledge swung himself inside, realizing as he did that he'd damaged his elbow fighting to hold on to the motorcar's door. Ignoring the pain, he began to roll and heard Barber swear as he struggled to join him, sprawling across the stack of boxes in his way. As Rutledge reversed the van and started out the London road, they could hear the van's owner screaming at them from the tea shop door.

Barber said, almost out of breath, "I don't think he's ever killed anyone. Jessup. But it's been a near run thing, a time or two."

"I want Morrison alive."

"But how did you know?"

"A curate by the name of Morrison tried to visit young Fowler in hospital. An alert constable kept a list of all callers. They were afraid the killer might come back. And he did. Only no one guessed. Later he wrote an anonymous note."

"But Morrison was here, wasn't he?"

"No. He accepted St. Edward's when he learned somehow that Fowler was going to be sent to River's Edge. He's cagey about the time he arrived in Essex. But I'll have London document the date and his background, now that we know where to look."

"Why did he kill the others?"

"Morrison had killed the Fowlers out of jealousy. But when Justin survived and came to River's Edge to live with a new family, it must have seemed doubly unfair. Two families when he had none. He made certain that Mrs. Russell died first, a warning to Fowler that he would be next. And when Russell finally came back to River's Edge, another opportunity presented itself. The man was clever enough to be patient. He'd got away with murder before and he intended to get away with it again. Look—Jessup is just turning into the Rectory drive! We're in time."

But Morrison saw the motorcar, came to the cottage door, and then frowned when he realized that Jessup was driving.

"What's happened?" he called. "Where's Rutledge?" He turned to stare at the van barreling toward them.

Jessup was out the motorcar door, and Rutledge saw that he had the heavy torch that lived under the passenger seat.

Rutledge brought the van to a skidding stop and raced to intercept Jessup. Morrison, looking from one to the other as Rutledge used his shoulder to slam into the older man, took himself inside the Rectory, slamming the door shut.

With a roar of rage, Jessup recovered his balance and ran the short distance to the cottage door, hitting it with his own shoulder and bursting inside. Rutledge and Barber were just behind him, but he'd already cornered Morrison, who was standing with his back to the wall, glaring at Jessup. It was impossible to tell if he was armed or not. Rutledge prayed all three revolvers were still at River's Edge, safe in the gun case.

"What's this all about?" he demanded, looking to Rutledge for his answer. "I thought—"

"I'm arresting you for the murders of Justin Fowler's parents," Rutledge broke in, putting himself between Jessup and Morrison. "He's my prisoner," he said, turning to Jessup, "you can't touch him."

And then everything happened at once. Barber yelled something and then there was a deafening explosion almost in Rutledge's ear. He was momentarily back in the trenches, stunned into memory. Only vaguely aware of Jessup swearing and Barber racing past him, he fought to hold on to the present. Then Morrison fired again, and Barber was stumbling backward, his hands outstretched, as if to ward off a blow.

The third shot, meant for Rutledge, went wild as he shook off the war and grappled with Morrison for the revolver. Morrison fought with all the violence of a cornered animal, growling incoherently as

Rutledge reached out for the weapon. It went off again, and Rutledge heard a window breaking, glass raining down on the floor.

And then he had Morrison's wrist, driving him back against the wall and battering his arm against the low mantel. Morrison cried out in pain but held on to the weapon. It took all the strength he could muster for Rutledge to bring the arm down hard on the oak edge of the mantelpiece, expecting to hear it snap. Instead, Morrison's fingers flew open as the blow hit a nerve instead, and the revolver went thudding to the floor. Morrison fell back, nursing his arm, and for good measure, Rutledge hit him hard on the edge of his jaw. The rector slid down the wall, unconscious, sprawling there in a heap.

Wheeling to examine the injured, he heard Barber say with an effort, "See to Jessup. I think I'll make it." But his face was already pale with the pain, and he was clenching and unclenching a fist.

Jessup was still, and Rutledge bent over him. The shot had struck him in the stomach, but as Rutledge examined him, he said, "It's bad. I've seen worse. We need to get him to hospital as soon as possible."

He turned to look at Barber's chest wound, but it was high enough that he said, "You're right. You'll live. With care."

"Damn good thing he was a poor shot. That close? By rights we should all be dead."

"A knife is his weapon," Rutledge said grimly, busy doing what he could for both men, using whatever linens he could find in the cottage.

He got Barber into the motorcar, and the man said, "What will we do about the van? And there's my wife."

"There's no time to worry about it. I'll deal with it later when I come back to Furnham."

"And Morrison?"

"I'll leave him here until I can retrieve him. I don't want him in the motorcar."

Jessup was a big man, and it was harder to carry him outside, but then he opened his eyes, appeared to know what Rutledge was trying to do, and managed to get himself into the seat, his face pale and clammy from the cost in pain.

Morrison was only just coming to his senses when Rutledge was tying his hands and feet, looping the ropes through the pair of open windows and back again. Standing to one side, he regarded his handiwork. There was no way for the man to free himself without ripping out the heavy boards that separated the two windows. He didn't think Jessup and Barber together could break them.

He took up the revolver—there was one shot left—and stowed it in the boot of his motorcar.

He drove carefully on the rutted road, avoiding the deeper holes where he could. Listening to the grunts of pain from Jessup and Barber, he could still hear the low growl of warning from Hamish, crowded from his accustomed place.

Rutledge tried to think what he had overlooked, and failed. Shutting out everything except making the best time he could, he concentrated on his driving. His elbow was hurting like the very devil, and every time the wheel shook in his hands over a particularly rough patch, he could feel the knifing pain. But he shut that out as well.

There was a Casualty Ward in Tilbury, accustomed to dealing with men injured on the docks. He walked in and asked a nursing sister for help with two men suffering from gunshot wounds. It was an unpleasant reminder of bringing Russell to a similar ward in London. There would have to be a retraction in the *Times* about that, Rutledge reminded himself ruefully. The newspaper wouldn't care for it, but he hoped Fowler would see it, wherever he was hiding.

He got the two fishermen inside, and a doctor arrived to examine both of them. He looked up at Rutledge. "How did this happen?"

"Apprehending a killer. These men were caught in the cross fire." Wincing, he pulled out his identification and showed it to the doctor.

"You did a fair job of bandaging them. In the war, were you?"

"Yes."

The doctor nodded. "Field dressing. I recognize it. Sit down, you don't look very good yourself."

"I'm all right," Rutledge protested, but the doctor wouldn't take no for an answer.

Someone brought him a cup of tea and insisted he drink it. Then the doctor was back. "They will survive. Both men have serious but not life-threatening injuries. We can deal with them. Any next of kin to notify?"

"I'll see to it. Thank you."

"Are you hurt?" the doctor said, looking him up and down.

"I'm all right," Rutledge said again, and the doctor reluctantly let him go.

But he was stopped once more as he was about to leave the ward. A very angry man stood on the threshold, asking for the gunshot victims.

He was Inspector Hayes of the Tilbury Constabulary, and he'd been in the maternity ward with his wife when he heard there had been a shooting.

It took Rutledge another quarter of an hour to pacify him. "It's Inspector Robinson's case, in Colchester," Rutledge said. "If you disagree, take it up with him."

And as he walked out the door, he was fairly certain that Hayes would indeed contact Robinson.

Once more in his motorcar, he cursed Hayes for wasting precious time. He was fairly sure that Morrison would be unable to escape, but he felt an urgency he couldn't explain.

He was already into the turning for Furnham and the River Hawking, when he saw the van coming toward him. He didn't know the driver, but he recognized the van. He'd left it sitting outside the Rectory.

Someone from the village had found it, and he had a sinking feeling that whoever it was had found Morrison as well.

Picking up speed, driving with attention fueled by the certainty that he was too late, he covered the miles as best he could. But he could see even before he'd reached the Rectory that Morrison was free. His bonds lay scattered across the grass, and the cottage was empty when he stepped inside.

Rutledge took the time to search each room as well as the back garden, alert for an ambush at any moment.

Where had Morrison gone? To the village?

No, he couldn't be sure who beside Jessup and Barber knew the truth. The village was for all intents and purposes a trap.

"In the van," Hamish said. "As far away as he can go."

Possible. Very possible. Still, he hadn't been driving. And Rutledge had a feeling he hadn't chosen to go that far. Not yet. There was unfinished business to attend to first. He knew Rutledge would be coming back for him, and he intended to choose his ground for that encounter.

Rutledge had taken Morrison's revolver. But there were other guns in the case in the house at River's Edge.

Had the van carried him that far? Or had he gone by way of a shortcut through the marshes? He'd said once that he didn't know his way through them, but that had been a lie. The only way he could have reached River's Edge ahead of Major Russell was to take an even shorter path.

Retrieving his torch from where Jessup had dropped it, Rutledge went back to his motorcar.

When he reached River's Edge, he left his motorcar by the gates for what he hoped would be the last time. And after removing the revolver from the boot and shoving it under his coat, he walked up the overgrown drive.

There were shotguns in the glass case in the study. The question was, did Morrison know where to find the shells?

"Ye ken, he was in and oot of yon house often enough. It wouldna' take him verra' long to find them and load."

As carefully as he'd trod the dark approaches to No Man's Land, looking for snipers, Rutledge walked toward the house.

The sun was bright, but not bright enough to penetrate the deeper shadows. He moved cautiously, watching for movement, for the slightest sign that he had been seen. There was nothing he could do about the upper windows overlooking the drive. And so he ignored them. The undergrowth and the untrimmed trees offered more immediate danger.

The final sprint across the open lawn leading to the main door took him to the shelter of the house, and he pressed himself against the warm brick while he caught his breath.

Still no sign of Morrison.

Perhaps, Rutledge thought, I was wrong. He was in that van, out of sight among the crates and boxes.

But he had to be sure, and after two minutes, when nothing had happened, he quietly moved around the house toward the riverfront and the terrace, ducking under windows where a watcher could see him.

He reached the corner of the house, pausing again before leaning forward to peer around the edge.

He stopped, moving back out of sight.

For down by the water, at the landing, a launch he'd seen before was tied up and swinging gently with the current.

# 24

Cynthia Farraday had chosen today of all days to return to the house on the River Hawking. Because of the *Times* article, because she mourned Russell?

Rutledge swore under his breath, his eyes scanning the lawns and the edges of the marshes.

Where the hell was she?

And where was Morrison?

He waited, forcing himself to stop and to think. His mind was tired, Hamish hammering at the back of it.

If he'd been wrong about Morrison, if the man had cut his losses and escaped while he could, she was safe enough.

If he'd been right, was Cynthia Farraday already dead? Shot or stabbed, it wouldn't matter if Morrison had found her there. He would kill her, just as he'd killed the others. Rutledge needed to find out before he could know what his options were.

If Morrison was still expecting him, the launch was there waiting when it was over—or as a last resort if everything went wrong. If there was sufficient petrol in it, Morrison could very easily reach France or farther down the coast, past the mouth of the Thames and into Kent.

Were they inside?

It was where Rutledge would wait, in the same circumstances. There was no other way into the house without breaking a window or forcing a locked door and alerting his quarry. If Morrison had found the shotgun shells, he could wait in the garden room and control his field of fire.

The alternative was the first-floor master bedroom, with its long windows looking down to the water, giving a wide view of the lawns and the edges of the marsh.

There was no escape for Morrison from either place, if he himself could get in the first shot. But there was only one cartridge left in the revolver beneath his coat.

He could feel the rush of adrenaline now, as he had on the battle-field as he went over the top. Knowing what was waiting for him out there, knowing what his chances of survival were. But until he knew where Cynthia Farraday was, whether she was alive or dead, his hands were tied.

There was nothing for it but to walk out into the open and challenge Morrison.

Rutledge had taken the first step out into the open when he heard voices. Someone had come out onto the terrace. He moved swiftly back into the shelter of the house and pressed himself against the wall.

He could just hear Cynthia Farraday saying, "But I don't wish to sit in that chair. Bring me another."

She was alive, then, and being used as a Judas goat. Rutledge waited.

"You'll sit where you're told. I shan't kill you until he's dead. Or at least I hadn't planned to. Push me too far, and I won't wait."

"He isn't coming. You said yourself he had taken those other men to hospital. He won't leave until he's certain they'll live. Those men are his witnesses, don't you see?"

"He's not the sort to leave a prisoner tied to a post any longer than needful. It's hot today. He'll remember I have no water. No shade. He'll arrive at the Rectory and discover that I've escaped. Then he'll come here. He knows me very well, Rutledge does. But I know him even better. He'll die to save you. Wait and see. I have only to say, *Show yourself, and I'll let her live.* He'll step out then, and you'll walk down to the launch, as I told you to do. He won't know I've disabled it. He'll watch you go, he'll stand there and watch you step into the launch. And then I'll kill him. It's quite simple."

A silence fell.

Then she said, "You can't watch both of us. I can swim, I can leap out of the boat and you'll never find me in the marshes."

"I'll come back for you one day. As I did for Justin Fowler. Remember that. You will never know when. My life had taught me patience. Russell learned that too."

"Did you kill Mrs. Russell?"

"Oh, yes. I had to be quiet about it, so I cut her throat and then tied her to a stone. She's still down there on the river bottom, as far as I know. It's important that you understand me. Wherever you go, I shall find you. Eventually. Or now. It doesn't matter to me when you die. I'll even let you choose."

"That's very kind of you," she said with heavy irony.

Another silence fell. It lasted longer this time. Rutledge weighed the distance, and how quickly Morrison would react.

He didn't know how Morrison was armed. He didn't know whether he had brought out both shotguns or only one. Far more urgent was the question of what Cynthia Farraday would do. Whether he could depend on her to stay out of the way. It was just as likely she would try to throw Morrison off balance, and in that instant, put herself directly into his own line of fire.

There was no way to plan. No way to calculate the odds. Once he stepped out in plain sight, there would be chaos, with no chance to do anything but try for a kill with the first shot. After two years, was he still quick enough?

"You canna' fash yourself over the lass. If Morrison brings ye doon, she willna' live verra' long afterward. Ye canna save her. You mustna' even consider it."

"Not by my shot, please God." But Hamish was right. He had to stop Morrison any way he could. If he wanted to protect Cynthia Farraday, he himself would have to survive.

Bringing out the revolver, he checked again to be sure. One shot. That was all he had.

Then he put it back again.

One deep breath to steady himself, and then he walked out of the shelter at the corner of the house and into the open.

He heard Cynthia Farraday gasp. And Morrison turned to look his way.

There was no time to think, he'd been right about that. Waiting had dulled Morrison's wits. Danger had sharpened his.

Before the shotgun could swing up and be aimed, Rutledge had retrieved the revolver and fired.

The upward motion of the shotgun hadn't stopped. Rutledge had no defense.

He watched the man's finger close spasmodically on the trigger and prepared to throw himself to one side. Cynthia Farraday had her hands in the air, and then he realized in the same instant what she was doing.

Pulling the long pin from her hat, she rammed it into Morrison's side.

He didn't cry out. But his fingers clenched prematurely, and the shotgun went off even as his knees buckled and he went down. Rutledge could hear the shot raining down somewhere to the left of him, but he was already in a dead run toward the terrace.

Morrison had died by the time he got to the man, Rutledge's shot in his heart. In some far corner of his mind, he could hear Cynthia Farraday crying, and peripherally he could see that her hands had covered her face.

Rutledge's shot had been true. He wasn't sure how he had managed it, there had been no time to take careful aim. Still, he'd used his revolver all through the war, he had learned to make every shot count.

He was not proud of the skill.

Pushing the shotgun to one side with his foot, he turned to Cynthia. She pulled her hands down.

"I wanted him to *hang*," she cried, staring at Rutledge with horror-filled eyes. "He murdered *my* family too. Why did you kill him?"

He reached out to her, but she spun away, running down the steps, across the lawns to the water. She leapt into the launch, and when she failed to start it, she sat down and stared at him numbly.

Leaving Morrison where he lay, Rutledge walked down to the landing and said, "Let me drive you back to London. There are some things you need to know."

"I don't want to hear anything," she told him, turning her back on him. "Why won't this launch *start*?"

"He told you. He disabled it. Leave it. It can be brought in later." He squatted on the landing, next to the launch. "Listen to me. Wyatt Russell is alive. Notice of his death was a way of advertising for information to help us find this man."

She half turned her head and said, "Is it true?"

"I'll take you to him. He's in my flat at present."

After a moment, she said, "I think you're the cruelest man I've ever known."

"The motorcar is by the gates. I'll meet you there. There's something I must attend to first."

She wouldn't take his hand. Stepping out of the launch herself, she started toward the house.

He walked as far as the terrace with her, then without speaking, she veered to the nearest side of the house and left him to do what he had to do.

He returned the chairs to the garden room, spread a dust cloth over Morrison's body, and closed the house door, taking the shotgun and the revolver with him.

The drive to London was made in a tense silence. There was one stop on the road, and that was in Tilbury, where he spoke again to the doctor in the casualty ward.

"Both men are out of danger. Did you reach Mrs. Barber?"

He had not. But his day hadn't ended.

He also begged the use of the only telephone, and put in a call to Inspector Robinson in Colchester.

He caught the man just leaving for his dinner.

Rutledge said, "Your murderer is lying on a terrace behind River's Edge." He gave directions to the house. "I'm sorry. I had to kill him. There was a hostage."

There was a pause at the other end of the line. "He's dead, you say? Damn it, Rutledge, I wanted him to stand trial."

Rutledge rang off, rubbing his aching elbow.

Leaving the Casualty Ward, he debated telling Cynthia Farraday the truth about Justin Fowler.

And then he decided that it was not his truth to tell. Fowler had made a life for himself in the north of England. He was content. He was safe. Best to leave it that way.

"Ye must tell him so."

That too could be done, an unsigned letter to a tobacco shop in Chester.

Cynthia Farraday looked away as he turned the crank and got in beside her.

It would be after midnight before he reached Furnham again, he realized, hearing a church clock in the distance striking the hour. He hoped to be in time to meet Inspector Robinson there, after speaking to Abigail Barber.

As he drove through the familiar outskirts of London, Cynthia Farraday said, "I have a confession to make."

"Go on. I'm listening."

"In the beginning, when I believed you were a solicitor for the Russell family, I liked you very much. I told you I wanted to buy River's Edge so that I'd have an excuse to see you again. I was flattered when you tried to follow me to my house. I thought it meant you liked me as well. Instead, you dragged me into a murder inquiry."

"You were involved long before I came on the scene," he told her.

"Did you know he held a knife to my throat when he caught me inside the house? I smiled at him when I first saw him in the doorway, thinking he'd come because he was looking out for River's Edge. That he had heard about Wyatt and wanted to offer comfort. He told me he'd hurt his arm and had walked up to the house, hoping to find something to use as a sling. I could see it for myself, it was red, bruised. And when I turned to look for a strip of cloth, he came up behind me and I felt the coldness of metal against my skin. I couldn't imagine what he wanted, I was afraid—but later he told me he'd cut Aunt Elizabeth's throat. I had no idea you were coming for him until he took out the shotgun. He was the *rector*. I'd known him for years, trusted him, and yet he told me he was going to kill me. I thought Wyatt loved me. And yet he burst into my house and shouted at me and even slapped me. That was your fault too. In the past few hours I have learned to hate you."

He said, his voice tired, "Then why did you stab him with your hat pin, to stop him from shooting me as he went down?"

"For the same reason I wanted him to hang. I wanted him to feel the pain he'd made the rest of us feel. Justin, Wyatt, Aunt Elizabeth. Me." She took off the hat and tossed it into the back of the motorcar, discarding it as she was discarding the truth. "You showed me how evil people are. You showed me how impossible it is to trust anyone ever again. You showed me that I can't even trust my own judgment. Even the war hadn't showed me those things."

There was nothing he could say. And so he drove on to his flat and signaled the nursing sister to allow Miss Farraday to come inside.

That done, he started for Furnham, to face another woman's anger, even though it was not his fault that Jessup and Barber were shot.

He had almost reached the corner of his street when he heard someone calling his name.

Turning his head, he saw that Miss Farraday had come out of his flat and was running down the street toward him. He waited where he was, and as she got closer he could see that she was flushed, her eyes bright.

He took it for anger. And he didn't think he could endure another denunciation.

"Please? I'm sorry—so sorry," she said, stumbling over her words as she caught the door of the motorcar with one hand. "I was—it was—you saved my life and I never even thanked you." She broke off, bit her lip, and walked slowly back toward his flat, her head down.

He watched her until she had stepped inside and closed the door.

# Epilogue

As he made his way out of London, Rutledge remembered the boxes that were in his sister's attic. He hadn't had an opportunity to tell Cynthia Farraday about them. Tomorrow, when he took her statement, would be soon enough. He would have to explain as well that they held what must be the only remaining copy of Willet's third and last book. Whether she chose to see that it was sent to France was her decision to make. He was of two minds about its publication.

He stopped briefly in Tilbury, was told that both patients were resting comfortably, and drove on toward the Hawking. Passing the gates of River's Edge, he didn't look down the drive. He didn't want to see the ghosts that must inhabit it now. He didn't believe in ghosts. Still, he did not look for them.

He wondered if the house would ever be opened again. Too much had happened there, and memory could be an uneasy companion. But he rather thought that if Cynthia Farraday wanted it opened, Wyatt Russell would do that for her. After her ordeal today, perhaps her love for the marshes was tainted too.

He didn't want to think about the dead man lying on the terrace. That would come later. He must come to terms with shooting a man. Not a German in the war but a murder suspect, and he went through those last seconds once more, to judge himself. There had been only one cartridge left in the revolver. He'd had to shoot to kill, he couldn't be certain of disabling Morrison. Even so, he had been lucky that it had hit its mark. That didn't make the fact easier to live with.

In some ways, he thought, Willet and Morrison had been alike. Selfish enough to go after what they wanted with little regard to the consequences in the lives of others. Willet knew his second and third books would anger everyone in Furnham, but he had written both of them anyway, and at the end of his life had salved his conscience by reporting Fowler's death instead of going home and facing his family. It would have been easier for him to die alone in Paris.

Passing the turning that led to the Rectory, such as it was, and thence to the burned-out shell of the old church, he considered Morrison. The man could have put the education his mother had blackmailed Fowler into providing for her son to better use. He could even have become a good priest. And yet he had hidden behind his calling, comforting Abigail Barber even though he had killed her brother. Believing the lies he'd been told because he wanted to think of himself as the neglected child of a rich man instead of the son of a felon who died in prison.

Ahead lay the lane that led to Abigail Barber's house. She must be frantic with worry, but at least he could assure her that her husband and her uncle would live.

A small victory. He accepted it as he turned off the headlamps and prepared his tired mind for the hour ahead.

Hamish said as Rutledge left the motorcar and walked toward Barber's house, "Ye must put this inquiry aside. Ye canna' hold on to it."

And Rutledge realized that that was precisely what he'd done. Held on. Seeking absolution?

He remembered Cynthia Farraday's flushed face as she had thanked him for saving her life. That would have to serve.

He felt a flickering of peace as he knocked lightly on the door and heard anxious footsteps hurrying to answer the summons.

Insights,
Interviews
& More . . .

# Meet the Author

CHARLES TODD is the *New York Times* bestselling author of the Inspector Ian Rutledge mysteries, the Bess Crawford mysteries, and two stand-alone novels. A mother-and-son writing team, they live in Delaware and North Carolina, respectively.

www.charlestodd.com ∾

# The Spell of London
## An Essay from
## Charles Todd

LONDON IS JUST RIGHT for mystery novels.

There is something about those gas-lit lamps, like disembodied halos in the thick fog, streets wet with rain, and footsteps echoing against the sooty walls of ancient buildings that speak of Jack the Ripper and Sherlock Holmes. Granted, London is very different today—the gas lamps are gone, buildings are cleaner, and the smog is rare. It is now the world of Dalgliesh and Lindley—bright, modern, very with it. Nevertheless, there is still that mystique, that sense that here evil things can happen.

It is also the home of Scotland Yard. I remember the first time I saw the sign for New Scotland Yard. I was not a mystery writer then, I was a mystery fan. Later, when Charles went to London for the first time, that sign was on our list of things to see. Just a sign, of course—but it was evocative of so much we had read in books and seen in films.

It was natural, really, to put our first protagonist to work there. Moreover, the Yard suited Rutledge; it gave him position and influence in the matter of solving murders. That card identified him as one of the ▶

66 Moreover, the Yard suited Rutledge; it gave him position and influence in the matter of solving murders. 99

3

**The Spell of London** *(continued)*

elite in law enforcement in his time. However, there was another reason. In the golden age of mysteries, the Scotland Yard inspector was always grateful for the assistance given him by the likes of Sherlock Holmes, Peter Wimsey, and Hercule Poirot. Miss Marple had a slightly different touch with the pros, almost motherly, but it still seemed that with all the might and power of the Yard behind them, few inspectors in these stories solve a murder on their own. Enter Rutledge, who does. Even Inspector Pitt relies on Charlotte's knowledge and input.

Well, you ask, if that's how you feel about London, why does Rutledge spend so much of his time outside the city? The answer is two-fold. First of all, as you'd expect by 2011, the masters have been there before us. London is a character, and an important one, in many great mystery novels. Rutledge works and solves cases in London, as he should, but for greater variety in plot, we move to villages where the motive for murder grows out of quite different surroundings. Our interest is in psychological suspense—the *why* in murder rather than the how and when, and the tighter-knit village offers more compressed emotions as well as settings that contribute to the atmosphere or geography or history

66 Our interest is in psychological suspense—the *why* in murder rather than the how and when ... 99

of that particular place. Ordinary people who turn to murder as the only solution to a problem are often influenced by the fact that they can't escape their environment. London too has "villages," as Rumpole and Inspector Pitt know very well, but they are beginning to blur by 1919, and "big city" crime is taking on different overtones.

We were walking through a neighborhood near the Imperial War Museum not long ago, and thinking how little London had changed since Rutledge's day in some parts of the city. Then we turned a corner and saw The Eye, the giant Ferris wheel, in the distance. That's London's charm. History walks here, and the riverboats plying the Thames may look different, but they have all carried kings and commoners up river and down, as well as thieves, spies, murderers, and victims. However, London is not a dead city, living on the past. It changes with every visit.

We went to the Ceremony of the Queen's Keys late one misty night threatening rain to watch the Tower of London closing. As the keys are collected by the Yeoman Warders, their voices echoing in the darkness from the stone walls, and the Last Post rings out across the black ▶

vastness of the Thames just beyond, you can feel yourself back in the time of the Little Princes, or the captive Princess Elizabeth, or the condemned Anne Boleyn waiting for the last dawn she would ever see. Back in our hotel rooms we sat down to write another chapter of the manuscript we were working on at that time, and the lingering sounds of boots on stone, great keys clanking in the hands of men wearing a uniform of another era, and the bleak, silent walls all around us led to some of our best writing.

Rutledge hunted the Green Park Killer in London. *A Fearsome Doubt* brought back his prewar career at the Yard and a closed case, after a woman's hysterical claim that he helped convict an innocent man. He has interviewed suspects and witnesses here in London, and he remembers where once he walked the beat as a green constable. Much of *The Red Door* takes place in the city, as does an encounter with the War Office in *A Pale Horse*, which is important in learning why a man had disappeared. In *A Long Shadow*, Rutledge is at a dinner party in London when he first discovers that someone is dogging his footsteps. In addition, it is here that he meets Meredith Channing. A vital part of

> 66 The lingering sounds of boots on stone, great keys clanking in the hands of men wearing a uniform of another era, and the bleak, silent walls all around us led to some of our best writing. 99

*A Matter of Justice* brings him to London as well. It is his city, even when he must leave it to deal with an inquiry elsewhere, and the clues essential to his work draw him back again and again.

And just as war forever altered Rutledge, it has also made its mark on London over the centuries. The fighting that Cadfael knew in Shrewsbury had touched London. Rumpole was old enough to remember World War II, and so was She Who Must Be Obeyed. They were famous London residents in the world of modern mystery. His chambers were here, and although he sometimes took over the defense in provincial cases, the backbone of his work came from the families of London's petty criminals, who always looked to Mr. Rumpole to see them right. His practice was a glimpse into a very different London.

James Bond was headquartered in London. He was expected to come to London to see M and Q and of course Moneypenny. Smiley knew London very well. It was a center of the Cold War, and more than one spy—and spy catcher—walked the dark streets.

Lynley and Barbara Havers have dealt with cases in London, Lynley arriving in his Bentley and Barbara in her battered little car. Lynley loses ▶

his wife in London, and the child killer lived there as well in one of the most poignant books of the series, a study in desperation and how life fails some of its most vulnerable children.

Dalgliesh travels in style now, having been promoted. He handles special cases, now. One took place in a publishing house that looked like a Venetian palace. Stylish is the word for those mysteries. As for Lynley and Rutledge, this is home, wherever he may be sent.

Poirot lived in London too. The TV series shows his building as very modern for his time, indicating that he has not lost touch. Miss Marple frequents villages, but one longs to know what comparisons she might have found between London and St. Mary Mead.

Morse came to London for the opera, not for murder. Wimsey hung out in London. But the policemen of Ian Rankin, Val McDermid, Ruth Rendell, Catherine Aird, Ellis Peters, and Caroline Graham mainly worked elsewhere in their particular patch. The bloody imagination of Minette Walters flourished here. Who can forget those tales?

Of late, we have become hooked by *Law & Order: UK*, a classy version of the American show, and we have found it interesting that many of the cast conversations take place outside, not inside, giving vignette glimpses of their London. It is probably a cost-cutting measure, but it has been fun to try to guess where they are.

There are other examples, famous and not so. They all prove a point, that when it comes to crime, you cannot beat London for mystery. Its spell most certainly touched us, and shaped our decisions when it came to creating our characters. ∽

> " When it comes to crime, you cannot beat London for mystery. "

# Reading Group Guide

1. How would you react if someone confessed to you that he had committed a crime? Could Rutledge have handled this situation in any other way than he did?

2. Why are the Furnham villagers so unwilling to talk to strangers? Would they have been more forthcoming if Rutledge had not been a policeman, and if not, why not? What part does geography play in their actions?

3. How does the gold locket that was around the neck of the dead man at Gravesend help Rutledge in his search for answers?

4. In what way do office politics at Scotland Yard hinder or aid Rutledge in his investigation? What do you think of the way he handles the restrictions?

5. What examples can you give of Rutledge's determination in solving the crimes? Does he have any other choice if he wanted to bring the murderer to justice?

6. What function does Hamish serve in this novel?

7. This story takes place a few years after World War I ended. What part did the war play in the

commission of the crimes? The war has also had a profound effect on Rutledge, but has it changed his essential character? Why or why not?

8. Does the identity of the killer surprise you, and if so, in what way? Which of the seven deadly sins drove him, and do you think that there were any other reasons for his actions?

9. At the end of the novel, what does Rutledge mean when he wonders if River's Edge is haunted? ∽

# The History of Inspector Ian Rutledge
## A Complete Timeline of Major Events Leading up to *Proof of Guilt*

### June 1919—*A Test of Wills*

Ian Rutledge, returned home from the trenches of the Great War, loses his fiancée, Jean, after long months in hospital with what is now called PTSD, and faces a bleak future. Fighting back from the edge of madness, he returns to his career at Scotland Yard. But Chief Superintendent Bowles is determined to break him. And so Rutledge finds himself in Warwickshire, where the only witness to the murder of Colonel Harris is a drunken ex-soldier suffering from shell shock. Rutledge is fighting his own battles with the voice of Corporal Hamish MacLeod in his head, survivor's guilt after the bloody 1916 Battle of the Somme. The question is, will he win this test of wills with Hamish—or is the shell-shocked witness a mirror of what he'll become if he fails to keep his madness at bay?

### July 1919—*Wings of Fire*

Rutledge is sent to Cornwall because the Home Office wants to be reassured that Nicholas Cheney wasn't murdered. But Nicholas committed suicide with his half-sister Olivia. And she's written a body of war poetry under the name of O. A. Manning. Rutledge, who had used her poetry in the trenches to keep his mind functioning, is shocked to discover she never saw France—and may well be a cold-blooded killer. And yet even dead, she makes a lasting impression that he can't shake.

## August 1919—*Search the Dark*

An out-of-work ex-soldier, sitting on a train in a Dorset station, suddenly sees his dead wife and two small children standing on the platform. He fights to get off the train and, soon thereafter, the woman is found murdered and the children are missing. Rutledge is sent to coordinate a search, and finds himself attracted to Aurore, a French war bride who will lie to protect her husband and may have killed because she was jealous of the murder victim's place in her husband's life.

## September 1919—*Legacy of the Dead*

Just as Rutledge thinks he's coming to terms—of a sort—with the voice that haunts him, he's sent to northern England to find the missing daughter of a woman who once slept with a ▶

13

king. Little does he know that his search will take him to
Scotland, and to the woman Hamish would have married,
if he'd lived. But Fiona is certain to hang for murdering
a mother to steal her child, and she doesn't know that
Rutledge killed Hamish on the battlefield when she turns
to him for help. He couldn't save Hamish—but Rutledge
is honor bound to protect Fiona and the small child named
for him.

### October 1919—*Watchers of Time*

Still recovering from the nearly fatal wound he received in
Scotland, Rutledge is sent to East Anglia to discover who
murdered a priest, and what the priest's death had to do
with a dying man who knew secrets about the family
that owns the village. But there's more to the murder
than hearing a deathbed confession. And the key might
well be a young woman as haunted as Rutledge is, because
she survived the *Titanic*'s sinking and carries her own guilt
for failure to save a companion.

### November 1919—*A Fearsome Doubt*

A case from 1912 comes back to haunt Rutledge. Did he send
an innocent man to the gallows? Meanwhile, he's trying to
discover who has poisoned three ex-soldiers, all of them
amputees in a small village in Kent. Mercy killings—or
murder? And he sees a face across the Guy Fawkes' Day
bonfire that is a terrifying reminder of what happened to
him at the end of the war . . . something he is ashamed of,
even though he can't remember why. What happened in the
missing six months of his life?

### December 1919—*A Cold Treachery*

Rutledge is already in the north and the closest man to
Westmorland, where, at the height of a blizzard, there has
been a cold-blooded killing of an entire family, save one

child, who is missing in the snow. But as the facts unfold, it's possible that the boy killed his own family. And where is he? Dead in the snow, or hiding? And there are secrets in this isolated village of Urskdale that can lead to more deaths.

## January 1920—*A Long Shadow*

A party that begins innocently enough ends with Rutledge finding machine gun casings engraved with death's-heads—a warning. But he's sent to Northamptonshire to discover why someone shot Constable Ward with an arrow in what the locals call a haunted wood. He discovers there are other deaths unaccounted for, and there's also a woman who knows too much about Rutledge for his own comfort. Then whoever has been stalking him comes north after him, and Rutledge knows if he doesn't find the man, he'll die. Hamish, pushing him hard, is all too aware that Rutledge's death will mean his own. . . .

## March 1920—*A False Mirror*

A man is nearly beaten to death, his wife is taken hostage by his assailant, and Rutledge is sent posthaste to Hampton Regis to find out who wanted Matthew Hamilton dead. But the man who may be guilty is someone Rutledge knew in the war, a reminder that some were lucky enough to be saved, while Hamish was left to die. But this is a story of love gone wrong, and the next two deaths reek of madness. Are they? Or were the women mistaken for the intended victim?

## April 1920—*A Pale Horse*

In the ruins of Yorkshire's Fountains Abbey lies the body of a man wrapped in a cloak, the face covered by a gas mask. Next to him is a book on alchemy, which belongs to the schoolmaster, a conscientious objector in the Great War. Who is this man, and is the investigation into his death being manipulated by a thirst for revenge? Meanwhile, the ▸

British War Office is searching for a missing man of their own, someone whose war work was so secret that even Rutledge isn't told his real name or what he did. Here is a puzzle requiring all of Rutledge's daring and skill, for there are layers of lies and deception, while a ruthless killer is determined to hold on to freedom at any cost.

## May 1920—*A Matter of Justice*

At the turn of the century, in a war taking place far from England, two soldiers chance upon an opportunity that will change their lives forever. To take advantage of it, they will do the unthinkable, and then put the past behind them. Twenty years later, a successful London businessman is found savagely and bizarrely murdered in a medieval tithe barn on his estate in Somerset. Called upon to investigate, Rutledge soon discovers that the victim was universally despised. Even the man's wife—who appears to be his wife in name only—and the town's police inspector are suspect. But who, among the many, hated enough to kill?

## June 1920—*The Red Door*

In a house with a red door lies the body of a woman who has been bludgeoned to death. Rumor has it that two years earlier, she'd painted that door to welcome her husband back from the Front. Only he never came home. Meanwhile, in London, a man suffering from a mysterious illness goes missing and then just as suddenly reappears. Rutledge must solve two mysteries before he can bring a ruthless killer to justice: Who was the woman who lived and died behind the red door? Who was the man who never came home from the Great War, for the simple reason that he might never have gone? And what have they to do with a man who cannot break the seal of his own guilt without damning those he loves most?

### July 1920—*A Lonely Death*

Three men have been murdered in a Sussex village, and
Scotland Yard has been called in. The victims are soldiers,
each surviving the nightmare of World War I only to meet
a ghastly end in the quiet English countryside. Each man
has been garroted, with small ID discs left in their mouths,
yet no other clue suggests a motive or a killer. Rutledge
understands all too well the darkness that resides within
men's souls. Yet his presence on the scene cannot deter
a vicious and clever killer, and a fourth dead soldier is
discovered shortly after Rutledge's arrival. Now a horror
that strikes painfully close to home threatens to engulf the
investigator, and he will have to risk his career, his good
name, even his shattered life itself, to bring an elusive fiend
to justice.

### August 1920—*The Confession*

A man walks into Scotland Yard and confesses that he
killed his cousin five years ago during the Great War. When
Rutledge presses for details, the man evades his questions,
revealing only that he hails from a village east of London.
Less than two weeks later, the alleged killer's body is found
floating in the Thames, a bullet in the back of his head.
Rutledge discovers that the dead man was not who he
claimed to be. The only clue is a gold locket, found around
the victim's neck, that leads back to Essex and an insular
village that will do anything to protect itself from notoriety.

### September 1920—*Proof of Guilt* (coming January 2013)

An unidentified body appears to have been run down by a
motorcar, and a clue leads Rutledge to a firm, built by two
families, famous for producing and selling the world's best
Madeira wine. There he discovers the current head of the
English enterprise is missing. But is he the dead man? And
does either his fiancée or his jilted former lover have ▶

**The History of Inspector Ian Rutledge**
*(continued)*

anything to do with his disappearance? With a growing list of suspects, Rutledge knows that suspicion and circumstantial evidence are nothing without proof of guilt. But his new Acting Chief Superintendent doesn't agree and wants Rutledge to stop digging and settle on the tidy answer. Rutledge must tread very carefully, for it seems that someone has decided that he, too, must die so that justice can take its course. ⤳

Don't miss the next book by your favorite author. Sign up now for AuthorTracker by visiting www.AuthorTracker.com.